THE ELEVENTH

JEFFREY ARCHER, whose novels and short stories include *Not a Penny More, Not a Penny Less, Kane and Abel* and *A Twist in the Tale*, has topped the bestseller lists around the world, with sales of over 250 million copies.

He is the only author ever to have been a number one best-seller in fiction (fourteen times), short stories (four times) and non-fiction (*The Prison Diaries*).

The author is married with two sons and lives in London and Cambridge.

www.jeffreyarcher.com

Brooks
705 725 0243

ALSO BY JEFFREY ARCHER

NOVELS

Not a Penny More, Not a Penny Less

Shall We Tell the President?　Kane and Abel

The Prodigal Daughter　First Among Equals

A Matter of Honour　As the Crow Flies

Honour Among Thieves　The Fourth Estate

Sons of Fortune　False Impression

The Gospel According to Judas
(*with the assistance of Professor Francis J. Moloney*)

A Prisoner of Birth　Paths of Glory

SHORT STORIES

A Quiver Full of Arrows　A Twist in the Tale

Twelve Red Herrings　The Collected Short Stories

To Cut a Long Story Short　Cat O' Nine Tales

And Thereby Hangs a Tale

PLAYS

Beyond Reasonable Doubt　Exclusive　The Accused

PRISON DIARIES

Volume One – Belmarsh: Hell

Volume Two – Wayland: Purgatory

Volume Three – North Sea Camp: Heaven

SCREENPLAYS

Mallory: Walking Off the Map　False Impression

JEFFREY ARCHER

THE ELEVENTH COMMANDMENT

PAN BOOKS

First published in the UK 1998 by HarperCollins*Publishers*

This edition published 2010 by Pan Books
an imprint of Pan Macmillan, a division of Macmillan Publishers Limited
Pan Macmillan, 20 New Wharf Road, London N1 9RR
Basingstoke and Oxford
Associated companies throughout the world
www.panmacmillan.com

ISBN 978-1-4472-2665-9

1 3 5 7 9 8 6 4 2

A CIP catalogue record for this book is available from
the British Library.

Typeset by SetSystems Ltd, Saffron Walden, Essex
Printed and bound by CPI Group (UK) Ltd, Croydon, CR0 4YY

TO NEIL AND MONIQUE

ACKNOWLEDGEMENTS

I would like to thank the following for their help in researching this book:

The Hon. William Webster, former Director of the CIA and the FBI
The Hon. Richard Thornburgh, former United States Attorney-General
The Hon. Samuel Berger, United States National Security Advisor
Patrick Sullivan, United States Secret Service, Washington Field Office
Special Agent J. Patrick Durkin, United States Diplomatic Secret Service
Melanne Verveer, Chief of Staff to Hillary Rodham Clinton
John Kent Cooke Jr, owner, Washington Redskins
Robert Petersen, Superintendent, United States Senate Press Gallery
Jerry Gallegos, Superintendent, House Press Gallery
King Davis, Chief of Police, Sierra Madre, California

Mikhail Piotrovsky, Director, Hermitage Museum and the Winter Palace,
    St Petersburg
Dr Galina Andreeva, Keeper of the Department of Eighteenth and
    Nineteenth Century Painting, State Tretyakov Gallery, Moscow
Aleksandr Novoselov, Assistant to the Ambassador, Embassy of the Russian
    Federation, Washington DC
Andrei Titov
Three members of the St Petersburg Mafya who refused to allow their
    names to appear

Malcolm Van de Riet and Timothy Rohrbaug, Nicole Radner, Robert Van
    Hoek, Phil Hochberg, David Gries, Judy Lowe and Philip Verveer,
    Nancy Henrietta, Lewis K. Loss, Darrell Green, Joan Komlos, Natasha
    Maximova, John Wood and Chris Ellis.

And, in particular, Janet Brown, Commission on Presidential Debates; and
    Michael Brewer of the Brewer Consulting Group.

CONTENTS

BOOK ONE

THE TEAM PLAYER

1

As he opened the door the alarm went off.

The sort of mistake you would expect an amateur to make, which was surprising, as Connor Fitzgerald was considered by his peers to be the professional's professional.

Fitzgerald had anticipated that it would be several minutes before the local *policia* responded to a burglary in the San Victorina district.

There were still a couple of hours to go before the kick-off of the annual match against Brazil, but half the television sets in Colombia would already be switched on. If Fitzgerald had broken into the pawn shop after the game had started, the *policia* probably wouldn't have followed it up until the referee had blown the final whistle. It was well known that the local criminals looked upon the match as a ninety-minute parole period. But his plans for that ninety minutes would have the *policia* chasing their shadows for days. And it would be weeks, probably months, before anyone worked out the real significance of the break-in that Saturday afternoon.

The alarm was still sounding as Fitzgerald closed the back door and made his way quickly through the small store room towards the front of the shop. He ignored the rows of watches on their little stands, emeralds in their cellophane bags and gold objects of every size and shape displayed behind a fine-mesh grille. All were carefully marked with a name and date, so their impoverished owners could return within six months and reclaim their family heirlooms. Few ever did.

3

Fitzgerald swept aside the bead curtain that divided the store room from the shop, and paused behind the counter. His eyes rested on a battered leather case on a stand in the centre of the window. Printed on the lid in faded gold letters were the initials 'D.V.R.' He remained absolutely still until he was certain that no one was looking in.

When Fitzgerald had sold the hand-crafted masterpiece to the shopkeeper earlier that day, he had explained that as he had no intention of returning to Bogotá, it could go on sale immediately. Fitzgerald was not surprised that the piece had already been placed in the window. There wouldn't be another one like it in Colombia.

He was about to climb over the counter when a young man strolled past the window. Fitzgerald froze, but the man's attention was wholly occupied by a small radio he was pressing to his left ear. He took about as much notice of Fitzgerald as he would of a tailor's dummy. Once he was out of sight, Fitzgerald straddled the counter and walked to the window. He glanced up and down the road to check for any casual observers, but there were none. With one movement he removed the leather case from its stand and walked quickly back. He leapt over the counter and turned to look out of the window again to reassure himself that no inquisitive eyes had witnessed the burglary.

Fitzgerald swung round, pulled aside the bead curtain and strode on towards the closed door. He checked his watch. The alarm had been blaring away for ninety-eight seconds. He stepped into the alley and listened. Had he heard the whine of a police siren, he would have turned left and disappeared into the maze of streets that ran behind the pawnbroker's shop. But apart from the alarm, everything remained silent. He turned right and walked casually in the direction of Carrera Septima.

When Connor Fitzgerald reached the pavement he glanced left and then right, weaved through the light traffic and, without looking back, crossed to the far side of the street. He disappeared into a crowded restaurant, where a group of noisy fans were seated around a large-screen television.

Nobody gave him a glance. Their only interest was in watching endless replays of the three goals Colombia had scored the previous year. He took a seat at a corner table. Although he couldn't see the television screen clearly, he had a perfect view across the street. A battered sign with the words '*J. Escobar. Monte de Piedad, establecido 1946*' flapped in the afternoon breeze above the pawn shop.

Several minutes passed before a police car screeched to a halt outside the shop. Once Fitzgerald had seen the two uniformed officers enter the building, he left his table and walked nonchalantly out of the back door onto another quiet Saturday afternoon street. He hailed the first empty taxi and said in a broad South African accent, 'El Belvedere on the Plaza de Bolívar, *por favor*.' The driver nodded curtly, as if to make it clear that he had no wish to become involved in a prolonged conversation. As Fitzgerald slumped into the back of the battered yellow cab, he turned up the radio.

Fitzgerald checked his watch again. Seventeen minutes past one. He was running a couple of minutes behind schedule. The speech would have already begun, but as they always lasted for well over forty minutes, he still had more than enough time to carry out his real reason for being in Bogotá. He moved a few inches to his right, so as to be sure the driver could see him clearly in the rear-view mirror.

Once the *policia* began their enquiries, Fitzgerald needed everyone who had seen him that day to give roughly the same description: male, Caucasian, fiftyish, a shade over six foot, around 210 pounds, unshaven, dark unruly hair, dressed like a foreigner, with a foreign accent, but not American. He hoped that at least one of them would be able to identify the South African nasal twang. Fitzgerald had always been good at accents. In high school he had regularly been in trouble for mimicking his teachers.

The taxi's radio continued to pump out the views of expert after expert on the likely outcome of the annual fixture. Fitzgerald mentally switched off from a language he had little interest in mastering, although he had recently added '*falta*', '*fuera*' and '*gol*' to his limited vocabulary.

When the little Fiat drew up outside the El Belvedere seventeen minutes later, Fitzgerald handed over a ten-thousand-peso note, and had slipped out of the cab before the driver had a chance to thank him for such a generous tip. Not that the taxi drivers of Bogotá are well known for their overuse of the words '*muchas gracias*'.

Fitzgerald ran up the hotel steps, past the liveried doorman and through the revolving doors. In the foyer, he headed straight for the bank of elevators opposite the check-in desk. He had to wait only a few moments before one of the four lifts returned to the ground floor. When the doors slid open he stepped inside and pressed the button marked '8', and the 'Close' button immediately afterwards, giving no one a chance to join him. When the doors opened on the eighth floor, Fitzgerald walked down the thinly carpeted corridor to room 807. He pushed a plastic card into the slot and waited for the green light to glow before he turned the handle. As soon as the door opened, he placed the '*Favor de no Molestar*' sign on the outside knob, closed the door and bolted it.

He checked his watch yet again: twenty-four minutes to two. By now he calculated that the police would have left the pawn shop, having concluded that it was a false alarm. They would phone Mr Escobar at his home in the country to inform him that everything appeared to be in order, and would suggest that when he returned to the city on Monday, he should let them know if anything was missing. But long before then, Fitzgerald would have replaced the battered leather case in the window. On Monday morning the only items that Escobar would report stolen would be the several small packets of uncut emeralds that had been removed by the *policia* on their way out. How long would it be before he discovered the only other thing that was missing? A day? A week? A month? Fitzgerald had already decided he would have to leave the odd clue to help speed up the process.

Fitzgerald took off his jacket, hung it over the nearest chair and picked up the remote control from a table by the side of the bed. He pressed the 'On' button and sat down on the sofa in front of the television. The face of Ricardo Guzman filled the screen.

Fitzgerald knew that Guzman would be fifty next April, but at six foot one, with a full head of black hair and no weight problem, he could have told the adoring crowd that he had not yet turned forty, and they would have believed him. After all, few Colombians expected their politicians to tell the truth about anything, especially their age.

Ricardo Guzman, the favourite in the upcoming presidential election, was the boss of the Cali cartel, which controlled 80 per cent of the New York cocaine trade, and made over a billion dollars a year. Fitzgerald had not come across this information in any of Colombia's three national newspapers, perhaps because the supply of most of the country's newsprint was controlled by Guzman.

'The first action I shall take as your President will be to nationalise any company in which Americans are the majority shareholders.'

The small crowd that surrounded the steps of the Congress building on the Plaza de Bolívar screamed their approval. Ricardo Guzman's advisors had told him again and again that it would be a waste of time making a speech on the day of the match, but he had ignored them, calculating that millions of television viewers would be flicking through the channels in search of the soccer, and would come across him on their screens, if only for a moment. The same people would then be surprised, only an hour later, to see him striding into the packed stadium. Football bored Guzman, but he knew that his entrance moments before the home team were due to take the field would divert the crowd's attention away from Antonio Herrera, the Colombian Vice-President and his main rival in the election. Herrera would be seated in the VIP box, but Guzman would be in the midst of the crowd behind one of the goals. The image he wished to portray was of a man of the people.

Fitzgerald estimated that there was about six minutes of the speech left. He had already heard Guzman's words at least a dozen times: in crowded halls, in half-empty bars, on street corners, even in a coach station while the candidate had addressed the local citizens from the back of a bus. He pulled the leather case off the bed and onto his lap.

'. . . Antonio Herrera is not the Liberal candidate,' hissed Guzman, 'but the American candidate. He is nothing more than a ventriloquist's dummy, whose every word is chosen for him by the man who sits in the Oval Office.' The crowd cheered again.

Five minutes, Fitzgerald calculated. He opened the case and stared down at the Remington 700 that had been out of his sight for only a few hours.

'How dare the Americans assume that we will always fall in line with whatever is convenient for them?' Guzman barked. 'And simply because of the power of the God-almighty dollar. To hell with the God-almighty dollar!' The crowd cheered even more loudly as the candidate took a dollar bill from his wallet and tore George Washington into shreds.

'I can assure you of one thing,' continued Guzman, scattering the tiny pieces of green paper over the crowd like confetti.

'God isn't an American . . .' mouthed Fitzgerald.

'God isn't an American!' shouted Guzman.

Fitzgerald gently removed the McMillan fibreglass stock from the leather case.

'In two weeks' time, the citizens of Colombia will be given the opportunity to let their views be heard right across the world,' Guzman shouted.

'Four minutes,' murmured Fitzgerald, as he glanced up at the screen and mimicked the smile of the candidate. He took the Hart stainless steel barrel from its resting place and screwed it firmly into the stock. It fitted like a glove.

'Whenever summits are held around the world, Colombia will once again be sitting at the conference table, not reading about it in the press the following day. Within a year I will have the Americans treating us not as a Third World country, but as their equals.'

The crowd roared as Fitzgerald lifted the Leupold 10 Power sniper scope from its place and slid it into the two little grooves on the top of the barrel.

'Within a hundred days you will see changes in our country that Herrera wouldn't have believed possible in a hundred years. Because when I am your President . . .'

Fitzgerald slowly nestled the stock of the Remington 700 into his shoulder. It felt like an old friend. But then, it should have done: every part had been hand-crafted to his exact specifications.

He raised the telescopic sight to the image on the television screen, and lined up the little row of mil dots until they were centred an inch above the heart of the candidate.

'. . . conquer inflation . . .'

Three minutes.

'. . . conquer unemployment . . .'

Fitzgerald breathed out.

'. . . and thereby conquer poverty.'

Fitzgerald counted three . . . two . . . one, then gently squeezed the trigger. He could barely hear the click above the noise of the crowd.

Fitzgerald lowered the rifle, rose from the sofa and put the empty leather case down. It would be another ninety seconds before Guzman reached his ritual condemnation of President Lawrence.

He removed one of the hollow-point bullets from its little leather slot inside the lid of the case. He broke the stock and slipped the bullet into its chamber, then snapped the barrel shut with a firm upward movement.

'This will be a last chance for the citizens of Colombia to reverse the disastrous failures of the past,' cried Guzman, his voice rising with every word. 'So we must be sure of one thing . . .'

'One minute,' murmured Fitzgerald. He could repeat word for word the final sixty seconds of a Guzman speech. He turned his attention from the television and walked slowly across the room towards the french windows.

'. . . that we do not waste this golden opportunity . . .'

Fitzgerald pulled back the lace curtain that obscured the view of the outside world, and stared across the Plaza de Bolívar to the north side of the square, where the presidential candidate was standing on the top step of the Congress building, looking down on the crowd. He was about to deliver his *coup de grâce*.

Fitzgerald waited patiently. Never leave yourself in the open for longer than is necessary.

'*Viva la Colombia!*' Guzman cried. '*Viva la Colombia!*' the mob screamed back in a frenzy, although many of them were no more than paid flunkies strategically placed among the crowd.

'I love my country,' declared the candidate. Thirty seconds of the speech left. Fitzgerald pushed open the french windows, to be greeted by the full volume of the masses repeating Guzman's every word.

The candidate dropped his voice almost to a whisper: 'And let me make one thing clear – my love of my country is my only reason for wishing to serve as your President.'

For a second time, Fitzgerald pulled the stock of the Remington 700 slowly up into his shoulder. Every eye was looking at the candidate as he boomed out the words, '*Dios guarde a la Colombia!*' The noise became deafening as he raised both arms high in the air to acknowledge the roars of his supporters shouting back, '*Dios guarde a la Colombia!*' Guzman's hands remained triumphantly in the air for several seconds, as they did at the end of every speech. And, as always, for a few moments he remained absolutely still.

Fitzgerald lined up the tiny mil dots until they were an inch above the candidate's heart, and breathed out as he tightened the fingers of his left hand around the stock. 'Three . . . two . . . one,' he murmured under his breath, before gently squeezing the trigger.

Guzman was still smiling as the boat-tailed bullet tore into his chest. A second later he slumped to the ground like a stringless puppet, fragments of bone, muscle and tissue flying in every direction. Blood spurted over those who were standing nearest to him. The last Fitzgerald saw of the candidate was his outstretched arms, as if he were surrendering to an unknown enemy.

THE ELEVENTH COMMANDMENT

Fitzgerald lowered the rifle, broke the stock and quickly closed the french windows. His assignment was completed.

His only problem now was to make sure he didn't break the Eleventh Commandment.

2

'SHOULD I SEND a message of condolence to his wife and family?' asked Tom Lawrence.

'No, Mr President,' replied the Secretary of State. 'I think you should leave that to an Assistant Secretary for Inter-American Affairs. It now looks certain that Antonio Herrera will be the next President of Colombia, so he'll be the person you'll have to do business with.'

'Will you represent me at the funeral? Or should I send the Vice-President?'

'Neither of us, would be my advice,' replied the Secretary of State. 'Our Ambassador in Bogotá can represent you quite adequately. As the funeral will take place this weekend, we couldn't be expected to be available at such short notice.'

The President nodded. He had become accustomed to Larry Harrington's matter-of-fact approach to everything, including death. He could only wonder what line Larry would adopt were he himself to be assassinated.

'If you have a moment, Mr President, I think I should brief you in greater detail on our present policy in Colombia. The press may want to question you on the possible involvement of . . .'

The President was about to interrupt him when there was a knock on the door, and Andy Lloyd entered the room.

It must be eleven o'clock, thought Lawrence. He hadn't needed a watch since he had appointed Lloyd as his Chief of Staff.

'Later, Larry,' said the President. 'I'm about to give a press conference on the Nuclear, Biological, Chemical and Conventional Arms Reduction Bill, and I can't imagine many journalists will be interested in the death of a presidential candidate in a country that, let's face it, most Americans couldn't even place on a map.'

Harrington said nothing. He didn't feel it was his responsibility to point out to the President that most Americans still couldn't place Vietnam on a map either. But once Andy Lloyd had entered the room, Harrington knew that only the declaration of a world war would have given him priority. He gave Lloyd a curt nod and left the Oval Office.

'Why did I ever appoint that man in the first place?' Lawrence asked, his eyes fixed on the closed door.

'Larry was able to deliver Texas, Mr President, at a moment when our internal polls showed that the majority of southerners considered you a northern wimp who would quite happily appoint a homosexual as Chairman of the Joint Chiefs of Staff.'

'I probably would,' said Lawrence, 'if I thought he was the right man for the job.'

One of the reasons Tom Lawrence had offered his old college friend the post of White House Chief of Staff was that after thirty years, they had no secrets from each other. Andy told it as he saw it, without any suggestion of guile or malice. This endearing quality ensured that he could never hope to be elected to anything himself, and would therefore never be a rival.

The President flicked open the blue file marked 'IMMEDIATE' that Andy had left for him earlier that morning. He suspected that his Chief of Staff had been up most of the night preparing it. He began to go over the questions Andy considered were the most likely to be asked at the midday press conference:

How much taxpayers' money do you anticipate saving by this measure?

'I suppose Barbara Evans will be asking the first question, as usual,' said Lawrence, looking up. 'Do we have any idea what it might be?'

'No, sir,' Lloyd replied. 'But as she's been pressing for an

Arms Reduction Bill ever since the day you beat Gore in New Hampshire, she's hardly in a position to complain now that you're ready to deliver it.'

'True. But that won't necessarily stop her asking an unhelpful question.'

Andy nodded his agreement as the President glanced at the next question.

How many Americans will lose their jobs as a result of this?

Lawrence looked up. 'Is there anyone in particular you want me to avoid?'

'The rest of the bastards,' said Lloyd with a grin. 'But when you wrap it up, go to Phil Ansanch.'

'Why Ansanch?'

'He backed the Bill at every stage, and he's among your dinner guests tonight.'

The President smiled and nodded as he continued to run his finger down the list of anticipated questions. He stopped at number seven.

Isn't this another example of America losing its way?

He looked up at his Chief of Staff. 'Sometimes I think we're still living in the Wild West, the way certain members of Congress have reacted to this Bill.'

'I agree, sir. But as you know, 40 per cent of Americans still consider the Russians our greatest threat, and nearly 30 per cent expect us to go to war with Russia in their lifetime.'

Lawrence cursed, and ran a hand through his thick, prematurely grey hair before returning to the list of questions, stopping again when he reached nineteen.

'How much longer am I going to be asked questions about burning my draft card?'

'As long as you're the Commander-in-Chief, would be my guess,' replied Andy.

The President mumbled something under his breath and moved on to the next question. He looked up again. 'Surely there's no chance of Victor Zerimski becoming the next President of Russia?'

'Probably not,' said Andy, 'but he's moved up to third place in the latest opinion poll, and although he's still well behind Prime Minister Chernopov and General Borodin, his stand against organised crime is beginning to make a dent in their leads. Probably because most Russians believe Chernopov is financed by the Russian Mafya.'

'What about the General?'

'He's been losing ground, since most of the Russian army haven't been paid for months. The press have been reporting that soldiers are selling their uniforms to tourists on the streets.'

'Thank God the election's still a couple of years away. If it looked as if that fascist Zerimski had the slightest chance of becoming the next President of Russia, an Arms Reduction Bill wouldn't get past first base in either House.'

Lloyd nodded as Lawrence turned the page. His finger continued to run down the questions. He stopped at twenty-nine.

'How many members of Congress have weapons manufacturing and base facilities in their districts?' he asked, looking back up at Lloyd.

'Seventy-two Senators and 211 House members,' said Lloyd, without having to refer to his unopened file. 'You'll need to convince at least 60 per cent of them to support you to guarantee a majority in both Houses. And that's assuming we can count on Senator Bedell's vote.'

'Frank Bedell was demanding a comprehensive Arms Reduction Bill when I was still in high school in Wisconsin,' said the President. 'He has no choice but to support us.'

'He may still be in favour of the Bill, but he feels you haven't gone far enough. He's just demanded that you reduce our defence expenditure by over 50 per cent.'

'And how does he expect me to pull that off?'

'By withdrawing from NATO and allowing the Europeans to be responsible for their own defence.'

'But that's totally unrealistic,' said Lawrence. 'Even the Americans for Democratic Action would come out against that.'

'You know that, I know that, and I suspect that even the good Senator knows that. But it doesn't stop him appearing on every television station from Boston to Los Angeles, claiming that a 50 per cent reduction in defence expenditure would solve America's health-care and pension problems overnight.'

'I wish Bedell spent as much time worrying about the defence of our people as he does about their health care,' said Lawrence. 'How do I respond?'

'Lavish praise on him for his tireless and distinguished record of defending the interests of the elderly. But then go on to point out that, as long as you are Commander-in-Chief, the United States will never lower its defences. Your first priority will always be to ensure that America remains the most powerful nation on earth, *et cetera*, *et cetera*. That way we should keep Bedell's vote, and perhaps even sway one or two of the hawks as well.'

The President glanced at his watch before turning to the third page. He gave out a deep sigh when he came to question thirty-one.

How can you hope to get this Bill enacted, when the Democrats don't have a majority in either House?

'OK, Andy. What's the answer to that one?'

'You explain that concerned Americans are making it clear to their elected representatives right across the country that this Bill is long overdue, and no more than common sense.'

'I used that line last time, Andy. For the Drugs Enforcement Bill, remember?'

'Yes, I do remember, Mr President. And the American people backed you all the way.'

Lawrence let out another deep sigh before saying, 'Oh, to govern a nation that doesn't have elections every two years and isn't hounded by a press corps convinced it could do a better job than the democratically elected government.'

'Even the Russians are having to come to terms with the phenomenon of the press corps,' said Lloyd.

'Who would have believed we'd live to see that?' said Lawrence, as he scanned the final question. 'My hunch is that if Chernopov promised the Russian voters that he intended to be the first President to spend more on health care than on defence, he'd romp home.'

'You may be right,' said Lloyd. 'But you can also be certain that if Zerimski were elected, he'd start rebuilding Russia's nuclear arsenal long before he considered building new hospitals.'

'That's for sure,' said the President. 'But as there's no chance of that maniac being elected . . .'

Andy Lloyd remained silent.

3

FITZGERALD KNEW that the next twenty minutes would decide his fate.

He walked quickly across the room and glanced at the television. The crowd were fleeing from the square in every direction. Noisy elation had turned to blind panic. Two of Ricardo Guzman's advisors were bending over what remained of his body.

Fitzgerald retrieved the spent cartridge and replaced it in its slot inside the leather case. Would the owner of the pawn shop notice that one of the bullets had been used?

From the other side of the square, the unmistakable whine of a police siren rose above the noise of the screaming crowd. This time the response had been a lot quicker.

Fitzgerald unclipped the viewfinder and placed it in its sculpted slot. He then unscrewed the barrel, slipped it into position, and finally replaced the stock.

He glanced at the television screen for the last time and watched the local *policia* pouring into the square. He grabbed the leather case, pocketed a book of matches from an ashtray on top of the television, then crossed the room and opened the door.

He looked up and down the empty corridor, then walked quickly in the direction of the freight elevator. He jabbed the little white button on the wall several times. He had unlocked the window that led to the fire escape only moments before he left for the pawn shop, but he knew that if he had to fall back on his contingency plan, a posse of uniformed police would probably be waiting for him at the bottom of the rickety metal staircase. There would be no Rambo-type helicopter, blades whirring, offering him an escape to glory as bullets flew past his ears, hitting everything except him. This was the real world.

When the heavy lift doors slid slowly open, Fitzgerald came face to face with a young waiter in a red jacket carrying an overloaded lunch tray. He had obviously drawn the short straw, and not been given the afternoon off to watch the match.

The waiter was unable to hide his surprise at the sight of a guest standing outside the freight elevator. 'No, señor, perdone, no puede entrar,' he tried to explain as Fitzgerald brushed past him. But the guest had jabbed the button marked 'Planta Baja' and the doors had closed long before the young man could tell him that particular lift ended up in the kitchen.

When he reached the ground floor, Fitzgerald moved deftly between the stainless steel tables covered with row upon row of hors d'oeuvres waiting to be ordered, and bottles of champagne that would only be uncorked if the home side won. He had reached the far end of the kitchen, pushed his way through the swing doors and disappeared out of sight long before any of the white-clad staff could think of protesting. He ran down a poorly-lit corridor – he had removed most of the lightbulbs from their sockets the previous night – to a heavy door that led to the hotel's underground car park.

He removed a large key from his jacket pocket, closed the door behind him and locked it. He headed straight for a small black Volkswagen parked in the darkest corner. He took a second, smaller key from his trouser pocket, unlocked the car's door, slipped behind the wheel, placed the leather case under the passenger seat and turned on the ignition. The engine immediately sprang into life, even though it had not been used for the past three days. He revved the accelerator for a few seconds before easing the gear lever into first.

Fitzgerald manoeuvred the vehicle unhurriedly between the rows of parked cars and drove up the steep ramp out onto the street. He paused at the top of the slope. The policia were breaking into a parked car, and didn't even glance in his direction. He turned left and headed slowly away from the Plaza de Bolívar.

And then he heard the whining sound behind him. He glanced at the rear-view mirror to see two *policia* outriders bearing down on him, their flashing lights full on. Fitzgerald pulled over to the side of the road as the outriders and the ambulance carrying Guzman's lifeless body sped past him.

He took the next left down a side street and began a long, circuitous route to the pawn shop, often doubling back on himself. Twenty-four minutes later he drove into an alley and parked behind a truck. He retrieved the battered leather case from under the passenger seat and left the car unlocked. He planned to be back behind the wheel in less than two minutes.

He quickly checked up and down the alley. There was no one in sight.

Once again as Fitzgerald entered the building, the alarm went off. But this time he was not worried about the speedy arrival of a passing patrol – most of the *policia* would be fully occupied, either at the stadium, where the game was due to kick off in half an hour, or arresting anyone who was still within a mile of the Plaza de Bolívar.

Fitzgerald closed the back door of the pawn shop behind him. For the second time that day he moved quickly through the rear office and, sweeping back the bead curtains, stopped behind the counter. He checked for passers-by before returning the battered leather case to its original place in the window.

When Escobar returned to the shop on Monday morning, how long would it be before he discovered that one of the six boat-tailed magnum bullets had been fired, and only the casing remained in place? And even then, would he bother to pass on the information to the police?

Fitzgerald was back behind the wheel of the Volkswagen in less than ninety seconds. He could still hear the clanging alarm as he drove onto the main street and began to follow the signs for Aeropuerto El Dorada. No one showed the slightest interest in him. After all, the game was just about to kick off. In any case, what possible connection could there be between an alarm going off in a pawn shop in the San Victorina district and the assassination of a presidential candidate in the Plaza de Bolívar?

Once Fitzgerald had reached the highway, he stuck to the centre lane, never once exceeding the speed limit. Several police cars shot past him, on their way into the city. Even if anyone had stopped him to check his papers, they would have found that everything was in order. The packed suitcase on the back seat would reveal nothing unusual for a businessman who was visiting Colombia to sell mining equipment.

Fitzgerald slipped off the highway when he reached the exit for the airport. After a quarter of a mile he suddenly swung right and drove into the parking lot of the San Sebastian hotel. He opened the glove compartment and removed a much-stamped passport. With the book of matches he had taken from the El Belvedere, he set Dirk van Rensberg alight. When his fingers were about to be burnt, he opened the car door, dropped the remains of the passport on the ground and stamped out the flames, making sure the South African crest was still recognisable. He put the matches on the passenger seat, grabbed his suitcase from the back and slammed the door closed, leaving the keys in the ignition. He walked towards the front door of the hotel and deposited the remains of Dirk van Rensberg's passport and a large, heavy key in the litter bin at the bottom of the steps.

Fitzgerald pushed through the revolving doors behind a group of Japanese businessmen, and remained in their slipstream as they were ushered towards an open elevator. He was the only passenger to step out on the third floor. He headed straight for room 347, where he extracted another plastic card that unlocked another room, booked in another name. He tossed the suitcase onto the bed and checked his watch. One hour and seventeen minutes until take-off.

He removed his jacket and threw it over the only chair, then opened the suitcase and took out a washbag before disappearing into the bathroom. It was some time before the water was warm enough for him to place the plug in the basin. While he waited he cut his nails, then he scrubbed his hands as thoroughly as a surgeon preparing for an operation.

It took Fitzgerald twenty minutes to remove every trace of his week-old beard, and several handfuls of shampoo needed to be rubbed in firmly under the warm shower before his hair returned to its natural wavy state and sandy colour.

Fitzgerald dried himself as best he could with the single thin towel the hotel had provided, then returned to the bedroom and put on a clean pair of jockey shorts. He walked over to the chest of drawers on the far side of the room, pulled open the third drawer and felt about until he found the packet taped to the drawer above. Although he hadn't occupied the room for several days, he was confident that no one would have come across his hiding place.

Fitzgerald ripped open the brown envelope and quickly checked its contents. Another passport in yet another name. Five hundred dollars in used notes and a first-class ticket to Cape Town. Escaping assassins don't travel first class. Five minutes later he left room 347, his old clothes strewn all over the floor and a '*Favor de no Molestar*' sign on the door.

Fitzgerald took the guest elevator to the ground floor, confident that no one would give a fifty-one-year-old man in a blue denim shirt, striped tie, sports jacket and grey flannels a second look. He stepped out of the elevator and strolled across the lobby, making no attempt to check out. When he'd arrived eight days earlier, he had paid cash in advance for the room. He had left the mini-bar locked, and never once rung room service, made an outside call or watched a pay film. There would be no extra charges on this guest's account.

He only had to wait for a few minutes before the shuttle bus swept up to the entrance. He checked his watch. Forty-three minutes to take-off. He wasn't at all anxious about missing Aeroperu's Flight 63 to Lima. He felt sure nothing was going to run on time that day.

Once the bus had dropped him at the airport he made his way slowly in the direction of the check-in counter, where he was not surprised to be told that the flight to Lima had been held up by over an hour. Several *policia* in the overcrowded, chaotic departures hall were suspiciously eyeing every passenger, and although he was stopped and questioned several times, and his case searched twice, he was eventually allowed to proceed to Gate 47.

He slowed his pace when he saw a couple of backpackers being dragged off by airport security staff. He idly wondered just how many innocent unshaven male Caucasians would spend the night being questioned in cells because of his actions earlier that afternoon.

When Fitzgerald joined the queue that led to Passport Control, he repeated his new name under his breath. It was his third that day. The blue-uniformed official in the little cubicle flicked open the New Zealand passport and carefully studied the photograph inside, which bore an undeniable resemblance to the smartly dressed man standing in front of him. He handed back the passport and allowed Alistair Douglas, a civil engineer from Christchurch, to stroll through to the departure lounge. After a further delay, the flight was finally called. A stewardess guided Mr Douglas to his seat in the first-class section.

'Would you care for a glass of champagne, sir?'

Fitzgerald shook his head. 'No, thank you. A glass of still water will be just fine,' he replied, trying out his New Zealand accent.

He fastened his seatbelt, sat back and pretended to read the in-flight magazine as the aircraft began its slow progress down the bumpy runway. Because of the extended line of planes waiting to take off in front of them, there was enough time for Fitzgerald to choose the dishes he would eat and the movie he would watch long before the 727 began its acceleration for take-off. When the wheels finally left the ground, Fitzgerald started to relax for the first time that day.

Once the aircraft had reached its cruising altitude, he disposed of the in-flight magazine, closed his eyes, and began to think about what needed to be done once he landed in Cape Town.

'This is your captain speaking,' said a sombre voice. 'I have an announcement to make which I know will cause some of you considerable distress.' Fitzgerald sat bolt upright. The one eventuality he hadn't planned for was an unscheduled return to Bogotá.

'I'm sorry to have to inform you that a national tragedy has taken place in Colombia today.'

Fitzgerald lightly gripped the armrest of his seat and concentrated on breathing evenly.

The captain hesitated for a moment. 'My friends,' he declared gravely, 'Colombia has suffered a terrible loss.' He paused. 'Our national team has been defeated by Brazil, by two goals to one.'

An audible groan went through the cabin, as if crashing into the nearest mountain would have been a preferable alternative. Fitzgerald allowed the suggestion of a smile to cross his lips.

The stewardess reappeared by his side. 'Can I fix a drink for you now we're on our way, Mr Douglas?'

'Thank you,' Fitzgerald replied. 'I think I'll have that glass of champagne after all.'

4

As Tom Lawrence entered the packed room, the press corps rose to their feet.

'The President of the United States,' declared the Press Secretary, just in case there was a visitor from outer space.

Lawrence climbed the one step up to the podium and placed Andy Lloyd's blue file on the lectern. He waved at the assembled journalists in a now-familiar gesture to let them know they could resume their seats.

'I am delighted to announce,' began the President, sounding relaxed, 'that I will be sending to Congress a Bill which I promised the American people during the election campaign.'

Few of the senior White House correspondents seated in front of him wrote down a word, as most of them knew that if there was going to be a story worth printing, it was much more likely to come during the question-and-answer session than from any prepared statement. In any case, the President's opening remarks would be handed to them in a press kit as they left the room. Old pros only fell back on the prepared text when they had to fill extra column inches.

This did not stop the President from reminding them that the passing of an Arms Reduction Bill would allow him to release more revenue for long-term health care, so that elderly Americans could expect a better standard of living during their retirement.

'This is a Bill that will be welcomed by any decent, caring citizen, and I am proud to be the President who will guide it through Congress.' Lawrence looked up and smiled hopefully, feeling satisfied that his opening statement at least had gone well.

Shouts of 'Mr President!' came from every direction as Lawrence opened his blue file and glanced down at the thirty-one likely questions. He looked up and smiled at a familiar face in the front row. 'Barbara,' he said, pointing to the veteran UPI journalist whose right it was, as the doyenne of the press corps, to ask the first question.

Barbara Evans rose slowly to her feet. 'Thank you, Mr President.' She paused for a moment before asking, 'Are you able to confirm that the CIA had no involvement in the assassination of the Colombian presidential candidate, Ricardo Guzman, in Bogotá on Saturday?'

A buzz of interest rippled around the room. Lawrence stared down at the redundant thirty-one questions and answers, wishing he hadn't dismissed Larry Harrington's offer of a more detailed briefing quite so casually.

'I'm glad you asked that question, Barbara,' he responded, without missing a beat. 'Because I want you to know that while I'm President, such a suggestion doesn't even arise. This administration would never in any circumstances interfere with the democratic process of a sovereign state. In fact, only this morning, I instructed the Secretary of State to call Mr Guzman's widow and pass on my personal condolences.'

Lawrence was relieved that Barbara Evans had mentioned the dead man's name, because otherwise he wouldn't have been able to recall it. 'It may also be of interest to you to know, Barbara, that I have already asked the Vice-President to represent me at the funeral, which I understand will be held in Bogotá this weekend.'

Pete Dowd, the Secret Service agent in charge of the Presidential Protective Division, immediately left the room to warn the Vice-President before the press got to him.

Barbara Evans looked unconvinced, but before she could follow up with a second question the President had turned his attention to a man standing in the back row who, he hoped, would have no interest in the presidential election in Colombia. But once he had asked his question, Lawrence began to wish he had. 'What chance does your Arms Reduction Bill have of becoming law if Victor Zerimski looks likely to be the next Russian President?'

For the next forty minutes Lawrence answered several questions about the Nuclear, Biological, Chemical and Conventional Arms Reduction Bill, but they were interspersed with demands to be told about the CIA's current role in South America, and how he would deal with Victor Zerimski should he become the next Russian President. As it became all too apparent that Lawrence didn't know a great deal more than they did about either subject, the hacks, scenting blood, began to badger him on them to the exclusion of all others, including the Arms Reduction Bill.

When Lawrence at last received a sympathetic question from Phil Ansanch on the subject of the Bill, he gave a long, discursive reply, and then without warning wrapped up the press conference by smiling down at the baying journalists and saying, 'Thank you, ladies and gentlemen. It's been a pleasure, as always.' Without another word he turned his back on them, quickly left the room and headed in the direction of the Oval Office.

The moment Andy Lloyd had caught up with him, the President growled under his breath, 'I need to speak to Larry Harrington immediately. As soon as you've tracked him down, call Langley. I want the Director of the CIA in my office within the hour.'

'I wonder, Mr President, if it might be wiser . . .' began the Chief of Staff.

'Within the hour, Andy,' said the President, not even looking at him. 'If I find out that the CIA had any involvement in that assassination in Colombia, I'll hang Dexter out to dry.'

'I'll ask the Secretary of State to join you immediately, Mr President,' said Lloyd. He disappeared into a side office, picked up the nearest phone and dialled Larry Harrington at the State Department. Even over the phone the Texan was unable to disguise his pleasure at being proved right so quickly.

When Lloyd had put the phone down, he made his way back to his own office, closed the door and sat silently at his desk for a few moments. Once he had thought through exactly what he needed to say, he dialled a number that only one person ever answered.

'The Director,' was all Helen Dexter said.

—◇—

Connor Fitzgerald handed over his passport to the Australian customs official. It would have been ironic if the document had been challenged, because for the first time in three weeks he was using his real name. The uniformed officer tapped out the details on his keyboard, checked the computer screen, then pressed a few more keys.

Nothing untoward appeared, so he stamped the tourist visa and said, 'Hope you enjoy your visit to Australia, Mr Fitzgerald.'

Connor thanked him and walked through to the baggage hall, where he took a seat opposite the motionless console and waited for his luggage to appear. He never allowed himself to be the first to pass through customs, even when he had nothing to declare.

When he had landed in Cape Town the previous day, Connor had been met off the plane by his old friend and colleague Carl Koeter. Carl had spent the next couple of hours debriefing him before they enjoyed a long lunch discussing Carl's divorce and what Maggie and Tara were up to. It was the second bottle of 1982 Rustenberg Cabernet Sauvignon that nearly caused Connor to miss his flight to Sydney. In the duty-free shop he hurriedly chose presents for his wife and daughter that were clearly stamped 'Made in South Africa'. Even his passport gave no clue that he had arrived in Cape Town via Bogotá, Lima and Buenos Aires.

As he sat in the baggage collection zone waiting for the console to start up, he began to think about the life he had been leading for the past twenty-eight years.

—◇—

Connor Fitzgerald had been brought up in a family dedicated to the cause of law and order.

His paternal grandfather, Oscar, named after another Irish poet, had emigrated to America from Kilkenny at the turn of the century. Within hours of landing at Ellis Island he had headed straight for Chicago, to join his cousin in the police department.

During Prohibition Oscar Fitzgerald was among the small band of cops who refused to take bribes from the mob. As a result he failed to rise above the rank of sergeant. But Oscar did sire five Godfearing sons, and only gave up when the local priest told him it was the Almighty's will that he and Mary wouldn't be blessed with a daughter. His wife was grateful for Father O'Reilly's words of wisdom – it was difficult enough raising five strapping lads on a sergeant's salary. Mind you, if Oscar had ever given her one cent more than she was entitled to from his weekly pay packet, Mary would have wanted to know in great detail where it came from.

On leaving high school, three of Oscar's boys joined the Chicago PD, where they quickly gained the promotion their father had deserved. Another took holy orders, which pleased Mary, and the youngest, Connor's father, studied criminal justice at De Paul on the GI Bill. After graduating, he joined the FBI. In 1949 he married Katherine O'Keefe, a girl who lived two doors away on South Lowe Street. They only had one child, a son, whom they christened Connor.

Connor was born in Chicago General Hospital on 8 February 1951, and even before he was old enough to attend the local Catholic school it had become clear that he was going to be a gifted football player. Connor's father was delighted when his son became captain of the Mount Carmel High School team, but his mother still kept him working late into the night, to make sure he always completed his homework. 'You can't play football for the rest of your life,' she continually reminded him.

The combination of a father who stood whenever a woman entered the room and a mother who verged on being a saint had left Connor, despite his physical prowess, shy in the presence of the opposite sex. Several girls at Mount Carmel High had made it only too obvious how they felt about him, but he didn't lose his virginity until he met Nancy in his senior year. Shortly after he had led Mount Carmel to another victory one autumn afternoon, Nancy had taken him behind the bleachers and seduced him. It would have been the first time he'd ever seen a naked woman, if she'd taken off all her clothes.

About a month later, Nancy asked him if he'd like to try two girls at once.

'I haven't even had two girls, let alone at once,' he told her. Nancy didn't seem impressed, and moved on.

When Connor won a scholarship to Notre Dame, he didn't take up any of the numerous offers that came the way of all the members of the football team. His team-mates seemed to take great pride in scratching the names of the girls who had succumbed to their charms on the inside of their locker doors. Brett Coleman, the team's place-kicker, had seventeen names inside his locker by the end of the first semester. The rule, he informed Connor, was that only penetration counted: 'The locker doors just aren't big enough to include oral sex.' At the end of his first year, 'Nancy' was still the only name Connor had scratched up. After practice one evening he checked through the other lockers, and discovered that Nancy's name appeared on almost every one of them, occasionally bracketed with that of another girl. The rest of the team would have given him hell for his low scoring if he hadn't been the best freshman quarterback Notre Dame had seen for a decade.

It was during Connor's first few days as a sophomore that everything changed.

When he turned up for his weekly session at the Irish Dance Club, she was putting on her shoes. He couldn't see her face, but that didn't matter much, because he was unable to take his eyes off those long, slim legs. As a football hero, he had become used to girls staring at him, but now the one girl he wanted to impress didn't seem aware that he even existed. To make matters worse, when she stepped onto the dance floor, she was partnered by Declan O'Casey, who had no rival as a dancer. They both held their backs rigidly straight, and their feet moved with a lightness Connor could never hope to match.

When the number came to an end, Connor still hadn't discovered her name. And, worse, she and Declan had left before he could find some way of being introduced to her. In desperation, he decided to follow them back to the women's dorms, walking fifty yards behind and always remaining in the shadows, just as his father had taught him. He grimaced as they held hands and chatted happily. When they reached Le Mans Hall she kissed Declan on the cheek and disappeared inside. Why, he wondered, hadn't he concentrated more on dancing and less on football?

After Declan had headed off in the direction of the men's dorms, Connor began to stroll casually up and down the sidewalk below the dormitory windows, wondering if there was anything he could do. He finally caught a glimpse of her in a dressing gown as she drew the curtain, and hung around for a few more minutes before reluctantly returning to his room. He sat on the end of his bed and began composing a letter to his mother, telling her that he had seen the girl he was going to marry, although he hadn't actually spoken to her yet – and come to think of it, he didn't even know her name. As Connor licked the envelope, he tried to convince himself that Declan O'Casey was nothing more to her than a dancing partner.

During the week, he tried to find out as much as he could about her, but he picked up very little other than that she was called Maggie Burke, had won a scholarship to St Mary's, and was in her freshman year studying Art History. He cursed the fact that he had never entered an art gallery in his life; in fact the nearest he'd come to painting was whenever his father asked him to touch up the fence surrounding their little back yard on South Lowe Street. Declan, it turned out, had been dating Maggie since her last year at school, and was not only the best dancer in the club, but was also considered the university's brightest mathematician. Other institutions were already offering him fellowships to pursue a postgraduate degree, even before the results of his final exams were known. Connor could only hope that Declan would be offered an irresistible post far away from South Bend as soon as possible.

Connor was the first to turn up at the dance club the following Thursday, and when Maggie appeared from the changing room in her cream cotton blouse and short black skirt, the only question he had to consider was whether to stare up into those green eyes or down at her long legs. Once again she was partnered by Declan all evening, while Connor sat mutely on a bench, trying to pretend he wasn't aware of her presence. After the final number the two of them slipped off. Once again Connor followed them back to Le Mans Hall, but this time he noticed that she wasn't holding Declan's hand.

After a long chat and another kiss on the cheek, Declan disappeared off in the direction of the men's dorms. Connor slumped down on a bench opposite her window and stared up at the balcony of the girls' dormitory. He decided to wait until he had seen her draw the curtains, but by the time she appeared at the window, he'd dozed off.

The next thing he remembered was waking from a deep sleep in which he had been dreaming that Maggie was standing in front of him, dressed in pyjamas and a dressing gown.

He woke with a start, stared at her in disbelief, jumped up and thrust out his hand. 'Hi, I'm Connor Fitzgerald.'

'I know,' she replied as she shook his hand. 'I'm Maggie Burke.'

'I know,' he said.

'Any room on that bench?' she asked.

From that moment, Connor never looked at another woman.

On the following Saturday Maggie went to a football game for the first time in her life, and watched him pull off a series of remarkable plays in front of what was for him a packed stadium of one.

The next Thursday, she and Connor danced together all evening, while Declan sat disconsolately in a corner. He looked even more desolate when the two of them left together, holding hands. When they reached Le Mans Hall, Connor kissed her for the first time, then fell on one knee and proposed. Maggie laughed, turned bright red, and ran inside. On his way back to the men's dorms Connor also laughed, but only when he spotted Declan hiding behind a tree.

From then on Connor and Maggie spent every moment of their spare time together. She learned about touchdowns, end zones and lateral passes, he about Bellini, Bernini and Luini. Every Thursday evening for the next three years he fell on one knee and proposed to her. Whenever his team-mates asked him why he hadn't scratched her name on the inside of his locker, he replied simply, 'Because I'm going to marry her.'

At the end of Connor's final year, Maggie finally agreed to be his wife – but not until she had completed her exams.

'It's taken me 141 proposals to make you see the light,' he said triumphantly.

'Oh, don't be stupid, Connor Fitzgerald,' she told him. 'I knew I was going to spend the rest of my life with you the moment I joined you on that bench.'

They were married two weeks after Maggie had graduated *summa cum laude*. Tara was born ten months later.

5

'DO YOU EXPECT ME to believe that the CIA didn't even *know* that an assassination attempt was being considered?'

'That is correct, sir,' said the Director of the CIA calmly. 'The moment we became aware of the assassination, which was within seconds of it taking place, I contacted the National Security Advisor, who, I understand, reported directly to you at Camp David.'

The President began to pace around the Oval Office, which he found not only gave him more time to think, but usually made his guests feel uneasy. Most people who entered the Oval Office were nervous already. His secretary had once told him that four out of five visitors went to the rest room only moments before they were due to meet the President. But he doubted if the woman sitting in front of him even knew where the nearest rest room was. If a bomb had gone off in the Rose Garden, Helen Dexter would probably have done no more than raise a well-groomed eyebrow. Her career had outlasted three Presidents so far, all of whom were rumoured at some point to have demanded her resignation.

'And when Mr Lloyd phoned to tell me that you required more details,' said Dexter, 'I instructed my deputy, Nick Gutenburg, to contact our people on the ground in Bogotá and to make extensive enquiries as to exactly what happened on Saturday afternoon. Gutenburg completed his report yesterday.' She tapped the file on her lap.

Lawrence stopped pacing and came to a halt under a portrait

of Abraham Lincoln that hung above the fireplace. He looked down at the nape of Helen Dexter's neck. She continued to face straight ahead.

The Director was dressed in an elegant, well-cut dark suit with a simple cream shirt. She rarely wore jewellery, even on state occasions. Her appointment by President Ford as Deputy Director at the age of thirty-two was meant to have been a stopgap to placate the feminist lobby a few weeks before the 1976 election. As it was, Ford turned out to be the stopgap. After a series of short-term directors who either resigned or retired, Ms Dexter finally ended up with the coveted position. Many rumours circulated in the hothouse atmosphere of Washington about her extreme right-wing views and the methods she had used to gain promotion, but no member of the Senate dared to question her appointment. She had graduated *summa cum laude* from Bryn Mawr, followed by the University of Pennsylvania Law School, before joining one of New York's leading law firms. After a series of rows with the board over the length of time it took women to become partners, ending in litigation that was settled out of court, she had accepted an offer to join the CIA.

She began her life with the Agency in the office of the Directorate of Operations, eventually rising to become its Deputy. By the time of her appointment, she had made more enemies than friends, but as the years passed they seemed to disappear, or were fired, or took early retirement. When she was appointed Director she had just turned forty. The *Washington Post* described her as having blasted a hole through the glass ceiling, but that didn't stop the bookies offering odds on how many days she would survive. Soon they altered that to weeks, and then months. Now they were taking bets on whether she would last longer as the head of the CIA than J. Edgar Hoover had at the FBI.

Within days of Tom Lawrence taking up residence in the White House, he had discovered the lengths to which Dexter would go to block him if he tried to encroach on her world. If he asked for reports on sensitive subjects, it was often weeks before they appeared on his desk, and when they eventually did, they inevitably turned out to be long, discursive, boring and already out of date. If he called her into the Oval Office to explain unanswered questions, she could make a deaf mute appear positively forthcoming. If he pushed her, she would play for time, obviously assuming she would still be in her job long after the voters had turned him out of his.

But it was not until he proposed his nomination for a vacancy on the Supreme Court that he saw Helen Dexter at her most lethal. Within days, she had placed files on his desk that went to great lengths to point out why the nominee was unacceptable.

Lawrence had pressed on with the claims of his candidate – one of his oldest friends, who was found hanging in his garage the day before he was due to take up office. He later discovered that the confidential file had been sent to every member of the Senate Selection Committee, but he was never able to prove who had been responsible.

Andy Lloyd had warned him on several occasions that if he ever tried to remove Dexter from her post, he had better have the sort of proof that would convince the public that Mother Teresa had held a secret bank account in Switzerland regularly topped up by organised crime syndicates.

Lawrence had accepted his Chief of Staff's judgement. But he now felt that if he could prove the CIA had been involved in the assassination of Ricardo Guzman without even bothering to inform him, he could have Dexter clearing her desk within days.

He returned to his chair and touched the button under the rim of his desk which would allow Andy to listen in on the conversation, or pick it up off the tape later that evening. Lawrence realised that Dexter would know exactly what he was up to, and he suspected that the legendary handbag which never left her side lacked the lipstick, perfume and compact usually associated with her sex, and had already recorded every syllable that had passed between them. Nevertheless, he still needed his version of events for the record.

'As you seem to be so well informed,' the President said as

he sat down, 'perhaps you could brief me in more detail on what actually happened in Bogotá.'

Helen Dexter ignored his sarcastic tone, and picked up a file from her lap. The white cover bearing a CIA logo had printed across it the words 'FOR THE PRESIDENT'S EYES ONLY'. Lawrence wondered just how many files she had stashed away across the river marked 'FOR THE DIRECTOR'S EYES ONLY'.

She flicked the file open. 'It has been confirmed by several sources that the assassination was carried out by a lone gunman,' she read.

'Name one of these sources,' snapped the President.

'Our Cultural Attaché in Bogotá,' replied the Director.

Lawrence raised an eyebrow. Half the Cultural Attachés in American embassies around the world had been placed there by the CIA simply to report back directly to Helen Dexter at Langley without any consultation with the local Ambassador, let alone the State Department. Most of them would have thought the Nutcracker Suite was a dish to be found on the menu of an exclusive restaurant.

The President sighed. 'And who does *he* think was responsible for the assassination?'

Dexter flicked over a few pages of the file, extracted a photograph and pushed it across the Oval Office desk. The President looked down at a picture of a well-dressed, prosperous-looking middle-aged man.

'And who's this?'

'Carlos Velez. He runs the second-largest drug cartel in Colombia. Guzman, of course, controlled the biggest.'

'And has Velez been charged?'

'Unfortunately he was killed only a few hours after the police had obtained a warrant to arrest him.'

'How convenient.'

The Director didn't blush. Not possible in her case, thought Lawrence: after all, blushing requires blood.

'And did this lone assassin have a name? Or did he also die only moments after a court order was . . .'

'No, sir, he's still very much alive,' the Director replied firmly. 'His name is Dirk van Rensberg.'

'What's known about him?' asked Lawrence.

'He's South African. Until recently he lived in Durban.'

'Until recently?'

'Yes. He went underground immediately after the assassination.'

'That would be quite easy to do, if you were never above ground in the first place,' said the President. He waited for the Director to react, but she remained impassive. Eventually he said, 'Do the Colombian authorities go along with your account of what happened, or is our Cultural Attaché your only source of information?'

'No, Mr President. We picked up the bulk of our intelligence from Bogotá's Chief of Police. In fact, he already has in custody one of van Rensberg's accomplices, who was employed as a waiter at the El Belvedere hotel, the building from which the shot was fired. He was arrested in the corridor only moments after he had helped the assassin to escape in the freight elevator.'

'And do we know anything of van Rensberg's movements following the assassination?'

'He seems to have taken a flight to Lima in the name of Alistair Douglas, and then continued on to Buenos Aires, using the same passport. We lost track of him after that.'

'And I doubt if you'll ever find him again.'

'Oh, I wouldn't be that pessimistic, Mr President,' said Dexter, ignoring Lawrence's tone. 'Hired assassins tend to be loners who often disappear for several months following a job of this importance. Then they reappear once they feel the heat is off.'

'Well,' said the President, 'let me assure you that in this case I intend to keep the heat on. When we next meet, I may well have a report of my own for you to consider.'

'I shall look forward to reading it,' said Dexter, sounding like the school bully who had no fear of the headmaster.

The President pressed a button under his desk. A moment

later there was a tap on the door and Andy Lloyd entered the room.

'Mr President, you have a meeting with Senator Bedell in a few minutes,' he said, ignoring Dexter's presence.

'Then I'll leave you, Mr President,' said Dexter, rising from her place. She put the file on the President's desk, picked up her handbag and left the room without another word.

The President didn't speak until the Director of the CIA had closed the door behind her. Then he turned to his Chief of Staff. 'I don't believe a word of it,' he muttered as he dropped the file into the out tray. Lloyd made a mental note to retrieve it as soon as his boss had left the room. 'I guess the best we can hope for is that we've put the fear of God in her, and that she won't consider carrying out another operation like that while I'm in the White House.'

'Remembering the way she treated you when you were a Senator, Mr President, I wouldn't put a lot of money on that.'

'As I can hardly employ an assassin to remove her, what do you suggest I do?'

'In my opinion she has left you with two choices, Mr President. You can either sack her and face the inevitable Senate inquiry, or accept defeat, go along with her version of what took place in Bogotá, and hope you can get the better of her next time.'

'There could be a third choice,' the President said quietly.

Lloyd listened intently, making no attempt to interrupt his boss. It quickly became clear that the President had given considerable thought to how he might remove Helen Dexter from her post as Director of the CIA.

<><

Connor collected his thoughts as he glanced up at the baggage arrivals screen. The console was beginning to spew out the luggage from his flight, and some passengers were already stepping forward to pick up the first bags.

It still saddened him that he had not been present at his

daughter's birth. While he had doubts about the wisdom of the United States's policy in Vietnam, Connor shared his family's patriotism. He volunteered for military service, and completed officers' candidate school while he waited for Maggie to graduate. They ended up only having time for a wedding and a four-day honeymoon before Second Lieutenant Fitzgerald left for Vietnam in July 1972.

Those two years in Vietnam were now a distant memory. Being promoted to first lieutenant, captured by the Vietcong, escaping while saving another man's life – it all seemed so long ago that he was almost able to convince himself that it had never actually happened. Five months after he returned home, the President awarded him the nation's highest military decoration, the Medal of Honor, but after eighteen months as a prisoner of war in Vietnam he was just happy to be alive and reunited with the woman he loved. And the moment he saw Tara, he fell in love for a second time.

Within a week of returning to the States, Connor began to look for a job. He had already been interviewed for a position at the CIA's Chicago field office when Captain Jackson, his old company commander, turned up unannounced and invited him to be part of a special unit that was being set up in Washington. Connor was warned that should he agree to join Jackson's elite team, there would be aspects of the job he could never discuss with anyone, including his wife. When he learned what was expected of him, he told Jackson that he would need a little time to think about it before he came to a decision. He discussed the problem with Father Graham, the family priest, who simply advised him: 'Never do anything you consider dishonourable, even if it's in the name of your country.'

When Maggie was offered a job at the Admissions Office at Georgetown University, Connor realised just how determined Jackson was to recruit him. He wrote to his old company commander the following day and said he would be delighted to join 'Maryland Insurance' as an executive trainee.

That was when the deception had begun.

A few weeks later Connor, Maggie and Tara moved to

Georgetown. They found a small house on Avon Place, the deposit being covered by the Army paycheques Maggie had deposited in Connor's account, refusing to believe he was dead.

Their only sadness during those early days in Washington was that Maggie suffered two miscarriages, and her gynaecologist advised her to accept that she could have only one child. It took a third miscarriage before Maggie finally accepted his advice.

Although they had now been married for thirty years, Maggie was still able to arouse Connor simply by smiling and running her hand down his back. He knew that when he walked out of customs and saw her waiting for him in the arrivals hall, it would be as if it was for the first time. He smiled at the thought that she would have been at the airport for at least an hour before the plane was scheduled to land.

His case appeared in front of him. He grabbed it from the conveyor and headed towards the exit.

Connor passed through the green channel, confident that even if his luggage was searched, the customs officer wouldn't be that interested in a wooden springbok marked clearly on the foot 'Made in South Africa'.

When he stepped out into the arrivals hall, he immediately spotted his wife and daughter standing among the crowd. He quickened his pace and smiled at the woman he adored. Why had she even given him a second look, let alone agreed to be his wife? His smile broadened as he took her in his arms.

'How are you, my darling?' he asked.

'I only come alive again when I know you're safely back from an assignment,' she whispered. He tried to ignore the word 'safely' as he released her and turned to the other woman in his life. A slightly taller version of the original, with the same long red hair and flashing green eyes, but a calmer temperament. Connor's only child gave him a huge kiss on the cheek that made him feel ten years younger.

At Tara's christening, Father Graham had asked the Almighty that the child might be blessed with the looks of Maggie and the brains of – Maggie. As Tara had grown up, her grades in high school, and the turned heads of young men, had proved Father

Graham not only to be a priest, but a prophet. Connor had soon given up fighting off the stream of admirers who had knocked on the front door of their little house in Georgetown, or even bothering to answer the phone: it was almost invariably another tongue-tied youth who hoped his daughter might agree to a date.

'How was South Africa?' Maggie asked as she linked arms with her husband.

'It's become even more precarious since Mandela's death,' Connor replied – he'd had a full briefing from Carl Koeter on the problems facing South Africa over their long lunch in Cape Town, supplemented by a week of local papers that he read during the flight to Sydney. 'The crime rate's so high in most of the major cities that it's no longer against the law to drive through a red light after dark. Mbeki is doing his best, but I'm afraid I'm going to have to recommend that the company cut back its investment in that part of the world – at least until we're confident that the civil war is under control.'

'"*Things fall apart; the centre cannot hold; mere anarchy is loosed upon the world*",' Maggie said.

'I don't think Yeats ever visited South Africa,' said Connor.

How often he had wanted to tell Maggie the whole truth, and explain why he had lived a lie for so many years. But it was not that easy. She may have been his mistress, but they were his masters, and he had always accepted the code of total silence. Over the years, he had tried to convince himself that it was in her best interests not to know the whole truth. But when she unthinkingly used words like 'assignment' and 'safely', he was aware that she knew far more than she ever admitted. Did he talk in his sleep? Soon, though, it would no longer be necessary to continue deceiving her. Maggie didn't know it yet, but Bogotá had been his last mission. During the holiday he would drop a hint about an expected promotion that would mean far less travelling.

'And the deal?' Maggie asked. 'Were you able to settle it?'

'The deal? Oh, yes, it all went pretty much to plan,' said Connor. That was the nearest he would get to telling her the truth.

Connor began to think about spending the next two weeks basking in the sun. As they passed a news-stand, a small headline in a right-hand column of the *Sydney Morning Herald* caught his eye.

American Vice-President to Attend Funeral in Colombia

Maggie let go of her husband's arm as they walked out of the Arrivals hall into the warm summer air and headed for the parking lot.

'Where were you when the bomb went off in Cape Town?' Tara asked.

Koeter hadn't mentioned anything about a bomb in Cape Town. Would he ever be able to relax?

6

HE INSTRUCTED HIS DRIVER to take him to the National Gallery.

As the car pulled away from the White House staff entrance, a Secret Service Uniformed Division officer in the guard booth opened the reinforced metal gate and raised a hand to acknowledge him. The driver turned onto State Place, drove between the South Grounds and the Ellipse, and past the Department of Commerce.

Four minutes later, the car drew up outside the gallery's east entrance. The passenger walked quickly across the cobbled driveway and up the stone steps. When he reached the top step, he glanced back over his shoulder to admire the vast Henry Moore sculpture that dominated the other side of the square, and checked to see if anyone was following him. He couldn't be sure, but then he wasn't a professional.

He walked into the building and turned left up the great marble staircase that led to the second-floor galleries where he had spent so many hours in his youth. The large rooms were crowded with schoolchildren, which was not unusual on a weekday morning. As he walked into Gallery 71, he looked around at the familiar Homers, Bellows and Hoppers, and began to feel at home – a sensation he never experienced in the White House. He moved on to Gallery 66, to admire once again August Saint-Gaudens' *Memorial to Shaw and the 54th Massachusetts Regiment.* The first time he'd seen the massive life-size frieze he had stood in front of it, mesmerised, for over an hour. Today he could only spare a few moments.

Because he couldn't stop stopping, it took him another quarter of an hour to reach the rotunda at the centre of the building. He walked quickly past the statue of Mercury and down the stairs, doubled back through the bookstore, ran down another flight of stairs and along the underground concourse before finally emerging in the East Wing. Taking one flight of steps up, he passed below the large Calder mobile hanging from the ceiling, then pushed his way through the revolving doors out of the building onto the cobbled driveway. By now he was confident no one was following him. He jumped into the back of the first taxi in the queue. Glancing out of the window, he saw his car and driver on the far side of the square.

'A.V.'s, on New York Avenue.'

The taxi turned left on Pennsylvania, then headed north up Sixth Street. He tried to marshal his thoughts into some sort of coherent order, grateful that the driver didn't want to spend the journey offering him his opinions on the Administration or, particularly, on the President.

They swung left onto New York Avenue and the taxi immediately began to slow down. He passed a ten-dollar bill to the driver even before they had come to a halt, then stepped out onto the street and shut the back door of the cab without waiting for the change.

He passed under a red, white and green awning which left no doubt of the proprietor's origins, and pushed open the door. It took a few moments for his eyes to grow accustomed to the light, or lack of it. When they did, he was relieved to find that the place was empty except for a solitary figure seated at a small table at the far end of the room, toying with a half-empty glass of tomato juice. His smart, well-cut suit gave no indication that he was unemployed. Although the man still had the build of an athlete, his prematurely balding dome made him look older than the age given in his file. Their eyes met, and the man nodded. He walked over and took the seat opposite him.

'My name is Andy . . .' he began.

'The mystery, Mr Lloyd, is not who you are, but why the President's Chief of Staff should want to see me in the first place,' said Chris Jackson.

-◄o►-

'And what *is* your specialist field?' Stuart McKenzie asked.

Maggie glanced at her husband, knowing he wouldn't welcome such an intrusion into his professional life.

Connor realised that Tara couldn't have warned the latest young man to fall under her spell not to discuss her father's work.

Until that moment, he couldn't remember enjoying a lunch more. Fish that must have been caught only hours before they had sat down at the corner table in the little beach café at Cronulla. Fruit that had never seen preservatives or a tin, and a beer he hoped they exported to Washington. Connor took a gulp of coffee before leaning back in his chair and watching the surfers only a hundred yards away – a sport he wished he'd discovered twenty years before. Stuart had been surprised by how fit Tara's father was when he tried out the surfboard for the first time. Connor bluffed by telling him that he still worked out two or three times a week. Two or three times a day would have been nearer the truth.

Although he would never consider anyone good enough for his daughter, Connor had to admit that over the past few days he had come to enjoy the young lawyer's company.

'I'm in the insurance business,' he replied, aware that his daughter would have told Stuart that much.

'Yes, Tara said you were a senior executive, but she didn't go into any details.'

Connor smiled. 'That's because I specialise in kidnap and ransom, and have the same attitude to client confidentiality that you take for granted in your profession.' He wondered if that would stop the young Australian pursuing the subject. It didn't.

'Sounds a lot more interesting than most of the run-of-the-mill cases I'm expected to advise on,' said Stuart, trying to draw him out.

'Ninety per cent of what I do is fairly routine and boring,' Connor said. 'In fact, I suspect I have even more paperwork to deal with than you do.'

'But I don't get trips to South Africa.'

Tara glanced anxiously in her father's direction, knowing that he wouldn't be pleased that this information had been passed on to a relative stranger. But Connor showed no sign of being annoyed.

'Yes, I have to admit my job has one or two compensations.'

'Would it be breaking client confidentiality to take me through a typical case?'

Maggie was about to intervene with a line she had used many times in the past, when Connor volunteered, 'The company I work for represents several corporate clients who have large overseas interests.'

'Why don't those clients use companies from the country involved? Surely they'd have a better feel for the local scene.'

'Con,' interrupted Maggie, 'I think you're burning. Perhaps we ought to get back to the hotel before you begin to look like a lobster.'

Connor was amused by his wife's unconvincing intervention, especially as she had made him wear a hat for the past hour.

'It's never quite that easy,' he said to the young lawyer. 'Take a company like Coca-Cola, for example – whom, I should point out, we don't represent. They have offices all over the world, employing tens of thousands of staff. In each country they have senior executives, most of whom have families.'

Maggie couldn't believe that Connor had allowed the conversation to go this far. They were fast approaching the question that always stopped any further enquiry dead in its tracks.

'But we have people well qualified to carry out such work in Sydney,' said Stuart, leaning forward to pour Connor some more coffee. 'After all, kidnap and ransom isn't unknown even in Australia.'

'Thank you,' said Connor. He took another gulp while he considered this statement. Stuart's scrutiny didn't falter – like a good prosecuting counsel, he waited patiently in the hope that the witness would at some stage offer an unguarded response.

'The truth is that I'm never called in unless there are complications.'

'Complications?'

'Let's say, for example, that a company has a large presence in a country where crime is rife and kidnap and ransom fairly common. The chairman of that company – although it's more likely to be his wife, because she will have far less day-to-day protection – is kidnapped.'

'That's when you move in?'

'No, not necessarily. After all, the local police may well be experienced at handling such problems, and there aren't many firms that welcome outside interference, especially when it comes from the States. Often I'll do no more than fly in to the capital city and start carrying out my own private enquiries. If I've visited that part of the world before and built up a rapport with the local police, I might make my presence known, but even then I'd still wait for them to ask me for assistance.'

'What if they don't?' asked Tara. Stuart was surprised that she had apparently never asked her father that question before.

'Then I have to go it alone,' said Connor, 'which makes the process all the more precarious.'

'But if the police aren't making any headway, why wouldn't they want to enlist your help? They must be aware of your particular expertise,' said Stuart.

'Because it's not unknown for the police to be involved at some level themselves.'

'I'm not sure I understand,' said Tara.

'The local police could be receiving part of the ransom,' suggested Stuart, 'so they wouldn't welcome any outside interference. In any case, they might think the foreign company involved could well afford to pay it.'

Connor nodded. It was quickly becoming clear why Stuart

had landed a job with one of the most prestigious criminal practices in Sydney.

'So what do you do if you think the local police might be taking a cut?' asked Stuart.

Tara began to wish she had warned Stuart not to push his luck too far, although she was fast coming to the conclusion that Australians had no idea where 'too far' was.

'When that happens you have to consider opening negotiations yourself, because if your client is killed, you can be sure that the ensuing investigation won't exactly be thorough, and it's unlikely that the kidnappers will ever be caught.'

'And once you've agreed to negotiate, what's your opening gambit?'

'Well, let's assume that the kidnapper demands a million dollars – kidnappers always ask for a round figure, usually in US dollars. Like any professional negotiator, my primary responsibility is to get the best possible deal. And the most important element of that is making sure that the company's employee comes to no harm. But I would never allow things to reach the negotiation stage if I felt that my client could be released without the company having to hand over a penny. The more you pay out, the more likely it is that the criminal will repeat the exercise a few months later, sometimes kidnapping exactly the same person.'

'How often do you reach the negotiating stage?'

'About 50 per cent of the time. That's the point when you discover whether or not you're dealing with professionals. The longer you can stretch out the negotiations, the more likely it is that amateurs will become anxious about being caught. And after a few days they often grow to like the person they've kidnapped, which makes it almost impossible for them to carry out their original plan. In the Peruvian Embassy siege, for example, they ended up holding a chess competition, and the terrorists won.'

All three of them laughed, which helped Maggie to relax a little.

'Is it the pros or the amateurs who send ears through the post?' asked Stuart with a wry smile.

'I'm happy to say I didn't represent the company that negotiated on behalf of Mr Getty's grandson. But even when I'm dealing with a pro, some of the best cards will still be in my hand.' Connor hadn't noticed that his wife and daughter had allowed their coffee to go cold.

'Please continue,' said Stuart.

'Well, the majority of kidnaps are one-off affairs, and although they're nearly always carried out by a professional criminal, he may have little or no experience of how to negotiate in a situation like that. Professional criminals are almost always over-confident. They imagine they can handle anything. Not unlike a lawyer who thinks he can open a restaurant simply because he eats three meals a day.'

Stuart smiled. 'So what do they settle for once they realise they're not going to get the mythical million?'

'I can only speak from my own experience,' said Connor. 'I usually end up handing over around a quarter of the sum demanded – in used, traceable notes. On a few occasions I've parted with as much as half. Only once did I agree to hand over the full amount. But in my defence, counsel, on that particular occasion even the island's Prime Minister was taking a cut.'

'How many of them get away with it?'

'Of the cases I've handled over the past seventeen years, only three, which works out at roughly 8 per cent.'

'Not a bad return. And how many clients have you lost?'

They were now entering territory even Maggie hadn't ventured onto before, and she began to shift uneasily in her chair.

'If you do lose a client, the company backs you to the hilt,' said Connor. He paused. 'But they don't allow anyone to fail twice.'

Maggie rose from her place, turned to Connor and said, 'I'm going for a swim. Anyone care to join me?'

'No, but I'd like another go on the board,' said Tara, eagerly assisting her mother's attempt to end the interrogation.

'How many times did you fall in this morning?' Connor

asked, confirming that he also thought it had gone quite far enough.

'A dozen or more,' said Tara. 'That was the worst one.' She pointed proudly to a large bruise on her right thigh.

'Why did you let her go that far, Stuart?' asked Maggie, sitting back down to take a closer look at the bruise.

'Because it gave me the chance to rescue her and look heroic.'

'Be warned, Stuart, she'll have mastered surfing by the end of the week, and she'll end up rescuing you,' said Connor with a laugh.

'I'm well aware of that,' Stuart replied. 'But the moment it happens I plan to introduce her to bungee jumping.'

Maggie turned visibly white, and quickly looked in Connor's direction.

'Don't worry, Mrs Fitzgerald,' Stuart added quickly. 'You'll all be back in America long before then.' None of them wanted to be reminded.

Tara grabbed Stuart by the arm. 'Let's go, Superman. It's time to find another wave you can rescue me from.'

Stuart leapt up. Turning to Connor, he said, 'If you ever discover your daughter's been kidnapped, I won't be demanding a ransom, and I won't be willing to settle – in US dollars or any other currency.'

Tara blushed. 'Come on,' she said, and they ran down the beach towards the breakers.

'And for the first time, I don't think I'd try to negotiate,' Connor said to Maggie, stretching and smiling.

'He's a nice young man,' said Maggie, taking his hand. 'It's just a pity he's not Irish.'

'It could have been worse,' said Connor, rising from his chair. 'He might have been English.'

Maggie smiled as they began walking towards the surf. 'You know, she didn't get home until five this morning.'

'Don't tell me you still lie awake all night whenever your daughter goes out on a date,' said Connor with a grin.

'Keep your voice down, Connor Fitzgerald, and try to remember she's our only child.'

'She's not a child any longer, Maggie,' he said. 'She's a grown woman, and in less than a year she'll be Dr Fitzgerald.'

'And you don't worry about her, of course.'

'You know I do,' said Connor, taking her in his arms. 'But if she's having an affair with Stuart – which is none of my business – she could have done a lot worse.'

'I didn't sleep with you until the day we were married, and even when they told me you were missing in Vietnam, I never looked at another man. And it wasn't because of a lack of offers.'

'I know, my darling,' said Connor. 'But by then you'd realised I was irreplaceable.'

Connor released his wife and ran towards the waves, making sure he always remained just one stride ahead of her. When she finally caught up with him, she was out of breath.

'Declan O'Casey proposed to me long before . . .'

'I know, my darling,' he replied, looking down into her green eyes and brushing back a stray wisp of hair. 'And never a day goes by when I'm not thankful that you waited for me. It was the one thing that kept me alive after I'd been captured in 'Nam. That and the thought of seeing Tara.'

Connor's words reminded Maggie of the sadness she had felt at her miscarriages and the knowledge that she couldn't have any more children. She had been brought up in a large family, and longed to have a brood herself. She could never accept her mother's simple philosophy – it's God's will.

While Connor had been away in Vietnam, she had spent many happy hours with Tara. But the moment he returned the young madam had transferred her affections overnight, and although she remained close to her daughter, Maggie knew that she could never have the same relationship with Tara that Connor enjoyed.

When Connor signed up with Maryland Insurance as a management trainee, Maggie had been puzzled by his decision. She had always thought that, like his father, Connor would want to be involved in law enforcement. That was before he explained who he would really be working for. Although he didn't go into great detail, he did tell her who his paymaster was, and the significance of being a non-official cover officer, or NOC. She kept his secret loyally over the years, though not being able to discuss her husband's profession with her friends and colleagues was sometimes a little awkward. But she decided this was a minor inconvenience, compared with what so many other wives were put through by husbands only too happy to discuss their work in endless detail. It was their extracurricular activities they wanted to keep secret.

All she really hoped was that one day her daughter would find someone willing to wait on a park bench all night just to see her draw a curtain.

7

JACKSON LIT A CIGARETTE, and listened carefully to every word the man from the White House had to say. He made no attempt to interrupt him.

When Lloyd eventually came to the end of his prepared piece, he took a sip of the *acqua minerale* in front of him and waited to hear what the former Deputy Director of the CIA's first question would be.

Jackson stubbed out his cigarette. 'May I ask why you thought I was the right person for this assignment?'

Lloyd was not taken by surprise. He had already decided that if Jackson asked that particular question, he would simply tell the truth. 'We know that you resigned your post with the CIA because of a . . . difference of opinion' – he emphasised the words – 'with Helen Dexter, despite the fact that your record with the Agency had been exemplary, and until then you were considered her natural successor. But since resigning for reasons that on the face of it seem somewhat bizarre, I believe you have not been able to find a job worthy of your qualifications. We suspect that Dexter also has something to do with that.'

'It only takes one phone call,' said Jackson, 'off the record, of course – and suddenly you find you've been removed from any shortlist. I've always been wary of speaking ill of the living, but in the case of Helen Dexter, I'm happy to make an exception.' He lit another cigarette. 'You see, Dexter believes that Tom Lawrence has the second most important job in America,' he continued. '*She* is the true defender of the faith, the nation's last bastion, and to her elected politicians are nothing more than a temporary inconvenience who will, sooner or later, be ejected by the voters.'

'The President has been made aware of that on more than one occasion,' Lloyd said, with some feeling.

'Presidents come and go, Mr Lloyd. My bet is that, like the rest of us, your boss is human, and therefore you can be sure that Dexter will have a file on him which is filled with the reasons why Lawrence isn't qualified for a second term. And by the way, she'll have one almost as thick on you.'

'Then we'll have to start building up our own file, Mr Jackson. I can think of no one better qualified to carry out the task.'

'Where would you like me to begin?'

'By investigating who was behind the assassination of Ricardo Guzman in Bogotá last month,' said Lloyd. 'We have reason to believe that the CIA might have been involved, directly or indirectly.'

'Without the President's knowledge?' said Jackson in disbelief.

Lloyd nodded, removed a file from his briefcase and slid it across the table. Jackson flicked it open.

'Take your time,' said Lloyd, 'because you're going to have to memorise everything.'

Jackson began reading, and started making observations even before he had come to the end of the first page.

'If we assume that it was a lone gunman, trying to get any reliable information will be virtually impossible. That sort of character doesn't leave a forwarding address.' Jackson paused. 'But if it *is* the CIA we're dealing with, then Dexter has a ten-day start on us. She's probably already turned every avenue that might lead to the assassin into a blind alley – unless . . .'

'Unless . . . ?' echoed Lloyd.

'I'm not the only person that woman has crossed over the years. It's just possible that there might be someone else based in Bogotá who – ' He paused. 'How long have I got?'

'The new President of Colombia is making an official visit to

Washington in three weeks' time. It would help if we had something by then.'

'It's already beginning to feel like the old days,' said Jackson as he stubbed out his cigarette. 'Except this time there's the added pleasure of Dexter being officially on the other side.' He lit another cigarette. 'Who will I be working for?'

'Officially you're freelance, but unofficially you work for me. You'll be paid at the same level as you were when you left the Agency, your account credited on a monthly basis, although for obvious reasons your name won't appear on any books. I'll contact you whenever . . .'

'No you won't, Mr Lloyd,' said Jackson. 'I'll contact *you* whenever I have anything worthwhile to report. Two-way contacts only double the chance of someone stumbling across us. All I'll need is an untraceable phone number.'

Lloyd wrote down seven figures on a cocktail napkin. 'This gets straight through to my desk, bypassing even my secretary. After midnight it's automatically transferred to a phone by the side of my bed. You can call me night or day. You needn't bother about the time difference when you're abroad, because I don't care about being woken up.'

'That's good to know,' said Jackson. 'Because I don't think Helen Dexter ever sleeps.'

Lloyd smiled. 'Have we covered everything?'

'Not quite,' said Jackson. 'When you leave, turn right and then take the next right. Don't look back, and don't hail a taxi until you've walked at least four blocks. From now on you're going to have to think like Dexter, and be warned, she's been at it for thirty years. There's only one person I know who's better than she is.'

'I hope that's you,' said Lloyd.

'I'm afraid not,' said Jackson.

'Don't tell me he already works for Dexter.'

Jackson nodded. 'Even though he's my closest friend, if Dexter ordered him to kill me, there isn't an insurance company in town that would take out a policy on my life. If you expect me to beat both of them, you'd better hope I haven't gone rusty over the past eight months.'

The two men rose. 'Goodbye, Mr Lloyd,' said Jackson as they shook hands. 'I'm sorry that this will be our first and last meeting.'

'But I thought we agreed – ' said Lloyd, looking anxiously at his new recruit.

'To work together, Mr Lloyd, not to meet. You see, Dexter wouldn't consider two meetings a coincidence.'

Lloyd nodded. 'I'll wait to hear from you.'

'And Mr Lloyd,' said Jackson, 'don't visit the National Gallery again, unless it's for the sole purpose of seeing the paintings.'

Lloyd frowned. 'Why not?' he asked.

'Because the half-asleep guard in Gallery 71 was planted there on the day of your appointment. It's all in your file. You go there once a week. Is Hopper still your favourite artist?'

Lloyd's mouth went dry. 'Then Dexter already knows about this meeting?'

'No,' said Jackson. 'You got lucky this time. It's the guard's day off.'

—◇—

Although Connor had seen his daughter cry many times when she was younger, over a cut leg, a bruised ego or simply not getting her own way, this was quite different. While she clung to Stuart he pretended to be absorbed in a rack of bestselling books at the news-stand, and reflected on one of the most enjoyable holidays he could remember. He'd put on a couple of pounds and had managed to almost master the surfboard, although he had rarely experienced more pride before more falls. During the past fortnight he had come first to like, and later to respect Stuart. And Maggie had even stopped reminding him every morning that Tara hadn't returned to her room the previous night. He took that to be his wife's reluctant seal of approval.

Connor picked up the *Sydney Morning Herald* from the news-stand. He flicked over the pages, only taking in the headlines until he came to the section marked 'International News'. He glanced towards Maggie, who was paying for some souvenirs that they would never display or even consider giving as presents, and which would undoubtedly end up in Father Graham's Christmas sale.

Connor lowered his head again. 'Landslide for Herrera in Colombia' was the headline running across three columns at the foot of the page. He read about the new President's one-sided victory over the National Party's last-minute replacement for Ricardo Guzman. Herrera, the article went on to say, planned to visit America in the near future to discuss with President Lawrence the problems Colombia was currently facing. Among the subjects uppermost . . .

'Do you think this would be all right for Joan?'

Connor glanced across at his wife, who was holding up a Ken Done print of Sydney Harbour.

'A bit modern for her, I would have thought.'

'Then we'll have to get her something from duty free once we're on the plane.'

'This is the last call for United Airlines Flight 816 to Los Angeles,' said a voice that echoed around the airport. 'Will all those who have not yet boarded the aircraft please make their way immediately to Gate 27.'

Connor and Maggie began walking in the direction of the large departure sign, trying to stay a few paces in front of their daughter and Stuart, who were locked together as if they were in a three-legged race. Once they had gone through passport control, Connor hung back, while Maggie carried on towards the departure lounge to tell the gate agent that the last two passengers would be following shortly.

When Tara reluctantly appeared round the corner a few moments later, Connor placed an arm gently around her shoulders. 'I know it's not much of a consolation, but your mother and I think he's . . .' Connor hesitated.

'I know,' she said between sobs. 'As soon as I get back to Stanford, I'm going to ask if they'll allow me to complete my

thesis at Sydney University.' Connor spotted his wife talking to a
stewardess by the gate to the aircraft.

'Is she that afraid of flying?' the stewardess whispered to
Maggie when she saw the young woman sobbing.

'No. She just had to leave something behind that they
wouldn't let her take through customs.'

—◇—

Maggie slept almost the entire fourteen-hour flight from Sydney
to Los Angeles. Tara always marvelled at how she managed it.
She could never do more than doze during a flight, however
many pills she took. She held her father's hand firmly. He smiled
at her but didn't speak.

Tara returned his smile. For as long as she could remember,
he had been the centre of her world. It never worried her that
she might not meet a man who could take his place; more
that when she did, he wouldn't be able to accept it. Now that it
had happened, she was relieved to discover just how supportive
he was. If anything, it was her mother who was proving to be
the problem.

Tara knew that if her mother had her way, she would still be
a virgin, and probably still living at home. It wasn't until the
eleventh grade that she stopped believing that if you kissed a
boy you'd become pregnant. That was when a classmate passed
on to her a much-thumbed copy of *The Joy of Sex*. Each night,
curled up under the sheets with a torch, Tara would turn the
pages.

But it was only after her graduation from Stone Ridge that
she lost her virginity – and if everyone else in her class had been
telling the truth, she must have been the last. Tara had joined
her parents for a long-promised visit to her great-grandfather's
birthplace. She fell in love with Ireland and its people within
moments of landing at Dublin. Over dinner in their hotel on the
first night, she told her father that she couldn't understand why
so many of the Irish were not content to remain in their homeland, but had to emigrate.

59

The young waiter who was serving them looked down at her and recited:

> *'Ireland never was contented.'*
> *'Say you so? You are demented.*
> *Ireland was contented when*
> *All could use the sword and pen.'*

'Walter Savage Landor,' Maggie said. 'But do you know the next line?'

The waiter bowed.

> *'And when Tara rose so high . . .'*

Tara blushed, and Connor burst out laughing. The waiter looked puzzled.

'It's my name,' Tara explained.

He bowed again before clearing away the plates. While her father was settling the bill and her mother was collecting her coat, the waiter asked Tara if she would like to join him for a drink at Gallagher's when he came off duty. Tara happily agreed.

She spent the next couple of hours watching an old movie in her room, before creeping downstairs just after midnight. The pub Liam had suggested was only a few hundred yards down the road, and when Tara walked in she found him waiting at the bar. Liam wasted no time in introducing her to the joys of Guinness. She wasn't surprised to discover that he had taken the job as a waiter during the holidays before he completed his final year at Trinity College, studying the Irish poets. Liam was surprised, however, to find how well she could quote Yeats, Joyce, Wilde and Synge.

When he took her back to her room a couple of hours later, he kissed her gently on the lips and asked, 'How long are you staying in Dublin?'

'Two more days,' she replied.

'Then don't let's waste a moment of it.'

After three nights during which she hardly slept, Tara

departed for Oscar's birthplace in Kilkenny, feeling qualified to add a footnote or two to *The Joy of Sex*.

As Liam carried their bags down to the hire car, Connor gave him a large tip and whispered, 'Thank you.' Tara blushed.

At Stanford in her sophomore year, Tara had what might have been described as an affair with a medical student. But it wasn't until he proposed that she realised she didn't want to spend the rest of her life with him. It hadn't taken her a year to reach a very different conclusion about Stuart.

They had first met when they bumped into each other. It was her fault – she wasn't looking when she crossed his path as he swooped down the face of a large wave. Both of them went flying. When he lifted her out of the water, Tara waited for a richly deserved tirade of abuse.

Instead he just smiled and said, 'In future, try and keep out of the fast lane.' She performed the same trick later that afternoon, but this time on purpose, and he knew it.

He laughed and said, 'You've left me with two choices. Either I start giving you lessons, or we can have a coffee. Otherwise our next meeting might well be in the local hospital. Which would you prefer?'

'Let's start with the coffee.'

Tara had wanted to sleep with Stuart that night, and by the time she was due to leave ten days later, she wished she hadn't made him wait three days. By the end of the week . . .

'This is your captain speaking. We're now beginning our descent into Los Angeles.'

Maggie woke with a start, rubbed her eyes and smiled at her daughter. 'Did I fall asleep?' she asked.

'Not until the plane took off,' Tara replied.

After they'd collected their luggage, Tara said goodbye to her parents and went off to join her connecting flight to San Francisco. As she disappeared into the crowd of arriving and departing passengers, Connor whispered to Maggie, 'It wouldn't surprise me if she turned round and took the next plane back to Sydney.' Maggie nodded.

They headed off in the direction of the domestic terminal,

and climbed aboard the 'red-eye'. This time Maggie was asleep even before the video describing the safety drill had been completed. As they flew across the States, Connor tried to dismiss Tara and Stuart from his thoughts, and to concentrate on what needed to be done once he was back in Washington. In three months' time he was due to be taken off the active list, and he still had no idea which department they planned to transfer him to. He dreaded the thought of being offered a nine-to-five job at headquarters, which he knew would consist of giving lectures to young NOCs on his experiences in the field. He had already warned Joan that he would resign if they didn't have anything more interesting to offer him. He wasn't cut out to be a teacher.

During the past year there had been hints about one or two front-line posts for which he was being considered, but that was before his boss had resigned without explanation. Despite twenty-eight years of service and several commendations, Connor was aware that now Chris Jackson was no longer with the Company, his future might not be quite as secure as he'd imagined.

8

'ARE YOU CERTAIN Jackson can be trusted?'

'No, Mr President, I'm not. But I am certain of one thing: Jackson loathes – I repeat, loathes – Helen Dexter as much as you do.'

'Well, that's as good as a personal recommendation,' said the President. 'What else made you pick him? Because if loathing Dexter was the primary qualification for the job, there must have been a fairly large number of candidates.'

'He also has the other attributes I was looking for. There's his record, as an officer in Vietnam and as head of counter-intelligence, not to mention his reputation as Deputy Director of the CIA.'

'Then why did he suddenly resign when he still had such a promising career ahead of him?'

'I suspect that Dexter felt it was a bit too promising, and he was beginning to look like a serious contender for her post.'

'If he can prove that she gave the order to assassinate Ricardo Guzman, he still might be. It looks as if you've chosen the best man for the job, Andy.'

'Jackson told me there was one better.'

'Then let's recruit him as well,' said the President.

'I had the same idea. But it turns out that he's already working for Dexter.'

'Well, at least he won't know Jackson's working for us. What else did he have to say?'

Lloyd opened the file and began to take the President

through the conversation he had had with the former Deputy Director of the CIA.

When he'd finished, Lawrence's only comment was, 'Are you telling me I'm expected to just sit around twiddling my thumbs while we wait for Jackson to come up with something?'

'Those were his conditions, Mr President, if we wanted him to take on the assignment. But I have a feeling that Mr Jackson isn't the sort of person who sits around twiddling *his* thumbs.'

'He'd better not be, because every day Dexter's at Langley is a day too many for me. Let's hope Jackson can supply us with enough rope to hang her publicly. And while we're at it, let's hold the execution in the Rose Garden.'

The Chief of Staff laughed. 'That might have the double advantage of getting a few more Republicans to vote with us on the Safe Streets and Crime Reduction Bill.'

The President smiled. 'Who's next?' he asked.

Lloyd glanced at his watch. 'Senator Bedell has been waiting in the lobby for some time.'

'What does he want now?'

'He was hoping to talk you through his latest set of proposed amendments to the Arms Reduction Bill.'

The President frowned. 'Did you notice how many points Zerimski has picked up in the latest opinion poll?'

◄○►

Maggie began dialling the 650 number moments after she had turned the key in the lock of their little house in Georgetown. Connor started to unpack, listening to one end of the conversation between his wife and his daughter.

'Just phoned to let you know that we've arrived back safely,' Maggie tried as an opener.

Connor smiled at the unconvincing ploy. Tara was far too acute to fall for it, but he knew that she would play along.

'Thanks for calling, Mom. It's good to hear you.'

'Everything all right at your end?' asked Maggie.

'Yes, fine,' Tara said, before spending the next few minutes trying obliquely to assure her mother that she wasn't about to do something impetuous. When she was convinced that Maggie was convinced, she asked, 'Is Dad around?'

'He's right here.' She handed the phone across the bed to Connor.

'Can you do me a favour, Dad?'

'You bet.'

'Please explain to Mom that I'm not about to do anything silly. Stuart's already rung twice since I got back, and as he's planning to' – she hesitated – 'to come over to the States for Christmas, I'm pretty sure I can hang on until then. By the way, Dad, I thought I'd better warn you that I already know what I'd like for Christmas.'

'And what's that, my darling?'

'That you'll pay for my overseas calls for the next eight months. I have a feeling that might end up being more expensive than buying that used car you promised me if I get my PhD.'

Connor laughed.

'So you'd better get that promotion you mentioned when we were in Australia. Bye, Dad.'

'Bye, darling.'

Connor hung up, and gave Maggie a reassuring smile. He was about to tell her for the tenth time to stop worrying, when the phone rang again. He picked up the receiver, assuming it would be Tara again. It wasn't.

'Sorry to call the moment you arrive back,' said Joan, 'but I've just heard from the boss, and it sounds like an emergency. How quickly can you come in?'

Connor checked his watch. 'I'll be with you in twenty minutes,' he said, and put the phone down.

'Who was that?' asked Maggie, as she continued unpacking.

'Joan. She just needs me to sign a couple of outstanding contracts. Shouldn't take too long.'

'Damn,' said Maggie. 'I forgot to get her a present on the plane.'

'I'll find her something on the way to the office.'

Connor quickly left the room, and ran down the stairs and out of the house before Maggie could ask any more questions.

He climbed into the old family Toyota, but it was some time before he could get the engine to splutter into life. He eventually eased the 'old tank', as Tara described it, out onto Twenty-Ninth Street. Fifteen minutes later he turned left on M Street, before taking another left and disappearing down a ramp into an unmarked underground carpark.

As Connor entered the building, the security guard touched the rim of his peaked hat and said, 'Welcome back, Mr Fitzgerald. I wasn't expecting to see you until Monday.'

'That makes two of us,' said Connor, returning the mock-salute and heading towards the bank of elevators. He took one to the seventh floor. When he stepped out into the corridor, he was greeted by a smile of recognition from the receptionist who sat at a desk below the boldly printed caption 'Maryland Insurance Company'. The directory on the ground floor stated that the distinguished firm occupied the seventh, eighth, ninth and tenth floors.

'How nice to see you, Mr Fitzgerald,' said the receptionist. 'You have a visitor.'

Connor smiled and nodded before continuing down the corridor. As he turned the corner, he spotted Joan standing by the door of his office. From the expression on her face, he suspected she had been waiting there for some time. Then he remembered Maggie's words just before he left home – not that Joan looked as if a present was uppermost in her thoughts.

'The boss arrived a few minutes ago,' Joan said, holding the door open for him.

Connor strode into his office. Sitting on the other side of his desk was someone he'd never known to take a holiday.

'I'm sorry to have kept you waiting, Director,' he said. 'I only . . .'

'We have a problem,' was all Helen Dexter said, pushing a file across the desk.

◄◦►

'Just give me one decent lead, and I'll do all the groundwork,' said Jackson.

'I only wish I could, Chris,' replied Bogotá's Chief of Police. 'But it has already been made clear to me by one or two of your former colleagues that you are now *persona non grata*.'

'I've never thought of you as someone who gave a damn about such niceties,' said Jackson as he poured the Police Chief another whisky.

'Chris, you have to understand that when you were a representative of your government, it was all above board.'

'Including your kickbacks, if I remember correctly.'

'But of course,' said the policeman nonchalantly. 'You'll be the first to appreciate that expenses still have to be met.' He took a gulp from his crystal glass. 'And as you know only too well, Chris, inflation in Colombia remains extremely high. My salary doesn't cover even my day-to-day expenses.'

'From that little homily,' said Jackson, 'am I to understand that the rate remains the same, even if one is *persona non grata*?'

The Chief of Police downed his last drop of whisky, wiped his moustache and said, 'Chris, Presidents come and go in both our countries – but not old friends.'

Jackson gave him a thin smile before removing an envelope from an inside pocket and sliding it under the table. The Chief of Police glanced inside it, unbuttoned a tunic pocket and slipped the envelope out of sight.

'I see that your new masters have not, alas, allowed you the same degree of latitude when it comes to – expenses.'

'One decent lead, that's all I ask,' repeated Jackson.

The Chief of Police held up his empty glass and waited until the barman had filled it to the brim. He took another long gulp. 'I have always believed, Chris, that if you're looking for a bargain, there's no better place to start than a pawn shop.' He smiled, drained his glass and rose from the table. 'And remembering the dilemma you are currently facing, my old friend, I would begin in the San Victorina district, and I wouldn't bother to do much more than window-shop.'

Once Connor had finished reading the details of the confidential memorandum, he passed the file back to the Director.

Her first question took him by surprise. 'How long is it before you're due to retire from the service?'

'I come off the active list on the first of January next year, but naturally I hope to remain with the Company.'

'It may not be quite that easy to accommodate your particular talents at the present time,' Dexter said matter-of-factly. 'However, I do have a vacancy I would feel able to recommend you for.' She paused. 'As director of our Cleveland office.'

'Cleveland?'

'Yes.'

'After twenty-eight years' service with the Company,' said Connor, 'I was rather hoping you might be able to find me something in Washington. I'm sure you know that my wife is the Dean of Admissions at Georgetown. It would be almost impossible for her to find an equivalent post in . . . Ohio.'

A long silence followed.

'I'd like to help,' Dexter said in the same flat tone, 'but there's nothing suitable for you at Langley at the present time. If you did feel able to take up the appointment in Cleveland, it might be possible to bring you back in a couple of years.'

Connor stared across the table at the woman he had served for the past twenty-six years, painfully aware that she was now using the same lethal blade on him as she had on so many of his colleagues in the past. But why, when he had always carried out her orders to the letter? He glanced at the file. Had the President demanded that someone should be sacrificed after he had been questioned so closely about the CIA's activities in Colombia? Was Cleveland to be his reward for all his years of service?

'Is there any alternative?' he asked.

The Director didn't hesitate. 'You could always opt for early retirement.' She sounded as if she was suggesting the replacement of a sixty-year-old janitor in her apartment building.

Connor sat in silence, unable to believe what he was hearing. He'd given his whole life to the Company, and like so many of its officers, he'd put that life on the line several times.

Helen Dexter rose from her place. 'Perhaps you'd let me know when you've reached a decision.' She left the room without another word.

Connor sat alone at his desk for some time, trying to take in the full implications of the Director's words. He recalled that Chris Jackson had told him of an almost identical conversation he had had with her eight months before. In his case, the position he'd been offered was in Milwaukee. 'It could never happen to me,' he remembered telling Chris at the time. 'After all, I'm a team player, and no one would suspect me of wanting her job.' But Connor had committed an even graver sin. By carrying out Dexter's orders, he had unwittingly become the cause of her possible downfall. If he were no longer around to embarrass her, she might survive yet again. How many other good officers had been sacrificed over the years, he wondered, on the altar of her ego?

Connor's thoughts were interrupted when Joan entered the room. She didn't need to be told that the meeting had gone badly.

'Anything I can do?' she asked quietly.

'No, not a thing, thanks, Joan.' After a short silence he added, 'You know I'm due to come off the active list soon.'

'On the first of January,' she said. 'But with your record, the Company's certain to offer you a large desk, civilised hours for a change, and perhaps a long-legged secretary thrown in.'

'It seems not,' said Connor. 'The only job the Director had in mind for me was to head up the office in Cleveland, and there certainly wasn't any mention of a long-legged secretary.'

'Cleveland?' repeated Joan incredulously.

Connor nodded.

'The bitch.'

Connor glanced up at his long-serving secretary, unable to hide a look of surprise. This was the strongest language he had heard her use about anyone in nineteen years, let alone the Director.

Joan looked him in the eye and said, 'What will you tell Maggie?'

'I don't know. But as I've been deceiving her for the past twenty-eight years, I'm sure I'll be able to come up with something.'

◄○►

As Chris Jackson opened the front door, a bell rang to warn the shopkeeper that someone had entered the premises.

There are more than a hundred pawn shops in Bogotá, most of them in the San Victorina district. Jackson hadn't done so much footwork since he had been a junior agent. He even began to wonder if his old friend the Chief of Police had sent him off on a wild goose chase. But he kept going, because he knew that this particular policeman always made sure there would be another envelope stuffed full of notes at some time in the future.

Escobar looked up from behind his evening paper. The old man reckoned that he could always tell, even before a customer had reached the counter, if he was a buyer or a seller. The look in their eyes, the cut of their clothes, even the way they walked towards him. It took only a glance at this particular gentleman to make him feel pleased that he hadn't closed early.

'Good evening, sir,' Escobar said, rising from his stool. He always added 'sir' when he thought it was a buyer. 'How may I assist you?'

'The gun in the window . . .'

'Ah, yes. I see that you are most discerning. It is indeed a collector's item.' Escobar lifted the counter lid and walked across to the window. He removed the case, placed it on the counter, and allowed his customer to have a closer look at its contents.

Jackson only needed a cursory glance at the handcrafted rifle to know its provenance. He wasn't surprised to find that one of the cartridges had been fired.

'How much are you asking for it?'

'Ten thousand dollars,' replied Escobar, having identified the American accent. 'I cannot let it go for any less. I have already received so many enquiries.'

After three days of traipsing round the hot and humid city,

Jackson was in no mood to bargain. But he didn't have that amount of cash on him, and he couldn't just write out a cheque or present a credit card.

'Can I leave a down-payment,' he asked, 'and pick it up first thing in the morning?'

'Certainly, sir,' said Escobar. 'Although for this particular item, I would require a 10 per cent deposit.'

Jackson nodded, and removed a wallet from his inside pocket. He extracted some used notes and passed them across the counter.

The shopkeeper counted the ten hundred-dollar bills slowly, then placed them in the cash register and wrote out a receipt.

Jackson looked down at the open case, smiled, removed the spent cartridge and put it in his pocket.

The old man was puzzled, not by Jackson's action, but because he could have sworn that all twelve bullets had been in place when he had bought the rifle.

'I'd pack up everything and join you tomorrow,' she said, 'if it weren't for my parents.'

'I'm sure they'd understand,' said Stuart.

'Maybe,' said Tara. 'But it wouldn't stop me feeling guilty about all the sacrifices my father's made over the years so I could finish my PhD. Not to mention my mother. She'd probably have a heart attack.'

'But you said you'd find out if your Faculty Advisor would allow you to finish off your doctorate in Sydney.'

'My Faculty Advisor isn't the problem,' said Tara. 'It's the Dean.'

'The Dean?'

'Yes. When my Faculty Advisor discussed the idea with him yesterday, he told her it was out of the question.' There was a long silence before Tara said, 'Are you still there, Stuart?'

'Sure am,' he said, followed by a sigh that would have done credit to a Shakespearean lover.

'It's only another eight months,' Tara reminded him. 'In fact, I can even tell you how many days. And don't forget, you'll be over here for Christmas.'

'I'm looking forward to that,' said Stuart. 'I only hope your parents don't feel I'm imposing on them. After all, they won't have seen you for some time.'

'Don't be silly. They were delighted when I told them you'd be joining us. Mom adores you, as you well know, and you're the first man Dad has ever had a good word for.'

'He's a remarkable man.'

'What do you mean?'

'I suspect you know exactly what I mean.'

'I'd better hang up, or Dad will need a raise just to cover my phone bills. By the way, it's your turn next time.'

Stuart pretended he hadn't noticed how suddenly Tara had changed the subject.

'It always seems strange to me,' she continued, 'that you're still at work while I'm fast asleep.'

'Well, I can think of one way of changing that,' said Stuart.

◄○►

When he opened the door, the alarm went off. A carriage clock in the outer office struck twice as he swept aside the bead curtain and stepped into the shop. He stared across at the stand in the window. The rifle was no longer in its place.

It took him several minutes to find it, hidden under the counter.

He checked each item, and noted that one cartridge was missing, placed the case under his arm and left as quickly as he had entered. Not that he had any anxiety about being caught: the Chief of Police had assured him that the break-in would not be reported for at least thirty minutes. He glanced at the carriage clock before closing the door behind him. It was twelve minutes past two.

The Chief of Police could hardly be blamed if his old friend didn't have enough cash on him to buy the rifle. And in any case, he did so like being paid twice for the same piece of information. Especially when the currency was dollars.

◆

She poured him a second cup of coffee.

'Maggie, I'm considering resigning from the company and looking for a job that means I don't have to travel so much.' He glanced across the kitchen table and waited to see how his wife would react.

Maggie replaced the coffee pot on the warmer and took a sip from her own cup before she spoke. 'Why now?' she asked simply.

'The Chairman has told me I'm to be taken off kidnap and ransom and replaced by a younger man. It's company policy at my age.'

'But there must be plenty of other jobs in the company for someone with your experience.'

'The Chairman did come up with a suggestion,' said Connor. 'She offered me the chance to head up our field office in Cleveland.'

'Cleveland?' said Maggie in disbelief. She remained silent for some time, then said quietly, 'Why is the Chairman suddenly so keen to see the back of you?'

'Oh, it's not that bad. After all, if I turn the offer down, I'm still eligible for a full retirement package,' said Connor, making no attempt to answer her question. 'In any case, Joan assures me there are several large insurance companies in Washington who would be only too happy to employ someone with my experience.'

'But not the one you're currently working for,' said Maggie, still looking directly at her husband. Connor met her eyes, but couldn't think of a convincing reply. There followed an even longer silence.

'Don't you think the time has come to tell me the whole truth,' said Maggie. 'Or am I simply expected to go on believing every word you say, like a dutiful wife?'

Connor lowered his head and remained silent.

'You've never hidden the fact that "Maryland Insurance" is nothing more than a front for the CIA. And I've never pressed you on the subject. But lately even your well-disguised trips have left a little mud on your shoes.'

'I'm not sure I understand,' Connor said lamely.

'When I picked up your suit from the dry cleaners, they told me they'd found this in the pocket.' Maggie placed a tiny coin on the table. 'I'm told it has no value outside Colombia.'

Connor stared at a ten-peso piece, that would cover a local call in Bogotá.

'Many wives would immediately jump to one conclusion, Connor Fitzgerald,' Maggie continued. 'But don't forget, I've known you for over thirty years, and I'm well aware you're not capable of that particular deception.'

'I promise you, Maggie . . .'

'I know, Connor. I've always accepted that there had to be a good reason why you haven't been completely candid with me over the years.' She leaned across, took her husband's hand and said, 'But if you're now to be dumped on the scrapheap for no apparent reason, don't you feel I have a right to be told exactly what you've been up to for the past twenty-eight years?'

◄o►

Jackson asked the taxi driver to pull up outside the pawn shop and wait. He would only be a few minutes, he said, and then he wanted to be taken on to the airport.

As soon as he entered the shop, Escobar came scurrying through from the outer office. He looked agitated. When he saw who the customer was, he bowed his head and without a word pressed a key on the cash register and pulled open the drawer. He slowly extracted ten hundred-dollar bills and handed them across the counter.

'I must apologise, sir,' he said, looking up at the tall American, 'but I fear the rifle was stolen at some time during the night.'

Jackson didn't comment.

'The funny thing about it,' continued Escobar, 'is that who-ever stole it didn't take any cash.'

Jackson still said nothing. Escobar couldn't help thinking, after his customer had left the shop, that he hadn't seemed all that surprised.

As the taxi headed towards the airport, Jackson placed a hand in his jacket pocket and removed the spent cartridge. He might not be able to prove who had pulled the trigger, but he was now in no doubt who had given the order to assassinate Ricardo Guzman.

9

THE HELICOPTER LANDED SOFTLY on a patch of grass by the Reflecting Pool between the Washington and Lincoln Memorials. As the rotor blades slowed, a short flight of steps unfolded. The door of *Nighthawk* swung open and President Herrera appeared, sporting a full-dress uniform that made him look like a minor character in a B-movie. He stood to attention and returned the salute of the waiting Marines, then walked the short distance to his armoured Cadillac limousine. As the motorcade proceeded up Seventeenth Street, every flagstaff was flying the Colombian, American and District of Columbia flags.

Tom Lawrence, Larry Harrington and Andy Lloyd were waiting for him at the south portico of the White House. 'The better-tailored the outfit, the more colourful the sash, the more numerous the medals, the less significant the country,' Lawrence thought as he stepped forward to greet his visitor.

'Antonio, my dear old friend,' said Lawrence as Herrera embraced him, though they had only met once before. When Herrera eventually released his host, Lawrence turned to introduce him to Harrington and Lloyd. Cameras flashed and videotapes whirred as the presidential party made its way into the White House. Several more 'grip and grin' pictures were taken in the long corridor below a full-length portrait of George Washington.

After the requisite three-minute photo-op the President ushered his guest into the Oval Office. While Colombian coffee was being served and yet more photographs taken, they discussed nothing of significance. When they were eventually left alone, the Secretary of State began to guide the conversation on to the current relationship between the two countries. Lawrence was grateful for the briefing he had received from Larry earlier that morning. He felt able to speak authoritatively about extradition agreements, this year's coffee crop, the drug problem, even the new metro being constructed in Bogotá by an American company as part of an overseas aid package.

As the Secretary of State broadened the discussion to take in the repayment of extended dollar loans and the disparity of exports and imports between the two countries, Lawrence found his mind wandering to the problems he would have to face later that day.

The Arms Reduction Bill was getting bogged down in committee, and Andy had already warned him that the votes just weren't stacking up. He would probably need to see several Congressmen individually if he was to have any chance of pushing it through. He was aware that these ritual visits to the White House were usually nothing more than ego-massaging, so that the elected representatives could return to their districts and inform the voters – if they were Democrats – how close their relationship was with the President, or – if they were Republicans – how the President was dependent on their support to get any legislation through. With the mid-term elections less than a year away, Lawrence realised that there would have to be quite a few unscheduled meetings during the coming weeks.

He was brought back to the present with a jolt when Herrera said, '. . . and for that I must thank you particularly, Mr President.' A large smile appeared on the face of Colombia's leader as the three most powerful men in America stared at him in disbelief.

'Would you care to repeat that, Antonio?' said the President, not quite sure that he had heard his visitor correctly.

'As we are in the privacy of the Oval Office, Tom, I just wanted to say how much I appreciated the personal role you played in my election.'

◄◊►

'How long have you been working for Maryland Life, Mr Fitzgerald?' asked the Chairman of the Board. It was his first question in an interview that had already lasted for over an hour.

'Twenty-eight years in May, Mr Thompson,' replied Connor, looking directly at the man who sat at the centre of the large table facing him.

'Your record is most impressive,' said the woman sitting on the Chairman's right. 'And your references are impeccable. I'm bound to ask why you want to leave your present job. And, perhaps more important, why Maryland Life seems willing to let you go.'

Connor had discussed how he should answer this question with Maggie over dinner the previous evening. 'Just tell them the truth,' she had said. 'And don't bother with any guile; you've never been any good at it.' He hadn't expected any different advice.

'My only immediate chance of promotion would have meant moving to Cleveland,' he answered, 'and I felt I couldn't ask my wife to give up her job at Georgetown University. It would be hard for her to find an equivalent post in Ohio.'

The third member of the interviewing board nodded. Maggie had briefed him that one member of the panel had a son who was in his senior year at Georgetown.

'I don't think that we need to detain you any longer,' said the Chairman. 'I'd just like to thank you, Mr Fitzgerald, for coming to see us this afternoon.'

'My pleasure,' said Connor, standing to leave.

To his surprise the Chairman rose from behind the long table and came round to join him. 'Would you and your wife care to have dinner with us one evening next week?' he asked as he escorted Connor to the door.

'We'd be delighted, sir,' Connor replied.

'Ben,' said the Chairman. 'Nobody at Washington Provident calls me sir, and certainly not my senior executives.' He smiled and shook Connor warmly by the hand. 'I'll ask my secretary to phone your office tomorrow morning and fix a date. I look forward to meeting your wife – Maggie, isn't it?'

'Yes, sir,' Connor replied. He paused. 'And I look forward to meeting Mrs Thompson, Ben.'

◄◊►

The White House Chief of Staff picked up the red phone, but didn't immediately recognise the voice.

'I have some information you might find useful. I'm sorry it's taken so long.'

Lloyd quickly grabbed a blank yellow pad and flicked the top off a felt-tip pen. He didn't need to press any buttons – every conversation that took place on that particular phone was automatically recorded.

'I've just returned from ten days in Bogotá, and someone down there was making sure that doors were not only slammed in my face, but locked and bolted.'

'So Dexter must have found out what you were up to,' said Lloyd.

'Within minutes of my speaking to the local Chief of Police, would be my bet.'

'Does that mean she also knows who you're working for?'

'No, I covered myself on that front, which is why I've taken so long getting back to you. And I can promise you that after the wild goose chase I led one of her junior officers on, she'll never be able to fathom who I'm reporting back to. Our Cultural Attaché in Bogotá is now following up every known drug baron, every junior official in the narcotics department, and half the local police force. His report will fill so many pages it will take them a month just to read it, let alone figure out what the hell I was doing down there.'

'Did you come up with anything we could pin on Dexter?' Lloyd asked.

'Nothing she wouldn't be able to explain away with the usual smoke and mirrors. But all the evidence suggests that the CIA was behind the assassination.'

'We already know that,' said Lloyd. 'The President's problem is that, although our informant's credentials are impeccable, he could never appear on the stand, because he's the person who directly benefited from the assassination. Do you have anything that could stand up in court?'

'Only Bogotá's Chief of Police, and his credentials certainly aren't impeccable. If he were to stand up in court, you could never be certain which side he'd end up supporting.'

'Then how can you be so sure the CIA was involved?'

'I saw the rifle that I'm confident was used to kill Guzman. I even got hold of the spent cartridge of the bullet that hit him. What's more, I'm fairly sure I know the man who made the gun. He's the best in the business, and he's contracted to work for a small number of NOCs.'

'NOCs?'

'Non-official cover officers, unattached to any government agency. That way the CIA can deny all knowledge of their activities if anything goes wrong.'

'So the assassin is a serving officer of the CIA,' said Lloyd.

'It looks that way. Unless it turns out to be the one Dexter pensioned off a few days ago.'

'Well there's one person we ought to have on our payroll.'

There was a long silence before Jackson finally said, 'That may be the way you do things at the White House, Mr Lloyd, but this man wouldn't betray a former employer, however large a bribe you offered him. Threatening him won't work either: he wouldn't give you the time of day if you put a gun to his head.'

'How can you be so sure?'

'He served under me in 'Nam, and even the Vietcong couldn't get anything out of him. If you really want to know, he's about the only reason I'm still alive. In any case, Dexter will already have convinced him that her orders came direct from the White House.'

'We could tell him she was lying,' said Lloyd.

'That would only put his own life in danger. No, I have to be able to prove Dexter's involvement without him finding out what we're up to. And that won't be easy.'

'So how do you intend to do it?'

'By going to his retirement party.'

'Are you serious?'

'Yes, because there'll be one person there who loves him even more than she loves her country. And she might just be willing to talk. I'll be in touch.'

The phone went dead.

◄o►

When Nick Gutenburg, the Deputy Director of the CIA, entered the drawing room of the Fitzgeralds' home, the first person he saw was his predecessor Chris Jackson, deep in conversation with Joan Bennett. Was he telling her who he'd been working for in Bogotá? Gutenburg would have liked to overhear what they were talking about, but first he had to say hello to his host and hostess.

'I'll do another nine months with the company,' Joan was saying. 'By then I'll be eligible for my full pension. After that, I'm hoping to join Connor in his new job.'

'I've only just heard about that,' said Jackson. 'It sounds ideal. From what Maggie was telling me, he won't have to spend quite so much time travelling.'

'That's right, but his appointment isn't official yet,' said Joan. 'And you know how Connor feels about things being cut and dried. But as the Chairman of Washington Provident has invited him and Maggie to dinner tomorrow night, I think we can assume he's landed the job. Unless, of course, Mr Thompson simply wants to make up a bridge four.'

'Good of you to come, Nick,' said Connor warmly, passing the Deputy Director a glass of Perrier. He didn't need to be reminded that Gutenburg never allowed alcohol to pass his lips.

'Wouldn't have missed it for the world, Connor,' replied Gutenburg.

Turning to his wife, Connor said, 'Maggie, this is Nick Gutenburg, a colleague of mine. He works in . . .'

'Loss adjustment,' Gutenburg interjected quickly. 'We're all going to miss your husband at Maryland Life, Mrs Fitzgerald,' he said.

'Well, I'm sure your paths will cross again,' said Maggie, 'now that Connor's taking up another job in the same line of business.'

'It hasn't been confirmed yet,' said Connor. 'But as soon as it is, Nick, you'll be the first to hear about it.'

Gutenburg's eyes returned to Jackson, and when he moved away from Joan Bennett, Gutenburg slipped across the room to join her.

'I was delighted to hear that you'll be staying with the company, Joan,' were his opening words. 'I thought you might be leaving us to join Connor in his new job.'

'No, I'll be remaining with the firm,' said Joan, uncertain how much the Deputy Director knew.

'I just thought that as Connor's continuing in the same line of business . . .'

You're on a fishing trip, thought Joan. 'I wouldn't know,' she said firmly.

'Who's Chris Jackson talking to?' Gutenburg asked.

Joan looked across the room. She would like to have been able to say she had no idea, but she knew she wouldn't get away with it. 'That's Father Graham, the Fitzgeralds' local parish priest from Chicago, and Tara, Connor's daughter.'

'And what does she do?' asked Gutenburg.

'She's completing a PhD at Stanford.'

Gutenburg realised that he was wasting his time trying to get any real information out of Connor's secretary. After all, she had worked for Fitzgerald for nearly twenty years, so there wasn't much doubt where her loyalties lay – though there was nothing in her file to suggest that their relationship was anything but professional. And, looking at Miss Bennett, he suspected she might be the last forty-five-year-old virgin left in Washington. When Connor's daughter went over to the drinks table to refill her glass, Gutenburg left Joan without another word.

'My name's Nick Gutenburg,' he told her, thrusting out his hand. 'I'm a colleague of your father's.'

'I'm Tara,' she said. 'Do you work at the downtown office?'

'No, I'm based in the suburbs,' said Gutenburg. 'Are you still on the West Coast doing graduate work?'

'That's right,' Tara replied, looking a little surprised. 'And what about you? Which branch of the company do you work for?'

'Loss adjustment. It's rather boring compared with what your father does, but someone has to stay at home and do the paperwork,' he said, letting out a little laugh. 'By the way, I was delighted to hear about your dad's new appointment.'

'Yes, Mom was pleased that such a prestigious firm snapped him up so quickly. Although it's still not official.'

'Will he be working out of Washington?' Gutenburg asked, sipping his Perrier.

'Yes, the company's based just a couple of blocks from his old office . . .' Tara stopped talking when she heard a sharp noise. She turned to see Chris Jackson banging the table to bring the guests to order.

'Excuse me,' she whispered. 'That's my cue to resume my official duties for the evening.' She walked quickly away, and Gutenburg turned to listen to his predecessor at Langley.

'Ladies and gentlemen,' Chris began. He waited until everyone was silent before he continued. 'It's my privilege to propose a toast to two of my oldest friends, Connor and Maggie. Over the years, Connor has consistently proved to be the one man most likely to get me into a scrape.'

The guests laughed. One called out, 'Only too true,' and another added, 'I know the problem.'

'But once you're in a scrape, I don't know anyone better to get you out of it.' This was greeted by warm applause. 'We first met . . .'

Gutenburg felt his pager buzz, and quickly pulled it off his belt. 'troy asap', it read. He flicked it off, and slipped out of the room into the hall. He picked up the nearest phone as if he was in his own home and dialled a number that wasn't in any directory. It hadn't even rung before a voice said, 'The Director.'

'I got your message, but I'm on a non-secure line.' He didn't need to announce who he was.

'What I have to tell you, everyone in the world will know about in a few hours.'

Gutenburg didn't speak. It wasted time.

'Yeltsin died of a heart attack seventeen minutes ago,' said Helen Dexter. 'Report to my office immediately, and cancel everything you're doing for the next forty-eight hours.' The line went dead. No call from a non-secure line to Dexter's office ever lasted more than forty-five seconds. She kept a stop-watch on her desk.

Gutenburg replaced the phone and slipped out of the front door without bothering to say goodbye to his hostess. He was being driven down the Parkway on his way back to Langley by the time Chris raised his glass and said, 'To Connor and Maggie, and whatever the future holds for them.'

All the guests raised their glasses. 'To Connor and Maggie.'

10

'I'LL TELL YOU EXACTLY where my information came from,' said Tom Lawrence. 'From the President of Colombia himself. He thanked me personally for "the role I played in his election".'

'That's hardly proof,' Helen Dexter said, showing no sign of emotion.

'Are you doubting my word?' The President made no attempt to hide his anger.

'Certainly not, Mr President,' said Dexter calmly. 'But if you're accusing the Agency of carrying out covert operations without your knowledge, I hope it's not going to be simply on the word of a South American politician.'

The President leaned forward. 'I suggest that you listen carefully to a recording of a conversation that took place in this office quite recently,' he said. 'Because what you're about to hear struck me as having a ring of truth about it – something I suspect you haven't had much exposure to in recent years.'

The Director remained impassive, although Nick Gutenburg, seated on her right, shifted uneasily in his seat. The President nodded in the direction of Andy Lloyd, who reached over and pressed a button on a tape recorder that had been placed on the corner of the President's desk.

'Would you care to go into greater detail?'

'Of course, although I'm sure I can't tell you anything you don't already know. My only real rival, Ricardo Guzman, was conveniently removed from the contest just two weeks before the election.'

'*Surely you're not suggesting . . .*' It was Lawrence's voice.

'*Well, if it wasn't your people, it certainly wasn't mine,*' Herrera cut in before the President could finish his sentence.

There followed such a long silence that Gutenburg began to wonder if the conversation had come to an end, but as Lawrence and Lloyd didn't move, he assumed there was more to follow.

'*Do you have any actual evidence to link the assassination with the CIA?*' asked Lloyd eventually.

'*The bullet that killed him was traced to a rifle that had been sold to a pawn shop before the assassin fled the country. The rifle was later removed from the shop by one of your operatives and shipped back to America via the diplomatic pouch.*'

'*How can you be so sure of that?*'

'*My Chief of Police is obviously a lot more forthcoming with me than the CIA are with you.*'

Andy Lloyd flicked off the tape recorder. Helen Dexter looked up to find the President's eyes boring into hers.

'Well?' Lawrence asked. 'What simple explanation do you have this time?'

'From that conversation there is absolutely no proof of any CIA involvement in Guzman's assassination,' she said evenly. 'All it suggests to me is that Herrera is trying to shield the person who carried out his orders.'

'I assume you're referring to the "lone assassin" who has since conveniently disappeared somewhere in South Africa,' said the President sarcastically.

'The moment he surfaces, Mr President, we'll find him, and then I'll be able to supply the proof you've asked for.'

'An innocent man shot in a back street in Johannesburg will not be enough proof for me,' said Lawrence.

'Nor me,' said Dexter. 'When I produce the man who was responsible for the assassination, there won't be any doubt about who he was working for.' There was a slight edge to her voice.

'If you fail to do so,' said the President, 'I wouldn't be surprised if this tape' – he tapped the recorder – 'ended up in the hands of a certain reporter at the *Washington Post* who isn't exactly known for his love of the CIA. We can leave it to him to decide if Herrera is covering himself, or simply telling the truth. Either way, you're going to have to answer an awful lot of awkward questions.'

'If that were ever to happen, you might have to answer one or two yourself, Mr President,' said Dexter, not flinching.

Lawrence rose angrily from his chair and glared down at her. 'Let me make it clear that I still require positive proof of the existence of your missing South African. And if you fail to produce it within twenty-eight days, I'll expect both of your resignations on my desk. Now get out of my office.'

The Director and her Deputy rose to leave the room without another word. Neither of them spoke until they were seated in the back of Dexter's car. Once they had been driven out of the grounds of the White House, she touched a button on her armrest and a smoked-glass window slid up so that the driver – a senior operative – was unable to hear the conversation taking place behind him.

'Have you found out which company it was that interviewed Fitzgerald?'

'Yes,' replied Gutenburg.

'Then you're going to have to give their Chairman a call.'

—<o>—

'My name is Nick Gutenburg. I'm the Deputy Director of the CIA. You may wish to call me back. The switchboard number at the Agency is 703 482 1100. If you give the operator your name, she will put you straight through to my office.' He put the phone down.

Gutenburg had found over the years that not only were such calls invariably returned, usually in under a minute, but that the little subterfuge nearly always gave him the upper hand.

He sat at his desk, waiting. Two minutes passed, but he wasn't concerned. He knew that this particular gentleman would want to verify the number. Once he had confirmed that it was the CIA's switchboard, Gutenburg would be in an even stronger position.

When the phone eventually rang three minutes later, Gutenburg let it continue for some time before answering it. 'Good morning, Mr Thompson,' he said, not waiting to hear who it was. 'I'm grateful to you for calling back so promptly.'

'My pleasure, Mr Gutenburg,' said the Chairman of Washington Provident.

'I fear it's a delicate matter that I need to speak to you about, Mr Thompson. I wouldn't be making such a call unless I felt it was in your best interests.'

'I appreciate that,' said Thompson. 'How can I help?'

'You have recently been interviewing candidates to head up your kidnap and ransom department. A post that demands the highest standards of integrity.'

'Of course,' said Thompson. 'But I think we've found the ideal person for the position.'

'I have no idea who you've selected for the job, but I should let you know that we are currently investigating one of the applicants, and should the case end up in court, it might not reflect too well on your firm. However, Mr Thompson, if you are confident that you have found the right man, the CIA certainly has no desire to stand in his way.'

'Now wait a moment, Mr Gutenburg. If you're aware of something I should know about, I'll be only too happy to listen.'

Gutenburg paused before saying, 'May I ask, in the strictest confidence, the name of the candidate to whom you are thinking of offering this position?'

'You most certainly can, because I'm in no doubt about his reputation, background or propriety. We are about to sign a contract with a Mr Connor Fitzgerald.' There was a long silence before Thompson said, 'Are you still there, Mr Gutenburg?'

'I am, Mr Thompson. I wonder if you could find the time to visit me at Langley? I think I should brief you more fully on the fraud investigation we are presently undertaking. You might also want to examine some confidential papers that have come into our possession.'

This time it was Thompson's turn to remain silent. 'I'm very sorry to hear that. I don't think a visit will be necessary,' said the Chairman quietly. 'He seemed like such a good man.'

'I'm equally distressed to have had to make this call in the first place, Mr Thompson. But you would have been more angry with me if I hadn't, and the whole sorry affair had ended up on the front page of the *Washington Post*.'

'I can't disagree with that,' said Thompson.

'May I add,' said the Deputy Director, 'though of course it's not pertinent to the case we're investigating, that I've been a policyholder with Washington Provident since the day I began working for the CIA.'

'I'm glad to hear that, Mr Gutenburg. I'd just like to say how much I appreciate the thoroughness with which you people carry out your job.'

'I only hope I've been of some service, Mr Thompson. Goodbye, sir.'

Gutenburg replaced the receiver, and immediately pressed '1' on the phone nearest to him.

'Yes?' said a voice.

'I don't think Washington Provident will be offering Fitzgerald a job after all.'

'Good. Why don't we leave it for three days, then *you* can tell him about his new assignment.'

'Why wait three days?'

'You've obviously never read Freud's paper on maximum vulnerability.'

◀◇▶

We are sorry to inform you . . .

Connor was reading the letter for the third time when the phone on his desk rang. He felt numb with disbelief. What could possibly have gone wrong? The dinner at the Thompsons' home couldn't have been more agreeable. When he and Maggie left a few minutes before midnight, Ben had suggested a round of golf at Burning Tree the following weekend, and Elizabeth Thompson had asked Maggie to drop by for coffee while the men were out chasing little white balls. The next day his lawyer had rung to say that the contract Washington Provident had sent for his approval needed no more than a few minor adjustments.

Connor picked up the phone.

'Yes, Joan.'

'I have the Deputy Director on the line.'

'Put him through,' he said wearily.

'Connor?' said a voice he had never trusted. 'Something important has come up, and the Director's asked me to brief you immediately.'

'Of course,' said Connor, not really taking in Gutenburg's words.

'Shall we make it three o'clock, the usual place?'

'Of course,' Connor repeated. He was still holding the phone long after he had heard the click. He read the letter for a fourth time, and decided not to tell Maggie about it until he had been shortlisted for another job.

◄○►

Connor was the first to arrive in Lafayette Square. He sat down on a bench facing the White House. A few minutes later Nick Gutenburg took a seat on the other end of the bench. Connor took care not to even glance in his direction.

'The President himself requested that you should take on this assignment,' murmured Gutenburg, looking fixedly in the direction of the White House. 'He wanted our best man.'

'But I'm due to leave the Company in ten days' time,' said Connor.

'Yes, the Director told him. But the President insisted that we do everything in our power to convince you to stay until this assignment has been completed.'

Connor remained silent.

'Connor, the outcome of the elections in Russia could affect the future of the free world. If that lunatic Zerimski is elected, it would mean a return to the Cold War overnight. The President could forget his Arms Reduction Bill, and Congress would be demanding an increase in the defence budget that could bank-rupt us.'

'But Zerimski's still way behind in the polls,' said Connor. 'Isn't Chernopov expected to win comfortably?'

'That's how it may look right now,' said Gutenburg. 'But there are still three weeks to go, and the President' – he emphasised the word while continuing to stare at the White House – 'feels that with an electorate that volatile, anything could happen. He'd be a lot happier knowing you were out there, just in case your particular expertise is needed.'

Connor didn't respond.

'If it's your new job you're worrying about,' continued Gutenburg, 'I'd be happy to have a word with the Chairman of the company you're joining and explain to him that it's only a short-term assignment.'

'That won't be necessary,' said Connor. 'But I'll need a little time to think about it.'

'Of course,' said Gutenburg. 'When you've made up your mind, please call the Director and let her know your decision.' He rose and walked away in the direction of Farragut Square.

Three minutes later, Connor strolled off in the opposite direction.

◄○►

Andy Lloyd picked up the red phone. This time he recognised the voice immediately.

'I'm almost certain I know who carried out the assignment in Bogotá,' said Jackson.

'Was he working for the CIA?' Lloyd asked.

'Yes, he was.'

'Do you have enough proof to convince the Congressional Select Committees on Intelligence?'

'No, I don't. Almost all the evidence I have would be thrown out as circumstantial. But when it's all put together, there are far too many coincidences for my liking.'

'For example?'

'The agent who I suspect pulled the trigger was sacked shortly after the President saw Dexter in the Oval Office and demanded to know who was responsible for Guzman's assassination.'

'Not even admissible as evidence.'

'Perhaps not. But the same agent was about to take up a new appointment with Washington Provident as head of their kidnap and ransom department when suddenly, without any explanation, the job offer was withdrawn.'

'A second coincidence.'

'There's a third. Three days later, Gutenburg met the agent in question on a park bench in Lafayette Square.'

'Why would they want to take him back?'

'To carry out a one-off assignment.'

'Do we have any idea what that assignment is?'

'No. But don't be surprised if it takes him a long way from Washington.'

'Have you any way of finding out where?'

'Not at the moment. Even his wife doesn't know.'

'OK, let's look at it from their point of view,' said Lloyd. 'What do you think Dexter will be doing right now to make sure her ass is covered?'

'Before I could begin to answer that I'd need to know the outcome of her last meeting with the President,' said Jackson.

'He gave her and Gutenburg twenty-eight days to prove that the Agency wasn't involved in the assassination of Guzman, and to provide cast-iron proof of who *did* kill him. He also left them in no doubt that if they fail, he'll demand their resignations and release all the evidence in his possession to the *Washington Post*.'

There was a long silence before Jackson said, 'That means the agent in question has less than a month to live.'

'She'd never eliminate one of her own people,' said Lloyd in disbelief.

'Don't forget that he's an NOC. The section of the CIA he works for doesn't even exist officially, Mr Lloyd.'

'This guy's a good friend of yours, isn't he?' said Lloyd.

'Yes,' replied Jackson quietly.

'Then you'd better make sure he stays alive.'

◄○►

'Good afternoon, Director. It's Connor Fitzgerald.'

'Good afternoon, Connor. How nice to hear from you,' Dexter said in a warmer tone than the one she had adopted at their previous meeting.

'The Deputy Director asked me to call you once I'd come to a decision on the matter he and I discussed on Monday.'

'Yes,' said Dexter, reverting to her normal clipped style.

'I'm willing to take the assignment.'

'I'm glad to hear that.'

'On one condition.'

'And what's that?'

'I will require proof that the operation has been sanctioned by the President.'

There was a long silence before Dexter said, 'I'll inform the President of your request.'

◄○►

'So how does it work?' asked the Director. She couldn't remember when she had last visited the OTS lab at Langley.

'It's quite simple really,' said Professor Ziegler, the CIA's Director of Technical Services. He turned to a bank of computers and pressed some keys. Tom Lawrence's face appeared on the screen.

After Dexter and Nick Gutenburg had listened to the words of the President for a few moments, she said, 'What's so remarkable about that? We've all heard Lawrence making a speech before.'

'Maybe, but you've never heard him make that particular speech,' said Ziegler.

'What do you mean?' asked Gutenburg.

An almost childlike smile of satisfaction spread across the professor's face. 'I have stored in my computer – codename "Tommy" – over a thousand speeches, television and radio interviews and telephone conversations the President has given or taken part in during the past two years. Every word or phrase he has used in that time is stored in this memory bank. That means I can make him deliver a speech on any subject you choose. I can even decide what his position is on any given issue.'

Dexter began to consider the possibilities. 'If Tommy were to be asked a question, could he give a convincing reply?' she asked.

'Not spontaneously,' admitted Ziegler. 'But if you had some idea of the questions he might be expected to answer, I believe I could fool Lawrence's own mother.'

'So all we have to do,' said Gutenburg, 'is anticipate what the other party is likely to say.'

'Which may not be as difficult as you might think,' said Ziegler. 'After all, if *you* were to receive a call from the President, you'd be unlikely to ask him about the strength of the dollar, or what he had for breakfast, would you? In most cases you'd know the reason he was calling. I have no idea why you might need Tommy, but if you were to prepare opening and closing remarks, as well as – say – the fifty questions or statements he was most likely to have to respond to, I could almost guarantee he could conduct a plausible conversation.'

'I'm sure we can do that,' said Gutenburg.

The Director nodded her agreement, then asked Ziegler: 'Why did we develop this piece of equipment in the first place?'

'It was set up in case the President died while America was at war, and we needed the enemy to believe he was still alive. But Tommy has many other uses, Director. For example . . .'

'I'm sure he does,' interrupted Dexter.

Ziegler looked disappointed, aware that the Director was coming to the end of her attention span.

'How long would it take you to prepare a specific programme?' Gutenburg asked.

'How long will it take you to work out what the President needs to say?' replied Ziegler, the childlike smile returning to his face.

—◦—

She kept her finger on the buzzer until Connor finally picked up the phone on his desk.

'What's the problem, Joan? I'm not going deaf.'

'I've got Ruth Preston, the President's personal secretary, on the line.'

The next voice Connor heard was a woman's. 'Is that Connor Fitzgerald?'

'Speaking,' Connor replied. He could feel the sweat in the palm of the hand holding the phone. That never happened when he was waiting to pull the trigger.

'I have the President on the line for you.'

He heard a click. 'Good afternoon,' a familiar voice said.

'Good afternoon, Mr President.'

'I think you know why I'm calling.'

'Yes, sir, I do.'

Professor Ziegler pressed 'Opening Statement'. The Director and Deputy Director held their breath.

'I felt I had to call and let you know just how important I consider this assignment to be.' *Pause.* 'Because I have no doubt that you're the right person to carry it out.' *Pause.* 'So I hope you will agree to take on the responsibility.'

Ziegler pressed the 'Wait' button.

'I appreciate your confidence in me, Mr President,' said Connor, 'and I'm grateful to you for taking the time to phone personally . . .'

'*Number 11*,' said Ziegler, who knew all the replies by heart.

'I felt it was the least I could do in the circumstances.' *Pause.*

'Thank you, Mr President. Although Mr Gutenburg assured me of your involvement, and the Director herself called later that afternoon to confirm it, as you know, I still felt unable to take on the assignment unless I was certain that the order had come directly from you.'

'*Number 7.*'

'I can quite understand your anxiety.' *Pause.*

'*Number 19.*'

'Perhaps when this is all over you and your wife would come

and visit me at the White House – that is, if the Director will allow it.' *Pause*.

'*Number 3*,' said Ziegler sharply. There was a burst of loud laughter.

Connor moved the phone slightly away from his ear. 'We would be honoured, sir,' he said once the laughter had died away.

'*Closing statement*,' said Ziegler.

'Good. I'll look forward to seeing you as soon as you return.' *Pause*. 'I often think it's sad that America doesn't always appreciate its unsung heroes.' *Pause*. 'It was good talking to you. Goodbye.'

'Goodbye, Mr President.'

Connor was still holding the phone when Joan came into the room. 'So that's another myth exploded,' she said as Connor replaced the receiver. He looked up at her and raised an enquiring eyebrow.

'That the President always calls everyone by their first name.'

11

GUTENBURG HANDED HIM a large brown envelope containing four passports, three airline tickets and a bundle of notes in different currencies.

'Don't I have to sign for all this?' asked Connor.

'No. As it's all been a bit rushed, we'll deal with the paperwork when you get back. Once you arrive in Moscow, you're to go to Zerimski's campaign headquarters and show them your credentials as a freelance reporter from South Africa. They'll give you a press pack detailing his schedule for the run-up to the election.'

'Do I have a contact in Moscow?'

'Yes. Ashley Mitchell.' Gutenburg hesitated. 'It's his first big assignment, and he's been briefed strictly on a need-to-know basis. He's also been instructed only to get in touch with you if it's a green light, in which case he'll supply you with the weapon.'

'Make and model?'

'The usual custom-made Remington 700,' said Gutenburg. 'But if Chernopov stays ahead in the polls, I don't expect your services will be needed, in which case you're to return to Washington the day after the election. I'm afraid this mission may turn out to be a bit of a non-event.'

'Let's hope so,' said Connor, and left the Deputy Director without shaking hands.

'I'm afraid my arm was twisted so far up my back that I couldn't say no,' said Connor, putting another blue shirt in his suitcase.

'You could have refused,' said Maggie. 'Starting a new job on the first of the month would have been a convincing enough excuse.' She paused. 'What was Ben Thompson's reaction?'

'He's been very understanding,' said Connor. 'He has no problem with me starting a month later. It seems December is always a quiet time.' Connor pressed his clothes down, wondering how he would fit his spongebag in. He was already wishing he had allowed Maggie to pack for him, but hadn't wanted her to come across several items that didn't tie in with his story. He sat down heavily on the suitcase lid. Maggie snapped the lock shut, and they fell on the bed, laughing. He took her in his arms and held on to her a little too long.

'Is everything all right, Connor?' she asked quietly.

'Everything's just fine, honey,' he said, releasing her.

He picked up the case and carried it downstairs. 'I'm sorry I won't be here for Thanksgiving. Don't forget to tell Tara I'm looking forward to seeing her at Christmas,' he said as Maggie followed him out of the front door. He stopped beside a car she had never seen before.

'And Stuart too,' she reminded him.

'Yes, of course,' he said as he placed the suitcase in the boot. 'It will be good to see him again.' Once more he took his wife in his arms. This time he made sure he didn't hold on too long.

'Heavens, what are we going to give Tara for Christmas?' Maggie suddenly said. 'I haven't even thought about it.'

'If you'd seen her latest phone bill, you wouldn't have to think about it,' said Connor, climbing behind the wheel.

'I don't remember this car,' said Maggie.

'It's one of the company's,' he explained as he turned on the ignition. 'By the way, could you let Father Graham know he'll have to find someone else to make up his bridge four on Saturday? Goodbye, honey.'

Without another word he put the car into drive and eased it out onto the road. He hated saying goodbye to Maggie, and always tried to keep their farewells as short as possible. He checked in the rear-view mirror. She was standing at the end of the drive, waving, as he turned the corner onto Cambridge Place and headed for the airport.

When he reached the end of the Dulles access road, he didn't need to look for the arrow pointing to the long-term parking lot. He drove down the ramp and took a ticket from the machine, then parked in a far corner. He locked the car and headed towards the airport entrance, then took the escalator up one flight to the United Airlines check-in desk.

'Thank you, Mr Perry,' said the uniformed assistant who checked his ticket. 'Flight 918 is almost ready for boarding. Please make your way to Gate C7.'

After clearing security, Connor boarded a mobile lounge to the mid-field terminal. In the waiting area he sat in the far corner, and when the passengers were asked to board he took his usual window seat near the back. Twenty minutes later he was listening to the captain explaining that although they would not be taking off on time, they would somehow miraculously still be arriving on schedule.

Back in the terminal, a young man in a dark blue suit dialled a number on his cellphone.

'Yes?' said a voice.

'Agent Sullivan calling from "Coach House". The bird has flown.'

'Good. Report in again as soon as you've carried out the rest of your assignment.' The line went dead.

The young man switched off his phone and took the escalator to the ground floor. He walked over to a car in the far corner of the long-term carpark, unlocked it, drove out of the lot, paid the parking ticket, and headed east.

Thirty minutes later he returned the keys to the car pool and signed the daily log. It showed that the vehicle had been checked out in his name and returned in his name.

—◦—

'Can you be absolutely sure there'll be no trace of his ever having existed?' asked the Director.

'No trace whatsoever,' said Gutenburg. 'Don't forget that as an NOC he was never on the Company's books in the first place.'

'But what about his wife?'

'Why should she suspect anything? His monthly pay-cheque has been paid into their joint account. She won't give it a second thought. As far as she's concerned, he's resigned from his present position and will be joining Washington Provident on the first of January.'

'There's still his former secretary.'

'I've had her transferred to Langley so I can keep an eye on her.'

'What division?'

'Middle East.'

'Why Middle East?'

'Because she'll have to be at the office during their working hours, from six in the evening until three in the morning. And for the next eight months I'm going to work her so hard that she'll be too tired to think about anything other than what she's going to do once she retires.'

'Good. Where's Fitzgerald at this moment?'

Gutenburg checked his watch. 'Halfway across the Atlantic. He'll be landing at London Heathrow in about four hours.'

'And the car?'

'Has already been returned to the pool. It's currently being resprayed and given a new set of plates.'

'What about his office on M Street?'

'It will be stripped overnight, and that floor will be placed in the hands of real estate agents on Monday.'

'You seem to have thought of everything except what happens when he returns to Washington,' said the Director.

'He isn't going to return to Washington,' replied Gutenburg.

◄○►

Connor joined the long queue waiting to go through passport control. When he eventually reached the front, an official checked his passport and said, 'I hope you have an enjoyable fortnight in Britain, Mr Perry.'

In the little box asking 'How long do you intend to stay in the United Kingdom?' Mr Perry had written 'Fourteen days.' But then, it would be Mr Lilystrand who returned to the airport the following morning.

Two men watched him as he left Terminal Three and boarded the bus for Victoria Coach Station. Forty-two minutes later, the same two men saw him join the queue at a taxi rank. Separately they followed the black cab to the Kensington Park Hotel, where one of them had already left a package for him in reception.

'Any messages for me?' Connor asked as he signed the registration form.

'Yes, Mr Lilystrand,' said the concierge. 'A gentleman left this for you this morning.' He handed Connor an enormous brown envelope. 'Your room number is 211. The porter will bring up your luggage.'

'I can manage it myself, thank you,' he said.

As soon as Connor entered the room, he tore open the envelope. Inside was a ticket to Geneva in the name of Theodore Lilystrand, and a hundred Swiss francs. He slipped off his jacket and lay down on the bed, but despite being exhausted he was unable to sleep. He turned on the television and flicked through endless programmes – what Tara called channel surfing – but it didn't help.

He had always disliked the waiting game. That was the only time doubts ever set in. He kept reminding himself that this would be his last mission. He began to think about Christmas with Maggie and Tara – and, yes, Stuart. He disliked not being allowed to carry photographs with him, always having to visualise them in his mind. Most of all, he hated not being able to just pick up a phone and talk to either of them whenever he felt like it.

Connor didn't stir from his bed until it was dark. Then he emerged from his overnight prison cell to go in search of a meal.

He bought an *Evening Standard* from a corner news-vendor and strolled into a small Italian restaurant on High Street, Kensington that was only half full.

The waiter showed him to a quiet table in the corner. The light was barely strong enough for him to read the paper. He ordered a Diet Coke with lots of ice. The British would never understand the meaning of 'lots of ice', and he was not surprised when the waiter returned a few minutes later bearing a long glass with three small ice cubes floating in it, and a tiny piece of lemon.

He ordered cannelloni and a side salad. Funny how he picked Maggie's favourite dishes whenever he was abroad. Anything to remind him of her.

'The one thing you have to do before you start your new job is find a decent tailor,' Tara had said to him when they last spoke. 'And I want to come with you so I can pick your shirts and ties.'

'Your new job.' Once again he thought about that letter. *I am sorry to have to inform you . . .* However many times he went over it, he still couldn't think of a reason for Thompson to have changed his mind. It simply didn't add up.

He began to read the front page of the paper: nine candidates were contesting an election to be the first Mayor of London. That's odd, thought Connor: haven't they always had a Mayor – what about Dick Whittington? He looked at the photographs of the contenders and their names, but they meant nothing to him. One of them would be running England's capital in a couple of weeks' time. He wondered where he would be then.

He paid the bill in cash and left a tip that would not give the waiter any reason to remember him. When he was back in his hotel room he switched on the television and watched a few minutes of a comedy that didn't make him laugh. After trying a couple of movies, he slept intermittently. But he was comforted by the thought that at least he was better off than the two men stationed outside on the pavement, who wouldn't sleep at all. He had spotted them within moments of landing at Heathrow.

He checked his watch. A few minutes after midnight – a few minutes after seven in Washington. He wondered what Maggie would be doing that evening.

-◦-

'And how's Stuart?' Maggie asked.

'Still hanging in there,' Tara replied. 'He arrives in LA in fifteen days. I can't wait.'

'Will you both be flying straight here?'

'No, Mom,' said Tara, trying not to sound exasperated. 'As I've told you several times already, we're going to rent a car and drive up the West Coast. Stuart's never been to America, and he wants to see LA and San Francisco. Remember?'

'Do drive carefully, won't you?'

'Mother, I've been driving for nine years without even a ticket, which is more than can be said for you or Dad. Now, will you stop worrying and tell me what you're doing this evening?'

'I'm going to hear Placido Domingo in *La Bohème*. I decided to wait until your father was out of town before I went, because I know he'd fall asleep before the first act was over.'

'Are you going on your own?'

'Yes.'

'Well, be careful, Mother, and make sure you don't sit in the first six rows.'

'Why not?' asked Maggie innocently.

'Because some rich, handsome man might leap out of one of the boxes and ravish you.'

Maggie laughed. 'I consider myself properly chastised.'

'Why don't you ask Joan to go with you? Then you can both talk about Dad all night.'

'I called her at the office, but the number seems to be out of order. I'll try her at home later.'

'Bye, Mom, talk to you tomorrow,' said Tara. She knew her mother would call every day while Connor was away.

Whenever Connor travelled abroad or took an evening off to partner Father Graham at the bridge club, Maggie would catch up with some of her university activities. Anything from GULP, the Georgetown University Litter Patrol, of which she was a founder member, to the Alive Women's Poetry Society and the Irish dance class, where she gave lessons. The sight of the young students dancing, their backs straight, their feet tapping away, brought back memories of Declan O'Casey. He was now a distinguished professor, with a chair at the University of Chicago. He had never married, and still sent her a card every Christmas, and an unsigned one on Valentine's Day. The old typewriter with the crooked 'e' always gave away his identity.

She picked up the phone again and dialled Joan's home number, but there was no reply. She fixed herself a light salad, which she ate alone in the kitchen. After she had put the plate in the dishwasher she rang Joan again. There was still no answer, so she set off for the Kennedy Center. A single ticket was always easy to come by, however celebrated the guest tenor happened to be.

Maggie was transfixed by the first act of *La Bohème*, and only wished she had someone with whom to share the experience. When the curtain came down, she joined the throng heading for the foyer. As she approached the crowded bar, Maggie thought she caught a glimpse of Elizabeth Thompson. She remembered that she had invited her for coffee, but had never followed it up. She had been surprised, because the offer had sounded so genuine at the time.

When Ben Thompson turned and caught her eye, Maggie smiled and walked over to join them.

'How nice to see you, Ben,' she said.

'And you too, Mrs Fitzgerald,' he replied, but not in the warm voice she remembered from dinner a fortnight before. And why hadn't he called her Maggie?

Undaunted, she ploughed on. 'Domingo is magnificent, don't you think?'

'Yes, and we were extremely lucky to lure Leonard Slatkin from St Louis,' said Ben Thompson. Maggie was surprised that he didn't offer to buy her a drink, and when she finally ordered an orange juice, she was even more puzzled when he made no attempt to pay for it.

'Connor is so looking forward to joining you all at Washington Provident,' she said, taking a sip of her juice. Elizabeth Thompson appeared surprised, but didn't comment.

'He's particularly grateful to you, Ben, for allowing him to put it off for a month so he could complete that unfinished contract for his old firm.'

Elizabeth was just about to say something when the three-minute bell sounded.

'Well, we'd better get back to our seats,' said Ben Thompson, although his wife had only half-finished her drink. 'Nice to have seen you again, Mrs Fitzgerald.' He took his wife firmly by the arm and guided her towards the auditorium. 'I hope you enjoy the second act.'

Maggie didn't enjoy the second act. She couldn't concentrate, as the conversation that had just taken place in the foyer kept running through her mind. But however many times she went over it, she couldn't reconcile his attitude with what had taken place at the Thompsons' only a fortnight before. If she had known how to get in touch with Connor, she would have broken the rule of a lifetime and phoned him. So she did the next best thing. The moment she arrived home, she called Joan Bennett again.

The phone rang and rang.

◄○►

The following morning Connor rose early. He had settled his bill in cash, hailed a taxi and was on his way to Heathrow before the duty porter even realised he'd left. At seven forty he boarded Swissair Flight 839 to Geneva. The flight took just under two hours, and he readjusted his watch to ten thirty as the wheels of the aircraft touched the ground.

During the stopover he took advantage of Swissair's offer to take a shower. He entered the 'exclusive facility' – the description in their in-flight magazine – as Theodore Lilystrand, an investment banker from Stockholm, and emerged forty minutes later as Piet de Villiers, a reporter with the *Johannesburg Mercury*.

Even though he still had over an hour to kill, Connor did not browse in any of the duty-free shops, buying only a croissant and a cup of coffee from one of the most expensive restaurants in the world.

Eventually he walked across to Gate 23. There wasn't a long queue for the Aeroflot flight to St Petersburg. When the passengers were called a few minutes later, he made his way to the back of the aircraft. He began to think about what needed to be done the following morning, once the train had pulled in to Moscow's Raveltay station. He went over the Deputy Director's final briefing again, wondering why Gutenburg had repeated the words, 'Don't get caught. But if you are, deny absolutely that you have anything to do with the CIA. Don't worry – the Company will always take care of you.'

Only raw recruits were ever reminded of the Eleventh Commandment.

◄○►

'The flight to St Petersburg has just taken off, and our package is on board.'

'Good,' said Gutenburg. 'Anything else to report?'

'I don't think so,' replied the young CIA agent. He hesitated. 'Except . . .'

'Except what? Come on, spit it out.'

'It's just that I thought I recognised someone else who boarded the plane.'

'Who was it?' snapped Gutenburg.

'I can't remember his name, and I'm not that certain it was him. I couldn't risk taking my eyes off Fitzgerald for more than a few seconds.'

'If you remember who it was, call me immediately.'

'Yes, sir.' The young man switched off his phone and made his way to Gate 9. In a few hours he would be back behind his desk in Berne, resuming his role as Cultural Attaché at the American Embassy.

◄○►

'Good morning. This is Helen Dexter.'

'Good morning, Director,' replied the White House Chief of Staff stiffly.

'I thought the President would want to know immediately that the man he asked us to track down in South Africa is on the move again.'

'I'm not sure I follow you,' said Lloyd.

'The head of our Johannesburg office has just informed me that Guzman's killer boarded a South African Airways flight to London two days ago. He was carrying a passport in the name of Martin Perry. He only stayed in London overnight. The following morning he took a Swissair flight to Geneva, using a Swedish passport in the name of Theodore Lilystrand.'

Lloyd didn't interrupt her this time. After all, he could play the tape back if the President wanted to hear exactly what she had said.

'At Geneva he boarded an Aeroflot flight to St Petersburg. This time he was carrying a South African passport in the name of Piet de Villiers. From St Petersburg, he took the overnight train to Moscow.'

'Moscow? Why Moscow?' asked Lloyd.

'If I recall correctly,' said Dexter, 'an election is about to take place in Russia.'

—◦—

When the plane landed in St Petersburg, Connor's watch claimed that it was five fifty. He yawned, stretched and waited for the aircraft to taxi to a halt before altering the hands to local time. He looked out of the window at an airport that was in semi-darkness because half the lightbulbs were missing. Light snow was falling, but didn't settle. The hundred weary passengers had to wait another twenty minutes before a bus arrived to transport them to the terminal. Some things simply didn't change, whether the KGB or organised criminals were in charge. Americans had come to refer to them as the Mafya, to avoid confusion with the Italian version.

Connor was the last to leave the aircraft, and the last to get off the bus.

A man who had travelled first class on the same flight rushed to the front of the queue to be sure of being the first through immigration and customs. He was grateful that Connor followed the textbook routine. Once the man had stepped off the bus, he never looked back. He knew Connor's eyes would always be moving.

When Connor walked out of the airport onto the pot-holed road thirty minutes later, he hailed the first available taxi and asked to be taken to Protsky station.

The first-class traveller followed Connor into the booking hall, which looked more like an opera house than a railway station. He watched closely to see which train he would be boarding. But there was another man standing in the shadows who even knew the number of the sleeping compartment he would be occupying.

The American Cultural Attaché in St Petersburg had passed up an invitation to the Kirov Ballet that evening so he could inform Gutenburg when Fitzgerald had boarded the overnight train to Moscow. It wouldn't be necessary to accompany him on the journey, as Ashley Mitchell, his colleague in the capital, would be waiting on Platform 4 the following morning to confirm that Fitzgerald had reached his destination. It had been made clear to the Attaché that this was Mitchell's operation.

'One first-class sleeper to Moscow,' said Connor in English to the booking clerk.

The man pushed a ticket across the wooden counter, and was disappointed when the customer handed over a ten-thousand-rouble note. He had been hoping that this passenger would give him an opportunity to make a small turn on the exchange rate – his second that night.

Connor checked his ticket before making his way towards the Moscow express. He walked down the crowded platform, passing several old green carriages that looked as if they predated the 1917 Revolution, stopped at Coach K and presented his ticket to a woman standing by the open door. She clipped it and stood aside to allow him to climb aboard. Connor strolled down the corridor, looking for booth Number 8. Once he had found it, he switched on the light and locked himself in; not because he was afraid of being robbed by bandits, as was so often reported in the American press, but because he needed to change his identity once again.

He had seen the fresh-faced youth standing under the arrivals board at Geneva airport, and had wondered where they were recruiting them from these days. He didn't bother trying to spot the agent in St Petersburg: he knew someone would be there to check on his arrival, and someone else would be waiting on the platform in Moscow. Gutenburg had already briefed him fully on Agent Mitchell, who he had described as fairly raw, and unaware of Fitzgerald's status as an NOC.

The train left St Petersburg at exactly one minute to midnight, and the gentle, rhythmic sound of the carriage wheels clattering over the tracks soon made Connor feel drowsy. He woke with a start, and checked his watch: four thirty-seven. The most sleep he'd managed in the past three nights.

Then he recalled his dream. He had been sitting on a bench in Lafayette Square, facing the White House and talking with someone who never once looked in his direction. The meeting he'd had with the Deputy Director the previous week was being replayed word for word, but he couldn't recall what it was about the conversation that continued to nag away at him. Just as Gutenburg came to the sentence he wanted to hear repeated, he had woken up.

He was no nearer to solving the problem when the train pulled in to Raveltay station at eight thirty-three that morning.

–◄o►–

'Where are you?' asked Andy Lloyd.

'A phone booth in Moscow,' Jackson replied. 'Via London, Geneva and St Petersburg. As soon as he got off the train he led us all on a wild goose chase. He managed to lose our man in

Moscow in less than ten minutes. If it hadn't been me who taught him the doubling-back technique in the first place, he would have shaken me off as well.'

'Where did he end up?' asked Lloyd.

'He checked into a small hotel on the north side of the city.'

'Is he still there?'

'No, he left about an hour later, but he was so well disguised that I nearly missed him myself. If it hadn't been for the walk, he might have given me the slip.'

'Where did he go?' asked Lloyd.

'He took another circuitous route, and ended up at the campaign headquarters of Victor Zerimski.'

'Why Zerimski?'

'I don't know yet, but he came out of the building carrying all Zerimski's campaign literature. Then he bought a map from a news-stand and had lunch in a nearby restaurant. In the afternoon, he hired a small car and returned to his hotel. He hasn't left the building since.'

'Oh my God,' said Lloyd suddenly. 'It's going to be Zerimski this time.'

There was a long pause at the other end of the line before Jackson said, 'No, Mr Lloyd, that's not possible.'

'Why not?'

'He'd never agree to carry out such a sensitive assignment unless the order had come directly from the White House. I've known him long enough to be certain of that.'

'Try not to forget that your friend carried out exactly the same assignment in Colombia. No doubt Dexter was able to convince him that that operation had also been sanctioned by the President.'

'There could be an alternative scenario,' said Jackson quietly.

'Namely?'

'That it's not Zerimski they're planning to kill, but Connor.'

Lloyd wrote the name down on his yellow pad.

BOOK TWO

THE LONER

12

'AMERICAN?'

'Yes,' said Jackson, not looking down at the source of the piping voice.

'You need anything?'

'No thanks,' he said, still not taking his eyes off the front door of the hotel.

'You must need something. Americans always need something.'

'I don't need anything. Now go away,' said Jackson firmly.

'Caviar? Russian dolls? General's uniform? Fur hat? Woman?'

Jackson looked down at the boy for the first time. He was draped from head to toe in a sheepskin jacket three sizes too large for him. On his head he wore a cap made out of rabbitskin that Jackson felt he needed more every minute. The boy's smile revealed two missing teeth.

'A woman? At five o'clock in the morning?'

'Good time for woman. But perhaps you prefer man?'

'How much do you charge for your services?'

'What type of services?' asked the boy, looking suspicious.

'As a runner.'

'Runner?'

'Helper, then.'

'Helper?'

'Assistant.'

'Ah, you mean partner, like in American movies.'

'OK, so now we've agreed on your job description, wiseguy, how much do you charge?'

'Per day? Per week? Per month?'

'Per hour.'

'How much you offer?'

'Quite the little entrepreneur, aren't we?'

'We learn from Americans,' said the boy, with a grin that stretched from ear to ear.

'One dollar,' said Jackson.

The boy began laughing. 'I may be wiseguy, but you are comedian. Ten dollars.'

'That's nothing less than extortion.'

The boy looked puzzled for the first time.

'I'll give you two.'

'Six.'

'Four.'

'Five.'

'Agreed,' said Jackson.

The boy raised the palm of his right hand high in the air, something else he'd seen in American movies. Jackson slapped it. The deal was struck. The boy immediately checked the time on his Rolex watch.

'So, what's your name?' Jackson asked.

'Sergei,' replied the boy. 'And yours?'

'Jackson. How old are you, Sergei?'

'How old you want me to be?'

'Cut the crap and tell me your age.'

'Fourteen.'

'You're not a day over nine.'

'Thirteen.'

'Ten.'

'Eleven.'

'OK,' said Jackson. 'I'll settle for eleven.'

'And how old are you?' demanded the boy.

'Fifty-four.'

'I'll settle for fifty-four,' said Sergei.

Jackson laughed for the first time in days. 'How come your

English is so good?' he asked, still keeping an eye on the hotel door.

'My mother live with American for long time. He return to States last year, but not take us.'

This time Jackson believed he was telling the truth.

'So what's the job, partner?' asked Sergei.

'We're keeping an eye on someone who's staying at that hotel.'

'Is a friend or enemy?'

'Friend.'

'Mafya?'

'No, he works for the good guys.'

'Don't treat me like child,' said Sergei, with an edge to his voice. 'We're partners, remember.'

'OK, Sergei. He's a friend,' said Jackson, just as Connor appeared in the doorway. 'Don't move.' He placed a hand firmly on the boy's shoulder.

'Is that him?' asked Sergei.

'Yes, that's him.'

'He has kind face. Maybe better I work for him.'

―◇―

Victor Zerimski's day hadn't begun well, and it was still only a few minutes past eight a.m. He was chairing a meeting of the Central Council of the Communist Party which was being briefed by Dmitri Titov, his Chief of Staff.

'An international body of observers has arrived in Moscow to monitor the electoral process,' Titov was telling them. 'They are looking principally for any suggestion of ballot-rigging, but their chairman has already admitted that with an electorate so vast and so widespread, there is no way they can spot every irregularity.' Titov ended his report by saying that now that Comrade Zerimski had climbed to second place in the polls, the Mafya were pouring even more money into Chernopov's campaign.

Zerimski stroked his thick moustache as he looked in turn at each of the men seated round the table. 'When I am President,' he said, rising from his place at the head of the table, 'I'll throw those Mafya bastards in jail one by one. Then the only thing they'll count for the rest of their lives will be rocks.' The members of the Central Council had heard their leader lambast the Mafya many times before, though he never mentioned them by name in public.

The short, muscle-bound man thumped the table. 'Russia needs to return to the old-fashioned values the rest of the world used to respect us for.' The twenty-one men facing him nodded, despite having heard these words repeatedly over the past few months.

'For ten years we have done nothing but import the worst America has to offer.'

They continued to nod, and kept their eyes firmly fixed on him.

Zerimski ran a hand through his thick black hair, sighed, and slumped back into his chair. He looked across at his Chief of Staff. 'What am I doing this morning?'

'You're paying a visit to the Pushkin Museum,' said Titov. 'They're expecting you at ten o'clock.'

'Cancel it. A complete waste of time when there are only eight days until the election.' He banged the table again. 'I should be out on the streets where the people can see me.'

'But the director of the museum has applied for a grant from the government to restore the works of leading Russian artists,' said Titov.

'A waste of the people's money,' said Zerimski.

'And Chernopov has been criticised for cutting the arts subsidy,' continued the Chief of Staff.

'All right. I'll give them fifteen minutes.'

'Twenty thousand Russians visit the Pushkin every week,' Titov added, looking down at the typewritten notes in front of him.

'Make it thirty minutes.'

'And Chernopov accused you on television last week of being an uneducated thug.'

'He did *what*?' bellowed Zerimski. 'I was studying law at Moscow University when Chernopov was still a farm labourer.'

'That is of course true, Chairman,' said Titov, 'but our internal polls show that it is not the public perception, and that Chernopov is getting his message across.'

'Internal polls? Something else we have to thank the Americans for.'

'They put Tom Lawrence in office.'

'Once I'm elected, I won't need polls to keep me in office.'

—<o>—

Connor's love of art had begun when Maggie had dragged him around galleries while they were still at college. At first he had gone along just so he could spend more time in her company, but within weeks he became a convert. Whenever they travelled out of town together he would happily accompany her to any gallery she chose, and as soon as they moved to Washington they had become Friends of the Corcoran and Members of the Phillips. While Zerimski was being guided around the Pushkin by its director, Connor had to be careful not to become distracted by the many masterpieces, and to concentrate on observing the Communist leader.

When Connor had first been sent to Russia back in the 1980s, the nearest any senior politician got to the people was to stare down at them from the Praesidium during May Day parades. But now that the masses could make a choice on a ballot paper, it had suddenly become necessary for those who hoped to be elected to move among them, even to listen to their views.

The gallery was as crowded as Cooke Stadium for a Redskins game, and wherever Zerimski appeared, the crowds parted as if he were Moses approaching the Red Sea. The candidate moved slowly among the Muscovites, ignoring the paintings and sculptures in favour of their outstretched hands.

Zerimski was shorter than he looked in his photographs, and had surrounded himself with an entourage of even smaller aides so as not to emphasise the fact. Connor recalled President Truman's comment about size: 'When it comes down to inches, my boy, you should only consider the forehead,' he once told a

Missouri student. 'Better to have a spare inch between the top of your nose and the hairline than between the ankle and the kneecap.' Connor noticed that Zerimski's vanity hadn't affected his dress-sense. His suit was badly cut, and his shirt was frayed at the collar and cuffs. Connor wondered if it was wise for the director of the Pushkin to be wearing a hand-tailored suit that obviously hadn't been made in Moscow.

Although Connor was aware that Victor Zerimski was a shrewd and educated man, it soon became clear that his visits to art galleries over the years must have been infrequent. As he bustled through the crowd he occasionally jabbed a finger in the direction of a canvas and informed the onlookers of the name of the artist in a loud voice. He managed to get it wrong on several occasions, but the crowd still nodded their agreement. He ignored a magnificent Rubens, showing more interest in a mother standing in the crowd clinging to her child than in the genius with which the same scene was depicted behind her. When he picked up the child and posed for a picture with the mother, Titov suggested he should take a pace to the right. That way they would get the Virgin Mary into the photograph as well. No front page would be able to resist it.

Once he had walked through half a dozen galleries, and was sure that everyone visiting the Pushkin was aware of his presence, Zerimski became bored and switched his attention to the journalists following closely behind him. On the first-floor landing he began to hold an impromptu press conference.

'Go on, ask me anything you like,' he said, glowering at the pack.

'What is your reaction to the latest opinion polls, Mr Zerimski?' asked the Moscow correspondent of *The Times*.

'Heading in the right direction.'

'You now appear to be in second place, and therefore Mr Chernopov's only real rival,' shouted another journalist.

'By election day *he* will be *my* only real rival,' said Zerimski. His entourage laughed dutifully.

'Do you think Russia should return to being a Communist

state, Mr Zerimski?' came the inevitable question, delivered with an American accent.

The wily politician was far too alert to fall into that trap. 'If by that you mean a return to higher employment, lower inflation, and a better standard of living, the answer must be yes.' He sounded not unlike a Republican candidate during an American primary.

'But that's exactly what Chernopov claims is the government's present policy.'

'The government's present policy,' said Zerimski, 'is to make sure that the Prime Minister keeps his Swiss bank account overflowing with dollars. That money belongs to the Russian people, which is why he is not fit to be our next President. I'm told that when *Fortune* magazine next publishes its list of the ten richest people in the world, Chernopov will be in seventh place. Elect him as President and within five years he'll knock Bill Gates off the top spot. No, my friend,' he added. 'You are about to learn that the Russian people will vote resoundingly for a return to those days when we were the most respected nation on earth.'

'And the most feared?' suggested another journalist.

'I'd rather that than continue the present situation, where we are simply ignored by the rest of the world,' said Zerimski. Now the journalists were writing down his every word.

'Why is your friend so interested in Victor Zerimski?' whispered Sergei at the other end of the gallery.

'You ask too many questions,' said Jackson.

'Zerimski bad man.'

'Why?' asked Jackson, his eyes fixed on Connor.

'If elected, he put people like me in jail and we all go back to "the good old days", while he's in Kremlin eating caviar and drinking vodka.'

Zerimski began striding towards the gallery's exit, with the director and his entourage trying to keep up with him. The candidate stopped on the bottom step to be photographed in front of Goya's vast *Christ Descending from the Cross*. Connor was so moved by the painting that he was almost knocked over by the pursuing crowd.

'You like Goya, Jackson?' whispered Sergei.

'I haven't seen that many,' admitted the American. 'But yes,' he said, 'it's quite magnificent.'

'They have several more in the basement,' said Sergei. 'I could always arrange for one . . .' he rubbed his thumb against his fingers.

Jackson would have cuffed the boy if it wouldn't have drawn attention to them.

'Your man's on the move again,' said Sergei suddenly. Jackson looked up to see Connor disappearing out of a side entrance of the gallery with Ashley Mitchell in pursuit.

◄◦►

Connor sat alone in a Greek restaurant on the Prechinstenka and considered what he had seen that morning. Although Zerimski was always surrounded by a bunch of thugs, their eyes staring in every direction, he was still not as well protected as most Western leaders. Several of his strong-arm men might be brave and resourceful, but only three of them appeared to have any previous experience of protecting a world statesman. And they couldn't be on duty all the time.

He tried to digest a rather bad moussaka as he went over the rest of Zerimski's itinerary, right through to election day. The candidate would be seen in public on twenty-seven different occasions during the next eight days. By the time a waiter had placed a black coffee in front of him, Connor had shortlisted the only three locations worth considering if Zerimski's name needed to be removed from the ballot paper.

He checked his watch. That evening the candidate would address a Party gathering in Moscow. The following morning he would travel by train to Yaroslavl, where he would open a factory before returning to the capital to attend a performance by the Bolshoi Ballet. From there he would take the midnight train to St Petersburg. Connor had already decided to shadow Zerimski in Yaroslavl. He had also booked tickets for the ballet and the train to St Petersburg.

As he sipped his coffee he thought about Ashley Mitchell at the Pushkin, slipping behind the nearest pillar whenever Connor had glanced in his direction, and tried not to laugh. He had decided that he would allow Mitchell to follow him during the day – he might prove useful at some point – but he wouldn't let him find out where he slept at night. He glanced out of the window to see the Cultural Attaché seated on a bench, reading a copy of *Pravda*. He smiled. A professional should always be able to watch his prey without being seen.

◄○►

Jackson removed a wallet from inside his jacket, extracted a hundred-rouble note and passed it to the boy.

'Get us both something to eat, but don't go anywhere near that restaurant,' he said, nodding across the road.

'I've never been inside a restaurant. What would you like?'

'I'll have the same as you.'

'You catching on fast, Jackson,' said Sergei as he scurried away.

Jackson checked up and down the road. The man seated on the bench reading a copy of *Pravda* wasn't wearing an overcoat. He had obviously assumed that surveillance was only carried out in warm, comfortable surroundings, but having lost Fitzgerald the previous day, there was clearly no way he could risk moving. His ears were bright red, his face flushed with the cold, and he had no one to fetch him something to eat. Jackson doubted if they would be seeing him tomorrow.

Sergei returned a few minutes later, carrying two paper bags. He passed one up to Jackson. 'A big Mac with French fries and ketchup.'

'Why do I have a feeling that if Zerimski becomes President, he'll close down McDonald's?' said Jackson. He took a bite of the hamburger.

'And I thought you might need this,' said Sergei, handing him an officer's hat made of rabbit's fur.

'Did a hundred roubles cover all this?' asked Jackson.

'No, I stole the hat,' said Sergei matter-of-factly. 'I thought your need was greater than his.'

'You could get us both arrested.'

'Not likely,' said Sergei. 'There are over two million soldiers in Russia. Half of them haven't been paid for months, and most would sell you their sister for a hundred roubles.'

Jackson tried on the hat – it fitted perfectly. Neither of them spoke while they devoured their lunch, their eyes pinned on the restaurant.

'See that man sitting on the bench reading *Pravda*, Jackson?'

'Yes,' said Jackson between bites.

'He was at the gallery this morning.'

'You also catch on fast,' said Jackson.

'Don't forget that I have a Russian mother,' replied Sergei. 'By the way, which side is the bench man on?'

'I know who's paying him,' said Jackson, 'but I don't know which side he's on.'

13

CONNOR WAS AMONG THE LAST to arrive at the Lenin Memorial Hall. He took a seat at the back of the room in the section reserved for the press and tried to make himself as inconspicuous as possible. He couldn't help remembering the last time he'd attended a political meeting in Russia. On that occasion he had also come to listen to the Communist candidate, but that was in the days when there was only one name on the ballot paper. Which was possibly why the turnout on election day had been only 17 per cent.

Connor glanced around the hall. Although there was another fifteen minutes to go before the candidate was due to arrive, every seat had already been taken, and the gangways were almost full. At the front of the hall, a few officials were milling around on the stage, making sure everything would be as the leader expected it. An old man was placing a grandiose chair towards the back of the stage.

The gathering of Party faithful couldn't have been in greater contrast to an American political convention. The delegates, if that was what they were, were dressed in drab clothes. They looked undernourished, and sat in silence as they waited for Zerimski to appear.

Connor lowered his head and began scribbling some notes on his pad; he had no desire to get involved in a conversation with the journalist on his left. She had already told the correspondent on the other side of her that she represented the *Istanbul News*, the sole English-language paper in Turkey, and that her editor thought it would be a disaster if Zerimski were ever to become President. She went on to say she had recently reported that the Communist candidate might just pull it off. If she had asked Connor's opinion, he would have had to agree. The odds on his being required to carry out his assignment were shortening by the hour.

A few moments later, the Turkish journalist began sketching a portrait of Zerimski. Her paper obviously couldn't afford the luxury of a photographer, and was probably relying on wire services and whatever she came up with. He had to admit that the drawing was a good likeness.

Connor checked the room again. Would it be possible to assassinate someone in a room as crowded as this? Not if you hoped to escape. Getting at Zerimski while he was in his car was another option, although it was certain to be well protected. No professional would consider a bomb, which often ended up killing innocent people while failing to eliminate the target. If he was to have any chance of escaping, he would have to rely on a high-powered rifle in an open space. Nick Gutenburg had assured him that a customised Remington 700 would be safely in the US Embassy long before he arrived in Moscow – another misuse of the diplomatic pouch. If Lawrence gave the order, they would leave him to decide the time and place.

Now that he'd studied Zerimski's itinerary in detail, Connor had decided that his first choice would be Severodvinsk, where the Communist leader was addressing a rally in a shipyard two days before the election. Connor had already begun to study the various cranes which operated at Russian docks, and the possibility of remaining hidden inside one for a long period of time.

Heads were beginning to turn towards the back of the room, and Connor looked around. A group of men in badly cut suits with bulges under their arms were filling the back of the hall, scanning the room before their leader made his entrance.

Connor could see that their methods were primitive and ineffective, but like all security forces they probably hoped that their presence and sheer weight of numbers would make anyone think twice before trying anything. He checked the faces – all three of the professionals were back on duty.

Suddenly loud applause burst from the rear of the hall, followed by cheering. As Zerimski entered, the Party members rose as one to acclaim their leader. Even the journalists were forced to stand to catch a glimpse of him. Zerimski's progress toward the stage was continually held up as he stopped to clasp outstretched hands. When he finally reached the platform, the noise became almost deafening.

The elderly chairman who had been waiting patiently at the front of the hall led Zerimski up the steps and onto the stage, guiding him towards the large chair. Once Zerimski had sat down, he walked slowly forward to the microphone. The audience resumed their places and fell silent.

He didn't do a good job of introducing 'the next President of Russia', and the longer he spoke, the more restless the audience became. Zerimski's entourage, who were standing behind him, began to fidget and look annoyed. The old man's final flourish was to describe the speaker as 'the natural successor to Comrade Vladimir Ilyich Lenin'. He stood aside to make way for his leader, who didn't look at all certain that Lenin was the most fortunate comparison that could have been chosen.

As Zerimski rose from his place at the back of the stage and walked slowly forward, the crowd began to come alive again. He threw his arms high in the air, and they cheered more loudly than ever.

Connor's eyes never left Zerimski. He carefully noted his every movement, the stances he took, the poses he struck. Like all energetic men, he hardly remained still for a moment.

After Zerimski felt the cheering had gone on for long enough, he waved his audience back down into their seats. Connor noted that the whole process from start to finish had taken a little over three minutes.

Zerimski didn't begin to speak until everyone had resumed their places and he had complete silence.

'Comrades,' he began in a firm voice, 'it is a great honour for me to stand before you as your candidate. As each day passes, I become more and more aware that the Russian people are demanding a fresh start. Although few of our citizens wish to return to the old totalitarian regime of the past, the majority want to see a fairer distribution of the wealth that has been created by their skills and hard work.'

The audience began clapping again.

'Let us never forget,' Zerimski continued, 'that Russia can once again become the most respected nation on earth. If other countries entertain any doubt about that, under my presidency they will do so at their peril.'

The journalists scribbled away furiously, and the audience cheered even more loudly. Nearly twenty seconds passed before Zerimski was able to speak again.

'Look at the streets of Moscow, comrades. Yes, you will see Mercedes, BMWs and Jaguars, but who is driving them? Just a privileged few. And it is those few who are hoping that Chernopov will be elected so they can continue to enjoy a lifestyle no one in this room can ever hope to emulate. The time has come, my friends, for this wealth – *your* wealth – to be shared among the many, not the few. I look forward to the day when Russia no longer has more limousines than family cars, more yachts than fishing boats, and more secret Swiss bank accounts than hospitals.'

Once again the audience greeted his words with prolonged applause.

When the noise eventually died down, Zerimski dropped his voice, but every word still carried to the back of the hall. 'When I become your President, I shall not be opening bank accounts in Switzerland, but factories all over Russia. I shall not be spending my time relaxing in a luxurious dacha, but working night and day in my office. I shall be dedicating myself to your service, and be more than satisfied with the salary of a President, rather than taking bribes from dishonest businessmen whose only interest is in pillaging the nation's assets.'

This time the applause was so enthusiastic that it was over a minute before Zerimski was able to continue.

'At the back of the room,' he said, pointing a stubby finger at the assembled journalists, 'are the representatives of the world's press.' He paused, curled his lip and added, 'And may I say how welcome they are.'

No applause followed this particular remark.

'However, let me remind them that when I am President, they'll need to be in Moscow not only during the run-up to an election, but permanently. Because then Russia will not be hoping for handouts whenever the Group of Seven meet, but will once again be a major participant in world affairs. If Chernopov were elected, the Americans would be more concerned about the views of Mexico than those of Russia. In future, President Lawrence will have to listen to what *you* are saying, and not just soft-talk the world's press by telling them how much he likes Boris.'

Laughter spread around the hall.

'He may call everyone else by their first name, but he'll call me "Mr President".'

Connor knew that the American media would report that remark from coast to coast, and that every word of the speech would be raked over in the Oval Office.

'There are only eight days to go, my friends, before the people decide,' Zerimski said. 'Let us spend every moment of that time making sure we have an overwhelming victory on election day. A victory that will send out a message to the whole world that Russia is back as a power to be reckoned with on the global stage.' His voice was beginning to rise with every word. 'But don't do it for me. Don't even do it for the Communist Party. Do it for the next generation of Russians, who will then be able to play their part as citizens of the greatest nation on earth. Then, when you have cast your vote, you will have done so knowing that we can once again let the people be the power behind the nation.' He paused, and looked around the audience. 'I ask for only one thing – the privilege of being allowed to lead those people.' Dropping his voice almost to a whisper, he ended with the words, 'I offer myself as your servant.'

Zerimski took a pace backwards and threw his arms in the

air. The audience rose as one. The final peroration had taken forty-seven seconds, and not for a moment had he remained still. He had moved first to his right and then to his left, each time raising the corresponding arm, but never for more than a few seconds at a time. Then he bowed low, and after remaining motionless for twelve seconds he suddenly stood bolt upright and joined in the clapping.

He remained in the centre of the stage for another eleven minutes, repeating several of the same gestures again and again. When he felt he had milked every ounce of applause he could drag out of the audience, he descended the steps from the stage, followed by his entourage. As he walked down the centre aisle, the noise rose higher than ever, and even more arms were thrust out. Zerimski grabbed as many as he could during his slow progress to the back of the hall. Never once did Connor's eyes leave him. Even after Zerimski had left the hall, the cheering continued. It didn't die down until the audience began to leave.

Connor had noted several characteristic movements of the head and hands, small mannerisms that were often repeated. He could see already that certain gestures regularly accompanied certain phrases, and he knew that soon he would be able to anticipate them.

'Your friend just left,' said Sergei. 'I follow him?'

'That won't be necessary,' said Jackson. 'We know where he's spending the night. Mind you, that poor bastard a few paces behind him is going to be led a merry dance for the next hour or so.'

'What do we do next?' asked Sergei.

'You grab some sleep. I have a feeling tomorrow's going to be a long day.'

'You haven't paid me for today yet,' said Sergei, thrusting out his hand. 'Nine hours at $6 an hour is – $56.'

'I think you'll find it's eight hours at $5 an hour,' said Jackson. 'But nice try.' He passed $40 over to Sergei.

'And tomorrow?' his young partner asked after he had counted and pocketed the notes. 'What time you want me?'

'Meet me outside his hotel at five o'clock, and don't be late.

My guess is we'll be following Zerimski on his travels to Yaroslavl, and then returning to Moscow before going on to St Petersburg.'

'You're lucky, Jackson. I was born in St Petersburg, and there's nothing I don't know about the place. But remember, I charge double outside Moscow.'

'You know, Sergei, if you go on like this, it won't be long before you price yourself out of the market.'

14

MAGGIE DROVE OUT of the university parking lot at one minute past one. She swung left onto Prospect Street, braking only briefly at the first stop sign before accelerating away. She only ever took an hour for lunch, and if she failed to find a parking spot near the restaurant it would cut down their time together. And today she needed every minute of that hour.

Not that any of her staff in the Admissions Office would have complained if she had taken the afternoon off. After twenty-eight years working for the university – the last six as Dean of Admissions – if she had put in a backdated claim for overtime, Georgetown University would have had to launch a special appeal.

At least today the gods were on her side. A woman was pulling out of a spot a few yards from the restaurant where they had arranged to meet. Maggie put four quarters in the meter to cover an hour.

When she entered the Café Milano, Maggie gave the maître d' her name. 'Yes, of course, Mrs Fitzgerald,' he said, and guided her to a table by the window to join someone who had never been known to be late for anything.

Maggie kissed the woman who had been Connor's secretary for the past nineteen years, and took the place opposite her. Joan probably loved Connor as much as she had any man, and for that love she had never been rewarded with more than the occasional peck on the cheek and a gift at Christmas, which Maggie inevitably ended up buying. Though Joan was not yet fifty, her sensible tweeds, flat shoes and cropped brown hair revealed that she had long ago given up trying to attract the opposite sex.

'I've already decided,' Joan said.

'I know what I'm going to have too,' said Maggie.

'How's Tara?' asked Joan, closing her menu.

'Hanging in there, to use her own words. I only hope she'll finish her thesis. Although Connor would never say anything to her, he'll be very disappointed if she doesn't.'

'He speaks warmly of Stuart,' Joan said as a waiter appeared by her side.

'Yes,' said Maggie, a little sadly. 'It looks as if I'm going to have to get used to the idea of my only child living thirteen thousand miles away.' She looked up at the waiter. 'Cannelloni and a side salad for me.'

'And I'll have the angel-hair pasta,' said Joan.

'Anything to drink, ladies?' the waiter asked hopefully.

'No, thank you,' said Maggie firmly. 'Just a glass of water.' Joan nodded her agreement.

'Yes, Connor and Stuart got on well,' said Maggie once the waiter had left. 'Stuart will be joining us for Christmas, so you'll have a chance to meet him then.'

'I look forward to that,' said Joan.

Maggie sensed that she wanted to add something, but after so many years she had learned that there was no point in pressing her. If it was important, Joan would let her know when she was good and ready.

'I've tried to call you several times in the past few days. I hoped you might be able to join me at the opera or come for dinner one evening, but I seem to keep missing you.'

'Now that Connor's left the company, they've closed the office on M Street and moved me back to headquarters,' said Joan.

Maggie admired the way Joan had chosen her words so carefully. No hint of where she was working, no suggestion of for whom, not a clue about what her new responsibilities were now that she was no longer with Connor.

'It's no secret that he hopes you'll eventually join him at Washington Provident,' said Maggie.

'I'd love to. But there's no point in making any plans until we know what's happening.'

'What do you mean, "happening"?' asked Maggie. 'Connor's already accepted Ben Thompson's offer. He has to be back before Christmas, so he can start his new job at the beginning of January.'

A long silence followed before Maggie said quietly, 'So he didn't get the job with Washington Provident after all.'

The waiter arrived with their meals. 'A little parmesan cheese, madam?' he asked as he placed them on the table.

'Thank you,' said Joan, staring intently at her pasta.

'So that's why Ben Thompson cold-shouldered me at the opera last Thursday. He didn't even offer to buy me a drink.'

'I'm sorry,' said Joan, as the waiter left them. 'I just assumed you knew.'

'Don't worry. Connor would have let me know the moment he'd got another interview, and then told me it was a far better job than the one he'd been offered at Washington Provident.'

'How well you know him,' said Joan.

'Sometimes I wonder if I know him at all,' said Maggie. 'Right now I have no idea where he is or what he's up to.'

'I don't know much more than you do,' said Joan. 'For the first time in nineteen years, he didn't brief me before he left.'

'It's different this time, isn't it, Joan?' said Maggie, looking straight at her.

'What makes you say that?'

'He told me he was going abroad, but left without his passport. My guess is that he's still in America. But why . . .'

'Not taking his passport doesn't prove he isn't abroad,' said Joan.

'Possibly not,' said Maggie. 'But this is the first time he's hidden it where he knew I would find it.'

A few minutes later, the waiter reappeared and whisked away their plates.

'Would either of you care for dessert?' he asked.

'Not for me,' said Joan. 'Just coffee.'

'Me too,' said Maggie. 'Black, no sugar.' She checked her watch. She only had sixteen minutes left. She bit her lip. 'Joan, I've never asked you to break a confidence before, but there's something I have to know.'

Joan looked out of the window and glanced at the good-looking young man who had been leaning against the wall on the far side of the street for the past forty minutes. She thought she had seen him somewhere before.

When Maggie left the restaurant at seven minutes to two, she didn't notice the same young man take out a mobile phone and dial an unlisted number.

'Yes?' said Nick Gutenburg.

'Mrs Fitzgerald has just finished lunch with Joan Bennett at Café Milano on Prospect. They were together for forty-seven minutes. I've recorded every word of their conversation.'

'Good. Bring the tape in to my office immediately.'

As Maggie ran up the steps to the Admissions Office, the clock in the university courtyard was showing one minute to two.

—◦—

It was one minute to ten in Moscow. Connor was enjoying the finale of *Giselle*, performed by the Bolshoi Ballet. But unlike most of the audience, he didn't keep his opera glasses trained on the prima ballerina's virtuoso performance. From time to time he would glance down to the right and check that Zerimski was still in his box. Connor knew how much Maggie would have enjoyed the Dance of the Wilis, the spirits of thirty-six young brides dressed in their wedding gowns, pirouetting in the moonlight. He tried not to be mesmerised by their *pliés* and arabesques, and to concentrate on what was going on in Zerimski's box. Maggie often went to the ballet when he was out of town, and she would have been amused to know that the Russian Communist leader had achieved in a single evening what she had failed to do in thirty years.

Connor studied the men in the box. On Zerimski's right was Dmitri Titov, his Chief of Staff. On his left sat the elderly man who had introduced him before he gave his speech the previous evening. Behind him in the shadows stood three guards. Connor assumed that there would be at least another dozen in the corridor outside.

The vast theatre, with its beautiful tiered balconies and its stalls filled with gilt chairs covered in red velvet plush, was always sold out for weeks in advance. But the Maggie theory had also applied in Moscow – you can always pick up a single ticket, even at the last minute.

Moments before the conductor was due to arrive in the orchestra pit, a section of the crowd began to applaud. Connor had looked up from his programme to see one or two people pointing towards a box on the second tier. Zerimski had timed his entrance to perfection. He stood at the front of the box, waving and smiling. A little under half the audience rose and cheered loudly, while the rest remained seated, some clapping politely, others continuing their conversations as if he wasn't there. This seemed to confirm the accuracy of the opinion polls – that Chernopov was now leading his rival by only a few percentage points.

Once the curtain had risen, Connor quickly discovered that Zerimski showed about as much interest in ballet as he did in art. It had been another long day for the candidate, and Connor was not surprised to see him stifling the occasional yawn. His train had left for Yaroslavl early that morning, and he had immediately begun his programme with a visit to a clothes factory on the outskirts of the town. When he left the union officials an hour later, he had grabbed a sandwich before dropping in to a fruit market, then a school, a police station and a hospital, followed by an unscheduled walkabout in the town square. Finally he had been driven back to the station at speed and jumped onto a train that had been held up for him.

The dogma Zerimski proclaimed to anyone who cared to listen hadn't changed a great deal from the previous day, except that 'Moscow' had been replaced with 'Yaroslavl'. The thugs who surrounded him as he toured the factory looked even more amateurish than those who had been with him when he delivered his speech at the Lenin Memorial Hall. It was clear that the locals were not going to allow any Muscovites onto their territory. Connor concluded that an attempt on Zerimski's life would have a far better chance of succeeding outside the capital. It would need to be in a city that was large enough to disappear in, and proud enough not to allow the three professionals from Moscow to call the tune.

Zerimski's visit to the shipyard in Severodvinsk in a few days' time still looked his best bet.

Even on the train back to Moscow, Zerimski didn't rest. He called the foreign journalists into his carriage for another press conference. But before anyone could ask a question, he said, 'Have you seen the latest opinion polls, which show me running well ahead of General Borodin and now trailing Chernopov by only one point?'

'But you've always told us in the past to ignore the polls,' said one of the journalists bravely. Zerimski scowled.

Connor stood at the back of the mêlée and continued to study the would-be President. He knew he had to anticipate Zerimski's every expression, movement and mannerism, as well as be able to deliver his speech verbatim.

When the train pulled into Protsky station four hours later, Connor had a sense that someone on board was watching him, other than Mitchell. After twenty-eight years, he was rarely wrong about these things. He was beginning to wonder if Mitchell wasn't just a little too obvious, and if there might be someone more professional out there. If there was, what did they want? Earlier in the day, he'd had a feeling that someone or something had flitted across his path that he'd noticed before. He disapproved of paranoia, but like all professionals, he didn't believe in coincidences.

He left the station and doubled back to his hotel, confident that no one had followed him. But then, they wouldn't need to if they knew where he was staying. He tried to dismiss these thoughts from his mind as he packed his bag. Tonight he would lose whoever was trailing him – unless, of course, they already knew exactly where he was going. After all, if they knew why he was in Russia, they had only to follow Zerimski's itinerary. He checked out of the hotel a few minutes later, paying his bill in cash.

He had changed taxis five times before allowing the last one to drop him outside the theatre. He checked his bag in with an old woman seated behind a counter in the basement, and rented a pair of opera glasses. Leaving the bag gave the management confidence that the glasses would be returned.

When the curtain was finally lowered at the end of the performance, Zerimski rose and waved to the audience once again. The response was not quite so enthusiastic as before, but Connor thought he must have left feeling that his visit to the Bolshoi had been worthwhile. As he strode down the steps of the theatre he loudly informed the departing audience how much he had enjoyed the magnificent performance of Ekaterina Maximova. A line of cars awaited him and his entourage, and he slipped into the back of the third. The motorcade and its police escort whisked him off to another train waiting at another station. Connor noted that the number of motorcycle outriders had been increased from two to four.

Other people were obviously beginning to think he might be the next President.

–◦–

Connor arrived at the station a few minutes after Zerimski. He showed a security guard his press pass before purchasing a ticket for the eleven fifty-nine to St Petersburg.

Once he was inside his sleeping compartment he locked the door, switched on the light over his bunk and began to study the itinerary for Zerimski's visit to St Petersburg.

In a carriage at the other end of the train, the candidate was also going over the itinerary, with his Chief of Staff.

'Another first-thing-in-the-morning-to-last-thing-at-night sort of day,' he was grumbling. And that was before Titov had added a visit to the Hermitage.

'Why should I bother to go to the Hermitage when I'm only in St Petersburg for a few hours?'

'Because you went to the Pushkin, and not to go to Russia's most famous museum would be an insult to the citizens of St Petersburg.'

'Let's be thankful that we leave before the curtain goes up at the Kirov.'

Zerimski knew that by far the most important meeting of the day would be with General Borodin and the military high command at Kelskow Barracks. If he could persuade the General to withdraw from the presidential race and back him, then the military – almost two and a half million of them – would surely swing behind him, and the prize would be his. He had planned to offer Borodin the position of Defence Secretary until he discovered that Chernopov had already promised him the same post. He knew that Chernopov had been to see the General the previous Monday, and had left empty-handed. Zerimski took this as a good sign. He intended to offer Borodin something he would find irresistible.

Connor also realised that tomorrow's meeting with the military leader might decide Zerimski's fate. He switched off the light above his bunk a few minutes after two a.m., and fell asleep.

Mitchell had turned off his light the moment the train had pulled out of the station, but he didn't sleep.

Sergei had been unable to hide his excitement at the thought of travelling on the Protsky express. He had followed his partner to their compartment like a contented puppy. When Jackson pulled open the door, Sergei announced, 'It's bigger than my flat.' He leapt onto one of the bunks, kicked off his shoes and pulled the blankets over him without bothering to take off any clothes. 'Saves washing and changing,' he explained as Jackson hung his jacket and trousers on the flimsiest wire hanger he'd ever seen.

As the American prepared for bed, Sergei rubbed the steamed-up window with an elbow, making a circle he could peer through. He didn't say another word until the train began to move slowly out of the station.

Jackson climbed into his bunk and switched his light off.

'How many kilometres to St Petersburg, Jackson?'

'Six hundred and thirty.'

'And how long will it take us to get there?'

'Eight and a half hours. We've got another long day ahead of us, so try to get some sleep.'

Sergei switched off his light, but Jackson remained awake. He was now certain that he knew why his friend had been despatched to Russia. Helen Dexter obviously wanted Connor out of the way, but Jackson still didn't know how far she would go to save her own skin.

He had attempted to ring Andy Lloyd earlier that afternoon on his cellphone, but hadn't been able to get through. He didn't want to risk calling from the hotel, so he decided to try again after Zerimski had delivered his speech in Freedom Square the following day, by which time Washington would have woken up. Once Lloyd knew what was going on, Jackson was sure he would be given the authority to abort the whole operation before it was too late. He closed his eyes.

'Are you married, Jackson?'

'No, divorced,' he replied.

'There are now more divorces each year in Russia than in the States. Did you know that, Jackson?'

'No. But I've come to realise over the past couple of days that that's just the sort of useless information you carry around in that head of yours.'

'What about children? You have any?'

'None,' said Jackson. 'I lost . . .'

'Why don't you adopt me? Then I go back to America with you.'

'I don't think Ted Turner could afford to adopt *you*. Now go to sleep, Sergei.'

There was another long silence.

'One more question, Jackson?'

'Tell me how I'm going to stop you.'

'Why is this man so important to you?'

Jackson waited some time before answering. 'Twenty-nine years ago he saved my life in Vietnam, so I guess you could say I owe him for those years. Does that make any sense?'

Sergei would have replied, but he'd fallen fast asleep.

15

VLADIMIR BOLCHENKOV, St Petersburg's Chief of Police, had enough on his mind without having to worry about four mysterious phone calls. Chernopov had visited the city on Monday, and had brought the traffic to a standstill by demanding that his motorcade should be the same size as the late President's.

Borodin was refusing to allow his men to leave their barracks until they were paid, and now that it looked as if he was out of the race for President, rumours of a military coup were beginning to surface once again. 'It's not hard to work out which city Borodin will want to take over first,' Bolchenkov had warned the Mayor. He had set up a whole department to deal with the threat of terrorism during the election campaign. If any of the candidates were going to be assassinated, it wouldn't be on his territory. That week alone, the department had received twenty-seven threats on Zerimski's life. The Chief had dismissed them as the usual assortment of weirdos and lunatics – until a young lieutenant had rushed into his office earlier that morning, white-faced and talking far too quickly.

The Chief sat and listened to the recording the Lieutenant had made moments before. The first call had come through at nine twenty-four, fifty-one minutes after Zerimski had arrived in the city.

'There will be an attempt on Zerimski's life this afternoon,' said a male voice with an accent that Bolchenkov couldn't quite place. Mid-European, perhaps; certainly not Russian.

'While Zerimski is addressing the rally in Freedom Square,

a lone gunman hired by the Mafya will make the attempt. I will call back with more details in a few minutes' time, but I will speak only to Bolchenkov.' The line went dead. The brevity of the call meant there was no possibility of tracing it. Bolchenkov knew immediately that they were dealing with a professional.

Eleven minutes later the second call came through. The Lieutenant bluffed for as long as he could, claiming they were trying to find the Chief, but all the caller said was, 'I will phone again in a few minutes' time. Just be sure Bolchenkov is standing by the phone. It's your time that's being wasted, not mine.'

That was when the Lieutenant had burst into the Chief's office. Bolchenkov had been explaining to one of Zerimski's sidekicks why his motorcade couldn't be allocated the same number of police outriders as Chernopov's. He immediately stubbed out his cigarette and went to join his team in the terrorism unit. It was another nine minutes before the caller phoned again.

'Is Bolchenkov there?'

'This is Bolchenkov speaking.'

'The man you are looking for will be posing as a foreign journalist, representing a South African newspaper that doesn't exist. He arrived in St Petersburg on the express from Moscow this morning. He is working alone. I will call you again in three minutes.'

Three minutes later the whole department was assembled to listen to him.

'I'm sure that by now the entire anti-terrorism division of the St Petersburg Police are hanging on my every word,' was the caller's opening salvo. 'So allow me to give you a helping hand. The assassin is six foot one, has blue eyes and thick sandy hair. But he'll probably be disguised. I don't know what he will be wearing, but then you must do something to earn your wages.' The line went dead.

The whole unit listened to the tapes again and again over the next half-hour. Suddenly the Chief stubbed out another cigarette and said, 'Play the third tape again.' The young Lieutenant pressed a button, wondering what his boss had picked up that the rest of them had missed. They all listened intently.

'Stop,' said the Chief after only a few seconds. 'I thought so. Go back and start counting.'

Count what? the Lieutenant wanted to ask as he pressed the playback button. This time he heard the faint chime of a carriage clock in the background.

He rewound the tape and they listened once again. 'Two chimes,' said the Lieutenant. 'If it was two in the afternoon, our informant was calling from the Far East.'

The Chief smiled. 'I don't think so,' he said. 'It's more likely that the call was made at two in the morning, from the east coast of America.'

-◇-

Maggie picked up the phone by her bed and dialled a 650 number. It only rang a couple of times before it was picked up.

'Tara Fitzgerald,' said a brisk voice. No 'Hello, good evening,' or confirmation that the caller had dialled the correct number. Just the bold announcement of her name, so no one needed to waste any time. How like her father, Maggie thought.

'It's Mom, honey.'

'Hi, Mom. Has the car broken down again, or is it something serious?'

'Nothing, honey, I'm just missing your father,' she replied, laughing. 'I hoped you'd have time for a chat.'

'Well, at least you're only missing *one* man,' said Tara, trying to lighten the tone. 'I'm missing two.'

'Maybe, but at least you know where Stuart is, and can give him a call whenever you want to. My problem is that I haven't a clue where your father is.'

'There's nothing new about that, Mom. We all know the rules when Dad's away. The womenfolk are expected to sit at home dutifully waiting for their master to return. Typically Irish . . .'

'Yes, I know. But I have an uneasy feeling about this particular trip,' said Maggie.

'I'm sure there's no need to be anxious, Mother. After all, he's only been away for a week. Remember how many times in the past he's turned up when you least expected it. I've always assumed it was a dastardly plot to make sure you don't have a lover on the side.'

Maggie laughed unconvincingly.

'Something else is worrying you, isn't it, Mom?' said Tara quietly. 'Do you want to tell me about it?'

'I discovered an envelope addressed to me hidden in one of his drawers.'

'The old romantic,' said Tara. 'What did he have to say?'

'I've no idea. I haven't opened it.'

'Why not, for heaven's sake?'

'Because he's written clearly on the outside, "Not to be opened before 17 December".'

'Mom, it's probably just a Christmas card,' said Tara lightly.

'I doubt it,' said Maggie. 'I don't know many husbands who give their wives Christmas cards, and certainly not in a brown envelope hidden in a drawer.'

'If you're that anxious about it, Mom, I'm sure Dad would want you to open it. Then you might find out you've been worrying about nothing.'

'Not until 17 December,' said Maggie quietly. 'If Connor arrived home before then and discovered I'd opened it, he'd . . .'

'When did you find it?'

'This morning. It was among his sports clothes, in a drawer I hardly ever open.'

'I'd have opened it straight away if it had been addressed to me,' said Tara.

'I know you would,' said Maggie, 'but I still think I'd better leave it for a few more days before I do anything. I'll put it back in the drawer in case he suddenly turns up. Then he'll never know I'd even come across it.'

'Perhaps I should fly back to Washington.'

'Why?' asked Maggie.

'To help you open it.'

'Stop being silly, Tara.'

'No sillier than you just sitting there on your own fretting about what might be inside.'

'Perhaps you're right.'

'If you're so uncertain, Mother, why don't you give Joan a call and ask her advice?'

'I already have.'

'And what did she say?'

'Open it.'

—◇—

Bolchenkov sat on the desk at the front of the operations room and looked down at the twenty hand-picked men. He struck a match and lit his seventh cigarette of the morning.

'How many people are we expecting in the square this afternoon?' he asked.

'It's only a guess, Chief,' said the most senior uniformed officer present, 'but it could be as many as a hundred thousand.'

A murmur of whispered conversations broke out.

'Quiet,' said the Chief sharply. 'Why so many, Captain? Chernopov only managed seventy thousand.'

'Zerimski's a far more charismatic figure, and now that the polls are moving in his direction, I predict he'll prove a much bigger draw.'

'How many officers can you spare me on the ground?'

'Every available man will be in the square, Chief, and I've cancelled all leave. I've already issued the man's description, in the hope that we can pick him up before he even reaches the square. But not many of them have any experience of something this big.'

'If there are really going to be a hundred thousand people in the square,' said Bolchenkov, 'it will be a first for me as well. Have all your officers been issued with the description?'

'Yes, but he may be in disguise. In any case, there are a lot of tall foreigners with blue eyes and sandy hair out there. And don't forget, they haven't been told why he's wanted for questioning. We don't need a panic on our hands.'

'Agreed. But I don't want to frighten him off now, just to

give him a second chance later. Has anyone picked up any more information?'

'Yes, Chief,' replied a younger man leaning against the back wall. The Chief stubbed out his cigarette and nodded.

'There are three South African journalists officially covering the election. From the description given to us by our informant, I'm fairly confident it's the one who calls himself Piet de Villiers.'

'Anything on the computer about him?'

'No,' said the young officer. 'But the police in Johannesburg were extremely cooperative. They have three men on their files answering to that name, with crimes ranging from petty theft to bigamy, but none of them fitted the description, and in any case two of them are currently locked up. They've no idea of the whereabouts of the third. They also mentioned a Colombian connection.'

'What Colombian connection?'

'A few weeks ago the CIA circulated a confidential memo giving details about the murder of a presidential candidate in Bogotá. It seems they traced the assassin to South Africa, then lost him. I called my contact at the CIA, but all he could tell me was that they knew the man was on the move again, and that he was last seen boarding a plane for Geneva.'

'That's all I need,' said the Chief. 'I don't suppose there was any sign of de Villiers when Zerimski visited the Hermitage this morning?'

'No, Chief,' said another voice, 'not if he was with the press corps. There were twenty-three journalists there, and only two of them vaguely fitted the description. One was Clifford Symonds, an anchor with CNN, and the other I've known for years. I play chess with him.' Everyone in the room laughed, helping to break the tension.

'Rooftops and buildings?' said the Chief.

'I have a dozen men detailed to cover the rooftops around the square,' said the head of the small-arms unit. 'Most of the buildings are public offices, so I'll station plain-clothes officers at every entrance and exit. If anyone fitting the description tries to enter the square, or any of the buildings overlooking it, he'll be arrested on the spot.'

'Be careful you don't arrest some foreign dignitary and get us into even worse trouble. Any questions?'

'Yes, Chief. Have you considered calling off the rally?' asked a voice from the back.

'I have, and I decided against it. If I were to cancel a meeting every time I received a threat to a public figure, our telephone lines would be blocked with calls from every half-baked radical with nothing better to do than cause mayhem. In any case, it could still be a false alarm. And even if de Villiers is roaming around the city, when he sees our presence on the ground he might have second thoughts. Any more questions?'

No one stirred.

'If any of you picks up anything, and I mean anything, I want to know immediately. Heaven help the man who tells me afterwards, "I didn't mention it, Chief, because I didn't think it was important at the time."'

—◇—

Connor kept the television on while he shaved. Hillary Bowker was bringing viewers up to date with what was happening in the States. The Arms Reduction Bill had passed the House, squeaking home by a mere three votes. Tom Lawrence was nevertheless claiming the result as a triumph for common sense. The pundits, on the other hand, were already warning that the Bill would face a far tougher passage once it reached the floor of the Senate.

'Not at all,' the President had assured the assembled journalists at his morning press briefing. Connor smiled. 'The House was simply carrying out the will of the people, and I'm confident that the Senate will want to do exactly the same.'

The President was replaced by a pretty girl with bright red hair who reminded Connor of Maggie. In my line of work I should have married a newscaster, he had once told her.

'And now, to find out more about the upcoming elections in

Russia, we go over to Clifford Symonds, our correspondent in St Petersburg.'

Connor stopped shaving and stared at the screen.

'The opinion polls show that the two leading candidates, Prime Minister Grigory Chernopov and Communist Party leader Victor Zerimski, are now running neck and neck. The Communist candidate will be addressing a rally in Freedom Square this afternoon that the police are predicting could be attended by as many as a hundred thousand people. This morning Mr Zerimski will have a private meeting with General Borodin, who is expected shortly to announce his withdrawal from the race following his poor showing in the latest opinion polls. Uncertainty remains as to which of the two front-runners he will support, and on that decision could hang the result of the election. This is Clifford Symonds, CNN International, St Petersburg.'

Hillary Bowker's face reappeared on the screen. 'And now for the weather,' she said with a broad smile.

Connor flicked off the television, as he had no interest in being told the temperature in Florida. He rubbed some more lather into his stubble and continued shaving. He had already decided that he wasn't going to attend Zerimski's morning press conference, which would be nothing more than a panegyric from his press secretary about what his boss had achieved even before breakfast, or go to the Hermitage and spend most of his time avoiding Mitchell. He would concentrate on Zerimski's main public appearance that day. He had already found a convenient restaurant on the west side of the square. It wasn't known for its cuisine, but it did have the advantage of being on the second floor, and overlooking Freedom Square. More important, it had a rear door, so he wouldn't have to enter the square before it was necessary.

Once he had left his hotel, he called the restaurant from the nearest public phonebox and booked a corner table by the window for twelve o'clock. He then went in search of a rented car, which was even harder to find in St Petersburg than it had been in Moscow. Forty minutes later he drove into the centre of the city and left the vehicle in an underground carpark only a couple of hundred yards from Freedom Square. He had decided to drive back to Moscow after the speech. That way he would soon find out if anyone was following him. He walked up into the street, strolled into the nearest hotel and slipped the head porter a twenty-dollar bill, explaining that he needed a room for about an hour so that he could take a shower and change his clothes.

When he came back down in the lift a few minutes before twelve, the head porter didn't recognise him. Connor left a duffle bag with him and said he would be back to pick it up around four. When the porter placed the bag under the counter he noticed the briefcase for the first time. As each bore a label with the same name, he put them together.

Connor walked slowly up the side street next to Freedom Square. He passed two policemen who were questioning a tall, sandy-haired foreigner. They didn't give him a second glance as he slipped inside and took the lift to the second-floor restaurant. He gave the head waiter his name, and was immediately directed to a corner table. He sat so that he was shielded from most of the other diners, but still had a bird's-eye view of the square below.

He was thinking about Tom Lawrence, and wondering how late he would leave it before he made up his mind, when a waiter appeared by his side and handed him the menu. Connor glanced out of the window, and was surprised to find that the square was already filling up, although there were still two hours to go before Zerimski was due to deliver his speech. Among the crowd he spotted several plain-clothes policemen. One or two of the younger ones were already clinging to statues and checking carefully around the square. But what were they looking for? Was the Chief of Police being over-cautious, or did he fear there might be some form of demonstration during Zerimski's speech?

The head waiter returned. 'Could I please take your order, sir? The police have instructed us to close the restaurant before two o'clock.'

'Then I'd better have the minute steak,' said Connor.

16

'WHERE DO YOU THINK he is right now?' asked Sergei.

'He'll be out there somewhere, but if I know him he'll be damn near impossible to find in this crowd,' said Jackson. 'It will be like looking for a needle in a haystack.'

'Who ever lost a needle in a haystack?'

'Stop making smart-assed remarks and do what you're being paid for,' said Jackson. 'I'll give you a ten-dollar bonus if you can spot him. Remember, he's likely to be well disguised.'

Sergei suddenly took a far greater interest in the crowd milling around in the square. 'See that man on the top step in the north corner?' he said. 'Talking to a policeman.'

'Yes,' replied Jackson.

'That's Vladimir Bolchenkov, the Chief of Police. A fair man, even though he's the second most powerful person in St Petersburg.'

'Who's the first?' asked Jackson. 'The Mayor?'

'No, his brother Joseph. He's the city's Mafya boss.'

'Doesn't that cause a slight conflict of interest?'

'No. You only get arrested in St Petersburg if you're not Mafya.'

'Where do you get all your information?' asked Jackson.

'My mother. She's slept with both of them.'

Jackson laughed as they continued to watch the Chief talking to the uniformed officer. He would have liked to overhear their conversation. If it had been taking place in Washington, the CIA would have been able to play back every word that passed between them.

◄○►

'You see the young men draped around the statues?' said the senior police officer standing next to Bolchenkov.

'What about them?' said the Chief.

'Just in case you were wondering why I haven't arrested them, they're all members of my team, and have a better view of the crowd than anyone. Look behind you, Chief: the hotdog salesman, the two men on the flower barrows and the four news-vendors are also mine. And I've got twelve busloads of uniformed police less than a block away, who can be pulled in at a moment's notice. There will also be another hundred plain-clothes men drifting in and out of the square during the next hour. Every exit is covered, and anyone who has a view of the square will have one of my men within a few feet of him.'

'If he's as good as I think he is,' said the Chief, 'he'll have found somewhere you haven't thought of.'

◄○►

Connor ordered a cup of coffee and continued to watch the activity taking place in the square below. Although there were still thirty minutes to go before the candidate was due to arrive, the square was already packed with everyone from Zerimski-worshippers to the simply curious. He was amused by how hard the hotdog vendor was trying to disguise the fact that he was a policeman. The poor man had just received another voluble com-plaint – probably forgotten the ketchup. Connor turned his atten-tion to the far side of the square. The little stand erected for the press was now the only area that remained unoccupied. He won-dered why so many plain-clothes detectives were milling around, far more than was necessary to keep a casual passer-by from straying into a reserved area. Something didn't add up. He was distracted by a hot coffee being placed in front of him. He checked his watch. Zerimski should have finished his meeting with General Borodin by now. The outcome would lead the news on all the networks that evening. Connor wondered if he would be able to tell from Zerimski's manner if a deal had been struck.

He called for the bill, and while he waited he concentrated on the scene below him for the last time. No professional would ever have considered Freedom Square a suitable target area. Besides all the problems he had already identified, the Chief of Police's thoroughness was evident for anyone to see. Despite this, Connor felt that the sheer size of the crowd would give him his best opportunity yet to study Zerimski at close quarters, which was why he had decided not to sit among the press on this occasion.

He paid his bill in cash, walked slowly over to the girl seated in the little booth and passed her a ticket. She handed him his hat and coat, and he gave her a five-rouble note. Old people always leave small tips, he'd read somewhere.

He joined a large group of workers streaming out of offices on the first floor, who had obviously been given time off to attend the rally. Any managers within a mile of the square had probably accepted that not much work was going to be done that afternoon. Two plain-clothes policemen standing a few yards from the door were scrutinising the group of workers, but because of the freezing air they were revealing as little of themselves as possible. Connor found himself being borne along by the crowd as it flowed out onto the pavement.

Freedom Square was already packed as Connor tried to squeeze between the bodies and make his way towards the podium. The crowd must be well over seventy thousand strong. He knew that the Chief of Police would have been praying for a thunderstorm, but it was a typical winter's day in St Petersburg – cold, sharp and clear. He looked towards the roped-off press enclosure, which still seemed to have a considerable amount of activity going on around it. He smiled when he spotted Mitchell in his usual place, about ten feet from where he himself would normally have been seated. Not today, my friend. At least this time Mitchell was wearing a warm overcoat and the appropriate headgear.

⊷⊶

'Good day for pickpockets,' said Sergei, scanning the crowd.

'Would they risk it with this sort of police presence?' asked Jackson.

'You can always find a cop when you don't need one,' said Sergei. 'I've already seen some old lags leaving with wallets. But the police don't seem interested.'

'Perhaps they've got enough problems on their hands, what with a crowd of nearly a hundred thousand and Zerimski expected to arrive at any moment.'

Sergei's eyes settled on the Chief of Police. 'Where is he?' Bolchenkov was asking a sergeant with a walkie-talkie.

'He left the meeting with Borodin eighteen minutes ago, and is being driven down Preyti Street. He should be with us in about seven minutes.'

'Then in seven minutes our problems begin,' said the Chief, checking his watch.

'Don't you think it's possible our man might just try taking a shot at Zerimski while he's in the car?'

'Not a chance,' said the Chief. 'We're dealing with a pro. He wouldn't consider a moving target, especially one in a bulletproof car. In any case, he couldn't be certain which vehicle Zerimski was in. No, our man's out there in that crowd somewhere, I feel it in my bones. Don't forget, the last time he tried something like this, it was a standing target in the open. That way it's almost impossible to hit the wrong person; and with a big crowd you have a better chance of escaping.'

Connor was still edging his way slowly towards the platform. He cast an eye round the crowd, and identified several more plain-clothes policemen. Zerimski wouldn't mind, as they would only add to the numbers. All he would care about was having a larger turnout than Chernopov.

Connor checked the roofs. A dozen or so marksmen were scanning the crowd with binoculars. They couldn't have been more obvious if they'd been wearing yellow tracksuits. There were also at least a couple of hundred uniformed police standing around the perimeter of the square. The Chief obviously believed in the value of deterrence.

The windows of the buildings around the square were crammed with office-workers trying to get the best possible view of what was going on below them. Once again Connor glanced towards the roped-off press enclosure, which was now beginning to fill up. The police were checking everyone's credentials carefully – nothing unusual about that, except that some of the journalists were being asked to remove their headgear. Connor watched for a few moments. Everyone being challenged had two things in common: they were male, and they were tall. It caused him to stop in his tracks. Then, out of the corner of his eye, he caught sight of Mitchell a few paces away from him in the crowd. He frowned. How had the young agent recognised him?

Suddenly, without warning, a loud roar came from behind him, as if a rock star had arrived on stage. He turned and watched Zerimski's motorcade make its slow progress around three sides of the square, coming to a halt in the north-west corner. The crowd was applauding enthusiastically, although they couldn't possibly see the candidate, as the windows of all the cars were black. The doors of the Zil limousines were opened, but there was no way of knowing if Zerimski was among those who had stepped out, as he was surrounded by so many burly bodyguards.

When the candidate finally mounted the steps a few moments later, the crowd began cheering even louder, reaching a climax as he walked to the front of the stage. He stopped and waved first in one direction and then another. By now Connor could have told you how many paces he would take before he turned and waved again.

People were leaping up and down to get a better view, but Connor ignored the bedlam all around him. He kept his eye on the police, most of whom were looking away from the stage. They were searching for something, or someone, in particular. A thought flashed across his mind, but he dismissed it at once. No, it wasn't possible. Paranoia setting in. He'd once been told by a veteran agent that it was always at its worst on your last assignment.

But if you were in any doubt, the rule was always the same: get yourself out of the danger area. He looked around the square, quickly weighing up which exit he should take. The crowd was beginning to calm down as they waited for Zerimski to speak. Connor decided he would start moving towards the north end of the square the moment there was a burst of prolonged applause. That way it was less likely that he'd be noticed slipping through the crowd. He glanced, almost as a reflex action, to see where Mitchell was. He was still standing a few yards to his right, if anything a little closer than when he had first spotted him.

Zerimski approached the microphone with his hands raised, to let the crowd know that he was about to begin his speech.

'I've seen the needle,' said Sergei.

'Where?' demanded Jackson.

'There, about twenty paces from stage. He has different-coloured hair and walks like an old man. You owe me ten dollars.'

'How did you pick him out from this distance?' asked Jackson.

'He is the only one trying to leave the square.'

Jackson passed over a ten-dollar bill as Zerimski stopped in front of the microphone. The old man who had introduced him in Moscow sat alone at the back of the stage. Zerimski didn't allow that kind of mistake to happen a second time.

'Comrades,' he began resonantly, 'it is a great honour for me to stand before you as your candidate. As each day passes, I become more and more aware . . .'

As Connor scanned the crowd, he once again caught sight of Mitchell. He'd taken another step towards him.

'Although few of our citizens wish to return to the old totalitarian days of the past, the vast majority . . .'

Just the odd word change here and there, thought Connor. He noticed that Mitchell had taken another step towards him.

'. . . want to see a fairer distribution of the wealth that has been created by their skills and hard work.' As the crowd began to cheer, Connor quickly moved a few paces to his right. When the applause died down, he froze, not moving a muscle.

'Why is the man on the bench following your friend?' asked Sergei.

'Because he's an amateur,' said Jackson.

'Or a professional who knows exactly what he's doing?' suggested Sergei.

'My God, don't tell me I'm losing my touch,' said Jackson.

'So far he's done everything but kiss him,' said Sergei.

'Look at the streets of St Petersburg, comrades,' continued Zerimski. 'Yes, you will see Mercedes, BMWs and Jaguars, but who is driving them? Only the privileged few . . .'

When the crowd burst into applause again, Connor took a few more steps towards the north end of the square.

'I look forward to the day when this is not the only country on earth where limousines outnumber family cars . . .'

Connor glanced back to find that Mitchell had taken two or three more steps in his direction. What was he playing at?

'. . . and where there are more Swiss bank accounts than hospitals.'

He would have to lose him during the next burst of applause. He concentrated on Zerimski's words, to anticipate exactly when he would make his move.

'I think I've spotted him,' said a plain-clothes policeman who was sweeping the crowd through a pair of binoculars.

'Where, where?' demanded Bolchenkov, grabbing the glasses.

'Twelve o'clock, fifty yards back, not moving a muscle. He's in front of a woman wearing a red scarf. He doesn't look like his photograph, but whenever there's a burst of applause he moves too quickly for a man of that age.'

Bolchenkov began focusing the glasses. 'Got him,' he said. After a few seconds he added, 'Yes, it might just be him. Brief those two at one o'clock to move in and arrest him, and tell the pair twenty yards in front of him to cover them. Let's get it over with as quickly as possible.' The young officer looked anxious. 'If we've made a mistake,' said the Chief, 'I'll take the responsibility.'

'Let us never forget,' continued Zerimski, 'that Russia can once again be the greatest nation on earth . . .'

Mitchell was now only a pace away from Connor, who was studiously ignoring him. In just a few more seconds there would be an extended ovation when Zerimski told the crowd what he intended to do when he became President. No bank accounts supplied by the bribes of dishonest businessmen – that always got the loudest cheer of all. Then he'd be clean away, and would make sure that Mitchell was transferred to a desk job in some mosquito-infested backwater.

'. . . I shall be dedicating myself to your service, and be more than satisfied with the salary of a President, rather than taking bribes from dishonest businessmen whose only interest is in pillaging the nation's assets.'

The crowd erupted into cheers. Connor turned suddenly and began moving to his right. He had taken almost three strides when the first policeman grabbed his left arm. A second later another came at him from the right. He was thrown to the ground, but made no attempt to resist. Rule one: when you've nothing to hide, don't resist arrest. His hands were wrenched behind his back and a pair of handcuffs snapped around his wrists. The crowd began to form a little circle around the three men on the ground. They were now far more interested in the sideshow than in Zerimski's words. Mitchell hung back slightly, and waited for the inevitable 'Who is he?'

'Mafya hitman,' he whispered into the ears of those nearest him. He moved back towards the press enclosure, muttering the words 'Mafya hitman' periodically.

'Let me leave you good citizens in no doubt that if I were to be elected President, you can be sure of one thing . . .'

'You're under arrest,' said a third man whom Connor couldn't see because his nose was being pressed firmly against the ground.

'Take him away,' said the same authoritative voice, and Connor was bundled off towards the north end of the square.

Zerimski had spotted the disturbance in the crowd, but like an old pro he ignored it. 'If Chernopov were to be elected, the Americans would be more concerned about the views of Mexico than those of Russia,' he continued unfalteringly.

Jackson never took his eyes off Connor as the crowd quickly divided, making a path to allow the police through.

'My friends, there are only six days to go before the people decide . . .'

Mitchell walked quickly away from the commotion and headed towards the press stand.

'Don't do it for me. Don't even do it for the Communist Party. Do it for the next generation of Russians . . .'

The police car, surrounded by four motorcycles, began to make its way out of the square.

'. . . who will then be able to play their part as citizens of the greatest nation on earth. I ask for only one thing – the privilege of being allowed to lead those people.' This time he was silent until he was sure he had the attention of everyone in the square, before ending softly with the words, 'Comrades, I offer myself as your servant.'

He stood back, and suddenly the noise of the police sirens was obliterated by the roar of a hundred thousand voices.

Jackson looked towards the press enclosure. He could see that the journalists were far more interested in the disappearing police car than in Zerimski's frequently repeated words.

'Mafya hitman,' the Turkish journalist was informing a colleague – a 'fact' that she had picked up from someone in the crowd, whom she would later quote as 'an authoritative source'.

Mitchell was looking up at a row of television cameramen who were following the progress of the police car as it disappeared out of sight, its blue lamp flashing. His eyes settled on the one person he needed to speak to. He waited patiently for Clifford Symonds to look in his direction, and when he eventually did, Mitchell waved his arms to indicate that he needed to speak to him urgently. The CNN reporter quickly joined the American Cultural Attaché among the cheering throng.

Zerimski remained in the centre of the platform, soaking up the adulation of the crowd. He had no intention of leaving while they were still howling their approval.

Symonds listened carefully to what Mitchell had to tell him. He was due on air in twelve minutes. The smile on his face became broader by the second.

'Are you absolutely certain?' he asked, when Mitchell had finished speaking.

'Have I ever let you down in the past?' Mitchell asked, trying to sound offended.

'No,' said Symonds apologetically. 'You never have.'

'But you must keep this piece of information a million miles away from the Embassy.'

'Of course. But who shall I say is my source?'

'A resourceful and diligent police force. That's the last thing the Chief of Police is going to deny.'

Symonds laughed. 'I'd better get back to my producer if I'm going to lead on this for the morning newscast.'

'OK,' said Mitchell. 'Just remember – make sure it can't be traced back to me.'

'Have I ever let *you* down in the past?' retorted Symonds. He turned and dashed back towards the press enclosure.

Mitchell slipped away in the opposite direction. There was still one more receptive ear in which he needed to plant the story, and it would have to be done before Zerimski left the stage.

A protective line of bodyguards was barring any over-enthusiastic supporters from getting near the candidate. Mitchell could see his press secretary only a few yards away, basking in the cheers his leader was receiving.

Mitchell told one of the guards in perfect Russian who he needed to speak to. The thug turned around and shouted at the press secretary. If Zerimski was elected, thought Mitchell, it wasn't exactly going to be a subtle administration. The press secretary made an immediate sign to let the American through, and he entered the cordoned-off area and joined another of his chess partners. He briefed him quickly, telling him that de

Villiers had been disguised as an old man, and which hotel he'd been seen leaving just before he'd entered the restaurant.

By the end of the day, it would have dawned on Fitzgerald and Jackson that they had both been dealing with a real professional.

17

THE PRESIDENT and his Chief of Staff sat alone in the Oval Office, watching the early-morning news. Neither of them spoke as Clifford Symonds presented his report.

'An international terrorist was arrested in Freedom Square this afternoon during a speech given by the Communist leader Victor Zerimski. The as-yet unnamed man is being held in the notorious Crucifix Prison in the centre of St Petersburg. The local police are not ruling out the possibility that this may be the same man who was recently linked with the assassination of Ricardo Guzman, a presidential candidate in Colombia. The man who police have arrested is thought to have been following Zerimski for several days while he was campaigning around the country. Only last week he was described in *Time* magazine as the most expensive hired gun in the west. He is thought to have been offered a million dollars by the Russian Mafya to remove Zerimski from the presidential race. When the police tried to arrest him, it took four of them just to hold him down.'

Some footage followed of a man being arrested in the crowd and hustled away, but the best shot they had managed was the back of a head covered in a fur hat. Symonds' face reappeared on the screen.

'The Communist candidate continued to deliver his speech, although the arrest took place only a few yards in front of the platform. Zerimski later praised the St Petersburg police for their diligence and professionalism, and vowed that however many attempts were made on his life, nothing would deter him from his fight against organised crime. Zerimski is currently running neck and neck with Prime Minister Chernopov in the opinion polls, but many observers feel that today's incident will give a boost to his popularity in the final run-up to the election.

'A few hours before Zerimski addressed the rally, he held a private meeting with General Borodin at his headquarters on the north side of the city. No one knows the outcome of those talks, but the General's spokesmen are not denying that he will soon be making a statement about whether he intends to continue his campaign for President, and perhaps more importantly, which of the two remaining candidates he would pledge to support were he to withdraw. The election has suddenly been thrown wide open. This is Clifford Symonds, CNN International, in Freedom Square, St Petersburg.'

'On Monday the Senate will continue to debate the Nuclear, Biological, Chemical and Conventional Arms Reduction . . .'

The President pressed a button on his remote control, and the screen went blank.

'And you're telling me that the man they've arrested has no connection with the Russian Mafya, but is a CIA agent?'

'Yes. I'm waiting for Jackson to call in and confirm that it's the same man who killed Guzman.'

'What do I say to the press if they question me about this?'

'You'll have to bluff, because we don't need anyone to know that the man they're holding is one of ours.'

'But it would finish off Dexter and her little shit of a Deputy once and for all.'

'Not if you claimed you knew nothing about it, because then half the population would dismiss you as a CIA dupe. But if you admit you did know, the other half would want you impeached. So for now I suggest you confine yourself to saying that you are awaiting the result of the Russian elections with interest.'

'You bet I am,' said Lawrence. 'The last thing I need is for that evil little fascist Zerimski to become President. We'd be back to Star Wars overnight.'

'I expect that's exactly why the Senate is holding out on your

Arms Reduction Bill. They won't want to make a final decision until they know the outcome of the election.'

Lawrence nodded. 'If it's one of ours they've got holed up in that goddamn jail, we've got to do something about it, and quickly. Because if Zerimski does become President, then God help him. I certainly wouldn't be able to.'

—◁○▷—

Connor didn't speak. He was wedged between two officers in the back of the police car. He knew these young men had neither the rank nor the authority to question him. That would come later, and from someone with a lot more braid on his lapel.

As they drove through the vast wooden gates of the Crucifix prison and into a cobbled yard, the first thing Connor saw was the reception party. Three massive men in prisoners' garb stepped forward, almost pulled the car's back door off its hinges and dragged him out. The young policemen who had been sitting on either side of him looked terrified.

The three thugs quickly bundled the new prisoner across the yard and into a long, bleak corridor. That was when the kicking and punching began. Connor would have protested, but their vocabulary seemed to consist only of grunts. When they reached the far end of the corridor, one of them pulled open a heavy steel door and the other two threw him into a tiny cell. He made no effort to struggle when they removed first his shoes, then his watch, wedding ring and wallet – from which they would learn nothing. They left, slamming the cell door closed behind them.

Connor rose slowly to his feet and warily stretched his limbs, trying to discover if any bones had been broken. There didn't seem to be any permanent damage, he decided, although the bruises were already beginning to appear. He looked around the room, which wasn't much larger than the sleeping compartment he'd travelled in from Moscow. The green brick walls looked as if they hadn't seen a splash of paint since the turn of the century.

Connor had spent eighteen months in a far more restricted

space in Vietnam. Then his orders had been clear: when questioned by the enemy, give only your name, rank and serial number. The same rules did not apply to those who lived by the Eleventh Commandment:

> *Thou shalt not get caught. But if you are, deny absolutely*
> *that you have anything to do with the CIA. Don't*
> *worry – the Company will always take care of you.*

Connor realised that in his case he could forget 'the usual diplomatic channels', despite Gutenburg's reassurances. Lying on the bunk in his tiny cell, it now all fell so neatly into place.

He hadn't been asked to sign for the cash, or for the car. And he now remembered the sentence he'd been trying to recall from the recesses of his mind. He went over it word by word:

'*If it's your new job you're worrying about, I'd be happy to have a word with the Chairman of the company you're joining and explain to him that it's only a short-term assignment.*'

How did Gutenburg know he'd been interviewed for a new job, and that he was dealing directly with the Chairman of the company? He knew because he'd already spoken to Ben Thompson. That was the reason they had withdrawn their offer. '*I'm sorry to inform you . . .*'

As for Mitchell, he should have seen through that angelic choirboy façade. But he was still puzzled by the phone call from the President. Why had Lawrence never once referred to him by name? And the sentences had been a little disjointed, the laugh a little too loud.

Even now he found it hard to believe the lengths to which Helen Dexter was willing to go to save her own skin. He stared up at the ceiling. If the President had never made the phone call in the first place, he realised he had no hope of being released from the Crucifix. Dexter had successfully removed the one person who might expose her, and Lawrence could do nothing about it.

Connor's unquestioning acceptance of the CIA operative's code had made him a willing pawn in her survival plan. No

Ambassador would be making diplomatic protests on his behalf. There would be no food parcels. He would have to take care of himself, just as he had in Vietnam. And he had already been told by one of the young officers who'd arrested him of another problem he would face this time: no one had escaped from the Crucifix in eighty-four years.

The cell door suddenly swung open, and a man dressed in a light blue uniform covered in gold braid walked in. He took his time lighting a cigarette. His fifteenth that day.

◄○►

Jackson remained in the square until the police car was out of sight. He was furious with himself. He finally turned and marched off, leaving the cheering mob behind him, walking so quickly that Sergei had to run to keep up with him. The young Russian had already decided that this was not a time to be asking questions. The word 'Mafya' was on the lips of everyone they passed in the street. Sergei was relieved when Jackson stopped and hailed a taxi.

Jackson could only admire how well Mitchell – no doubt guided by Dexter and Gutenburg – had carried out the whole operation. It was a classic CIA sting, but with a difference: this time it was one of their own they had ruthlessly left languishing in a foreign jail.

He tried not to think about what they would be putting Connor through. Instead he concentrated on the report he was about to make to Andy Lloyd. If only he had been able to contact him the previous night, he might have got the go-ahead to pull Connor out. His cellphone still wasn't working, so he was going to have to risk using the phone in his hotel room. After twenty-nine years, he had been given one chance to balance the books. And he had been found wanting.

The taxi stopped outside Jackson's hotel. He paid the fare and ran inside. Not bothering to wait for the elevator, he leapt up the stairs until he reached the first floor and then sprinted down the corridor to Room 132. Sergei had only just caught up with him by the time he had turned the key and opened the door.

The young Russian sat on the floor in the corner of the room and listened to one half of a conversation Jackson had with someone called Lloyd. When he eventually put the phone down, Jackson was white and trembling with rage.

Sergei spoke for the first time since they had left the square: 'Maybe it's time I called one of my mother's customers.'

◄○►

'Congratulations,' said Dexter the moment Gutenburg entered her office. The Deputy Director smiled as he took the seat opposite his boss and placed a folder on her desk.

'I've just been watching the headlines on ABC and CBS,' she said. 'They've both run with Symonds' version of what took place in Freedom Square. Is there any feel yet as to how big the press are going to play the story tomorrow?'

'They're already losing interest. Not a shot was fired, not even a punch was thrown, and the suspect turned out to be unarmed. And no one's suggesting that the man they've arrested might be an American. By this time tomorrow, the story will only be making the front pages in Russia.'

'How are we responding to any press enquiries?'

'We're saying that it's an internal problem for the Russians, and that in St Petersburg hired gunmen come cheaper than a decent wristwatch. I tell them they only have to read *Time*'s piece on the Russian Godfather last month to appreciate the problems they're facing. If they push me, I point them in the direction of Colombia. If they keep on pushing, I throw in South Africa. That gives them several column inches to feed their hungry editors.'

'Did any of the networks show footage of Fitzgerald after he'd been arrested?'

'Only the back of his head, and even then he was surrounded by police. Otherwise you can be sure they'd have run it over and over.'

'What chance is there of him appearing in public and making a statement that would compromise us, and that the press might follow up?'

'Virtually none. If they ever do hold a trial, the foreign press will certainly be excluded. And if Zerimski's elected, Fitzgerald will never set foot outside the Crucifix again.'

'Have you prepared a report for Lawrence?' asked Dexter. 'Because you can be sure he'll be trying to make two and two equal six.'

Gutenburg leant forward and tapped the file he had placed on the Director's desk.

She flicked it open and began reading, showing no sign of emotion as she turned the pages. When she reached the end, she closed the file and allowed a flicker of a smile to cross her face before passing it back across the table.

'See that it's signed in your name and sent over to the White House immediately,' she said. 'Because whatever doubts the President may have at this moment, if Zerimski becomes President, he will never want to refer to the subject again.'

Gutenburg nodded his agreement.

Helen Dexter looked across the desk at her deputy. 'It's a pity we had to sacrifice Fitzgerald,' she said. 'But if it helps to get Zerimski elected, it will have served a double purpose. Lawrence's Arms Reduction Bill will be rejected by Congress, and the CIA will have far less interference from the White House.'

◄○►

Connor swung his legs off the bunk, placed his bare feet on the stone floor and faced his visitor. The Chief took a long drag on his cigarette and blew the smoke high into the air. 'Filthy habit,' he said, in flawless English. 'My wife never stops telling me to give it up.'

Connor showed no emotion.

'My name is Vladimir Bolchenkov. I am the Chief of Police of this city, and I thought we might have a little chat before we think about putting anything on the record.'

'My name is Piet de Villiers. I am a South African citizen working for the *Johannesburg Journal,* and I wish to see my Ambassador.'

'Now there's my first problem,' said Bolchenkov, the cigarette dangling from the corner of his mouth. 'You see, I don't believe your name is Piet de Villiers, I'm fairly sure you're not South African, and I know for certain that you don't work for the *Johannesburg Journal*, because there's no such paper. And just so we don't waste too much of each other's time, I have it on the highest authority that you were not hired by the Mafya. Now, I admit that I don't yet know who you are, or even which country you come from. But whoever it is that sent you has, to use a modern colloquialism, dropped you in deep shit. And, if I may say so, from a very great height.'

Connor didn't even blink.

'But I can assure you that they are not going to do the same thing to me. So if you feel unable to assist with my enquiries, there is nothing I can do except leave you here to rot, while I continue to bask in the glory that is currently being undeservedly heaped upon me.'

Connor still didn't react.

'I see that I'm not getting through to you,' said the Chief. 'I feel it's my duty to point out that this isn't Colombia, and that I will not be switching my allegiance according to who I've spoken to most recently, or who offers me the thickest wad of dollars.' He paused and drew on his cigarette again before adding, 'I suspect that's one of the many things we have in common.'

He turned and began walking towards the cell door, then stopped. 'I'll leave you to think it over. But if I were in your shoes, I wouldn't wait too long.'

He banged on the door. 'Let me assure you, whoever you are,' he added as the door was opened, 'there will be no thumbscrews, no rack, or any other, more sophisticated forms of torment while I'm St Petersburg's Chief of Police. I don't believe in torture; it's not my style. But I cannot promise you everything will be quite so friendly if Victor Zerimski is elected as our next President.'

The Chief slammed the cell door closed, and Connor heard a key turn in the lock.

18

THREE WHITE BMWs drew up outside the hotel. The man seated next to the driver in each car leapt out onto the pavement and checked up and down the road. Once they were satisfied, the back door of the middle car was opened to allow Alexei Romanov to step out. The tall young man was wearing a long black cashmere coat, and didn't look to either side as he walked quickly into the hotel. The other three men followed, forming a semi-circle around him.

From the description he had been given over the phone, Romanov immediately recognised the tall American standing in the middle of the hall, looking as if he was waiting for someone.

'Mr Jackson?' enquired Romanov in a guttural accent.

'Yes,' Jackson replied. He would have shaken hands if Romanov had not simply turned round and headed straight back towards the entrance.

The three cars' engines were running and their doors were still open when Jackson stepped out onto the street. He was ushered towards the back door of the centre vehicle, and sat between the man who hadn't been willing to shake hands with him and another equally silent but more heavily built man.

The three cars slipped into the centre lane, and as if by magic every other vehicle moved out of their path. Only the traffic lights didn't seem to know who they were.

As the little motorcade swept through the city, Jackson cursed himself again. None of this would have been necessary if he had been able to get through to Lloyd twenty-four hours earlier. But that was hindsight, he thought – a gift only politicians are born with.

–◄◦►–

'You need to meet Nicolai Romanov,' Sergei had said. He had dialled his mother's number, and when the phone was eventually answered, he behaved in a way Jackson had not witnessed before. He was respectful, listened attentively, and never once interrupted. Twenty minutes later he put the phone down.

'I think she'll make the call,' he said. 'The problem is that you can't become a member of the "Thieves in Law" – or the Mafya, as you call them – until you're fourteen. It was the same even for Alexei, the Czar's only son.'

Sergei went on to explain that he had asked that Jackson should be granted a meeting with the Czar, the leader of the Thieves in Law. The organisation had been founded at the time when Russia was ruled by a real Czar, and had survived to become the most feared and respected criminal organisation in the world.

'My mother is one of the few women the Czar will talk to. She will ask him to grant you an audience,' said Sergei.

The phone rang, and he immediately picked it up. As he listened carefully to what his mother had to say, he turned white and began to tremble. He hesitated for some time, but finally agreed to whatever she was suggesting. His hand was still shaking when he put the receiver down.

'Has he agreed to see me?' asked Jackson.

'Yes,' said Sergei quietly. 'Two men come to pick you up tomorrow morning: Alexei Romanov, the Czar's son, who will succeed him when he dies, and Stefan Ivanitsky, Alexei's cousin, who is third in command.'

'Then what's the problem?'

'As they do not know you, they make one condition.'

'And what's that?'

'If the Czar thinks you waste his time, the two men will come back and break one of my legs, to remind me not to bother them again.'

'Then you'd better make sure you're not around when I get back.'

'If I'm not here they pay a call on my mother and break her leg. And when they catch me, they break both my legs. It is the unwritten code of the Mafya.'

Jackson wondered if he should cancel the meeting. He didn't want to be responsible for Sergei ending up on crutches. But the boy told him it was too late. He had already accepted their terms.

◄○►

One glance at Stefan Ivanitsky, the Czar's nephew, who was seated on his right, was enough to convince Jackson that breaking a leg would take him only a moment, and would be forgotten even more quickly.

Once the BMWs had passed the city boundaries, the little motorcade quickly accelerated to sixty miles per hour. As they climbed the winding roads up into the hills, they met few other vehicles. They sped past peasants on the side of the road with their heads bowed, and no sign in their faces that they cared about either the past or the future. Jackson began to understand why Zerimski's words might excite any last flicker of hope left in them.

Without warning, the leading car suddenly swung left and stopped outside a massive wrought-iron gate dominated by a crest with a black falcon's outstretched wings. Two men holding Kalashnikovs stepped forward, and the first driver lowered a smoked-glass window to allow them to peer in. It reminded Jackson of arriving outside the CIA's headquarters – except that at Langley the guards had to be satisfied with side-arms that remained in their holsters.

After all three cars had been inspected, one of the guards nodded and the wings of the falcon split open. The motorcade proceeded at a more stately pace along a gravel drive that wound through a thick forest. It was another five minutes before Jackson caught his first glimpse of the house – though house it was not. A century before it had been the palace of an Emperor's first-born. It was now inhabited by a remote descendant who also believed in his hereditary position.

'Don't speak to the Czar unless he speaks first,' Sergei had warned him. 'And always treat him like his imperial ancestors.' Jackson preferred not to tell Sergei that he had no idea how to treat a member of the Russian Royal Family.

The cars crunched to a halt outside the front door. A tall, elegant man in a long black tailcoat, white shirt and bow tie stood waiting on the top step. He bowed to Jackson, who tried to look as if he was used to this sort of treatment. After all, he had once met Richard Nixon.

'Welcome to the Winter Palace, Mr Jackson,' said the butler. 'Mr Romanov awaits you in the Blue Gallery.'

Alexei Romanov and Stefan Ivanitsky accompanied Jackson through the open door. Jackson and the young Romanov followed the butler down a long marble corridor, while Ivanitsky remained standing by the entrance. Jackson would have liked to stop and admire the paintings and statues that would have graced any museum in the world, but the steady pace of the butler did not allow it. The butler stopped when he reached two white doors at the end of the corridor that stretched almost to the ceiling. He knocked, opened one of the doors, and stood aside to allow Jackson to enter.

'Mr Jackson,' he announced, and left the room, closing the door quietly behind him.

Jackson stepped into a vast, lavishly furnished drawing room. The floor was covered by a single carpet a Turk would have traded his life for. From a Louis XIV winged chair of red velvet rose an elderly man in a blue pin-striped suit. His hair was silver, and the pallor of his skin suggested that he had suffered a long illness. His thin body was slightly stooped as he took a step forward to shake hands with his guest.

'It is kind of you to come all this way to see me, Mr Jackson,' he said. 'You must forgive me, but my English is a little rusty. I was forced to leave Oxford in 1939, soon after the war broke out, although I was only in my second year. You see, the British never really trusted the Russians, even though we were later to become allies.' He smiled sweetly. 'I'm sure they show much the same attitude when dealing with the Americans.'

Jackson wasn't sure how to react.

'Do have a seat, Mr Jackson,' said the old man, gesturing towards the twin of the chair he had been sitting in.

'Thank you,' said Jackson. They were the first words he had spoken since leaving the hotel.

'Now, Mr Jackson,' said Romanov, lowering himself slowly into his chair, 'if I ask you a question, be sure to answer it accurately. If you are in any doubt, take your time before replying. Because should you decide to lie to me – how shall I put it? – you will find that it's not only this meeting that will be terminated.'

Jackson would have walked out there and then, but he knew that the old man was probably the one person on earth who could get Connor out of the Crucifix prison alive. He gave a curt nod to show that he understood.

'Good,' said Romanov. 'And now I should like to learn a little more about you, Mr Jackson. I can tell at a glance that you work for a law enforcement agency, and as you are in my country' – he emphasised the word *my* – 'I assume it has to be the CIA rather than the FBI. Am I right?'

'I worked for the CIA for twenty-eight years, until quite recently when I was – replaced.' Jackson chose his words carefully.

'It's against the rules of nature to have a woman as your boss,' commented Romanov, without even the suggestion of a smile. 'The organisation I control would never indulge in such stupidity.'

The old man leant across to a table on his left and picked up a small glass full of a colourless liquid that Jackson hadn't noticed until that moment. He took a sip, and replaced the glass on the table before asking his next question.

'Are you currently working for another law enforcement agency?'

'No,' said Jackson firmly.

'So you have gone freelance?' suggested the old man.

Jackson didn't reply.

'I see,' he said. 'From your silence I am bound to deduce that you are not the only person who doesn't trust Helen Dexter.'

Again Jackson said nothing. But he was quickly learning why it wouldn't pay to lie to Romanov.

'Why did you want to see me, Mr Jackson?'

Jackson suspected that the old man knew exactly why, but played along with the charade. 'I came on behalf of a friend of mine who, because of my stupidity, has been arrested and is currently locked up in the Crucifix Prison.'

'An establishment that isn't known for its humanitarian record, especially when it comes to considering appeals or granting parole.'

Jackson nodded his agreement.

'I am aware that it was not your friend who was responsible for informing the press that my organisation had offered him a million dollars to remove Zerimski from the presidential race. Had that been the case, he would have been found hanging in his cell long before now. No, I suspect that the person peddling that particular piece of misinformation,' Romanov continued, 'is one of Helen Dexter's minions. If only you had come to me a little earlier, Mr Jackson, I could have warned you about Mitchell.' He took another sip from his glass and added, 'One of the few of your countrymen I would consider recruiting into my organisation. I see you are surprised by the extent of my knowledge.'

Jackson thought he hadn't moved a muscle.

'Mr Jackson, surely you wouldn't be shocked to learn that I have my own people well placed in the upper echelons of both the CIA and the FBI?' The thin smile returned to his face. 'And if I thought it would prove useful, I would also have someone working for me in the White House. But as President Lawrence will reveal anything he is asked at his weekly news conference, it's hardly necessary. Which leads on to my next question. Your friend works for the CIA?'

Jackson didn't reply.

'Ah, I see. Just as I thought. Well, I think he can be confident that Helen Dexter will not be riding to his rescue on this occasion.'

Jackson still said nothing.

'Good,' said the old man. 'So now I know exactly what you expect of me.' He paused. 'But I am at a loss to understand what you have to offer in return.'

'I have no idea what the going rate is,' said Jackson.

The old man began laughing. 'You can't believe for one moment, Mr Jackson, that I dragged you out here to discuss money, can you? Look around and you will see that however much you have to offer, it wouldn't be enough. *Time* was well short of the mark when it speculated on the extent of my power and wealth. Last year alone my organisation had a turnover of $187 billion, more than the economy of Belgium or Sweden. We now have fully operational branches in 142 countries. A new one opens every month, to paraphrase McDonald's slogan. No, Mr Jackson, I do not have enough days left on earth to waste any of them discussing money with a penniless man.'

'Then why did you agree to see me in the first place?' asked Jackson.

'You don't ask questions, Mr Jackson,' said Romanov sharply. 'You only answer them. I'm surprised that you don't appear to have been properly briefed.'

The old man took a further sip of the colourless liquid before spelling out exactly what he expected in return for assisting Connor to escape. Jackson knew he didn't have the authority to accept Romanov's terms on Connor's behalf, but as he had been instructed not to ask questions, he remained silent.

'You may need a little time to think over my proposition, Mr Jackson,' continued the old man. 'But should your friend agree to my terms and then fail to carry out his side of the bargain, he must be made fully aware of the consequences of his actions.' He paused to draw breath. 'I do hope, Mr Jackson, that he's not the sort of person who, having signed an agreement, then relies on some clever lawyer to identify a loophole that will get him out of honouring it. You see, in this court I am both judge and jury, and I shall be appointing my son Alexei as prosecuting counsel. I have made it his personal responsibility to see that this particular contract is carried out to the letter. I have already given orders that he will accompany you both back to the United States, and he will not return until the agreement has been honoured. I hope I make myself clear, Mr Jackson.'

◄○►

Zerimski's office could not have been in greater contrast to the Czar's country palace. The Communist leader occupied the third floor of a dilapidated building in a northern suburb of Moscow – although anyone who was invited to stay at his dacha on the Volga quickly became aware that Zerimski was no stranger to luxury.

The last vote had been cast at ten o'clock the previous evening. Now all Zerimski could do was sit and wait for the officials from the Baltic to the Pacific to count the ballot papers. He knew only too well that in some districts people would have voted several times. In others the ballot boxes would simply never reach the town hall. But he was confident that once he had agreed terms with Borodin, and the General had withdrawn from the race, he was in with a real chance of winning. But he was enough of a realist to know that, with the Mafya backing Chernopov, he would need to poll well over half of the votes cast to have the slightest chance of being declared the winner. For that reason he had decided to make an ally in the Czar's camp.

The result of the election would not be known for a couple of days, as they still tallied the votes by hand in most parts of the country. He didn't need to be reminded of Stalin's oft-quoted remark that it doesn't matter how many people vote, only who counts them.

Zerimski's inner circle were working the phones as they tried to keep track of what was happening across the vast nation. But all the state chairmen were willing to say was that it looked too close to call. The Communist leader thumped the table more times that day than he had during the past week, and remained closeted in his room for long periods of time making private calls.

'That's good news, Stefan,' Zerimski was saying. 'As long as you can take care of the problem of your cousin.' He was listening to Ivanitsky's response when there was a knock on the door. He put the phone down the moment he saw his Chief of Staff enter the room. He had no desire for Titov to find out who he had been talking to.

'The press are wondering if you'll speak to them,' said Titov, hoping it might keep his master occupied for a few minutes. The last time Zerimski had seen the vultures, as he referred to them, was the previous morning, when they had all turned out to watch him cast his vote in Koski, the district of Moscow in which he was born. It would have been no different if he had been running for President of the United States.

Zerimski nodded reluctantly, and followed Titov down the stairs and out onto the street. He had instructed his staff never to allow a member of the press to enter the building, for fear that they would discover just how inefficient and understaffed his organisation was. That was something else which would change once he got his hands on the state coffers. He hadn't told even his Chief of Staff that if he won, this would be the last election the Russian people would vote in while he was alive. And he didn't give a damn how many protests there were in foreign newspapers and magazines. In a very short time they would have a zero circulation east of Germany.

When Zerimski stepped out onto the pavement, he was met by the largest gathering of journalists he'd seen since the campaign had begun.

'How confident are you of victory, Mr Zerimski?' someone shouted, before he even had a chance to say good afternoon.

'If the winner is the man who the most people have voted for, I will be the next President of Russia.'

'But the chairman of the international panel of observers says that this has been the most democratic election in the history of Russia. Do you not accept that judgement?'

'I will if I'm declared victor,' replied Zerimski. The journalists laughed politely at his little pun.

'If elected, how long will it be before you visit President Lawrence in Washington?'

'Soon after he has visited me in Moscow,' came back the immediate reply.

'If you become President, what will happen to the man who was arrested in Freedom Square and accused of plotting to assassinate you?'

'That will be a decision for the courts. But you can be sure he will receive a fair trial.'

Zerimski suddenly became bored. Without warning he turned and disappeared back into the building, ignoring the questions shouted at his retreating back.

'Have you offered Borodin a post in your cabinet?'

'What will you do about Chechnya?'

'Will the Mafya be your first target?'

As he wearily climbed the worn stone stairs to the third floor he decided that, win or lose, that was the last occasion he would ever speak to the press. He didn't envy Lawrence trying to run a country where journalists expected to be treated as equals. When he reached his office he slumped into the only comfortable chair in the room, and slept for the first time in days.

—◇—

The key turned in the lock, and the cell door swung open. Bolchenkov entered, carrying a large duffel bag and a battered leather briefcase.

'As you see, I have returned,' said St Petersburg's Chief of Police, sitting down opposite Connor. 'From which you can assume that I want another off-the-record chat. Though I am bound to say I hope it will be a little more productive than our last encounter.'

The Chief stared down at the man sitting on the bunk. Connor looked as if he had lost several pounds in the past five days.

'I see that you haven't yet become accustomed to our

nouvelle cuisine,' said Bolchenkov, lighting a cigarette. 'I must confess that it does take a few days even for the low life of St Petersburg to fully appreciate the Crucifix's menu. But they come round to it once they realise that they're here for the rest of their lives, and that there is no *à la carte* alternative.' He drew deeply on his cigarette and blew the smoke out of his nose.

'In fact,' he continued, 'you may have read in the press quite recently that one of our inmates ate a fellow prisoner. But what with the food shortage and the problem of overcrowding, we didn't think it worth making a fuss about.'

Connor smiled.

'Ah, I see you are alive after all,' said the Chief. 'Now, I have to tell you that there have been one or two interesting developments since our last meeting, which I have a feeling you will want to know about.'

He placed the duffel bag and the briefcase on the floor. 'These two pieces of luggage were reported as unclaimed by the head porter of the National Hotel.'

Connor raised an eyebrow.

'Just as I thought,' said the Chief. 'And to be fair, when we showed him your photograph, the porter confirmed that although he remembered a man fitting your description leaving the bag, he couldn't recall the briefcase. Nevertheless, I suspect you won't need to have its contents described to you.'

The Chief flicked up the knobs of the case and lifted the lid to reveal a Remington 700. Connor stared straight ahead, feigning indifference.

'Although I'm sure you have handled this type of weapon before, I'm confident that you have never seen this particular rifle, despite the initials P.D.V. being so conveniently printed on the case. Even a raw recruit could work out that you have been set up.'

Bolchenkov drew deeply on his cigarette.

'The CIA must think we have the dumbest police force on earth. Did they imagine for a moment that we don't know what Mitchell's real job is? Cultural Attaché!' he snorted. 'He probably thinks the Hermitage is a department store. Before you say anything, I have another piece of news that might be of interest to you.' He inhaled again, allowing the nicotine to reach down into his lungs. 'Victor Zerimski has won the election, and will be installed as President on Monday.'

Connor smiled weakly.

'And as I can't imagine that he'll be offering you a front-row seat for the inauguration,' said the Chief, 'perhaps the time has come for you to tell us your side of the story, Mr Fitzgerald.'

19

PRESIDENT ZERIMSKI swaggered into the room. His colleagues immediately rose from their places around the long oak table and applauded until he had taken his seat below a portrait of Stalin, resurrected from the basement of the Pushkin where it had languished since 1956.

Zerimski was dressed in a dark blue suit, white shirt and red silk tie. He looked quite different from the other men seated round the table, who were still garbed in the ill-fitting clothes they had worn throughout the election campaign. The message was clear – they should all visit a tailor as soon as possible.

Zerimski allowed the applause to continue for some time before waving down his colleagues as if they were just another adoring crowd.

'Although I do not officially take office until next Monday,' he began, 'there are one or two areas where I intend to make some immediate changes.' The President looked around at those supporters who had stood by him through the lean years, and were about to be rewarded for their loyalty. Many of them had waited half a lifetime for this moment.

He turned his attention to a short, squat man who was staring blankly in front of him. Joseph Pleskov had been promoted from Zerimski's bodyguard to a full member of the Politburo the day after he had shot three men who had tried to assassinate his boss while he was on a visit to Odessa. Pleskov had one great virtue, which Zerimski would require of any cabinet minister: as long as he understood his orders, he would carry them out.

'Joseph, my old friend,' Zerimski said. 'You are to be my Minister of the Interior.' Several faces around the table tried not to show surprise or disappointment; most of them knew they were far better qualified to do the job than the former docker from the Ukraine, and some suspected he couldn't even spell 'interior'. The short, thickset man beamed at his leader like a child who had been given an unexpected toy.

'Your first responsibility, Joseph, will be to deal with organised crime. I can think of no better way of setting about that task than by arresting Nicolai Romanov, the so-called Czar. Because there will be no room for Czars, imperial or otherwise, while I am President.'

One or two of the faces that had looked sullen only a moment before suddenly cheered up. Few of them would have been willing to take on Nicolai Romanov, and none of them believed Pleskov was up to it.

'What shall I charge him with?' asked Pleskov innocently.

'Anything you like, from fraud to murder,' said Zerimski. 'Just be sure it sticks.'

Pleskov was already looking a little apprehensive. It would have been easier if the boss had simply ordered him to kill the man.

Zerimski's eye circled the table. 'Lev,' he said, turning to another man who had remained blindly loyal to him. 'I shall give you responsibility for the other half of my law and order programme.'

Lev Shulov looked nervous, unsure if he should be grateful for what he was about to receive.

'You are to be my new Justice Minister.'

Shulov smiled.

'Let me make it clear that there is far too much of a logjam in the courts at present. Appoint a dozen or so new judges. Be sure they are all long-standing Party members. Begin by explaining to them that I have only two policies when it comes to law and order: shorter trials and longer sentences. And I am keen to make an example of someone newsworthy in the first few days of my presidency, to leave no doubt about the fate of those who cross me.'

'Did you have anyone in mind, Mr President?'

'Yes,' replied Zerimski. 'You will remember . . .' There was a quiet knock on the door. Everyone turned to see who dared to interrupt the new President's first cabinet meeting. Dmitri Titov entered noiselessly, gambling that Zerimski would have been even more annoyed not to be interrupted. The President drummed his fingers on the table as Titov walked the length of the room, then bent down and whispered in his ear.

Zerimski immediately burst out laughing. The rest of them wanted to join in, but were unwilling to until they had heard the joke. He looked up at his colleagues. 'The President of the United States is on the line. It seems that he wishes to congratulate me.' Now they all felt able to join in the laughter.

'My next decision as your leader is whether I should put him on hold – for another three years . . .' They all laughed even louder, except for Titov, '. . . or whether I should take the call.'

No one offered an opinion.

'Shall we find out what the man wants?' asked Zerimski. They all nodded. Titov picked up the phone by his side and handed it to his boss.

'Mr President,' said Zerimski.

'No, sir,' came back the immediate reply. 'My name is Andy Lloyd. I am the White House Chief of Staff. May I put you through to President Lawrence?'

'No, you may not,' said Zerimski angrily. 'Tell your President next time he calls to be on the end of the line himself, because I don't deal with messenger boys.' He slammed the phone down, and they all laughed again.

'Now, what was I saying?'

Shulov volunteered. 'You were about to tell us, Mr President, who should be made an example of in order to demonstrate the new discipline of the Justice Department.'

'Ah, yes,' said Zerimski, the smile returning to his lips just as the phone rang again.

Zerimski pointed at his Chief of Staff, who picked up the receiver.

'Would it be possible,' a voice enquired, 'to speak to President Zerimski?'

'Who's calling him?' asked Titov.

'Tom Lawrence.'

Titov handed the receiver to his boss. 'The President of the United States,' was all he said. Zerimski nodded and took the phone.

'Is that you, Victor?'

'This is President Zerimski. Who am I addressing?'

'Tom Lawrence,' said the President, raising an eyebrow to the Secretary of State and the White House Chief of Staff, who were listening in on their extensions.

'Good morning. What can I do for you?'

'I was just calling to add my congratulations to all the others you must be receiving after your impressive' – Lawrence had wanted say 'unexpected', but the State Department had counselled against it – 'victory. A very close-run thing. But everyone in politics experiences that problem from time to time.'

'It's not a problem I will experience again,' said Zerimski. Lawrence laughed, assuming this was meant to be funny. He wouldn't have done so if he could have seen the stony-faced looks of those seated around the cabinet table in the Kremlin.

Lloyd whispered, 'Keep going.'

'The first thing I'd like to do is get to know you a little better, Victor.'

'Then you will have to start by understanding that only my mother calls me by my first name.'

Lawrence looked down at the notes spread across his desk. His eye settled on Zerimski's full name, Victor Leonidovich. He underlined 'Leonidovich', but Larry Harrington shook his head.

'I'm sorry,' said Lawrence. 'How would you like me to address you?'

'The same way you would expect anyone *you* don't know to address you.'

Though they could hear only one side of it, those seated

around the table in Moscow were enjoying the first encounter between the two leaders. Those in the Oval Office were not.

'Try a different tack, Mr President,' suggested the Secretary of State, cupping a hand over his phone.

Tom Lawrence glanced down at Andy Lloyd's prepared questions and skipped a page. 'I was hoping it wouldn't be too long before we could find an opportunity to meet. Come to think of it,' he added, 'it's rather surprising that we haven't bumped into each other before now.'

'It's not all that surprising,' said Zerimski. 'When you last visited Moscow, in June, your Embassy failed to issue me or any of my colleagues with an invitation to the dinner that was held for you.' There were murmurs of support from around the table.

'Well, I'm sure you know only too well that on overseas trips one is very much in the hands of one's local officials . . .'

'I shall be interested to see which of those local officials you feel need replacing after such a fundamental miscalculation.' Zerimski paused. 'Starting with your Ambassador, perhaps.'

There followed another long silence while the three men in the Oval Office checked through the questions they had assiduously prepared. So far they had not anticipated one of Zerimski's replies.

'I can assure you,' Zerimski added, 'that I will not be allowing any of my officials, local or otherwise, to overrule *my* personal wishes.'

'Lucky man,' said Lawrence, giving up bothering with any of the prepared answers.

'Luck is not a factor I ever take into consideration,' said Zerimski. 'Especially when it comes to dealing with my opponents.'

Larry Harrington was beginning to look desperate, but Andy Lloyd scribbled a question on a pad and pushed it under the President's nose. Lawrence nodded.

'Perhaps we should try to arrange an early meeting so that we can get to know each other a little better?'

The White House trio sat waiting for the offer to be robustly rejected.

'I'll give that my serious consideration,' said Zerimski, to everyone's surprise, at both ends. 'Why don't you tell Mr Lloyd to get in touch with Comrade Titov, who is responsible for organising my meetings with foreign leaders.'

'I certainly will,' said Lawrence, feeling relieved. 'I'll ask Andy Lloyd to call Mr Titov in the next couple of days.' Lloyd scribbled another note, and handed it to him. It read: 'And of course I would be happy to visit Moscow.'

'Goodbye, Mr President,' said Zerimski.

'Goodbye – Mr President,' Lawrence replied.

As Zerimski put the phone down, he stalled the inevitable round of applause by quickly turning to his Chief of Staff and saying, 'When Lloyd rings, he will propose that I visit Washington. Accept the offer.'

His Chief of Staff looked surprised.

'I am determined,' said the President, turning back to his colleagues, 'that Lawrence should realise as soon as possible what sort of man he is dealing with. More importantly, I wish the American public to find out for themselves.' He placed his fingers together. 'I intend to begin by making sure that Lawrence's Arms Reduction Bill is defeated on the floor of the Senate. I can't think of a more appropriate Christmas present to give . . . Tom.'

This time he allowed them to applaud him briefly, before silencing them with another wave of his hand.

'But we must return for the moment to our domestic problems, which are far more pressing. You see, I believe it is important that our own citizens are also made aware of the mettle of their new leader. I wish to provide them with an example that will leave no one in any doubt about how I intend to deal with those who consider opposing me.' They all waited to see who Zerimski had selected for this honour.

He turned his gaze to the newly appointed Justice Minister. 'Where is that Mafya hitman who tried to assassinate me?'

'He's locked up in the Crucifix,' said Shulov. 'Where I assume you'll want him to remain for the rest of his life.'

'Certainly not,' said Zerimski. 'Life imprisonment is far too lenient a sentence for such a barbarous criminal. This is the ideal person to put on trial. We will make him our first public example.'

'I'm afraid the police haven't been able to come up with any proof that he . . .'

'Then manufacture it,' said Zerimski. 'His trial isn't going to be witnessed by anyone except loyal Party members.'

'I understand, Mr President,' said the new Justice Minister. He hesitated. 'What did you have in mind?'

'A quick trial, with one of our new judges presiding and a jury made up exclusively of Party officials.'

'And the sentence, Mr President?'

'The death penalty, of course. Once the sentence has been passed, you will inform the press that I shall be attending the execution.'

'And when will that be?' asked the Justice Minister, writing down Zerimski's every word.

The President flicked over the pages of his diary and began searching for a fifteen-minute gap. 'Eight o'clock next Friday morning. Now, something far more important – my plans for the future of the armed forces.' He smiled at General Borodin, who was seated on his right, and who hadn't yet opened his mouth

'For you, Deputy President, the greatest prize of all . . .'

20

As a prisoner in the Nan Dinh camp, Connor had developed a system for counting the days he'd been in captivity.

At five every morning a Vietcong guard would appear carrying a bowl of rice swimming in water – his only meal of the day. Connor would remove a single grain and place it inside one of the seven bamboo poles that made up his mattress. Every week he would transfer one of the seven grains to the beam above his bed, and then eat the other six. Every four weeks he would remove one of the grains from the beam above his bed and put it between the floorboards under his bed. The day he and Chris Jackson escaped from the camp, Connor knew he had been in captivity for one year, five months and two days.

But lying on a bunk in a windowless cell in the Crucifix, even he couldn't come up with a system to record how long he had been there. The Chief of Police had now visited him twice, and left with nothing. Connor began to wonder how much longer it would be before he became impatient with his simply repeating his name and nationality, and demanding to see his Ambassador. He didn't have to wait long to find out. Only moments after Bolchenkov had left the room the second time, the three men who had greeted him on the afternoon of his arrival came charging into his cell.

Two of them dragged him off the bunk and threw him into the chair recently occupied by the Chief. They wrenched his arms behind his back and handcuffed him.

That was when Connor first saw the cut-throat razor. While

two of them held him down, the third took just fourteen strokes of the rusty blade to shave every hair off his head, along with a considerable amount of skin. He hadn't wasted any time applying soap and water. The blood continued to run down Connor's face and soak his shirt long after they had left him slumped in the chair.

He recalled the words of the Chief when they had first met: 'I don't believe in torture; it's not my style.' But that was before Zerimski had become President.

He eventually slept, but for how long he could not tell. The next thing he remembered was being pulled up off the floor, hurled back into the chair and held down for a second time.

The third man had replaced his razor with a long, thick needle, and used the same degree of delicacy he had shown as a barber to tattoo the number '12995' on the prisoner's left wrist. They obviously didn't believe in names when you booked in for room and board at the Crucifix.

When they returned a third time, they yanked him up off the floor and pushed him out of the cell into a long, dark corridor. It was at times like this that he wished he lacked any imagination. He tried not to think about what they might have in mind for him. The citation for his Medal of Honor had described how Lieutenant Fitzgerald had been fearless in leading his men, had rescued a brother officer, and had made a remarkable escape from a North Vietnamese prisoner of war camp. But Connor knew he had never come across a man who was fearless. In Nan Dinh he had held out for one year, five months and two days – but then he was only twenty-two, and at twenty-two you believe you're immortal.

When they hurled him out of the corridor and into the morning sun, the first thing Connor saw was a group of prisoners erecting a scaffold. He was fifty-one now. No one needed to tell him he wasn't immortal.

◄◦►

When Joan Bennett checked in for work at Langley that Monday, she knew exactly how many days she had served of her eight-month sentence, because every evening, just before she left home, she would feed the cat and cross off one more date on the calendar hanging on the kitchen wall.

She left her car in the west parking lot, and headed straight for the library. Once she had signed in, she took the metal staircase down to the reference section. For the next nine hours, with only a break for a meal at midnight, she would read through the latest batch of e-mailed newspaper extracts from the Middle East. Her main task was to search for any mention of the United States and, if it was critical, electronically copy it, collate it and e-mail it to her boss on the third floor, who would consider its consequences at a more civilised hour later that morning. It was tedious, mind-deadening work. She had considered resigning on several occasions, but was determined not to give Gutenburg that satisfaction.

It was just before her midnight meal-break that Joan spotted a headline in the *Istanbul News*: 'Mafya Killer to go on Trial'. She could still only think of the Mafia as being Italian, and was surprised to discover that the article concerned a South African terrorist on trial for the attempted murder of the new President of Russia. She would have taken no further interest if she hadn't seen the line drawing of the accused man.

Joan's heart began to thump as she carefully read through the lengthy article by Fatima Kusmann, the *Istanbul News*'s Eastern European correspondent, in which she claimed to have sat next to the professional killer during a rally in Moscow which Zerimski had addressed.

Midnight passed, but Joan remained at her desk.

◄○►

As Connor stood in the prison courtyard and stared up at the half-constructed scaffold, a police car drew up and one of the thugs shoved him into the back seat. He was surprised to find the Chief of Police waiting for him. Bolchenkov hardly recognised the gaunt, crop-headed man.

Neither of them spoke as the car made its way through the gates and out of the prison. The driver turned right and drove along the banks of the Neva at exactly fifty kilometres an hour.

They passed three bridges before swinging left and crossing a fourth that would take them into the centre of the city. As they crossed the river, Connor stared out of the side window at the pale green palace of the Hermitage. It couldn't have been in greater contrast to the prison he had just left. He looked up at the clear blue sky, and back down at the citizens walking up and down the streets. How quickly he had been made aware of how much he valued his freedom. Once they were on the south side of the river the driver swung right, and after a few hundred yards pulled up in front of the Palace of Justice. The car door was opened by a waiting policeman. If Connor had any thoughts of escape, the other fifty officers on the pavement would have caused him to think again. They formed a long reception line as he climbed the steps into the huge stone building.

He was marched to the front desk, where an officer pinned his left arm to the counter, studied his wrist and entered the number '12995' on the charge sheet. He was then taken down a marble corridor towards two massive oak doors. When he was a few paces away the doors suddenly swung open, and he entered a packed courtroom.

He looked around at the sea of faces, and it was obvious they had been waiting for him.

⊸◦⊱

Joan typed a search string into the computer: *attempt on Zerimski's life*. What press reports there were all seemed to agree on one thing: that the man who had been arrested in Freedom Square was Piet de Villiers, a South African hitman hired by the Russian Mafya to assassinate Zerimski. A rifle discovered among his belongings was identified as identical to that which had been used to assassinate Ricardo Guzman, a presidential candidate in Colombia, two months earlier.

Joan scanned the Turkish newspaper's line drawing of de Villiers into her computer, and enlarged it until it filled the entire screen. She then zoomed in on the eyes, and blew them up to life size. She was now certain of the true identity of the man about to go on trial in St Petersburg.

Joan checked her watch. It was a few minutes past two. She picked up the phone by her side and dialled a number she knew by heart. It rang for some time before a sleepy voice answered, 'Who's this?'

Joan said only, 'It's important that I see you. I'll be at your place in a little over an hour,' and replaced the phone.

A few moments later, someone else was woken by a ringing telephone. He listened carefully before saying, 'We'll just have to advance our original schedule by a few days.'

—◁○▷—

Connor stood in the dock, and looked around the courtroom. His eyes first settled on the jury. Twelve good men and true? Unlikely. Not one of them even glanced in his direction. He suspected that it hadn't taken long to swear them in, and that there wouldn't have been any requests for alternatives.

Everyone in the courtroom rose as a man in a long black gown emerged from a side door. He sat down in the large leather chair in the centre of the raised dais, below a full-length portrait of President Zerimski. The clerk of the court rose from his place and read out the charge, in Russian. Connor was barely able to follow the proceedings, and he certainly wasn't asked how he wished to plead. The clerk resumed his seat, and a tall, sombre-looking middle-aged man rose from the bench directly below the judge and began to address the jury.

Holding the lapels of his jacket, the prosecutor spent the rest of the morning describing the events that had led up to the arrest of the defendant. He told the jury how de Villiers had been seen stalking Zerimski for several days before he was apprehended in Freedom Square. And how the rifle with which the defendant had intended to assassinate their beloved President had been discovered among his personal belongings in a hotel lobby. 'Vanity got the better of the accused,' the prosecutor said. 'The case that contained the weapon had his initials clearly printed on it.' The judge allowed the rifle and the briefcase to be examined by the jury.

'Even more damning, a slip of paper was found secreted in

the accused's spongebag,' continued the prosecutor, 'which confirmed the transfer of one million US dollars to a numbered bank account in Geneva.' Again, the jury was given the chance to study this piece of evidence. The prosecutor went on to praise the diligence and resourcefulness of the St Petersburg police force for preventing this heinous act, and its professionalism in catching the criminal who had intended to perpetrate it. He added that the nation owed a considerable debt of gratitude to Vladimir Bolchenkov, the city's Chief of Police. Several members of the jury nodded their agreement.

The prosecutor completed his monologue by informing the jury that whenever the defendant had been asked if he had been hired to carry out the killing on behalf of the Mafya, he had refused to answer. 'You must make what you will of his silence,' he said. 'My own conclusion is that having heard the evidence, there can only be one verdict, and one sentence.' He smiled thinly at the judge and resumed his seat.

Connor looked around the courtroom to see who had been appointed to defend him. He wondered how his counsel would go about the task when they hadn't even met.

The judge nodded towards the other end of the bench, and a young man who looked as if he hadn't long been out of law school rose to address the court. He did not clasp the lapels of his jacket as he looked up towards the bench, or smile at the judge, or even address the jury. He simply said, 'My client offers no defence,' and resumed his seat.

The judge nodded, then turned his attention to the foreman of the jury, a grave-looking man who knew exactly what was expected of him. He rose from his place on cue.

'Having listened to the evidence in this case, Mr Foreman, how do you find the defendant?'

'Guilty,' said the man, delivering his one-word script without needing to be prompted or to consult any other member of the jury.

The judge looked at Connor for the first time. 'As the jury has reached a unanimous verdict, all that is left for me to do is pass sentence. And, by statute, there is only one penalty for your crime.' He paused, stared impassively at Connor and said, 'I sentence you to death by hanging.' The judge turned to the defence counsel. 'Do you wish to appeal against the sentence?' he asked rhetorically.

'No, sir,' came back the immediate response.

'The execution will take place at eight a.m. on Friday.'

Connor was surprised only that they were waiting until Friday to hang him.

-◁◦▷-

Before she left, Joan checked over several of the articles again. The dates exactly matched Connor's absences abroad. First the trip to Colombia, then the visit to St Petersburg. There were, to quote one of Connor's favourite maxims, just too many coincidences.

By three o'clock, Joan felt drained and exhausted. She didn't look forward to telling Maggie the results of her detective work. And if it really was Connor on trial in St Petersburg, there wasn't a moment to waste, because the Turkish papers were already a couple of days old.

Joan shut down her computer, locked her desk and hoped her boss wouldn't notice that his e-mail in-box was almost empty. She walked up the old staircase to the ground floor, inserted her electric pass-key in the exit security control, and passed the trickle of workers arriving for the early-morning shift.

Joan switched on her headlights and drove her brand-new car out of the parking lot and through the gate, turning east onto the George Washington Parkway. The road was still covered with patchy ice from the previous evening's storm, and highway crews were working to clear it before the morning rush-hour. Normally she enjoyed driving through Washington's deserted early-morning streets, past the magnificent monuments that commemorated the nation's history. At school in St Paul she had sat silently at the front of the class while her teacher regaled them with tales of Washington, Jefferson, Lincoln and Roosevelt. It was her admiration for these heroic figures that had fuelled her ambition to work in the public service.

After studying government at the University of Minnesota, she had filled in application forms for the FBI and the CIA. Both had asked to interview her, but once she had seen Connor Fitzgerald she had cancelled her appointment with the FBI. Here was a man who had returned from a futile war with a medal he never mentioned, and who continued to serve his country without fanfare or recognition. If she ever expressed these thoughts to Connor, he only laughed and told her she was being sentimental. But Tom Lawrence had been right when he had described Connor as one of the nation's unsung heroes. Joan would suggest to Maggie that she contact the White House immediately, as it was Lawrence who had asked Connor to take on this assignment in the first place.

Joan was trying to put her thoughts into some logical order when a large green sanding truck passed her on the outside and began moving across into her lane moments before it had fully overtaken her. She flashed her lights, but the truck didn't pull away as she expected. She checked her rear-view mirror and eased into the centre lane. The truck immediately began to drift across into her path, forcing her to veer sharply into the left-hand lane.

Joan had to decide in an instant whether to slam on her brakes or to try to accelerate past the thoughtless driver. Once again she checked her rear-view mirror, but this time she was horrified to see a large black Mercedes coming up fast behind her. She slammed her foot down on the accelerator as the highway banked steeply to the left near Spout Run. The little Golf responded immediately, but the sanding truck also accelerated, and she couldn't pick up enough speed to pass it.

Joan had no choice but to move further to her left, almost into the median strip. She looked into her rearview mirror and saw that the Mercedes had also drifted across, and was now close to her rear bumper. She could feel her heart pounding. Were the truck and the car working together? She tried to slow down, but the Mercedes just moved closer and closer to her rear bumper. Joan slammed her foot down on the accelerator again and her car leapt forward. Sweat was running down her forehead and into her eyes as she drew level with the front of the sanding truck, but even with her foot flat on the floor she just couldn't overtake it. She stared up into the cab and tried to attract the driver's attention, but he ignored her waving hand, and went on implacably easing the truck inch by inch further to his left, forcing her to slow down and fall in behind him. She checked her rear-view mirror: the Mercedes was, if anything, even closer to her bumper.

As she looked forward the truck's tailplate rose, and its load of sand began to pour out onto the road. Instinctively Joan slammed on her brakes, but the little car careered out of control, skidded across the ice-encrusted median strip and hurtled down the grass embankment towards the river. It hit the water like a flat stone, and after floating for a moment, disappeared out of sight. All that was left were the skidmarks on the bank and a few bubbles. The sanding truck moved back into the centre lane and continued its journey in the direction of Washington. A moment later the Mercedes flashed its lights, overtook the truck and accelerated away.

Two cars that were heading towards Dulles Airport came to a halt on the median strip. One of the drivers leapt out and slid down the bank towards the river to see if he could help, but by the time he reached the water there was no sign of the car. All that remained were the skidmarks on the snowy bank and a few bubbles. The other driver scribbled down the sanding truck's licence number. He handed it to the first cop to arrive on the scene, who punched it into his dashboard computer. After a few seconds he frowned. 'Are you sure you wrote down the correct number, sir?' he asked. 'The Washington Highway Department has no record of such a vehicle.'

◄◇►

When Connor was bundled into the back of the car, he found the Chief of Police waiting for him once again. As the driver began the return journey to the Crucifix, Connor couldn't resist asking Bolchenkov a question.

'I'm puzzled to know why they're waiting until Friday to hang me.'

'Bit of luck, really,' said the Chief. 'It seems our beloved President insisted on witnessing the execution.' Bolchenkov inhaled deeply on his cigarette. 'And he doesn't have a spare fifteen minutes in his schedule before Friday morning.'

Connor gave a wry smile.

'I'm glad you've found your tongue at last, Mr Fitzgerald,' continued the Chief. 'Because I think the time has come to let you know that there is an alternative.'

21

MARK TWAIN ONCE SAID of a friend, 'If he didn't turn up on time, you would know he was dead.'

Once four o'clock had come and gone, Maggie started checking her watch every few minutes. By four thirty she began to wonder if she had been so sleepy when Joan called that she might have misunderstood what she had said.

At five o'clock, Maggie decided it was time to give Joan a call at home. No answer, just a continual ringing tone. Next she tried her car phone, and this time she did get a message: 'This number is temporarily out of order. Please try again later.'

Maggie began pacing round the kitchen table, feeling sure that Joan must have some news of Connor. It had to be important, otherwise why would she have woken her at two in the morning? Had he been in contact with her? Did she know where he was? Would she be able to tell her when he was coming home? By six, Maggie had decided it was now an emergency. She switched on the television to check the exact time. Charlie Gibson's face appeared on the screen. 'In the next hour we'll talk about Christmas decorations that even the kids can help you with. But first we'll go over to Kevin Newman for this morning's news.'

Maggie began pacing round the kitchen as a reporter predicted that the President's Nuclear, Biological, Chemical and Conventional Arms Reduction Bill was almost certain to be voted down in the Senate now that Zerimski had been elected as the Russian leader.

She was wondering if she should break a lifetime's rule and try to ring Joan at Langley when a trailer appeared under Kevin Newman's image: '*GW Parkway crash involves sanding truck and Volkswagen – driver of car presumed drowned. Details on Eyewitness News at 6.30.*' The words crawled across the screen and disappeared.

Maggie tried to eat a bowl of cornflakes while the early-morning bulletin continued. Andy Lloyd appeared on the screen, announcing that President Zerimski would be making an official visit to Washington just before Christmas. 'The President welcomed the news,' said a reporter, 'and hoped it would go some way to convincing Senate leaders that the new Russian President wished to remain on friendly terms with America. However, the majority leader of the Senate said he would wait until Zerimski had addressed . . .'

When Maggie heard the little thud on the mat, she went out into the hall, picked up the seven envelopes lying on the floor and checked through them as she walked back into the kitchen. Four were for Connor; she never opened his letters while he was away. One was a Pepco bill; another was postmarked Chicago, and the letter 'e' on 'Maggie' was at an angle, so it could only have been Declan O'Casey's annual Christmas card. The last letter bore the distinctive handwriting of her daughter. She tossed the others to one side and tore it open.

Dear Mother,
Just a note to confirm that Stuart arrives in Los Angeles on Friday. We plan to drive up to San Francisco for a few days before flying to Washington on the fifteenth.

Maggie smiled.

We're both looking forward to spending Christmas with you and Dad. He hasn't phoned me, so I assume he isn't back yet.

Maggie frowned.

I've had a letter from Joan, who doesn't seem to be enjoying her new job. I suspect that, like all of us, she is missing Dad. She tells me she is buying a sexy new Volkswagen . . .

Maggie read the sentence a second time before her hand began trembling. 'Oh my God, no!' she said out loud. She checked her watch – six twenty. On the television, Lisa McRee was holding up a paperchain of holly and berries. 'Festive Christmas decorations the children can help with,' she declared brightly. 'Now we turn to the topic of Christmas trees.'

Maggie flicked over to Channel 5. Another newscaster was speculating about whether Zerimski's planned visit would influence Senate leaders before they cast their vote on the Arms Reduction Bill.

'Come on, come on,' said Maggie.

Finally the newscaster said, '*And now we have more on that accident on the George Washington Parkway. We go live to our on-the-spot correspondent, Liz Fullerton.*'

'*Thank you, Julie. I'm standing on the median of the George Washington Parkway, where the tragic accident took place at approximately three fifteen this morning. Earlier I interviewed an eye-witness who told Channel 5 what he had seen.*'

The camera focused on a man who clearly hadn't expected to be on television that morning.

'*I was headed into Washington,*' he told the reporter, '*when this sanding truck deposited its load on the highway, causing the car behind to swerve and run out of control. The car skidded right across the road, down the bank and into the Potomac.*' The camera swung across to show a wide angle of the river, focusing on a group of police divers before returning to the reporter.

'*No one seems to be quite sure exactly what happened,*' she continued. '*It's even possible that the driver of the sanding truck, sitting high up in his cab, continued on his journey unaware that an accident had taken place.*'

'No! No!' screamed Maggie. 'Don't let it be her!'

'*Behind me you can see police divers, who have already located the vehicle, apparently a Volkswagen Golf. They hope to bring it to the surface within the next hour. The identity of the driver is still unknown.'*

'No, no, no,' repeated Maggie. 'Please, God, not Joan.'

'The police are requesting that the driver of a black Mercedes who may have witnessed the accident should come forward to help with their enquiries. We hope to bring you more news on the hour, so until then . . .'

Maggie ran into the hall, grabbed her coat and rushed out of the front door. She leapt into her car, and was relieved when the old Toyota spluttered into life almost immediately. She eased it slowly out onto Avon Place, before accelerating down Twenty-Ninth Street and east on M Street in the direction of the Parkway.

If she had checked her rear-view mirror, she would have seen a small blue Ford making a three-point turn before chasing after her. The passenger in the front seat was dialling an unlisted number.

—◇—

'Mr Jackson, it is so good of you to come and see me again.'

Jackson was amused by Nicolai Romanov's elaborate courtesy, especially as it carried with it the pretence that he might have had some choice in the matter.

The first meeting had been at Jackson's request, and obviously hadn't been considered 'a waste of time', as Sergei was still running around on both legs. Each subsequent meeting had followed a summons from Romanov to bring Jackson up to date with the latest plans.

The Czar sank back in his winged chair, and Jackson noticed the usual glass of colourless liquid on the table by his side. He remembered the old man's reaction on the one occasion he had asked a question, and waited for him to speak.

'You'll be glad to hear, Mr Jackson, that with the exception of a single problem that still needs to be resolved, everything required to make good your colleague's escape has been arranged. All we need now is for Mr Fitzgerald to agree our terms. Should he find himself unable to do so, I can do nothing to prevent him from being hanged at eight o'clock tomorrow morning.' Romanov spoke without feeling. 'Allow me to take you through what we have planned so far, should he decide to go ahead. I am certain that, as a former Deputy Director of the CIA, your observations will prove useful.'

The old man pressed a button in the armrest of his chair, and the doors at the far end of the drawing room opened immediately. Alexei Romanov entered the room.

'I believe you know my son,' said the Czar.

Jackson glanced in the direction of the man who always accompanied him on his journeys to the Winter Palace, but rarely spoke. He nodded.

The young man pushed aside an exquisite fourteenth-century tapestry depicting the Battle of Flanders. Behind it was concealed a large television set. The flat silver screen looked somewhat incongruous in such magnificent surroundings, but no more so, Jackson thought, than its owner and his acolytes.

The first image to come up on the screen was an exterior shot of the Crucifix prison.

Alexei Romanov pointed to the entrance. 'Zerimski is expected to arrive at the jail at seven fifty. He will be in the third of seven cars, and will enter through a side gate situated here.' His finger moved across the screen. 'He will be met by Vladimir Bolchenkov, who will accompany him into the main courtyard, where the execution will take place. At seven fifty-two . . .'

The young Romanov continued to take Jackson through the plan minute by minute, going into even greater detail when it came to explaining how Connor's escape would be achieved. Jackson noticed that he seemed unconcerned by the one remaining problem, obviously confident that his father would come up with a solution before the following morning. When he had finished, Alexei switched off the television, replaced the tapestry and gave his father a slight bow. He then left the room without another word.

When the door had closed, the old man asked, 'Do you have any observations?'

'One or two,' said Jackson. 'First, let me say that I'm

impressed by the plan, and convinced it has every chance of succeeding. It's obvious you've thought of almost every contingency that might arise – that is, assuming Connor agrees to your terms. And on that, I must repeat, I have no authority to speak on his behalf.'

Romanov nodded.

'But you're still facing one problem.'

'And do you have a solution?' asked the old man.

'Yes,' replied Jackson. 'I have.'

◄○►

Bolchenkov spent nearly an hour spelling out Romanov's plan in great detail, then left Connor to consider his response. He didn't need to be reminded that he was faced with an unalterable time limit: Zerimski was due to arrive at the Crucifix in forty-five minutes.

Connor lay on his bunk. The terms could not have been expressed more explicitly. But even if he did accept those terms, and his escape was successfully engineered, he was not at all confident that he would be able to carry out his side of the bargain. If he failed, they would kill him. It was that simple – except that Bolchenkov had promised that it would not be the quick and easy death of the hangman's noose. He had also spelled out – in case Connor should be in any doubt – that all contracts made with the Russian Mafya and not honoured automatically became the responsibility of the offender's next of kin.

Connor could still see the cynical expression on the Chief's face as he extracted the photographs from an inside pocket and passed them over to him. 'Two fine women,' Bolchenkov had said. 'You must be proud of them. It would be a tragedy to have to shorten their lives for something they know nothing about.'

Fifteen minutes later the cell door swung open again, and Bolchenkov returned, an unlit cigarette dangling from his mouth. This time he didn't sit down. Connor continued to look up at the ceiling as if he wasn't there.

'I see that our little proposal is still presenting you with a dilemma,' said the Chief, lighting the cigarette. 'Even after our brief acquaintance, that does not surprise me. But perhaps when you hear my latest piece of news, you will change your mind.'

Connor went on gazing at the ceiling.

'It appears that your former secretary, Joan Bennett, has met with an unfortunate car accident. She was on her way from Langley to visit your wife.'

Connor swung his legs off the bed, sat up and stared at Bolchenkov.

'If Joan is dead, how could you possibly know she was on her way to see my wife?'

'The CIA aren't the only people who are tapping your wife's telephone,' replied the Chief. He took a last drag from his cigarette, allowed the stub to fall from his mouth and ground it out on the floor.

'We suspect that your secretary had somehow discovered who it was that we arrested in Freedom Square. And without putting too fine a point on it, if your wife is as proud and headstrong as her profile suggests, I think we can assume that it won't be long before she reaches the same conclusion. If that is the case, I fear Mrs Fitzgerald is destined to suffer the same fate as your late secretary.'

'If I agree to Romanov's terms,' Connor said, 'I wish to insert a clause of my own into the contract.'

Bolchenkov listened with interest.

◄o►

'Mr Gutenburg?'

'Speaking.'

'This is Maggie Fitzgerald. I'm the wife of Connor Fitzgerald, who I believe is currently abroad on an assignment for you.'

'I don't recall the name,' said Gutenburg.

'You attended his farewell party at our home in Georgetown only a couple of weeks ago.'

'I think you must have mistaken me for someone else,' replied Gutenburg calmly.

'I have not mistaken you for anyone else, Mr Gutenburg. In fact, at eight twenty-seven on the second of November, you made a phone call from my home to your office.'

'I made no such call, Mrs Fitzgerald, and I can assure you that your husband has never worked for me.'

'Then tell me, Mr Gutenburg, did Joan Bennett ever work for the Agency? Or has she also been conveniently erased from your memory?'

'What are you suggesting, Mrs Fitzgerald?'

'Ah, I've caught your attention at last. Allow me to repair your temporary loss of memory. Joan Bennett was my husband's secretary for nearly twenty years, and I have a feeling you would find it hard to deny that you knew she was on her way from Langley to see me when she met her death.'

'I was sorry to read of Miss Bennett's tragic accident, but I'm at a loss to understand what it has to do with me.'

'The press are apparently mystified about what actually took place on the George Washington Parkway yesterday morning, but they might be a step nearer to the solution if they were told that Joan Bennett used to work for a man who has disappeared from the face of the earth while carrying out a special assignment for you. I've always found in the past that journalists consider a story involving a Medal of Honor winner to be of interest to their readers.'

'Mrs Fitzgerald, I can't be expected to remember every one of the seventeen thousand people the CIA employs, and I certainly don't recall ever meeting Miss Bennett, let alone your husband.'

'I see I'll have to jog that failing memory of yours a little further, Mr Gutenburg. As it happens, the party you didn't attend and didn't telephone from was, fortunately or unfortunately, depending on your perspective, videotaped by my daughter. She'd hoped to surprise her father by giving him the tape for Christmas. I've just had another look at it, Mr Gutenburg, and although you play only a minor role, I can assure you that your tête-à-tête with Joan Bennett is there for all to see. This conversation is also being recorded, and I have a feeling that the networks will consider your contribution worth airing on the early evening news.'

This time Gutenburg didn't reply for some time. 'Perhaps it might be a good idea for us to meet, Mrs Fitzgerald,' he said eventually.

'I can see no purpose in that, Mr Gutenburg. I already know exactly what I require from you.'

'And what is that, Mrs Fitzgerald?'

'I want to know where my husband is at this moment, and when I can expect to see him again. In return for those two simple pieces of information, I will hand over the tape.'

'I'll need a little time . . .'

'Of course you will,' said Maggie. 'Shall we say forty-eight hours? And Mr Gutenburg, don't waste your time tearing my home apart searching for the tape, because you won't find it. It's been hidden somewhere that even a mind as devious as yours wouldn't think of.'

'But . . .' began Gutenburg.

'I should also add that if you decide to dispose of me in the same way you did Joan Bennett, I've instructed my lawyers that if I die in suspicious circumstances, they are to immediately release copies of the tape to all three major networks, Fox and CNN. If, on the other hand, I simply disappear, the tape will be released seven days later. Goodbye, Mr Gutenburg.'

Maggie put the phone down and collapsed onto the bed, bathed in sweat.

Gutenburg shot through the connecting door between his office and the Director's.

Helen Dexter glanced up from her desk, unable to hide her surprise that her Deputy had entered the room without bothering to knock.

'We have a problem,' was all he said.

22

THE CONDEMNED MAN ate no breakfast.

The kitchen staff always made an effort to remove the lice from the bread for a prisoner's last meal, but this time they had failed. He took one look at the offering and put the tin plate under his bunk.

A few minutes later, a Russian Orthodox priest entered the cell. He explained that although he was not of the same denomination as the prisoner, he would be happy to perform the last rites.

The holy sacrament was the only food he would eat that day. After the priest had performed the little ceremony, they knelt together on the cold stone floor. At the end of a short prayer the priest blessed him and left him to his solitude.

He lay on his bunk staring up at the ceiling, not for one moment regretting his decision. Once he had explained his reasons, Bolchenkov had accepted them without comment, even nodding curtly as he left the cell. It was the nearest the Chief would ever get to admitting that he admired a man's moral courage.

The prisoner had faced the prospect of death once before. It didn't hold the same horror for him a second time. On that occasion he had thought about his wife, and the child he would never see. But now he could only think of his parents, who had died within a few days of each other. He was glad that neither of them had gone to their graves with this as their final memory of him.

For them, his return from Vietnam had been a triumph, and they were delighted when he had told them that he intended to go on serving his country. He might even have become Director if a President in trouble hadn't decided to appoint a woman, in the hope that it would help his flagging campaign. It hadn't.

Although it was Gutenburg who had placed the knife firmly between his shoulderblades, there wasn't any doubt about who had handed him the weapon; she would have enjoyed playing Lady Macbeth. He would go to his grave knowing that few of his fellow countrymen would ever be aware of the sacrifice he had made. For him that only made it all the more worthwhile.

There would be no ceremonial farewell. No coffin draped with the American flag. No friends and relatives standing by the graveside to hear the priest extolling the dedication and public service which had been the hallmark of his career. No Marines raising their rifles proudly in the air. No twenty-one-gun salute. No folded flag given on behalf of the President to his next of kin.

No. He was destined to be just another of Tom Lawrence's unsung heroes.

For him, all that was left was to be hanged by the neck in an unloved and unloving land. A shaven head, a number on his wrist, and an unmarked grave.

Why had he made that decision which had so moved the usually passionless Chief of Police? He didn't have time to explain to him what had taken place in Vietnam, but that was where the die had been irrevocably cast.

Perhaps he should have faced the firing squad all those years ago in another far-off land. But he had survived. This time there was no one to rescue him at the last moment. And it was too late now to change his mind.

—<o>—

The Russian President woke in a foul mood that morning. The first person he took it out on was his chef. He swept his breakfast onto the floor and shouted, 'Is this the sort of hospitality I can expect when I come to Leningrad?'

He stormed out of the room. In his study, a nervous official placed on his desk documents for signing which would empower the police to arrest citizens without having to charge them with any crime. This did nothing to change Zerimski's black mood. He knew that it was merely a ploy to get a few pickpockets, dope peddlers and petty criminals off the streets. It was the Czar's head he wanted delivered to him on a platter. If the Minister for the Interior continued to fail him, he would have to consider replacing him.

By the time his Chief of Staff arrived, Zerimski had signed away the lives of another hundred men whose only crime had been to support Chernopov during the election campaign. Rumours were already circulating around Moscow that the former Prime Minister planned to emigrate. The day he left the country, Zerimski would sign a thousand such orders, and would imprison everybody who had ever served Chernopov in any capacity.

He threw his pen down on the desk. All this had been achieved in less than a week. The thought of the havoc he was going to cause in a month, a year, made him feel a little more cheerful.

'Your limousine is waiting, Mr President,' said a petrified official whose face he couldn't see. He smiled at the thought of what would undoubtedly be the highlight of his day. He had been looking forward to a morning at the Crucifix as others would anticipate an evening at the Kirov.

He left his study and strode down the long marble corridor of the newly commandeered office block towards the open door, his entourage moving swiftly ahead of him. He paused for a moment on the top step to look down at the gleaming motorcade. He had instructed Party officials that he must always have one more limousine than any previous President.

He climbed into the back of the third car and checked his watch: seven forty-three. The police had cleared the road an hour before so that the motorcade could proceed without encountering a single vehicle travelling in either direction. Holding up the traffic makes the local inhabitants aware that the President is in town, he explained to his Chief of Staff.

The traffic police estimated that the journey, which would normally have taken twenty minutes, should be completed in less than seven. As Zerimski shot through traffic lights of whatever colour and swung across the river, he didn't even glance in the direction of the Hermitage. Once they reached the other side of the Neva, the driver of the leading car pushed the speedometer up to a hundred kilometres an hour to be sure the President would be on time for his first official engagement that morning.

⊸∘⊱

As he lay on his bunk, the prisoner could hear the guards marching down the stone passageway towards him, the noise of their boots becoming a little louder with each step. He wondered how many of them there would be. They stopped outside his cell. A key turned in the lock and the door swung open. When you have only moments to live, you notice every detail.

Bolchenkov led them in. The prisoner was impressed that he had got back so quickly. He lit a cigarette and inhaled once before offering it to the prisoner. He shook his head. The Chief shrugged his shoulders, ground the cigarette out on the stone floor with his foot, and left to greet the President.

The next person to enter the cell was the priest. He was carrying a large open bible and softly chanting some words that meant nothing to the prisoner. Next were three men he recognised immediately. But this time there was no razor, no needle, just a pair of handcuffs. They stared at him, almost willing him to put up a fight, but to their disappointment he calmly placed his hands behind his back and waited. They slapped on the cuffs and pushed him out of the cell into the corridor. At the end of the long grey tunnel he could just make out a pinprick of sunlight.

The President stepped out of his limousine, to be welcomed by the Chief of Police. It amused him that he had awarded Bolchenkov the Order of Lenin on the same day as he had signed an order to arrest his brother.

Bolchenkov led Zerimski into the yard where the execution

would take place. No one suggested removing the President's fur-lined coat or hat on such a bitterly cold morning. As they crossed the courtyard, the small crowd huddled up against one wall began to applaud. The Chief saw a frown cross Zerimski's face. The President had expected far more people to turn up to witness the execution of a man who had been sent to kill him.

Bolchenkov had anticipated that this might present a problem, so he leaned over and whispered in the President's ear, 'I was instructed to permit only Party members to attend.' Zerimski nodded. Bolchenkov didn't add how difficult it had been to drag even the few people present into the Crucifix that morning. Too many of them had heard the stories of how, once you were in, you never got out.

The Chief came to a halt by a plush eighteenth-century chair that Catherine the Great had bought from the estate of the British Prime Minister Robert Walpole in 1779, and that had been requisitioned from the Hermitage the previous day. The President sank into the comfortable seat directly in front of the newly erected gallows.

After only a few seconds Zerimski began fidgeting impatiently as he waited for the prisoner to appear. He looked across at the crowd, and his eyes rested on a young boy who was crying. It didn't please him.

At that moment the prisoner emerged from the dark corridor into the stark morning light. The bald head covered in dried blood and the thin grey prison uniform made him look strangely anonymous. He appeared remarkably calm for someone who had only a few more moments to live.

The condemned man stared up into the morning sun and shivered as an officer of the guard marched forward, grabbed his left wrist and checked the number: 12995. The officer then turned to face the President and read out the court order.

While the officer went through the formalities, the prisoner looked around the yard. He saw the shivering crowd, most of them wary of moving a muscle for fear that they might be ordered to join him. His eyes settled on the boy, who was still weeping. If they had allowed him to make a will, he would have left everything to that child. He glanced briefly at the scaffold, then settled his gaze on the President. Their eyes met. Although he was terrified, the prisoner held Zerimski's gaze. He was determined not to let him have the satisfaction of knowing just how frightened he was. If the President had stopped staring back at him and looked down at the ground between his feet, he would have seen for himself.

The officer, having completed his commission, rolled up his scroll and marched away. This was the sign for two of the thugs to come forward, grab one of the prisoner's arms each, and lead him to the scaffold.

He walked calmly past the President and on towards the gallows. When he reached the first of the wooden steps, he glanced up at the clock tower. Three minutes to eight. Few people, he thought, ever know exactly how long they have left to live. He almost willed the clock to strike. He had waited twenty-eight years to repay his debt. Now, in these final moments, it all came back to him.

It had been a hot, sweaty May morning in Nan Dinh. Someone had to be made an example of, and as the senior officer, he had been singled out. His second-in-command had stepped forward and volunteered to take his place. And, like the coward he was, he had not protested. The Vietcong officer had laughed and accepted the offer, but then decided that both men should face the firing squad the following morning.

In the middle of the night, the same Lieutenant had come to his bedside and said they must try to escape. They would never have another chance. Security at the camp was always lax, because to the north lay a hundred miles of jungle occupied by the Vietcong, and to the south twenty-five miles of impenetrable swamp. Several men had tried their luck with that route before, and their luck had run out.

The Lieutenant said he would rather risk dying in the swamps than face the certainty of death by firing squad. As he stole away into the night, the Captain had reluctantly joined him. When the sun appeared above the horizon a few hours later, the camp was still within sight. Across the stinking, mosquito-infested swamp they could hear the guards laughing as they took turns to fire potshots at them. They had dived below the surface of the swamp, but after only a few seconds they had to come up and struggle on. Eventually, after the longest day of his life, darkness fell. He had begged the Lieutenant to carry on without him, but he had refused.

By the end of the second day, he wished he had been allowed to face the firing squad instead of dying in that godforsaken swamp in that godforsaken country. But on and on the young officer went. For eleven days and twelve nights they didn't eat, surviving only by drinking from the endless torrents of rain. On the twelfth morning they reached dry land and, delirious from illness and exhaustion, he collapsed. He later learned that for four more days the Lieutenant had carried him through the jungle to safety.

The next thing he recalled was waking in an army hospital.

'How long have I been here?' he asked the nurse who was tending him.

'Six days,' she said. 'You're lucky to be alive.'

'And my friend?'

'He's been up for the past couple of days. He's already visited you once this morning.'

He fell asleep again, and when he woke he asked the nurse for a pen and paper. He spent the rest of the day sitting in his hospital bed writing and rewriting the citation. When he had made a fair copy, he asked that it should be sent to the commanding officer.

Six months later, he had stood on the White House lawn between Maggie and her father and had listened to the citation being read out. Lieutenant Connor Fitzgerald stepped forward and the President had awarded him the Medal of Honor.

As he began to mount the steps of the gallows, he thought of the one man who would mourn him when he discovered the truth. He had warned them not to tell him, because if he found out, he would break the contract, give himself up and return to the Crucifix. 'You must understand,' he had explained to them, 'that you are dealing with a totally honourable man. So be sure that the clock has struck eight before he finds out he's been deceived.'

The first chime sent a shiver through his body, and his thoughts were brought back to the moment.

On the second chime, the little boy who had been crying ran up to the foot of the gallows and fell on his knees.

On the third, the Chief placed a restraining arm on a young Corporal who had taken a step forward to drag the child away.

On the fourth, the prisoner smiled down at Sergei as if he were his only son.

On the fifth, the two thugs pushed him forward so that he was standing directly below the dangling rope.

On the sixth, the hangman placed the noose around his neck.

On the seventh, he lowered his eyes and stared directly at the President of the Russian Republic.

On the eighth, the hangman pulled the lever and the trap-door opened.

As the body of Christopher Andrew Jackson swung above him, Zerimski began to applaud. Some of the crowd half-heartedly joined in.

A minute later the two thugs carried the lifeless body down from the gallows. Sergei rushed forward to help them lower his friend into the crude wooden coffin that lay on the ground beside the scaffold.

The Chief accompanied the President back to his limousine and the motorcade sped out of the prison gates even before the coffin lid had been nailed down. Four prisoners lifted the heavy casket onto their shoulders and headed towards the graveyard. Sergei walked by their side, out of the yard to a patch of rough ground at the back of the prison. Even the dead were not allowed to escape from the Crucifix.

If Sergei had looked back, he would have seen the rest of the crowd running out through the prison gates before they were slammed shut and the vast wooden bolts pushed back in place.

The pallbearers stopped by the side of an unmarked grave that other prisoners had just finished digging. They dropped the casket unceremoniously into the gaping hole and then, without a prayer or even a moment's pause, shovelled the recently dug sods of earth on top of it.

The boy didn't move until they had completed their task. A few minutes later, the guards herded the prisoners back to their cells. Sergei fell on his knees, wondering how long they would allow him to remain by the grave.

A moment later a hand was placed on the boy's shoulder. He looked up and saw the Chief standing above him. A fair man, he'd once told Jackson.

'Did you know him well?' the Chief asked.

'Yes, sir,' said Sergei. 'He was my partner.'

The Chief nodded. 'I knew the man he gave his life for,' he said. 'I only wish I had such a friend.'

23

'MRS FITZGERALD is not quite as clever as she thinks she is,' said Gutenburg.

'Amateurs rarely are,' said Helen Dexter. 'Does that mean you've got hold of the video?'

'No, although I have got a pretty good idea where it is,' said Gutenburg. He paused. 'But not *exactly* where.'

'Stop being a smartass,' said Dexter, 'and get to the point. You don't need to prove to me how clever you are.'

Gutenburg knew that this was about as near as he would ever get to receiving a compliment from the Director.

'Mrs Fitzgerald doesn't realise that her home and office have been bugged for the past month, and that we've had agents watching her since the day her husband flew out of Dulles three weeks ago.'

'So what have you found out?'

'Not a lot when the individual bits of information are taken in isolation. But if you piece them together, they start making a picture.' He pushed a file and a tape recorder across the table.

The Director ignored them. 'Talk me through it,' she said, beginning to sound a little irritated.

'During Mrs Fitzgerald's lunch with Joan Bennett at the Café Milano, the conversation was inconsequential until just before she left to return to work. It was then that she asked Bennett a question.'

'And what was that question?'

'Perhaps you'd like to hear for yourself.' The Deputy Director pressed the 'Play' button on the tape recorder and sat back.

'*Me too. Black, no sugar.*' Footsteps could be heard walking away. '*Joan, I've never asked you to break a confidence before, but there's something I have to know.*'

'*I hope I can help, but as I've already explained, if it concerns Connor, I'm probably as much in the dark as you are.*'

'*Then I need the name of someone who isn't in the dark.*'

There followed a long silence before Joan said, '*I suggest you look at the guest-list for Connor's farewell party.*'

'*Chris Jackson?*'

'*No. Unfortunately, he's no longer employed by the Company.*'

There was another long silence.

'*That smooth little man who left without saying goodbye? The one who said he worked in loss adjustment?*'

Gutenburg flicked off the tape.

'Why did you ever go to that party?' snapped Dexter.

'Because you instructed me to find out if Fitzgerald had landed a job that would keep him in Washington. Don't forget that it was his daughter who gave us the lead that made it possible to convince Thompson that it might not be wise to employ him. I'm sure you recall the circumstances.'

The Director frowned. 'What happened after Mrs Fitzgerald left the Café Milano?'

'Nothing significant until she returned home that night, when she made several calls – she never makes personal calls from the office – including one to Chris Jackson's cellphone.'

'Why would she do that, when she knew he'd left the Company?'

'They go back a long way. He and Fitzgerald served in Vietnam together. In fact, it was Jackson who recommended Fitzgerald for the Medal of Honor, and who recruited him as an NOC.'

'Did Jackson tell her about you?' asked Dexter in disbelief.

'No, he didn't have a chance,' replied Gutenburg. 'I gave an order to block his cellphone the moment we discovered he was in Russia.' He smiled. 'We can, however, still identify who's been trying to call him, and who he's been trying to call.'

'Does that mean you've found out who he's reporting back to?'

'Jackson has only dialled one number on that line since he landed in Russia, and I suspect he only risked that because it was an emergency.'

'Who did he call?' asked Dexter impatiently.

'An unlisted number at the White House.'

Dexter didn't even blink. 'Our friend Mr Lloyd, no doubt.'

'No doubt,' replied Gutenburg.

'Is Mrs Fitzgerald aware that Jackson is reporting directly to the White House?'

'I don't think so,' said Gutenburg. 'Otherwise I suspect she would have tried to contact him herself some time ago.'

Dexter nodded. 'Then we must make certain that she *never* finds out.'

Gutenburg showed no emotion. 'Understood. But I can't do anything about that until I've got my hands on the family video.'

'What's the latest status on that?' asked Dexter.

'We wouldn't have progressed an inch if we hadn't picked up a clue in an intercepted phone call. When Joan Bennett rang Mrs Fitzgerald from Langley at two in the morning to say she'd be with her in an hour, one of my people checked what she'd been calling up on the reference library's computer. It soon became clear that she must have stumbled on something that made her suspect it was her old boss who was in prison in St Petersburg. But, as you know, she never kept her appointment with Mrs Fitzgerald.'

'A little too close for comfort.'

'Agreed. But when she failed to turn up, Mrs Fitzgerald drove out to the GW Parkway and waited for the police to dredge up the car.'

'She probably saw a report on TV, or heard about it on the radio,' said Dexter.

'Yes, that's what we assumed – the story led the local news

that morning. Once she knew for certain it was Bennett in the car, she immediately phoned her daughter at Stanford. If she sounds a little sleepy, that's because it was only five o'clock in the morning in California.' He leant forward again and touched the 'Play' button on the tape recorder.

'Hi, Tara. It's Mom.'

'Hi, Mom. What time is it?'

'I'm sorry to call so early, darling, but I have some very sad news.'

'Not Dad?'

'No, Joan Bennett – she's been killed in a car crash.'

'Joan's dead? I can't believe it. Tell me it's not true.'

'I'm afraid it is. And I have a terrible feeling that in some way it's connected to the reason Connor hasn't returned home.'

'Come on, Mom, aren't you getting a little paranoid? After all, Dad's only been away for three weeks.'

'You may be right, but I've still decided to move that video you made of his farewell party to a safer place.'

'Why?'

'Because it's the only proof I have that your father ever met a man called Nick Gutenburg, let alone worked for him.'

The Deputy Director touched the 'Stop' button. 'The conversation continues for some time, but it doesn't add a great deal to our knowledge. When Mrs Fitzgerald left the house a few minutes later carrying a videotape, the officer listening in realised the significance of what he'd just heard, and tailed her to the university. She didn't go straight to the Admissions Office as usual, but dropped in at the library, where she went to the computer section on the first floor. She spent twenty minutes searching for something on one of the computers, and left with a printout of about a dozen pages. Then she took the elevator down to the audio-visual research centre on the ground floor. The officer didn't want to risk joining her in the elevator, so once he knew which floor she'd stopped at, he went to the computer she'd been working on and tried to call up the last file that had been opened.'

'She'd erased everything, of course,' said Dexter.

'Of course,' said Gutenburg.

'But what about the printout?'

'Again, no clue as to what was on it.'

'She can't have lived with Connor Fitzgerald for twenty-eight years and not picked up something about the way we work.'

'The officer left the library and waited in his car. After a few minutes Mrs Fitzgerald came out of the building. She was no longer carrying the tape, but she was . . .'

'She must have deposited it in the audio-visual centre.'

'Exactly my thought,' said Gutenburg.

'How many tapes does the university store in its library?'

'Over twenty-five thousand,' said Gutenburg.

'We don't have enough time to go through them all,' said Dexter.

'We wouldn't have, if Mrs Fitzgerald hadn't made her first mistake.'

Dexter didn't interrupt this time.

'When she left the library she didn't have the video, but she did have the printout. Our agent followed her to the Admissions Office, where I'm happy to say her principles got the better of her.'

Dexter raised an eyebrow.

'Before returning to her office, Mrs Fitzgerald called in at the recycling centre. She's not the Vice-President of GULP by accident.'

'GULP?'

'Georgetown University Litter Patrol. She dumped the print-out in the paper depository.'

'Good. So what did you find on it?'

'A complete list of the videos currently on loan and unlikely to be returned until the beginning of next term.'

'So she must have felt it was safe to leave her video in an empty box, because no one would come across it for weeks.'

'Correct,' said Gutenburg.

'How many videos are there that fall into that category?'

'Four hundred and seventy-two,' replied Gutenburg.

'Presumably you've requisitioned every one.'

'I thought about doing that, but if an inquisitive student or member of staff became aware of a CIA presence on the campus, all hell would break loose.'

'Good thinking,' said Dexter. 'So how do you intend to go about finding that video?'

'I've detailed a dozen hand-picked officers, all recent graduates, to check out every one of the titles on that list until they come across a home-made video in what should be an empty box. The problem is that, despite their being dressed like students, I can't afford to leave any one of them inside the library for longer than twenty minutes, or let them go there more than twice in a day, if they're not going to stick out like sore thumbs, especially as there's hardly anyone around at this time of year. So the exercise is proving rather time-consuming.'

'How long do you think it will be before they find it?'

'We could get lucky and come across it almost immediately, but my bet is that it will probably take a day or two, three at the most.'

'Don't forget you have to be back in touch with Mrs Fitzgerald in less than forty-eight hours.'

'I hadn't forgotten. But if we find the tape before then, that won't be necessary.'

'Unless Mrs Fitzgerald also recorded her phone conversation with you.'

Gutenburg smiled. 'She did, but it was erased within seconds of her replacing the receiver. You should have seen the pleasure it gave Professor Ziegler to demonstrate his latest toy.'

'Excellent,' said Dexter. 'Ring me the moment you get your hands on that video. Then there will be nothing to stop us eliminating the one person who could still . . .' The red phone on her desk began to ring, and she grabbed it without completing her sentence.

'The Director,' she said, pressing a button on her stopwatch. 'When did this happen? . . . Are you absolutely certain? . . . And Jackson? Where is he?' When she had heard the reply, she immediately put the phone down. Gutenburg noticed that the stopwatch had reached forty-three seconds.

'I do hope you find that videotape within the next forty-eight hours,' said the Director, looking across the desk at her Deputy.

'Why?' asked Gutenburg, looking anxious.

'Because Mitchell tells me that Fitzgerald was hanged at eight o'clock this morning St Petersburg time, and that Jackson has just boarded a United Airlines flight out of Frankfurt, bound for Washington.'

BOOK THREE

THE HIRED ASSASSIN

24

AT SEVEN A.M., the three thugs entered his cell and marched him off to the Chief's office. Once they had left the room Bolchenkov locked the door, and without a word went over to a wardrobe in the corner. Inside was a policeman's uniform, which he indicated Connor should change into. Because of his loss of weight over the past week, the clothes hung on him, and he was grateful for the braces. But with the aid of a wide-brimmed hat and a long blue coat, he managed to look like any of the thousand policemen who would be walking the beat in St Petersburg that morning. He left his prison clothes at the bottom of the wardrobe, wondering how the Chief would dispose of them. Still without saying a word, Bolchenkov ushered him out of his office and into a tiny anteroom, then locked him in.

After a long silence, Connor heard a door opening, then footsteps, followed by another door opening, which could have been the wardrobe in the Chief's office. He didn't move a muscle as he tried to work out what was going on. The first door opened again and two, possibly three, people rushed noisily into the office. They left a few seconds later, dragging something or someone out of the room and slamming the door behind them.

Moments later the door was unlocked, and Bolchenkov indicated that he should come out. They went through the office and back into the corridor. If the Chief turned left, they would be returning to his cell; but he turned right. Connor's legs felt very weak, but he followed as quickly as he could.

The first thing he saw when he stepped into the courtyard

was the scaffold, and someone placing a magnificent gilded chair with plush red upholstery a few paces in front of it. He didn't need to be told who would be sitting there. As he and Bolchenkov walked across the yard, Connor noticed a group of policemen dressed in long blue coats like the one he was wearing dragging passers-by off the street, presumably to witness the execution.

The Chief moved quickly across the gravel to a car on the far side of the courtyard. Connor was about to open the passenger door when Bolchenkov shook his head and pointed to the driver's seat. Connor took his place behind the wheel.

'Drive up to the gate and then stop,' said the Chief as he got into the passenger seat.

Connor kept the car in first gear as he drove slowly across the yard, stopping in front of two guards posted by the closed gate. One of them saluted the Chief and immediately began checking under the vehicle, while the other looked through the back window and inspected the boot.

The Chief leaned across and pulled down the sleeve on Connor's left wrist. When the guards had completed their search, they returned to their positions and saluted Bolchenkov once again. Neither of them took the slightest interest in the driver. The vast wooden bolts were removed and the great gates of the Crucifix Prison were pulled open.

'Get moving,' said the Chief under his breath as a small boy ran into the prison compound, looking as if he knew exactly where he was going.

'Which way?' Connor whispered.

'Right.'

Connor swung the car across the road and began driving alongside the Neva towards the city centre. There wasn't another car in sight.

'Cross the next bridge,' said Bolchenkov, 'then take the first left.'

As they passed the prison on the far side of the river, Connor glanced across at its high walls. The police were still trying to coax people in to add to the small crowd who had already gathered to witness his hanging. How was Bolchenkov going to get away with it?

Connor continued driving for another couple of hundred metres, until Bolchenkov said, 'Pull over here.' He slowed down and brought the car to a halt behind a large white BMW with one of its rear doors open.

'This is where we part company, Mr Fitzgerald,' said Bolchenkov. 'Let's hope we never meet again.'

Connor nodded his agreement. As he stepped out of the car, the Chief added, 'You are privileged to have such a remarkable friend.'

It was to be some time before Connor understood the full significance of his words.

◄○►

'Your flight leaves from Gate 11, Mr Jackson. It will be boarding in twenty minutes.'

'Thank you,' said Connor, as he picked up his boarding pass. He began walking slowly towards Departures, hoping the official wouldn't check his passport too closely. Although they had replaced Jackson's photograph with his, Chris was three years older than him, two inches shorter, and was bald. If he was asked to remove his hat, he would have to explain why his head was covered in Gorbachev-like marks. In California they would simply have assumed he was a cult member.

He handed his passport over with his right hand – if he had used his left, the sleeve would have risen to reveal the tattooed number on his wrist. Once he was back in America he would buy himself a wider watchstrap.

The official gave the passport only a cursory glance before allowing him through. His newly acquired suitcase, containing nothing more than a change of clothes and a spongebag, passed through security without hindrance. He picked it up and made his way to Gate 11, where he took a seat in the far corner of the lounge facing away from the exit that led to the plane.

In the twenty-four hours since he had left the Crucifix, Connor hadn't relaxed for one moment.

'*This is the first call for Finnair Flight 821 to Frankfurt,*' said a voice over the intercom.

Connor didn't move. If they had told him the truth, he would never have allowed Chris to take his place. He tried to piece together everything that had happened after he had left Bolchenkov.

He had got out of the police car and walked as quickly as he could to the waiting BMW. The Chief had already begun his return journey to the Crucifix by the time Connor climbed into the back of the car and sat beside a pale, thin young man wearing a long black cashmere coat. Neither he nor the two similarly-dressed men seated in the front of the car spoke, or even acknowledged his presence.

The BMW eased out onto the empty road and moved quickly away from the city. Once they joined the highway, the driver ignored the speed limit. As 8.00 flicked up on the dashboard clock, a road sign told Connor that they were 150 kilometres from the Finnish border.

As the distance on the signs dropped to a hundred kilometres, then fifty, then thirty, then ten, Connor began to wonder how they were going to explain the presence of a Russian policeman to the border guards. But no explanation proved necessary. When the BMW was about three hundred metres from the no man's land that divided the two countries, the driver flashed his lights four times. The barrier at the frontier rose immediately, allowing them to cross the border into Finland without even dropping their speed. Connor was beginning to appreciate the extent of the Russian Mafya's influence.

No one in the car had uttered a word since their journey had begun, and once again the road signs gave Connor the only clue as to where they were heading. He began to think Helsinki must be their destination, but a dozen kilometres before they reached the outskirts of the city, they took a slip road off the highway. The car slowed as the driver manoeuvred over potholes and around blind bends that led deeper and deeper into the country-side. Connor gazed at the barren landscape, covered in a thick layer of snow.

'This is the second call for Finnair Flight 821 to Frankfurt. Would all passengers please board the aircraft.'

Connor still didn't move.

Forty minutes after leaving the highway, the car turned into the yard of what appeared to be a deserted farmhouse. A door was opened even before they had come to a halt. The tall young man jumped out and led Connor into the house. He didn't acknowledge the cowering woman they passed as they marched in. Connor followed him up a flight of stairs to the first landing. The Russian opened a door, and Connor entered the room. The door was slammed behind him, and he heard another key turning in another lock.

He walked across the room and looked out of the only window. One of the bodyguards was standing in the yard, staring up at him. He moved away from the window, and noticed that a complete set of clothes and a black rabbit-skin hat had been laid out on a small, uncomfortable-looking bed.

Connor stripped off all his clothes and threw them over a chair by the bed. In a corner of the room was a plastic curtain, and behind it a rusty shower. With the aid of a rough bar of soap and a trickle of lukewarm water, Connor spent several minutes trying to remove the stench of the Crucifix from his body. He dried himself with two dishcloths. When he looked in the mirror he realised that it would be some time before the scars on his head would heal and his hair return to its natural length. But the number tattooed on his wrist would be with him for the rest of his life.

He dressed in the clothes that had been left on the bed. Although the trousers were a couple of inches too short, the shirt and jacket fitted quite well, even though he must have lost at least ten pounds while he was in prison.

There was a gentle knock on the door, and the key turned in the lock. The woman who had been in the hall when they'd arrived was standing there, holding a tray. She placed it on the side table and slipped back out before Connor could thank her. He looked down at the bowl of warm broth and the three bread rolls, and literally licked his lips. He sat down and began to attack the food, but after sipping a few spoonfuls of soup and devouring one of the rolls he felt full. Suddenly overcome by drowsiness, he slumped down on the bed.

'This is the third call for Finnair Flight 821 to Frankfurt. Would all remaining passengers please board the aircraft.'

Connor still remained in his place.

He must have fallen asleep, because the next thing he remembered was waking and finding the pale young man standing at the end of the bed, looking down at him.

'We leave for the airport in twenty minutes,' he had told him, and tossed a thick brown package onto the bed.

Connor sat up and tore open the envelope. It contained a first-class ticket to Dulles International, a thousand US dollars, and an American passport.

He flicked open the passport and read the name 'Christopher Andrew Jackson', above a photograph of himself. He looked up at the young Russian.

'What does this mean?'

'It means you're still alive,' said Alexei Romanov.

'This is the final call for Flight 821 for Frankfurt. Would any remaining passengers please take their seats immediately.'

Connor strolled across to the gate agent, handed over his boarding pass and made his way to the waiting plane. The steward checked his seat number and pointed to the front section of the aircraft. Connor didn't have to search for the window seat in the fifth row, because the tall young Russian was already strapped into the aisle seat. It was obviously his job not only to pick up the package, but also to deliver it and to make sure the contract was carried out. As Connor stepped over his escort's feet, a stewardess asked, 'Can I take your hat, Mr Jackson?'

'No, thank you.'

He leaned back in the comfortable seat, but didn't relax until the plane had taken off. Then it began to sink in for the first time that he really had escaped. But to what, he wondered. He glanced to his left: from now on someone would be with him night and day until he had carried out his side of the bargain.

During the flight to Germany, Romanov never once opened his mouth, except to eat a few morsels of the meal they put in front of him. Connor left an empty plate, and then passed the time by reading Finnair's in-flight magazine. By the time the plane landed in Frankfurt, he knew all about saunas, javelin throwers, and the Finns' dependence on the Russian economy.

As they walked into the transit lounge, Connor spotted the CIA agent immediately. He quickly detached himself from his escort, returning twenty minutes later, to Romanov's evident relief.

Connor knew it would be easy to shake off his minder once they were back on his own territory, but he also knew that if he tried to escape, they would carry out the threat the Chief had so vividly described. He shuddered at the thought of any of those thugs laying a finger on Maggie or Tara.

The United Airlines 777 took off for Dulles on schedule. Connor managed to eat most of the first and second courses of his lunch. The moment the stewardess removed his tray, he pressed the button in his armrest, reclined his seat and began to think about Maggie. How he envied the fact that she could always . . . A few moments later he fell asleep on a plane for the first time in twenty years.

When he woke, they were serving a snack. He must have been the only person on the flight to eat everything they put in front of him, including the two pots of marmalade.

In the final hour before they were due to land in Washington, his thoughts returned to Chris Jackson and the sacrifice he'd made. Connor knew he could never repay him, but he was determined not to let it be a worthless gesture.

His mind switched to Dexter and Gutenburg, who must now be assuming he was dead. First they had sent him to Russia to save their own skins. Next they had murdered Joan, because she just might have passed some information on to Maggie. How long would it be before they decided Maggie herself had become too great a risk, and that she also needed to be disposed of?

'*This is your captain speaking. We have been cleared to land at Dulles International Airport. Would the cabin crew please prepare for landing. On behalf of United Airlines, I'd like to welcome you to the United States.'*

Connor flicked open his passport. Christopher Andrew Jackson was back on his home soil.

25

MAGGIE ARRIVED AT Dulles Airport an hour early – a habit which used to drive Connor mad. She checked the arrivals screen, and was pleased to see that the flight from San Francisco was scheduled to land on time.

She picked up a copy of the *Washington Post* from the news-stand and wandered into the nearest coffee shop, perched herself on a stool at the counter and ordered a black coffee and a croissant. She didn't notice the two men occupying a table in the opposite corner, one of whom also had a copy of the *Washington Post* which he appeared to be reading. But however hard she'd looked, she wouldn't have seen the third man who was taking more interest in her than in the arrivals screen he was looking up at. He had already spotted the other two men in the corner.

Maggie read the *Post* from cover to cover, checking her watch every few minutes. By the time she had ordered her second coffee, she was delving into the supplement on Russia published in anticipation of President Zerimski's forthcoming visit to Washington. Maggie didn't like the sound of the Communist leader, who seemed to belong in the last century.

She had downed her third coffee twenty minutes before the plane was scheduled to land, so she slipped off the stool and headed for the nearest bank of phones. Two men followed her out of the restaurant, while a third slipped from one shadow into another.

She dialled a cellphone number. 'Good morning, Jackie,' she

said when her deputy answered. 'I'm just checking to see if everything's OK.'

'Maggie,' said a voice trying not to sound too exasperated, 'it's seven o'clock in the morning, and I'm still in bed. You called yesterday, remember? The university is in recess, no one is due back until the fourteenth of January, and after three years of being your deputy, I am just about capable of running the office in your absence.'

'Sorry, Jackie,' said Maggie. 'I didn't mean to wake you. I forgot how early it was. I promise not to bother you again.'

'I hope Connor gets back soon, and that Tara and Stuart keep you fully occupied for the next few weeks,' said Jackie. 'Have a good Christmas, and I don't want to hear from you again before the end of January,' she added with feeling.

Maggie put the phone down, realising she had only been killing time, and shouldn't have bothered Jackie in the first place. She chastised herself, and decided she wouldn't call her again until the New Year.

She walked slowly over to the arrivals gate and joined the growing number of people peering through the windows at the runway, where early-morning flights were taking off and landing. Three men who weren't checking the insignia of every aircraft that arrived continued to watch Maggie as she waited for the board to confirm that United's Flight 50 from San Francisco had landed. When the message finally appeared, she smiled. One of the three men punched eleven numbers into his cellphone, and passed the information back to his superior at Langley.

Maggie smiled again when a man wearing a 49ers cap emerged from the jetway – the first passenger off the 'red-eye'. She had to wait for another ten minutes before Tara and Stuart came through the door. She had never seen her daughter looking more radiant. The moment Stuart spotted Maggie, he gave her the huge grin that had become so familiar during their holiday in Australia.

Maggie hugged them in turn. 'It's wonderful to see you both,' she said. She took one of Tara's bags and led them towards the subway which led to the main terminal.

One of the men who had been watching her was already waiting in the short-term parking lot, in the passenger seat of a Toyota transporter with a load of eleven new cars. The other two were running across the lot.

Maggie, Tara and Stuart stepped into the cold morning air and walked over to Maggie's car. 'Isn't it time you got yourself something more up to date than this old scrapheap, Mom?' Tara asked in mock horror. 'I was still in high school when you bought it, and it was second-hand then.'

'The Toyota is the safest car on the road,' said Maggie primly, 'as *Consumer Reports* regularly confirms.'

'No thirteen-year-old car is safe on the road,' replied Tara.

'In any case,' said Maggie, ignoring her daughter's jibe, 'your father thinks we should hold on to it until he begins his new job, when he'll be given a company car.'

The mention of Connor brought a moment of awkward silence.

'I'm looking forward to seeing your husband again, Mrs Fitzgerald,' said Stuart as he climbed into the back seat.

Maggie didn't say, 'And so am I,' but satisfied herself with, 'So this is your first visit to America.'

'That's right,' Stuart replied as Maggie switched on the ignition. 'And already I'm not sure I'll ever want to return to Oz.'

'We have enough overpaid lawyers in the States already, without adding another one from down under,' said Tara as they waited in line to pay the parking fee.

Maggie smiled at her, feeling happier than she had for weeks.

'When do you have to go home, Stuart?'

'If you feel he's already outstayed his welcome, we could just turn round and take the next flight back, Mom,' said Tara.

'No, I didn't mean that, it's just . . .'

'I know – you do love to plan ahead,' said Tara with a laugh. 'If she could, Stuart, Mom would make students register for Georgetown at conception.'

'Why didn't I think of that?' said Maggie.

'I'm not expected back at my desk until the fifth of January,' said Stuart. 'I hope you'll be able to tolerate me for that long.'

'She's not going to be given a lot of choice,' said Tara, squeezing his hand.

Maggie handed a ten-dollar bill to the cashier before pulling out of the parking lot and onto the highway. She glanced in the rear-view mirror, but didn't notice a nondescript blue Ford about a hundred yards behind her, travelling at roughly the same speed. The man in the passenger seat was reporting in to his superior at Langley that the subject had left 'Kerbside' at seven forty-three and was headed in the direction of Washington with the two packages she had picked up.

'Did you enjoy San Francisco, Stuart?'

'Every moment,' he replied. 'We're planning to spend a couple more days there on my way back.'

When Maggie glanced in her rear-view mirror again, she saw a Virginia State patrol car coming up behind her, its lights flashing.

'Is he following me, do you think? I certainly wasn't speeding,' said Maggie, looking down to check her speedometer.

'Mom, this car is practically an antique, and should have been towed away years ago. It could be anything, from your brake lights to defective tyres. Just pull over.' Tara looked out the back window. 'And when the traffic cop speaks to you, be sure to flash that Irish smile of yours.'

Maggie pulled over as the blue Ford drove by in the centre lane.

'Shit,' said the driver, as he shot past them.

Maggie wound down her window as the two policemen stepped out of their patrol car and walked slowly towards them. The first officer smiled and said politely, 'May I see your licence, ma'am?'

'Certainly, officer,' said Maggie, returning his smile. She leaned over, opened her bag and began rummaging around inside as the second patrolman indicated to Stuart that he should also wind down his window. Stuart thought this was an odd request, as he could hardly have been guilty of any traffic offence, but as he wasn't in his own country, he thought it wiser to comply. He wound down the window just as Maggie located her driving licence. As she turned to hand it over, the second policeman drew his gun and fired three shots into the car.

The two of them walked quickly back to their patrol car. While one eased the car into the early-morning traffic, the other phoned the man in the passenger seat of the transporter. 'A Toyota has broken down, and is in need of your immediate assistance.'

Soon after the patrol car accelerated away, the transporter carrying eleven brand-new Toyotas drew up and stopped in front of the stationary vehicle. The man in the passenger seat, wearing a Toyota cap and blue overalls, leapt out of the cab and ran towards the stationary car. He opened the driver's door, lifted Maggie gently across to the passenger seat and pulled the lever that opened the car's bonnet, then leaned over to where Stuart was slumped, removed his wallet and passport from his jacket pocket and replaced them with another passport and a slim paperback book.

The driver of the transporter opened the Toyota's bonnet and checked underneath. He swiftly deactivated the tracking device and slammed the bonnet closed. His companion was now seated behind the wheel of the Toyota. He turned on the ignition, put the car into first gear and slowly drove up the transporter's ramp, taking the one space left. He switched off the ignition, put on the handbrake, fastened the car's wheels to the ramp and rejoined the driver in the cab. The entire exercise had taken less than three minutes.

The transporter resumed its journey towards Washington, but after half a mile it took the air freight exit and drove back in the direction of the airport.

The CIA officers in the blue Ford had come off the highway at the next exit, then doubled back and rejoined the morning traffic heading into Washington. 'She must have committed some minor offence,' the driver was saying to his superior at Langley. 'It wouldn't be surprising with a car that old.'

The officer in the passenger seat was surprised to find that the Toyota was no longer registering on his screen. 'They're probably on their way back to Georgetown,' he suggested. 'We'll call in the moment we regain contact.'

As the two agents sped towards Washington, the transporter carrying the twelve Toyotas turned left off the Dulles service road at a sign marked 'Cargo Only'. After a few hundred yards it turned right, through a high wire gate held open by two men in airport overalls, and drove down an old runway towards an isolated hangar. A lone figure stood at the entrance to guide them in, as if the transporter was a recently-landed aircraft.

The driver brought the vehicle to a halt next to an unmarked van. Seven men in white overalls quickly emerged from the back. One of them undid the chains that secured the old car to the transporter. Another took his place behind the wheel, released the handbrake and allowed the Toyota to roll slowly back down the ramp to the ground. The moment it came to a halt, its doors were opened and the bodies inside were carefully lifted out.

The man in the Toyota cap jumped out of the transporter and took the wheel of the old car. He threw it into first gear, swung round in a circle and shot out of the hangar as if he had been driving it all his life. As he passed through the open gate the bodies were being gently placed in the rear of the van, where three coffins were waiting for them. One of the men in overalls said, 'Don't put the lids on until you're approaching the plane.'

'OK, doc,' came the reply.

'And once the hold's been closed, remove the bodies and strap them into their seats.'

As another man nodded, the transporter backed out of the hangar and retraced its route down the old runway and out of the gates. When the driver reached the highway he turned left and headed towards Leesburg, where he would deliver eleven new Toyotas to the local dealer. His fee for six hours' unscheduled work would allow him to buy one of them.

The wire gate had already been locked and bolted by the time the van drove out of the hangar and began heading slowly towards the cargo docking area. The driver passed rows of cargo planes, finally stopping at the back of a 747 marked 'Air Transport International'. The hold was open, and two customs officials stood waiting at the bottom of the ramp. They began checking the paperwork just as the two CIA officers in the blue Ford drove past 1648 Avon Place. After cautiously circling the block, the agents reported back to Langley that there was no sign either of the car or the three packages.

The old Toyota came off Route 66 and joined the highway into Washington. The driver put his foot down hard on the accelerator and sped towards the city. Over his earphone he listened to the two officers in the Ford being instructed to go to Mrs Fitzgerald's office to see if the car was in her usual parking space behind the Admissions building.

Once the customs officials had satisfied themselves that the coroner's documents were in order, one of them said, 'OK. Remove the lids.'

They carefully checked through the clothes, and in the mouths and other orifices of all three bodies, then countersigned the documents. The lids were replaced, and the men in white overalls carried the coffins one by one up the ramp and laid them side by side in the hold.

The ramp of the 747 was being raised as the old Toyota drove past Christ Church. It sped up the hill for another three blocks before screeching to a halt in the driveway of 1648 Avon Place.

The driver had already slipped around the side of the house and let himself in through the back door by the time the doctor began checking the pulses of his three patients. He ran upstairs to the master bedroom, and opened the chest of drawers by the side of the bed. He rummaged among the sports shirts, took out the brown envelope marked 'Not to be opened before 17 December', and slipped it into an inside pocket. He pulled down two suitcases from the top of the wardrobe and quickly filled them with clothes. Next he removed a small cellophane packet from his overalls and slipped it into a cosmetics bag which he threw into one of the cases. Before he left the bedroom he switched on the bathroom light, then the light at the bottom of the stairs, and finally, using the remote control, the television in the kitchen, setting the volume to high.

He left the suitcases by the back door and returned to the Toyota, raised the bonnet and reactivated the tracking device.

The CIA officers had begun slowly circling the university parking lot for a second time when a blip reappeared on their screen. The driver quickly turned round and headed back towards the Fitzgeralds' home.

The man in the Toyota cap returned to the rear of the house, grabbed the suitcases and let himself out by the back gate. He spotted the taxi parked in front of Tudor Place, and jumped into the back just as the two agents returned to Avon Place. A relieved young man called Langley to report that the Toyota was parked in its usual place, and that he could see and hear a television on in the kitchen. No, he couldn't explain how the tracking device had been out of action for nearly an hour.

The taxi driver didn't even turn his head when the man jumped in the back of his cab carrying two suitcases. But then, he knew exactly where Mr Fitzgerald wanted to be taken.

26

'ARE YOU TELLING ME that all three of them have disappeared off the face of the earth?' said the Director.

'It looks that way,' replied Gutenburg. 'It was such a professional operation that if I didn't know he was dead, I would have said it had all the hallmarks of Connor Fitzgerald.'

'As we know that's impossible, who do you think it was?'

'My bet is still Jackson,' replied the Deputy Director.

'Well, if he's back in the country, Mrs Fitzgerald will know her husband is dead. So we can expect to see her home video on the early-evening news any day now.'

Gutenburg grinned complacently. 'Not a chance,' he said, passing a sealed package across the table to his boss. 'One of my agents finally found the tape, a few minutes before the university library closed last night.'

'That's one problem dealt with,' said the Director, tearing open the package. 'But what's to stop Jackson telling Lloyd who's really buried in the Crucifix?'

Gutenburg shrugged his shoulders. 'Even if he does, what use is the information to Lawrence? He's hardly going to phone up his pal Zerimski, a few days before he's due to arrive in Washington on a goodwill visit, to let him know that the man they hanged for planning his assassination wasn't a South African terrorist hired by the Mafya after all, but a CIA agent carrying out orders that had come directly from the White House.'

'Maybe not,' said Dexter. 'But as long as Jackson and the Fitzgerald women are out there, we still have a problem. So I suggest you deploy the best dozen agents we've got to track them down, and as quickly as possible – I don't care what sector they're working in or who they're assigned to. If Lawrence can prove what really happened in St Petersburg, he'll have more than enough excuse to call for someone's resignation.'

Gutenburg was unusually silent.

'And as it's your signature at the bottom of every relevant document,' continued the Director, 'I would, alas, be left with no choice but to let you go.'

Small beads of sweat appeared on Gutenburg's forehead.

‑<o>‑

Stuart thought he was coming out of a bad dream. He tried to recall what had happened. They had been picked up at the airport by Tara's mother, who had been driving them towards Washington. But the car had been stopped by a traffic cop, and he had been asked to wind down his window. And then . . . ?

He looked around. He was on another plane, but where was it going? Tara's head was resting on his shoulder; on her other side was her mother, also fast asleep. All the other seats were empty.

He began to go over the facts again, as he always did when preparing for a case. He and Tara had landed at Dulles. Maggie had been waiting for them at the gate . . .

His concentration was broken when a smartly dressed middle-aged man appeared by his side and leaned over to check his pulse.

'Where are we going?' asked Stuart quietly, but the doctor didn't reply. He carried out the same cursory examination on Tara and Maggie, then disappeared back up to the front of the plane.

Stuart unfastened his seatbelt, but hadn't enough strength to stand up. Tara had begun stirring, while Maggie remained resolutely asleep. He checked his pockets. They had taken his wallet and passport. He tried desperately to make some sense of it. Why should anyone go to these extremes for a few hundred dollars, some credit cards and an Australian passport? Even more strangely, they seemed to have replaced them with a slim volume of Yeats's poems. He had never read Yeats before he met Tara, but after she had returned to Stanford he had begun to enjoy his work. He opened the book at the first poem, 'A Dialogue of Self and Soul'. The words *I am content to live it all again, and yet again* were underlined. He flicked through the pages, and noticed that other lines had also been marked.

As he was considering the significance of this, a tall, heavily built man appeared by his side, towering menacingly over him. Without a word, he snatched the book from Stuart's hands and returned to the front of the plane.

Tara touched his hand. He quickly turned to her and whispered in her ear, 'Say nothing.' She glanced across at her mother, who still hadn't stirred, seemingly at peace with the world.

—◆—

Once Connor had placed the two suitcases in the hold and checked that all three passengers were alive and unharmed, he left the aircraft and climbed into the back of a BMW whose engine was already running.

'We continue to keep our side of the bargain,' said Alexei Romanov, who was sitting next to him. Connor nodded his agreement as the BMW drove out through the wire gates and began its journey to Ronald Reagan National Airport.

After his experience at Frankfurt, where the local CIA agent had nearly spotted him because Romanov and his two sidekicks did practically everything except publicly announce their arrival, Connor realised that if he was going to pull off his plan to rescue Maggie and Tara, he would have to run the operation himself. Romanov had finally accepted this when he had been reminded of the clause agreed by his father. Now Connor could only hope that Stuart was as resourceful as he had appeared to be when he had quizzed him on the beach in Australia. He prayed that Stuart would notice the words he'd underlined in the book he'd slipped into his pocket.

The BMW drew up outside the upper-level Departure entrance of Washington National Airport. Connor stepped out, with Romanov a pace behind. Two other men joined them and followed Connor as he strolled calmly into the airport and over to the ticket counter. He needed them all to relax before he made his next move.

When Connor handed over his ticket, the man behind the American Airlines desk said, 'I'm sorry, Mr Radford, but Flight 383 to Dallas is running a few minutes late, though we hope to make up the time *en route*. You'll be boarding at Gate 32.'

Connor walked casually in the direction of the lounge, but stopped when he reached a bank of telephones. He chose one with occupied booths on either side. Romanov and the two bodyguards hovered a few paces away, looking displeased. Connor smiled at them innocently, then slipped Stuart's international phone-card into the slot and dialled a Cape Town number.

The phone rang for some time before it was eventually answered.

'Yes?'

'It's Connor.'

There was a protracted silence. 'I thought it was only Jesus who could rise from the dead,' said Carl eventually.

'I spent some time in purgatory before I managed it,' Connor replied.

'Well, at least you're alive, my friend. What can I do for you?'

'First, as far as the Company is concerned, there will be no second coming.'

'Understood,' said Carl.

Connor was answering Carl's last question when he heard the final call for Flight 383 to Dallas. He put the phone down, smiled at Romanov again, and headed quickly for Gate 32.

◄○►

When Maggie eventually opened her eyes, Stuart leaned across and warned her to say nothing until she was fully awake. A few moments later a stewardess appeared and asked them to lower their tray tables. An inedible selection of food appeared, as if they were on a normal first-class flight.

As he contemplated a fish that should have been left in the

sea, Stuart whispered to Maggie and Tara, 'I haven't a clue why we're here or where we're going, but I have to believe that in some way it's connected with Connor.'

Maggie nodded, and quietly began to tell them everything she had found out since Joan's death.

'But I don't think the people holding us can be the CIA,' she said, 'because I told Gutenburg that if I was missing for more than seven days, that video would be released to the media.'

'Unless they've already found it,' said Stuart.

'That's not possible,' said Maggie emphatically.

'Then who the hell are they?' said Tara.

No one offered an opinion as the stewardess reappeared and silently removed their trays.

'Have we got anything else to go on?' Maggie asked after the stewardess had left them.

'Only that somebody put a book of Yeats's poems in my pocket,' said Stuart.

Tara noticed Maggie give a start.

'What's the matter?' she asked, looking anxiously at her mother, whose eyes were now filling with tears.

'Don't you understand what this means?'

'No,' said Tara, looking puzzled.

'Your father must still be alive. Let me see it,' said Maggie. 'He might have left a message in it.'

'I'm afraid I haven't got it any more. I'd hardly opened it before a heavy appeared from the front of the plane and snatched it away,' said Stuart. 'I did notice that a few words were underlined, though.'

'What were they?' asked Maggie urgently.

'I couldn't make much sense of them.'

'That doesn't matter. Can you remember any of them?'

Stuart closed his eyes and tried to concentrate. '"*Content*",' he said suddenly.

Maggie smiled. '"*I am content to live it all again, and yet again*".'

⊸◦⊶

243

Flight 383 did land in Dallas on time, and when Connor and Romanov stepped out of the airport another white BMW was waiting for them. Had the Mafya placed a bulk order? Connor wondered. The latest pair of thugs to accompany them looked as if they had been hired from central casting – even their shoulder holsters were bulging under their jackets.

He could only hope that the Cape Town branch was a recent subsidiary, although he found it hard to believe that Carl Koeter, with over twenty years' experience as the CIA's senior operative in South Africa, wouldn't be able to handle the latest new kid on the block.

The trip into downtown Dallas took just over twenty minutes. Connor sat silently in the back of the car, aware that he might be about to come face to face with someone else who had worked for the CIA for almost thirty years. Although they'd never met, he knew this was the biggest risk he had taken since arriving back in America. But if the Russians expected him to honour the most demanding clause in their contract, he had to have the use of the only rifle ideal for carrying out such an assignment.

After another silent journey they pulled up outside Harding's Big Game Emporium. Connor slipped quickly into the shop, with Romanov and his two new shadows dogging his every step. He went up to the counter, while they pretended to take a keen interest in a rack of automatic pistols on the far side of the shop.

Connor glanced around. His search needed to be quick, unobtrusive but thorough. After a few moments he was convinced there were no security cameras in the shop.

'Good afternoon, sir,' said a young assistant dressed in a long brown coat. 'How can I help you?'

'I'm out here on a shooting trip, and I'd like to buy a rifle.'

'Do you have any particular model in mind?'

'Yes, a Remington 700.'

'That should be no problem, sir.'

'It may need a few modifications,' said Connor.

The assistant hesitated. 'Excuse me for a moment, sir.' He disappeared through a curtain into a back room.

A few moments later an older man, also dressed in a long brown coat, appeared through the curtain. Connor was annoyed: he had hoped to purchase the rifle without having to meet the legendary Jim Harding.

'Good afternoon,' the man said, looking closely at his customer. 'I understand you're interested in a Remington 700.' He paused. 'With modifications.'

'Yes. You were recommended by a friend,' said Connor.

'Your friend must be a professional,' said Harding.

As soon as the word 'professional' was mentioned, Connor knew he was being tested. If Harding hadn't been the Stradivarius of gunsmiths, he would have left the shop without another word.

'What modifications did you have in mind, sir?' asked Harding, his eyes never leaving the customer's.

Connor described in detail the gun he had left in Bogotá, watching carefully for any reaction.

Harding's face remained impassive. 'I might have something that would interest you, sir,' he said, then turned and disappeared behind the curtain.

Once again, Connor considered leaving, but within seconds Harding reappeared carrying a familiar leather case, which he placed on the counter.

'This model came into our possession after the owner's recent death,' he explained. He flicked up the catches, opened the lid and swivelled the case round so that Connor could inspect the rifle. 'Every part is hand-made, and I doubt if you'll find a finer piece of craftsmanship this side of the Mississippi.' Harding touched the rifle lovingly. 'The stock is fibreglass, for lightness and better balance. The barrel is imported from Germany – I'm afraid the Krauts still produce the best. The scope is a Leupold 10 Power with mil dots, so you don't even have to adjust for wind. With this rifle you could kill a mouse at four hundred paces, never mind a moose. If you're technically minded, you would be capable of a half-minute of angle at one hundred yards.' He looked up to see if his customer understood what he was talking about, but Connor's expression gave him no clue. 'A

Remington 700 with such modifications is only sought after by the most discerning of customers,' he concluded.

Connor didn't remove any of the five pieces from their places, for fear Mr Harding would discover just how discerning a customer he was.

'How much?' he asked, realising for the first time that he had no idea of the price of a hand-crafted Remington 700.

'Twenty-one thousand dollars,' Harding said. 'Though we do have the standard model should you . . .'

'No,' said Connor. 'This one will be just fine.'

'And how will you be paying, sir?'

'Cash.'

'Then I will require some form of identification,' said Harding. 'I'm afraid there's even more paperwork since they passed the Instant ID and Registration Law to replace the Brady Bill.'

Connor took out a Virginia driver's licence he'd bought for a hundred dollars from a pickpocket in Washington the previous day.

Harding studied the licence and nodded. 'All we need now, Mr Radford, is for you to fill in these three forms.'

Connor wrote out the name, address and Social Security number of the assistant manager of a shoe store in Richmond.

As Harding entered the numbers into a computer, Connor tried to look bored, but he was silently praying that Mr Radford hadn't reported the loss of his driver's licence during the past twenty-four hours.

Suddenly Harding looked up from the screen. 'Is that a double-barrelled name?' he asked.

'No,' replied Connor, not missing a beat. 'Gregory is my first name. My mother had a thing about Gregory Peck.'

Harding smiled. 'Mine too.'

After a few more moments Harding said, 'That all seems to be in order, Mr Radford.'

Connor turned and nodded to Romanov, who strolled over and extracted a thick bundle of notes from an inside pocket. He spent some time ostentatiously peeling off hundred-dollar bills, counting out 210 of them before passing them across to Harding.

What Connor had hoped would appear no more than a casual purchase, the Russian was fast turning into a pantomime. The sidekicks might as well have stood out on the street and sold tickets for the performance.

Harding wrote out a receipt for the cash and handed it to Connor, who left without another word. One of the hoodlums grabbed the rifle and ran out of the shop onto the sidewalk as if he had just robbed a bank. Connor climbed into the back of the BMW and wondered if it was possible to attract any more attention to themselves. The car screeched away from the kerb and cut into the fast-moving traffic, setting off a cacophony of horns. Yes, Connor thought, they obviously could. He remained speechless as the driver broke the speed limit all the way back to the airport. Even Romanov began to look a little apprehensive. Connor was quickly discovering that the new Mafia in the States were still amateurish compared with their cousins from Italy. But it wouldn't be long before they caught up, and when they did, God help the FBI.

Fifteen minutes later, the BMW drew up outside the entrance to the airport. Connor stepped out and began walking towards the revolving door as Romanov gave instructions to the two men in the car, finally peeling off several more hundred-dollar bills and handing them over. When he joined Connor at the check-in counter, he whispered confidently, 'The rifle will be in Washington within forty-eight hours.'

'I wouldn't bet on it,' said Connor as they headed towards the departure lounge.

◄○►

'You know the whole of Yeats off by heart?' asked Stuart in disbelief.

'Um, most of it,' admitted Maggie. 'But then, I do reread a few poems almost every night before going to bed.'

'Darling Stuart, you've still got so much to learn about the Irish,' said Tara. 'Now, try to remember some more of the words.'

Stuart thought for a moment. '"*Hollow*"!' he said triumphantly.

'*"Through hollow lands and hilly lands"*?' asked Maggie.

'That's it.'

'So it can't be Holland we're headed for,' said Tara.

'Stop being facetious,' said Stuart.

'Then try to remember some more words,' said Tara.

Stuart began to concentrate once again. '*"Friend"*,' he said eventually.

'*"Always we'd have the new friend meet the old"*,' said Maggie.

'So we're about to meet a new friend in a new country,' said Tara.

'But who? And where?' said Maggie, as the plane continued its journey through the night.

27

WITHIN MOMENTS OF READING the priority message, Gutenburg was dialling the number in Dallas. When Harding came on the line, the Deputy Director of the CIA simply said, 'Describe him.'

'Six foot, possibly six one. He was wearing a hat, so I couldn't see his hair colour.'

'Age?'

'Fifty. Could be a year or two either way.'

'Eyes?'

'Blue.'

'Dress?'

'Sports jacket, khaki pants, blue shirt, penny loafers, no tie. Smart but casual. I assumed he was one of ours, until I noticed that he was accompanied by a couple of well-known local hoodlums, who he tried to pretend weren't with him. There was also a tall young man who never once opened his mouth, but he was the one who paid for the gun – in cash.'

'And the first man made it clear he wanted those particular modifications?'

'Yes. I'm pretty sure he knew exactly what he was looking for.'

'Right – hold on to the cash. We may be able to identify a fingerprint from one of the bills.'

'You won't find any of his prints on them,' said Harding. 'The young man paid, and one of the hoodlums carried the gun out of the shop.'

'Whoever it was obviously wasn't willing to risk taking it through airport security,' said Gutenburg. 'The two thugs must simply have been couriers. What name did he sign the forms in?'

'Gregory Peck Radford.'

'Identification?'

'Virginia driver's licence. The address and date of birth all tied in with the correct Social Security number.'

'I'll have an agent with you in under an hour. He can start by e-mailing me any details you have on the two hoodlums, and I'll need a police artist's computerised sketch of the main suspect.'

'That won't be necessary,' said Harding.

'Why not?'

'Because the whole transaction was recorded on video.' Gutenburg couldn't see Harding's smile of satisfaction as he added, 'Even you wouldn't have spotted the security camera.'

—◦—

Stuart continued to concentrate. '"*Find out*"!' he said suddenly.

'"*I will find out where she has gone*",' said Maggie with a smile.

'We're going to meet a new friend in a new country, and he'll find us,' said Tara. 'Can you remember anything else, Stuart?'

'"*All things fall . . .*"'

'"*. . . and are built again*",' Maggie whispered as the man who had snatched the book out of Stuart's hands reappeared by their side.

'Now listen, and listen carefully,' he said, looking down at them. 'If you hope to survive – and I don't give a damn either way – you will follow my instructions to the letter. Is that understood?' Stuart stared into the man's eyes and didn't doubt that he looked upon the three of them as just another job. He nodded.

'Right,' the man continued. 'When the plane lands, you will go directly to the baggage area, pick up your luggage and pass through customs without attracting any attention to yourselves. You will not, I repeat not, use the rest rooms. Once you're through customs and in the arrivals area, you will be met by two of my men who will accompany you to the house where you'll be staying for the foreseeable future. I will meet up with you again later this evening. Is that clear?'

'Yes,' said Stuart firmly on behalf of the three of them.

'If any of you is stupid enough to make a run for it, or tries to enlist any help, Mrs Fitzgerald will be killed immediately. And if she's not available for any reason, I get to choose between you two.' He looked at Tara and Stuart. 'Those were the terms Mr Fitzgerald agreed.'

'That's not possible,' began Maggie. 'Connor would never . . .'

'I think it might be wise, Mrs Fitzgerald, to allow Mr Farnham to speak on behalf of all of you in future,' said the man. Maggie would have corrected him if Tara hadn't quickly kicked her leg. 'You'll need these,' he said, handing over three passports to Stuart. He checked them and passed one to Maggie and another to Tara, as the man returned to the cockpit.

Stuart looked down at the remaining passport, which like the other two bore the American eagle on its cover. When he flicked it open he found his own photograph above the name 'Daniel Farnham'. Profession: University law professor. Address: 75 Marina Boulevard, San Francisco, California. He passed it across to Tara, who looked puzzled.

'I do like dealing with professionals,' said Stuart. 'And I'm beginning to realise that your father is one of the best.'

'Are you sure you can't remember any more words?' asked Maggie.

'I'm afraid not,' said Stuart. 'No, wait a moment – "*anarchy*".'

Maggie smiled. 'Now I know where we're going.'

—◦—

It's a long drive from Dallas to Washington. The two thugs who had dropped Connor and Romanov off at the airport had always planned to break the journey somewhere before continuing to the capital the following day. Just after nine o'clock that evening, having covered around four hundred miles, they pulled into a motel on the outskirts of Memphis.

The two senior CIA officers who watched them park their BMW reported back to Gutenburg forty-five minutes later. 'They've checked into the Memphis Marriott, rooms 107 and 108. They ordered room service at nine thirty-three, and are currently in Room 107 watching *Nash Bridges*.'

'Where's the rifle?' asked Gutenburg.

'It's handcuffed to the wrist of the man booked into Room 108.'

'Then you're going to need a waiter and a pass key,' said Gutenburg.

Just after ten o'clock, a waiter appeared in Room 107 and set up a table for dinner. He opened a bottle of red wine, poured two glasses and laid out the food. He told the guests he would return in about forty minutes to clear the table. One of them told him to cut up his steak into little pieces, as he only had the use of one hand. The waiter was happy to oblige. 'Enjoy,' he added, as he left the room.

The waiter then went straight to the carpark and reported to the senior officer, who thanked him, then made a further request. The waiter nodded, and the agent handed him a fifty-dollar bill.

'Obviously not willing to let go of it even when he's eating,' said the other agent once the waiter was out of earshot.

The waiter returned to the carpark a few minutes after midnight, to report that both men had gone to bed in their own rooms. He handed over a pass-key, and in return was given another fifty-dollar bill. He left feeling he'd done a good night's work. What he didn't know was that the man in Room 107 had taken the keys of the handcuffs, so as to be sure that no one would try and steal the briefcase from his partner while he was asleep.

When the guest in 107 woke the following morning, he felt unusually drowsy. He checked his watch, and was surprised to find how late it was. He pulled on his jeans and hurried through the connecting door to wake his partner. He came to a sudden halt, fell on his knees and began to vomit. Lying on the carpet in a pool of blood was a severed hand.

◄○►

As they stepped off the plane in Cape Town, Stuart was aware of the presence of two men watching their every move. An immigration officer stamped their passports, and they headed towards the baggage claim area. After only a few minutes, luggage began to appear on the carousel. Maggie was surprised to see two of her old suitcases coming down the chute. Stuart was starting to get used to the way Connor Fitzgerald operated.

Once they had retrieved their bags, Stuart put them all on a trolley and they walked towards the green customs exit. The two men filed in close behind them.

As Stuart was wheeling the trolley through customs, an officer stepped into his path, pointed to the red suitcase and asked if the owner would place it on the counter. Stuart helped Maggie lift it, as the two men following them reluctantly moved on. Once they had passed through the sliding doors they stationed themselves a few feet from the exit. Each time the doors opened, they could be seen peering back through. Within moments they were joined by two other men.

'Would you open the case, please, ma'am,' asked the customs officer.

Maggie flicked up the catches and smiled at the mess that greeted her. Only one person could have packed that case. The customs officer dug around among her clothes for a few moments, and eventually came out with a cosmetics bag. He unzipped it and removed a small cellophane packet which contained a white powdery substance.

'But that isn't . . .' began Maggie. This time it was Stuart who restrained her.

'I'm afraid we'll have to conduct a body search, ma'am,' said the officer. 'Perhaps, in the circumstances, your daughter would like to join you.'

Stuart wondered how the officer could possibly have known that Tara was Maggie's daughter, when he apparently didn't assume that he was her son.

'Would all three of you care to follow me,' said the officer. 'Please bring the case, and the rest of your luggage.' He lifted a section of the counter and ushered them through a door that led into a small, drab room with a table and two chairs. 'One of my colleagues will join you in a moment,' he said. He closed the door, and they heard the key turning in the lock.

'What's going on?' said Maggie. 'That bag wasn't . . .'

'I expect we're about to find out,' said Stuart.

A door on the far side of the room opened, and a tall, athletic-looking man, who didn't have a hair on his head although he couldn't have been a day over fifty, bounced into the room. He was dressed in blue jeans and a red sweater, and certainly didn't give the impression of being a customs officer. He went straight over to Maggie, took her right hand and kissed it.

'My name is Carl Koeter,' he said in a broad South African accent. 'This is a great honour for me, Mrs Fitzgerald. I've wanted for many years to meet the woman who was brave enough to marry Connor Fitzgerald. He called me yesterday afternoon and asked me to assure you that he's very much alive.'

Maggie would have said something, but the flow didn't stop.

'Of course I know far more about you than you do about me, but unhappily on this occasion we will not have time to remedy that.' He smiled at Stuart and Tara, and bowed slightly. 'Perhaps you would all be kind enough to follow me.'

He turned, and began to push the trolley through the door.

'"*Always we'd have the new friend meet the old*",' Maggie whispered. Stuart smiled.

The South African led them down a steep ramp and along a dark, empty passageway. Maggie quickly caught up with him, and immediately began to question him about his phone conversation with Connor. At the end of the tunnel they climbed up another ramp, and emerged on the far side of the airport. Koeter guided them quickly through security, where they were met with only the most cursory of checks. After another long trek they arrived in an empty departure lounge, where Koeter handed over three tickets to a gate agent and received three boarding passes for a Qantas flight to Sydney that had been mysteriously held up for fifteen minutes.

'How can we begin to thank you?' asked Maggie.

Koeter took her hand and kissed it again. 'Ma'am,' he replied, 'you will find people all over the world who will never be able to fully repay Connor Fitzgerald.'

◄◦►

They both sat watching the television. Neither of them spoke until the twelve-minute clip had come to an end.

'Could it be possible?' said the Director quietly.

'Only if he somehow changed places with him in the Crucifix,' replied Gutenburg.

Dexter was silent for some time before she said, 'Jackson would only have done that if he was willing to sacrifice his own life.'

Gutenburg nodded.

'And who's the man who paid for the rifle?'

'Alexei Romanov, the son of the Czar and the number two in the Russian Mafya. One of our agents spotted him at Frankfurt airport, and we suspect he and Fitzgerald are now working together.'

'So it must have been the Mafya who got him out of the Crucifix,' said Dexter. 'But if he needed a Remington 700, who's the target?'

'The President,' said Gutenburg.

'You could be right,' replied Dexter. 'But which one?'

28

THE PRESIDENT OF THE UNITED STATES and the Secretary of State were among the seventy-two officials lined up on the runway when the Russian Air Force Ilyushin 62 landed at Andrews Air Force Base just outside Washington DC. The red carpet had already been rolled out, a podium with a dozen microphones was in place, and a wide staircase was being towed towards the exact spot on the tarmac where the aircraft would taxi to a standstill.

As the door of the plane opened, Tom Lawrence shielded his eyes from the bright morning sun. A tall, slim stewardess was standing in the doorway. A moment later a short, squat man appeared next to her. Although Lawrence knew that Zerimski was only five foot four, standing next to the tall stewardess cruelly emphasised his lack of stature. Lawrence doubted if it would be possible for a man of Zerimski's height to become President of the United States.

As Zerimski slowly descended the steps, the massed ranks of photographers began clicking furiously. From behind their cordon, camera crews from every network focused on the man who would dominate the world's news for the next four days.

The US Chief of Protocol stepped forward to introduce the two Presidents, and Lawrence shook hands warmly with his guest. 'Welcome to the United States, Mr President.'

'Thank you, Tom,' said Zerimski, immediately wrong-footing him.

Lawrence turned to present the Secretary of State.

'Nice to meet you, Larry,' said Zerimski.

Zerimski appeared disarmingly affable and friendly as he was introduced to each new official: the Defense Secretary, the Commerce Secretary, the National Security Advisor. When he came to the end of the line, Lawrence touched his elbow and guided him towards the podium. As they walked across the runway, the American President leaned down and said, 'I'll just say a few words of welcome, Mr President, and then perhaps you'd like to reply.'

'Victor, please,' Zerimski insisted.

Lawrence stepped up onto the podium, extracted a single sheet of paper from an inside pocket and placed it on the lectern.

'Mr President,' he began; then, turning towards Zerimski, he smiled and said, 'Victor. May I begin by welcoming you to America. Today marks the opening of a new era in the special relationship between our two great countries. Your visit to the United States heralds . . .'

Connor sat in front of three television screens, watching the major networks' coverage of the ceremony. That night he would replay the tapes again and again. There was an even greater security presence on the ground than he had anticipated. The Secret Service seemed to have turned out a full Dignitary Protective Division for each President. But there was no sign of Gutenburg, or of any CIA operatives. Connor suspected that the Secret Service was unaware that a potential assassin was on the loose.

Connor wasn't at all surprised that the rifle he had bought in Dallas had never reached its destination. The two Mafya hoodlums had done everything to tip off the CIA except call them on their toll-free number. Had he been Deputy Director, Connor would have allowed them to deliver the rifle, in the hope that they would lead him to the person who intended to use it. Gutenburg had obviously considered that removing the weapon was more important. Perhaps he was right. Connor couldn't risk being put through another débâcle like the one in Dallas. They had made it necessary for him to come up with an alternative plan.

After the episode in the Memphis Marriott, it had become clear that Alexei Romanov wasn't willing to take the blame if anything else went wrong, and Connor now had overall control of the preparations for the assassination. Those shadowing him kept a respectful distance, although they never let him out of their sight – otherwise he would have been at Andrews Air Force Base that morning. Although he could still have shaken them off whenever he chose, Connor was made aware of their attitude to failure when he learned that the local Mafya boss in Dallas had chopped off the hoodlum's other hand, so that he couldn't make the same mistake twice.

The President came to the end of his welcoming speech and received a round of applause that had little impact in such a large open space. He stepped aside to allow Zerimski to respond, but when the Russian President took his place, he couldn't be seen above the bank of microphones. Connor knew that the press would remind the six foot one American President of this public relations disaster again and again over the next four days, and that Zerimski would assume it had been done intentionally to upstage him. He wondered which White House advance man's head would roll later that day.

Shooting a six-foot man would be much easier than one who was only five foot four, Connor reflected. He studied the agents from the Dignitary Protective Division who had been assigned to protect Zerimski during his visit. He recognised four of them, all of whom were as good as any in their profession. Any one of them could have brought a man down with a single shot at three hundred paces, and disarmed an attacker with one blow. Behind their dark glasses, Connor knew that their eyes were darting ceaselessly in every direction.

Although Zerimski could not be seen by those standing on the runway, his words could be heard clearly. Connor was surprised to find that the hectoring, bullying manner he had employed in Moscow and St Petersburg had been replaced by a far more conciliatory tone. He thanked 'Tom' for his warm welcome, and said that he was confident the visit would prove fruitful for both nations.

Connor was sure that Lawrence wouldn't be fooled by this outward display of warmth. This obviously wasn't the time or place for the Russian President to allow the Americans to discover his real agenda.

As Zerimski continued to read from his script, Connor glanced down at the four-day itinerary prepared by the White House and so conveniently catalogued minute by minute in the *Washington Post*. He knew from years of experience that even with the best-laid plans, such programmes rarely managed to keep to their original timetables. At some time during the visit, he had to assume that the unexpected would happen; and he had to be sure that it wasn't at the moment when he was lining up his rifle.

The two Presidents would be flown by helicopter from the Air Force base to the White House, where they would immediately go into a session of private talks, which would continue over lunch. After lunch, Zerimski would be taken to the Russian Embassy to rest, before returning to the White House in the evening for a black-tie dinner in his honour.

The following morning he would travel to New York to address the United Nations and have lunch with the Secretary-General, followed by a visit to the Metropolitan Museum in the afternoon. Connor had laughed out loud when he read that morning in the style section of the *Post* that Tom Lawrence had become aware of his guest's great love of the arts during the recent presidential campaign, in the course of which Zerimski had found time in his busy schedule to visit not only the Bolshoi, but also the Pushkin and the Hermitage Museums.

After the Russian President returned to Washington on Thursday night, he would have just enough time to rush to the Embassy and change into a dinner jacket before attending a performance of *Swan Lake* by the Washington Ballet at the Kennedy Center. The *Post* tactlessly reminded its readers that over half the *corps de ballet* were Russian immigrants.

On the Friday morning there would be extended talks at the White House, followed by lunch at the State Department. In the afternoon Zerimski would deliver an address to a joint session of Congress, which would be the high point of his four-day visit. Lawrence hoped that the legislators would be convinced that the Russian leader was a man of peace, and agree to back his Arms Reduction Bill. An editorial in the *New York Times* warned that this might be the occasion at which Zerimski would outline Russia's defence strategy for the next decade. The paper's diplomatic correspondent had contacted the press office at the Russian Embassy, only to be informed curtly that there would be no advance copies of that particular speech.

In the evening Zerimski would be the guest of honour at a US–Russia Business Council dinner. Copies of that speech had already been widely circulated, with a casual indifference to any embargo. Connor had been through every sentence, and knew that no self-respecting journalist would bother to print a word of it.

On the Saturday Zerimski and Tom Lawrence would go to Cooke Stadium in Maryland to watch the football game between the Washington Redskins and the Green Bay Packers, the team that Lawrence, who had been the senior Senator for Wisconsin, had supported all his life.

In the evening Zerimski would host a dinner at the Russian Embassy to return the hospitality of all those whose guest he had been during his visit.

The following morning he would fly back to Moscow – but only if Connor had failed to carry out the contract.

Nine venues for Connor to consider. But he had already dismissed seven of them before Zerimski's plane had touched down. Of the remaining two, the banquet on the Saturday night looked the most promising, especially after he'd been told by Romanov that the Mafya had the catering concession for all functions held at the Russian Embassy.

A smattering of applause brought Connor's attention back to the welcoming ceremony. Some of the people standing on the runway were unaware that Zerimski had completed his speech until he stepped down from the podium, so the reception he received was not quite as enthusiastic as Lawrence had hoped.

The two leaders walked across the tarmac to a waiting helicopter. Normally no Russian President would fly in a US military aircraft, but Zerimski had brushed aside any objections, telling his advisors he wanted to take every opportunity of wrong-footing Lawrence. They climbed on board and waved to the crowd. Moments later Marine One rose, hovered above the ground for a few seconds, then lifted away. Those women who had not attended a welcoming ceremony before were unsure whether to cling on to their hats or hold down their dresses.

In seven minutes Marine One would land on the South Lawn of the White House, to be met by Andy Lloyd and the White House senior staff.

Connor flicked off the three televisions, rewound the tapes and began considering the alternatives. He had already decided not to go to New York. The United Nations and the Metropolitan Museum offered virtually no possibility of escape. And he was aware that the Secret Service were trained to spot anyone who appeared on more than one occasion during a visit such as this one, including journalists and television crews. Added to that, at least three thousand of New York's finest would be guarding Zerimski every second of his visit.

He would use the time while Zerimski was out of town to check out the two most promising venues. The Mafya had already arranged for him to be a member of the catering team that would visit the Russian Embassy that afternoon so he could be taken through the details of Saturday night's banquet. The Ambassador had made it clear that he wanted it to be an occasion that neither President would ever forget.

Connor checked his watch, put on a coat and went downstairs. The BMW was waiting for him. He climbed into the back seat.

'Cooke Stadium,' was all he said.

No one in the car commented as the driver eased the car into the centre lane.

As a transporter laden with new cars passed on the other side of the road, Connor thought of Maggie and smiled. He had spoken to Carl Koeter earlier that morning, and had been reassured that all three of the kangaroos were safely in their pouches.

'By the way, the Mafya are under the impression that they were sent straight back to America,' Koeter had told him.

'How did you manage to pull that one off?' asked Connor.

'One of their guards tried to bribe a customs officer. He took the money and informed him they'd been caught with drugs, and had been "returned to their port of embarkation".'

'Do you think they fell for it?'

'Oh yes,' said Koeter. 'They were made to pay a lot of money for that piece of information.'

Connor laughed. 'I'll always be in your debt, Carl. Just let me know how I can repay you.'

'That won't be necessary, my friend,' Koeter had replied. 'I will simply look forward to meeting your wife again in more agreeable circumstances.'

Connor's watchdogs had made no mention of Maggie's disappearance, so he couldn't be certain whether they were too proud to admit that they'd lost her, Stuart and Tara, or whether they were still hoping to catch up with them before he found out the truth. Perhaps they were afraid he wouldn't carry out the job if he knew his wife and daughter were no longer in their hands. But Connor never doubted that if he failed to honour the agreement, Alexei Romanov would eventually track down Maggie and kill her, and if not Maggie, Tara. Bolchenkov had warned him that until the contract had been completed – one way or the other – Romanov wouldn't be allowed to return to his homeland.

As the driver swung onto the beltway, Connor thought about Joan, whose only crime was to have been his secretary. He clenched his fist, and wished that his contract with the Mafya had been to take out Dexter and her conniving Deputy. That was an assignment he would have carried out with relish.

The BMW passed the Washington city limits, and Connor sat back, thinking about just how much preparation still needed to be done. He would have to circle the stadium several times, checking every exit, before deciding if he would even enter it.

◄○►

Marine One landed gently on the South Lawn. The two Presidents stepped out of the helicopter, and were greeted by warm applause from the six hundred assembled White House members of staff.

When Lawrence introduced Zerimski to his Chief of Staff, he couldn't help noticing that Andy seemed preoccupied. The two leaders spent an unusually long time posing for the photographers before retiring to the Oval Office with their advisors to confirm the subjects that would be covered at the later meetings. Zerimski put forward no objections to the timetable Andy Lloyd had prepared, and seemed relaxed about the topics that would come under consideration.

When they broke for lunch, Lawrence felt the preliminary discussions had gone well. They moved into the Cabinet Room, and Lawrence told the story of when President Kennedy had dined there with eight Nobel Laureates, and had remarked that it was the greatest gathering of intellect there since Jefferson had dined alone. Larry Harrington laughed dutifully, although he had heard the President tell the story a dozen times before. Andy Lloyd didn't even attempt a smile.

After lunch Lawrence accompanied Zerimski to his limousine, which was waiting at the diplomatic entrance. As soon as the last car of the motorcade was out of sight – once again Zerimski had insisted he should have one more vehicle than any past Russian President – Lawrence hurried back to the Oval Office. A grim-faced Andy Lloyd was standing by his desk.

'I thought that went as well as could be expected,' said the President.

'Possibly,' said Lloyd. 'Although I wouldn't trust that man to tell the truth even to himself. He was far too cooperative for my liking. I just get the feeling that we're being set up.'

'Was that the reason you were so uncommunicative during lunch?'

'No. I think we've got a far bigger problem on our hands,' said Lloyd. 'Have you seen Dexter's latest report? I left it on your desk yesterday afternoon.'

'No, I haven't,' the President replied. 'I spent most of

yesterday holed up with Larry Harrington in the State Department.' He flicked open a file bearing the CIA emblem, and began reading.

He had sworn out loud on three occasions before he had reached the second page. By the time he'd come to the final paragraph, his face was drained of colour. He looked up at his oldest friend. 'I thought Jackson was supposed to be on our side.'

'He is, Mr President.'

'Then how come Dexter claims she can prove that he was responsible for the assassination in Colombia, then went to St Petersburg intending to kill Zerimski?'

'Because that way she clears herself of any involvement, and leaves us to explain why we hired Jackson in the first place. By now she'll have a cabinet full of files to prove that it was Jackson who killed Guzman, and anything else she wants the world to believe about him. Just look at these pictures she's supplied of Jackson in a Bogotá bar handing money over to the Chief of Police. What they don't show is that the meeting took place almost two weeks after the assassination. Never forget, sir, that the CIA are unrivalled when it comes to covering their asses.'

'It's not their asses I'm worried about,' said the President. 'What about Dexter's story that Jackson's back in America, and is working with the Russian Mafya?'

'Isn't that convenient,' said Lloyd. 'If anything goes wrong during Zerimski's visit, she already has someone lined up to take the rap.'

'Then how do you explain the fact that Jackson was recorded by a security camera in Dallas a few days ago buying a high-powered rifle of near-identical specifications to the one used to kill Guzman?'

'Simple,' said Lloyd. 'Once you realise it wasn't actually Jackson, everything else falls into place.'

'If it wasn't Jackson, then who the hell was it?'

'It was Connor Fitzgerald,' said Lloyd quietly.

'But you told me Fitzgerald was arrested in St Petersburg,

and then hanged. We'd even discussed how we might get him out.'

'I know, sir, but that was never going to be a possibility once Zerimski had been elected. Unless . . .'

'Unless?'

'Unless Jackson took his place.'

'Why on earth would he do that?'

'Remember that Fitzgerald saved Jackson's life in Vietnam, and has the Medal of Honor to prove it. When Fitzgerald returned from the war, it was Jackson who recruited him as an NOC. For the next twenty-eight years he served the CIA, and gained the reputation of being their most respected officer. Then, overnight, he disappears and can't be traced on their books. His secretary, Joan Bennett, who worked for him for nineteen years, suddenly dies in a mysterious car accident while she's on the way to see Fitzgerald's wife. Then his wife and daughter also vanish off the face of the earth. Meanwhile, the man we appoint to find out what's going on is accused of being an assassin and double-crossing his closest friend. But however carefully you search through Helen Dexter's numerous reports, you'll never find a single reference to Connor Fitzgerald.'

'How do you know all this, Andy?' asked Lawrence.

'Because Jackson called me from St Petersburg just after Fitzgerald had been arrested.'

'Do you have a recording of that conversation?'

'Yes, sir, I do.'

'Goddamn it,' said Lawrence. 'Dexter makes J. Edgar Hoover look like a Girl Scout.'

'If we accept that it was Jackson who was hanged in Russia, we have to assume it was Fitzgerald who flew to Dallas, with the intention of buying that rifle so he could carry out his present assignment.'

'Am I the target this time?' asked Lawrence quietly.

'I don't think so, Mr President. That's the one thing I think Dexter's being straight about – I still believe the target's Zerimski.'

'Oh my God,' said Lawrence, slumping into his chair. 'But why would an honourable man with a background and reputation as good as Fitzgerald's get involved in a mission like this? It just doesn't add up.'

'It does if that honourable man believes that the original order to assassinate Zerimski came from you.'

—◇—

Zerimski was running late when his plane took off from New York to fly him back to Washington, but he was in a good mood. His speech to the United Nations had been well received, and his lunch with the Secretary-General had been described in a communiqué issued by the Secretariat as 'wide-ranging and productive'.

During his visit to the Metropolitan Museum that afternoon, not only had Zerimski been able to name the Russian artist who had been given an exhibition in one of the upper galleries, but when he left the museum he had abandoned his itinerary and, to the consternation of his Secret Service minders, walked down to Fifth Avenue to shake hands with Christmas shoppers.

Zerimski had fallen an hour behind schedule by the time his plane touched down in Washington, and he had to change into his dinner jacket in the back of the limousine so that he didn't hold up the performance of *Swan Lake* at the Kennedy Center by more than fifteen minutes. After the dancers had taken their final bow, he returned to spend a second night at the Russian Embassy.

—◇—

While Zerimski slept, Connor remained awake. He could rarely sleep for more than a few minutes at a time during the build-up to an operation. He had cursed out loud when he'd seen the early evening news coverage of the walkabout on Fifth Avenue. It had reminded him that he should always be prepared for the unexpected: from an apartment on Fifth Avenue, Zerimski would have been an easy target, and the crowd would have been so large and out of control that he could have disappeared within moments.

He dismissed New York from his mind. As far as he was concerned, there were still only two serious venues to consider.

At the first, there was the problem that he wouldn't have the rifle he felt most at ease with, although with a crowd that large the getaway would be easier.

As for the second, if Romanov could supply a modified Remington 700 by the morning of the banquet and guarantee his getaway, it seemed the obvious choice. Or was it a little too obvious?

He began to write out lists of pros and cons for each site. By two o'clock the next morning, exhausted, he realised he would have to visit both venues again before he could make his final decision.

But even then he had no intention of letting Romanov know which one he'd chosen.

29

'PUG' WASHER – no one knew his real name – was one of those characters who is an expert on one subject. In his case it was the Washington Redskins.

Pug had worked for the Redskins, man and boy, for fifty years. He had joined the ground staff at the age of fifteen, when the team was still playing at Griffith Stadium. He had started life as a waterboy and had later taken over as the team's masseur, becoming the trusted friend and confidant of generations of Redskins players.

Pug had spent the year before his retirement in 1997 working alongside the contractor who was building the new Jack Kent Cooke Stadium. His brief was simple: to make sure that the Redskins' fans and players had every facility they would expect of the greatest team in the country.

At the opening ceremony, the senior architect told the assembled gathering that he would be forever indebted to Pug for the role he had played in the building of the new stadium. During his closing speech John Kent Cooke, the Redskins' President, announced that Pug had been elected to the team's Hall of Fame, a mark of distinction normally reserved only for the greatest players. Pug told the journalists, 'It doesn't get any better than this.' Despite his retirement, he never missed a Redskins game – home or away.

It took Connor two phone calls to track Pug down at his little apartment in Arlington, Virginia. When he explained to the old man that he had been commissioned to write an article for

Sports Illustrated on the significance of the new stadium to Skins fans, it was like turning on a tap.

'Perhaps you could spare an hour or two to show me around "the Big Jack",' suggested Connor. Pug's monologue dried up for the first time, and he remained silent until Connor suggested an honorarium of $100. He had already found out that Pug's usual fee for guided tours was fifty.

They agreed to meet at eleven o'clock the following morning.

When Connor arrived at one minute to eleven, Pug ushered him into the stadium as if he were the owner of the club. For the next three hours he regaled his guest with the complete history of the Redskins and answered every one of Connor's questions – from why the stadium had not been completed in time for the opening ceremony to how the management went about employing temporary labour on the day of a game. Connor learned that the Sony JumboTrons behind the end zones made up the largest video-screen system in the world, and that the front row of seats had been raised nine feet above the field of play so the fans could see over the television cameras and the bulky players roaming restlessly up and down the sidelines in front of them.

Connor had been a Redskins fan for almost thirty years, so he already knew that all the season tickets had been sold out since 1966, and that there was currently a waiting list of fifty thousand. He knew because he was one of them. He also knew that the *Washington Post* sold an extra twenty-five thousand copies whenever the Skins won a game. But he didn't know that there were thirty-five miles of steam-heated pipes under the field of play, that there was parking space for twenty-three thousand vehicles, and that a local band would be playing the national anthems of Russia and the United States before tomorrow's kick-off. Most of the information Pug came up with would be of no practical use to Connor, but he still produced a gem every few minutes.

As they strolled around the stadium, Connor could see the tight security checks that the White House advance staff were carrying out for the following day's game. The magnetometers through which everyone who entered the ground would have to pass, and which would detect if they were carrying anything that could be used as a weapon, were already in place. The nearer they got to the owner's box – from where the two Presidents would be watching the game – the more intense the checks became.

Pug was irate when he was stopped by a Secret Service agent guarding the entrance to the executive boxes. He explained forcefully that he was a member of the Redskins Hall of Fame, and that he would be among the guests who would meet the two Presidents the next day, but the agent still refused to let him in without a security pass. Connor tried to assure the furious Pug that it wasn't that important.

As they walked away, Pug muttered under his breath, 'Do I look like the sort of person who would want to assassinate the President?'

When the two men parted at two o'clock, Connor handed his guide $120. The old man had told him more in three hours than an entire Secret Service detail would have divulged in a lifetime. He would have given him $200, but that might have aroused Pug's suspicions.

Connor checked his watch, to find he was running a few minutes late for his appointment with Alexei Romanov at the Russian Embassy. As he was driven away from the stadium he switched on the radio, tuning in to C-SPAN, a station he rarely listened to.

A commentator was describing the atmosphere on the floor of the House, as the members waited for the Russian President to arrive. No one had any idea what Zerimski was going to say, as the press had not been issued with advance copies of the speech, and had been advised to check against delivery.

Five minutes before the speech was due to begin, Zerimski walked out onto the floor of the House, accompanied by his escort committee.

'Everyone present,' announced the commentator, 'has risen from their seats and is applauding the guest from Russia. President Zerimski is smiling and waving as he makes his way down the aisle through the packed House chamber to the dais, shaking outstretched hands.' The commentator went on to describe the applause as 'warm rather than rapturous'.

When Zerimski reached the podium he carefully placed his papers on the lectern, took out his spectacle case and put on his glasses. Kremlin-watchers immediately knew that the speech would be delivered word for word from a prepared text, and there would be none of the off-the-cuff remarks for which Zerimski had become notorious during his election campaign.

The Members of Congress, the Supreme Court and the Diplomatic Corps resumed their seats, unaware of the bombshell that was about to be dropped.

'Mr Speaker, Mr Vice-President and Mr Chief Justice,' Zerimski began. 'Let me begin by thanking you and your countrymen for the kind welcome and generous hospitality I have received on this, my first, visit to the United States. Let me assure you that I look forward to returning again and again.' At this point Titov had written 'PAUSE' in the margin – rightly, because there followed a round of applause.

Zerimski then delivered several flattering homilies concerning America's historic achievements, reminding his listeners that three times in the past century their two nations had fought together against a common enemy. He went on to describe 'the excellent relationship currently enjoyed by our two countries'. Tom Lawrence, who was watching the speech with Andy Lloyd on C-SPAN in the Oval Office, began to relax a little. After another few minutes, he even allowed a flicker of a smile to cross his lips.

That smile was wiped off his face as Zerimski delivered the next seventy-one words of his speech.

'I am the last person on earth who would want our two great nations to become embroiled in another pointless war.' Zerimski paused. 'Especially if we were not on the same side.' He looked up and beamed at the assembled gathering, although nobody present appeared to find his comment particularly funny. 'To be sure that such a calamity can never befall us again, it will be necessary for Russia to remain as powerful as the United States on the battlefield if it is to carry the same weight at the conference table.'

In the Oval Office, Lawrence watched as the television cameras scanned the sullen faces of the members of both Houses, and knew that it had taken Zerimski about forty seconds to destroy any chance of his Arms Reduction Bill becoming law.

The rest of Zerimski's speech was received in silence. When he stepped down from the podium there were no outstretched hands, and the applause was distinctly cool.

—◦—

As the white BMW drove up Wisconsin Avenue, Connor switched off the radio. When they reached the gates of the Russian Embassy, one of Romanov's henchmen checked them through security.

Connor was escorted into the white marble reception area for the second time in three days. He could immediately see what Romanov had meant when he said the Embassy's internal security was lax. 'After all, who would want to murder Russia's beloved President in his own Embassy?' he had remarked with a smile.

As they walked down a long corridor, Connor said to Romanov, 'You seem to have the run of the building.'

'So would you have, if you'd paid enough into the Ambassador's Swiss bank account to ensure that he never had to return to the motherland again.'

Romanov continued to treat the Embassy as if it were his own home, even unlocking the door to the Ambassador's study and letting himself in. As they entered the ornately furnished room, Connor was surprised to see a customised Remington 700 resting on the Ambassador's desk. He picked it up and studied it closely. He would have asked Romanov how he'd got his hands on it, if he thought there was any chance of being told the truth.

Connor gripped the stock and broke the breech. There was a single boat-tailed bullet in the chamber. He raised an eyebrow and glanced at Romanov.

'I assume that from that range you will only need one bullet,' said the Russian. He led Connor to the far corner of the room, and drew back a curtain to reveal the Ambassador's private lift. They stepped inside, pulled the gate shut and travelled slowly up to the gallery above the ballroom on the second floor.

Connor checked every inch of the gallery several times, then squeezed in behind the vast statue of Lenin. He looked through its cocked arm to check the sightline to the spot from which Zerimski would deliver his farewell speech, making sure that he would be able to see without being seen. He was thinking how easy it all seemed when Romanov touched him on the arm and ushered him back towards the lift.

'You will have to arrive several hours early, and work with the catering staff before the banquet begins,' Romanov said.

'Why?'

'We don't want anyone to become suspicious when you disappear just before Zerimski begins his speech.'

Romanov checked his watch. 'We should go. Zerimski is due back in a few minutes.'

Connor nodded, and they walked towards the rear entrance. As he climbed back into the BMW, he said, 'I'll let you know when I've decided which venue I've chosen.'

Romanov looked surprised, but said nothing.

Connor was driven out through the Embassy gates minutes before Zerimski was due to return from the Capitol. He switched the radio on in time to catch the early-evening news: 'Senators and Congressmen were falling over each other to grab the microphones and assure their constituents that after hearing President Zerimski's speech, they would not be voting for the Nuclear, Biological, Chemical and Conventional Arms Reduction Bill.'

In the Oval Office, Tom Lawrence was watching CNN's reporter speaking from the Senate press gallery: 'No statement has yet come from the White House,' he was saying, 'and the President . . .'

'And don't hang around waiting for one,' Lawrence said angrily as he switched off the television. He turned to his Chief of Staff. 'Andy, I'm not even sure I can face sitting next to that man for four hours tomorrow afternoon, let alone respond to his farewell speech in the evening.'

Lloyd didn't comment.

◄O►

'I am looking forward to sitting next to my dear friend Tom and watching him have to squirm in front of an audience of millions,' said Zerimski as his limousine entered the grounds of the Russian Embassy. Dmitri Titov remained impassive.

'I think I shall cheer for the Redskins. It would be an added bonus if Lawrence's team lost,' Zerimski smirked. 'A fitting prelude to the humiliation I have planned for him in the evening. Make sure you prepare a speech so flattering that it will appear all the more tragic in retrospect.' He smiled again. 'I have ordered the beef to be served cold. And even you will be surprised by what I have in mind for dessert.'

◄O►

Connor spent several hours that evening wondering if he could risk breaking the rule of a lifetime. He phoned Romanov a few minutes after midnight.

The Russian seemed delighted that they had both come to the same conclusion. 'I'll arrange for a driver to pick you up at three thirty so you can be at the Embassy by four.'

Connor put the phone down. If everything went to plan, the President would be dead by four.

◄O►

'Wake him up.'

'But it's four o'clock in the morning,' said the First Secretary.

'If you value your life, wake him up.'

The First Secretary threw on a dressing gown, ran out of his bedroom and down the corridor. He knocked on the door. There was no response, so he knocked again. A few moments later, a light appeared under the door.

'Come in,' said a sleepy voice. The First Secretary turned the handle and entered the Ambassador's bedroom.

'I am sorry to disturb you, Your Excellency, but there's a Mr Stefan Ivanitsky on the line from St Petersburg. He insists that we wake the President. He says he has an urgent message for him.'

'I'll take the call in my study,' said Pietrovski. He threw back the blanket, ignoring the groans of his wife, ran downstairs and told the night porter to transfer the call to his study.

The phone rang several times before it was eventually picked up by a slightly breathless Ambassador. 'Pietrovski speaking.'

'Good morning, Your Excellency,' said Ivanitsky. 'I asked to be put through to the President, not to you.'

'But it's four o'clock in the morning. Can't it wait?'

'Ambassador, I don't pay you to tell me the time. The next voice I want to hear is the President's. Do I make myself clear?'

The Ambassador put the receiver down on his desk and walked slowly back up the wide staircase to the first floor, trying to decide which of the two men he was more frightened of. He stood outside the door of the President's suite for some time, but the sight of the First Secretary hovering at the top of the stairs stiffened his resolve. He tapped gently on the door, but there was no response. He knocked a little louder, and tentatively opened it.

In the light from the landing the Ambassador and the First Secretary could see Zerimski stirring in his bed. What they didn't see was the President's hand slipping under the pillow, where a pistol was concealed.

'Mr President,' whispered Pietrovski as Zerimski switched on the light by the side of his bed.

'This had better be important,' said Zerimski, 'unless you want to spend the rest of your days as refrigerator inspectors in Siberia.'

'We have a call for you from St Petersburg,' said the Ambassador, almost in a whisper. 'A Mr Stefan Ivanitsky. He says it's urgent.'

'Get out of my room,' said Zerimski as he picked up the phone by his bed.

The two men stepped backwards into the corridor and the Ambassador quietly closed the door.

'Stefan,' said Zerimski. 'Why are you calling at this hour? Has Borodin staged a coup in my absence?'

'No, Mr President. The Czar is dead.' Ivanitsky spoke without emotion.

'When? Where? How?'

'About an hour ago, at the Winter Palace. The colourless liquid finally got him.' Ivanitsky paused. 'The butler has been on my payroll for almost a year.'

The President was silent for a few moments before saying, 'Good. It couldn't have worked out better for us.'

'I would agree, Mr President, were it not for the fact that his son is in Washington. There's very little I can do from this end until he returns.'

'That problem may resolve itself this evening,' said Zerimski.

'Why? Have they fallen into our little trap?'

'Yes,' said Zerimski. 'By tonight I shall have disposed of both of them.'

'Both of them?'

'Yes,' the President replied. 'I have learned an appropriate new expression since I've been over here – "killing two birds with one stone". After all, how many times does one have the chance to see the same man die twice?'

'I wish I was there to witness it.'

'I'm going to enjoy it even more than I did watching his friend dangling from a rope. All things considered, Stefan, this will have been a most successful trip, especially if . . .'

'It's all been taken care of, Mr President,' said Ivanitsky. 'I arranged yesterday for the income from the Yeltsin and Chernopov oil and uranium contracts to be diverted to your Zurich account. That is, unless Alexei countermands my orders when he returns.'

'If he doesn't return, he won't be able to, will he?' Zerimski put the phone down, switched off the light, and fell asleep again within moments.

◄○►

At five o'clock that morning Connor was lying motionless on his bed, fully dressed. He was going over his escape route when the wake-up call came through at six. He rose, pulled back a corner of the curtain and checked that they were still there. They were: two white BMWs parked on the far side of the street, as they had been since midnight the previous evening. By now their occupants would be drowsy. He knew they changed shifts at eight, so he planned to leave ten minutes before the hour. He spent the next thirty minutes carrying out some light stretching exercises to get rid of his stiffness, then stripped off his clothes. He allowed the cold jets of the shower to needle his body for some time before he turned it off and grabbed a towel. Then he dressed in a blue shirt, a pair of jeans, a thick sweater, a blue tie, black socks and a pair of black Nikes with the logo painted out.

He went into the small kitchenette, poured himself a glass of grapefruit juice and filled a bowl with cornflakes and milk. He always ate the same meal on the day of an operation. He liked routine. It helped him believe everything else would run smoothly. As he ate, he read over the seven pages of notes he had made following his meeting with Pug, and once again minutely studied an architect's plan of the stadium. He measured the girder with a ruler, and estimated that it was forty-two feet to the trapdoor. He mustn't look down. He felt the calm come over him that a finely-tuned athlete experiences when called to the starting line.

He checked his watch and returned to the bedroom. They had to be at the intersection of Twenty-First Street and DuPont Circle just as the traffic was building up. He waited a few more minutes, then put three hundred-dollar bills, a quarter and a thirty-minute audiocassette in the back pocket of his jeans. He then left the anonymous apartment for the last time. His account had already been settled.

30

ZERIMSKI SAT ALONE IN the Embassy dining room reading the *Washington Post* as a butler served him breakfast. He smiled when he saw the banner headline:

RETURN OF THE COLD WAR?

As he sipped his coffee, he mused for a moment on what the *Post* might lead with the following morning.

ATTEMPT TO ASSASSINATE
RUSSIAN PRESIDENT FAILS
Former CIA Agent Gunned Down
in Embassy Grounds

He smiled again, and turned to the editorial, which confirmed that Lawrence's Nuclear, Biological, Chemical and Conventional Arms Reduction Bill was now considered by all the leading commentators to be 'dead in the water'. Another useful expression he had picked up on this trip.

At a few minutes past seven he rang the silver bell by his side and asked the butler to fetch the Ambassador and the First Secretary. The butler hurried away. Zerimski knew both men were already standing anxiously outside the door.

The Ambassador and the First Secretary thought they should wait for a minute or two before joining the President. They were still uncertain if he was pleased to have been woken at four in the morning, but as neither of them had yet been fired, they assumed that they must have made the right decision.

'Good morning, Mr President,' said Pietrovski as he entered the dining room.

Zerimski nodded, folded the paper and placed it on the table in front of him. 'Has Romanov arrived yet?' he asked.

'Yes, Mr President,' said the First Secretary. 'He has been in the kitchen since six o'clock this morning, personally checking the food that's being delivered for tonight's banquet.'

'Good. Ask him to join us in your study, Mr Ambassador. I will be along shortly.'

'Yes, sir,' said Pietrovski, retreating backwards out of the room.

Zerimski wiped his mouth with a napkin. He decided to keep the three of them waiting for a few more minutes. That would make them even more nervous.

He returned to the *Washington Post*, smiling as he read the editorial's conclusion for a second time: 'Zerimski is the natural successor to Stalin and Brezhnev, rather than Gorbachev or Yeltsin.' He had no quarrel with that; in fact he hoped that before the day was out he would have reinforced that image. He rose from his chair and strolled out of the room. As he walked down the corridor towards the Ambassador's study, a young man coming from the opposite direction stopped in his tracks, rushed over to the door and opened it for him. A grandfather clock chimed as he entered the room. He instinctively checked his watch. It was exactly seven forty-five.

◄○►

At ten minutes to eight, Connor appeared at the entrance of the apartment building and walked slowly across the street to the first of the two BMWs. He climbed in beside a driver who looked a little surprised to see him so early – he'd been told that Fitzgerald wasn't expected at the Embassy until four o'clock that afternoon.

'I need to go downtown to pick up a couple of things,' said Connor. The man in the back nodded, so the driver put the car into first and joined the traffic on Wisconsin Avenue. The second car followed closely behind them as they turned left into P Street, which was thickly congested as a result of the construction work that plagued Georgetown.

As each day passed, Connor had noticed that his minders had become more and more relaxed. At roughly the same time every morning he had jumped out of the BMW at the corner of Twenty-First Street and DuPont Circle, bought a copy of the *Post* from a newsvendor and returned to the car. Yesterday the man in the back seat hadn't even bothered to accompany him.

They crossed Twenty-Third Street, and Connor could see DuPont Circle in the distance. The cars were now bumper to bumper, and had almost ground to a halt. On the other side of the street the traffic heading west was moving far more smoothly. He would need to judge exactly when to make his move.

Connor knew that the lights on P Street approaching the Circle changed every thirty seconds, and on average twelve cars managed to get across during that time. The most he'd counted during the week was sixteen.

When the light turned red, Connor counted seventeen cars ahead of them. He didn't move a muscle. The light switched to green and the driver changed into first gear, but the traffic was so heavy that it was some time before he was able to edge forward. Only eight cars crawled through the light.

He had thirty seconds.

He turned and smiled at his minder in the back, and pointed to the newsvendor. The man nodded. Connor stepped out onto the sidewalk and started walking slowly towards the old man wearing a fluorescent orange vest. He didn't once look back, so he had no idea if anyone from the second car was following him. He concentrated on the traffic moving in the opposite direction on the other side of the street, trying to estimate how long the line of cars would be when the light turned red again. When he reached the newsvendor, he already had a quarter in his hand. He gave it to the old man, who handed him a copy of the *Post*. As he turned and began to walk back towards the first BMW, the light turned red and the traffic came to a halt.

Connor spotted the vehicle he needed. He suddenly switched direction and started sprinting, darting in and out of the stationary traffic on the westbound side of the street until he reached an empty taxi, six cars away from the lights. The two men in the second BMW leaped out of the car and began running after him just as the light at DuPont Circle turned green.

Connor pulled open the door and threw himself into the back of the taxi. 'Straight ahead,' he shouted. 'You get $100 if you beat that light.'

The driver pressed the palm of his hand onto his horn and kept it there as he ran the red light. The two white BMWs executed screeching U-turns, but the lights had already changed, and their path was blocked by three stationary cars.

So far everything had gone to plan.

The taxi swung left onto Twenty-Third Street, and Connor instructed the driver to pull over. When the car had come to a halt he passed him a hundred-dollar bill and said, 'I want you to drive straight to Dulles Airport. If you spot a white BMW coming up behind you, don't let it overtake you. When you get to the airport, stop for thirty seconds outside Departures, then drive slowly back into town.'

'OK, man, anything you say,' said the driver, pocketing the hundred-dollar bill. Connor slipped out of the cab, darted across Twenty-Third Street and flagged down another cab heading in the opposite direction.

He slammed the door shut as the two BMWs swept past him in pursuit of the first taxi.

'And where would you like to go this fine morning?'

'Cooke Stadium.'

'I hope you got a ticket, man, otherwise I'll be bringing you straight back.'

<o>

The three men stood as Zerimski entered the room. He waved them down as if they were a large crowd, and took the chair behind the Ambassador's desk. He was surprised to see a rifle where the blotter would normally be, but he ignored it and turned to Alexei Romanov, who was looking rather pleased with himself.

'I have some sad news for you, Alexei,' said the President. Romanov's expression turned to apprehension, and then to anxiety, during the long silence Zerimski allowed to follow.

'I received a call earlier this morning from your cousin Stefan. It appears that your father suffered a heart attack during the night, and died on the way to hospital.'

Romanov bowed his head. The Ambassador and First Secretary glanced towards the President to see how they should react.

Zerimski rose, walked slowly over to Romanov and placed a consoling hand on his shoulder. The Ambassador and First Secretary looked suitably grief-stricken.

'I shall mourn him,' said Zerimski. 'He was a great man.' The two diplomats nodded their agreement as Romanov inclined his head to acknowledge the President's kind words.

'Now his mantle has passed on to you, Alexei; a most worthy successor.'

The Ambassador and the Chief Secretary continued to nod.

'And soon,' Zerimski said, 'you will be given an opportunity to demonstrate your authority in a way that will leave no one in Russia in any doubt who is the new Czar.'

Romanov raised his head and smiled, his brief period of mourning over.

'That is,' added Zerimski, 'assuming nothing goes wrong this evening.'

'Nothing can go wrong,' said Romanov emphatically. 'I spoke to Fitzgerald just after midnight. He's agreed to my plan. He will report to the Embassy at four o'clock this afternoon, while you are at the football game with Lawrence.'

'Why so early?' asked Zerimski.

'We need everyone to think he's simply another member of the catering team, so that when he slips out of the kitchen six hours later nobody will give it a second thought. He will remain in the kitchen under my supervision until a few minutes before you rise to make your farewell speech.'

'Excellent,' said Zerimski. 'And then what happens?'

'I will accompany him to this room, where he will collect the rifle. He will then take the private elevator to the gallery that overlooks the ballroom.'

Zerimski nodded.

'Once he is there, he will position himself behind the great statue of Lenin, where he will remain until you reach that section of your speech where you thank the American people for their hospitality and the warm welcome you have received everywhere, *et cetera*, *et cetera*, and particularly from President Lawrence. At that point, I have arranged for prolonged applause. Throughout it you must remain absolutely still.'

'Why?' demanded Zerimski.

'Because Fitzgerald won't squeeze the trigger if he thinks you're likely to make a sudden movement.'

'I understand.'

'Once he has fired, he will climb out onto the ledge by the cedar tree in the back garden. He made us repeat the whole exercise several times yesterday afternoon, but this evening he will discover there is a small difference.'

'And what is that?' asked Zerimski.

'Waiting under the tree will be six of my personal body-guards,' said Romanov. 'They will have gunned him down long before his feet touch the ground.'

Zerimski was silent for a moment before saying, 'But surely your plan has a minor flaw?'

Romanov looked puzzled.

'How am I expected to survive a shot from a marksman of Fitzgerald's reputation from such close range?'

Romanov rose from his chair and picked up the rifle. He removed a small piece of metal and handed it to the President.

'What is this?' Zerimski asked.

'The firing pin,' Romanov replied.

31

THE TWO WHITE BMWs sped west on Route 66, pursuing an empty taxi that exceeded the speed limit all the way to Dulles Airport. A second cab was travelling east at a more leisurely pace towards Cooke Stadium in Maryland.

Connor thought again about his decision to choose the stadium, with all its risks, rather than the Embassy. He had been allowed in and out of that building far too easily: no one was that lax about security, especially when their President was in town.

When Connor was dropped at the stadium, he knew exactly where to go. He walked up the wide gravel path towards the north entrance and the two long lines of people who hung around before every home game in the hope of a day's work. Some of them just needed the cash, while others, Pug had explained, were such fanatical Skins fans that they would resort to anything, including bribery, to get into the stadium.

'Bribery?' Connor had asked innocently.

'Oh yes. Someone has to serve in the executive suites,' said Pug with a wink. 'And they end up with the best view of the game.'

'Fascinating material for my article,' Connor had assured him.

The first queue was for those who wanted to work outside the stadium, organising the parking for the twenty-three thousand cars and buses or selling programmes, cushions and souvenirs to the seventy-eight thousand fans. The other was for those who hoped to work inside the stadium. Connor joined that queue, mostly made up of the young, the unemployed and what Pug had described as the early-retirement junkies, who simply enjoyed the regular outing. Pug had even described how this group dressed, so that no one would mistake them for the unemployed.

On this particular day, a handful of Secret Service men were eyeing the hopeful applicants. Connor kept reading the *Washington Post* as the line moved slowly forward. Most of the front page was devoted to Zerimski's speech to the joint session of Congress. The reaction from the members was universally hostile. When he turned to the editorial, he suspected Zerimski would be pleased with it.

He turned to the Metro section, and a wry smile crossed his face as he read of the premature death of a distinguished academic from his home town.

'Hi,' said a voice.

Connor glanced round at a smartly-dressed young man who had joined the queue behind him.

'Hi,' he responded briefly, before returning to his paper. He didn't want to get involved in an unnecessary conversation with someone who might later be called as a witness.

'My name's Brad,' the young man announced, thrusting out his right hand.

Connor shook it, but said nothing.

'I'm hoping to get a job on one of the lighting towers,' he added. 'How about you?'

'Why the lighting towers?' asked Connor, avoiding his question.

'Because that's where the Secret Service's Special Agent in Charge will be stationed, and I want to find out what the job's really like.'

'Why?' asked Connor, folding up his paper. This was clearly not a conversation he could easily cut short.

'I'm thinking about joining them when I leave college. I've already taken the graduate training course, but I want to see them working at close quarters. An agent told me the one job nobody wants is taking meals up to the guys on the lighting platforms behind the end zones. All those steps scare them off.'

All 172 of them, thought Connor, who had dismissed the idea of the lighting towers early on, not because of the steps, but because there was no escape route. Brad started to tell him his life story, and by the time Connor reached the front of the queue he knew which school the boy had been to, that he was now a senior at Georgetown studying criminology – that made him think of Maggie – and why he still couldn't decide whether to join the Secret Service or be a lawyer. 'Next,' said a voice. Connor turned round to the man seated behind a trestle table.

'What have you got left?' Connor asked.

'Not much,' said the man, looking down at a list covered with ticks.

'Anything in catering?' asked Connor. Like Brad, he knew exactly where he wanted to be.

'Washing dishes or serving meals to employees around the stadium is all I've got left.'

'That will be just fine.'

'Name?'

'Dave Krinkle,' said Connor.

'ID?'

Connor handed over a driver's licence. The man filled in a security pass and a photographer stepped forward and took a Polaroid of Connor, which seconds later was laminated onto the pass.

'OK, Dave,' the man said, handing it over. 'This pass will get you everywhere inside the stadium except the high-security area, which includes the executive suites, the club boxes and the VIP section. You won't need to go there anyway.' Connor nodded and clipped the pass onto his sweater. 'Report to Room 47, directly below Block H.' Connor moved off to the left. He knew exactly where Room 47 was.

'Next.'

It took him a lot longer to get through the three security checks, including the magnetometer, than it had the previous day, as they were now manned by Secret Service personnel rather than the usual rentacops. Once Connor was inside the stadium, he ambled slowly along the inner walkway, past the museum and

under a red banner declaring 'HAIL VICTORY', until he came
to a stairway with an arrow pointing down to 'Room 47, Private
Catering'. Inside the small room at the foot of the stairs he found
a dozen men lounging around. They all looked as if they were
familiar with the routine. He recognised one or two who had been
standing in the line in front of him. No one else in the room
looked as if they didn't need the money.

He took a seat in a corner and returned to the *Post*, rereading
a preview of the afternoon's game. Tony Kornheiser thought it
would be nothing less than a miracle if the Redskins beat the
Packers – the finest team in the country. In fact, he was
predicting a twenty-point margin. Connor was hoping for a
totally different outcome.

'OK,' said a voice, 'pay attention.' Connor looked up to see a
huge man wearing a chef's uniform standing in front of them.
He was about fifty, with an enormous double chin, and must
have weighed over 250 pounds.

'I'm the catering manager,' he said, 'and as you can see, I
represent the glamour end of the business.' One or two of the
old hands laughed politely.

'I can offer you two choices. You either wash dishes or you
serve stadium employees and security guys stationed around
the stadium. Any volunteers for the dishes?' Most of the men
in the room put their hands up. Dishwashing, Pug had explained,
was always popular because not only did the washers get the full
rate of $10 an hour, but for some of them the leftovers from the
executive boxes were the best meal they had all week.

'Good,' he said, picking out five of them and writing down
their names. When he had completed the list, he said, 'Now,
waiting. You can either serve the senior staff or the security
personnel. Senior staff?' he said, looking up from his clipboard.
Almost all the remaining hands shot up. Again the catering
manager wrote down five names. When he'd finished, he tapped
his clipboard. 'OK,' he said. 'Everyone on the list can now report
to work.' The old pros rose from their seats and shuffled past
him, through a door that Connor knew led to the kitchens. Only
he and Brad were still in the room.

'I've got two jobs left in Security,' said the catering manager. 'One great, one lousy. Which one of you is going to get lucky?' He looked hopefully at Connor, who nodded and placed a hand in his back pocket.

The catering manager walked up to him, not even glancing at Brad, and said, 'I have a feeling you'd prefer the comfort of the JumboTron.'

'Right first time,' said Connor, slipping him a hundred-dollar bill.

'Just as I thought,' said the catering manager, returning his smile.

Connor said nothing as the fat man pocketed the cash, exactly as Pug had predicted he would.

That man had been worth every cent of his fee.

◄o►

'I should never have invited him in the first place,' Tom Lawrence growled as he boarded Marine One to take him from the White House to the Redskins' stadium.

'And I have a feeling that our problems aren't over yet,' said Andy Lloyd, strapping himself into his seat.

'Why? What else can go wrong?' asked Lawrence as the helicopter blades slowly began to rotate.

'There are still two public events before Zerimski returns to Russia, and my bet is that Fitzgerald will be waiting for us at one of them.'

'This evening shouldn't be a problem,' said Lawrence. 'Ambassador Pietrovski has told the Secret Service on countless occasions that his people are quite capable of protecting their own President. In any case, who would take that sort of risk with so much security around?'

'The normal rules don't apply to Fitzgerald,' said Lloyd. 'He doesn't work by the book.'

The President glanced down at the Russian Embassy. 'It would be hard enough just getting into that building,' he said, 'without having to worry about how you'd get out of it.'

'Fitzgerald wouldn't have the same trouble this afternoon, in a stadium holding nearly eighty thousand spectators,' replied Lloyd. 'That's one place he would find it easy to slip in and out of.'

'Don't forget, Andy, there's only a thirteen-minute window when any problem could arise. Even then, everybody in the stadium will have passed through the magnetometers, so there's no way anyone could get a penknife in, let alone a gun.'

'You think Fitzgerald doesn't know that?' said Lloyd as the helicopter swung east. 'It's not too late to cancel that part of the programme.'

'No,' said Lawrence firmly. 'If Clinton could stand in the middle of the Olympic Stadium in Atlanta for the opening ceremony, I can do the same in Washington for a football game. Damn it, Andy, we live in a democracy, and I'm not going to allow our lives to be dictated to in that way. And don't forget that I'll be out there, taking exactly the same risk as Zerimski.'

'I accept that, sir,' said Lloyd. 'But if Zerimski were to be assassinated, no one would praise you for standing by his side, least of all Helen Dexter. She'd be the first to point out . . .'

'Who do you think will win this afternoon, Andy?' asked the President.

Lloyd smiled at a ploy his boss often fell back on if he didn't wish to continue discussing an unpalatable subject. 'I don't know, sir,' he replied. 'But until I saw how many of my staff were trying to cram themselves into the advance cars this morning, I had no idea we had so many Skins fans working at the White House.'

'Some of them might just have been Packers fans,' said Lawrence. He opened the file on his lap and began to study the short profiles of the guests he would be meeting at the stadium.

—◇—

'OK, pay attention,' said the catering manager. Connor gave the impression of listening intently.

'The first thing you do is collect a white coat and a Redskins cap, to show you're on the staff. Then you take the elevator to the seventh level and wait for me to put the food in the service elevator. The Secret Service agents have a snack at ten, and lunch – Coke, sandwiches, whatever else they want – at the start of the game. You press the button on the left-hand side,' he continued, as if he was addressing a ten-year-old, 'and it should be with you in about a minute.'

Connor could have told him that it took exactly forty-seven seconds for the service elevator to travel from the basement to the seventh level. But as there were two other levels – the second (club seats) and the fifth (executive suites) – which also had access to the service lift, he might have to wait until their orders were completed before the elevator reached him, in which case it could take as long as three minutes.

'Once your order arrives, you take the tray to the officer stationed inside the JumboTron at the eastern end of the ground. You'll find a door marked "Private" down the walkway to your left.' Thirty-seven paces, Connor recalled. 'Here's the key. You go through it, and down an enclosed walkway until you reach the back entrance of the JumboTron.' Seventy yards, thought Connor. In his footballing days he could have covered that distance in around seven seconds.

While the manager continued to tell him things he already knew, Connor studied the service elevator. It was two foot three by two foot seven, and inside were clearly printed the words: 'Maximum weight permitted 150 pounds'. Connor weighed 210 pounds, so he hoped the designer had allowed a bit of leeway. There were two other problems: he wouldn't be able to test it out, and there was nothing he could do to prevent it from being stopped at the fifth or second floors once he was on his way down.

'When you reach the door at the back of the JumboTron,' the catering manager was saying, 'you knock, and the agent on duty will unbolt it and let you in. Once you've handed him the tray, you can go to the back of the stadium and watch the first quarter. At the break you go and get the tray and take it to the service elevator. You press the green button and it will go back down to the basement. Then you can watch the rest of the game. Did you understand all that, Dave?'

Connor was tempted to say, No, sir. Would you be kind enough to run through it once again, but a little more slowly?

'Yes, sir.'

'Any questions?'

'No, sir.'

'OK. If the officer treats you good, I'll send him up a steak after full time. When he's finished that, report to me and collect your pay. Fifty dollars.' He winked.

Pug had explained that serious fans didn't bother to pick up their wages if they wanted to be offered the job again. 'Remember,' he had said, 'when the manager mentions the word "pay", just wink.'

Connor had no intention of collecting the $50, or of ever returning to the stadium. He winked.

32

'WHY IS LAWRENCE TRAVELLING to the game by helicopter when I'm stuck in the back of this car?' Zerimski asked as his nine-limousine motorcade swept out of the Embassy gates.

'He has to make sure he's there before you,' said Titov. 'He wants to be introduced to all the guests, so that by the time you arrive he can give the impression he's known them all his life.'

'What a way to run a country,' said Zerimski. 'Not that this afternoon is important.' He was silent for a moment. 'Do you know, I've even seen the rifle Fitzgerald plans to kill me with,' he said eventually. Titov looked surprised. 'He's using the same model the CIA planted on him in St Petersburg. But with a refinement.' He put a hand in his jacket pocket. 'What do you think this is?' he asked, holding up what looked like a bent nail.

Titov shook his head. 'I've no idea.'

'It's the firing pin of a Remington 700,' Zerimski replied. 'So we can even allow him to pull the trigger before the bodyguards begin to pump bullets into him.' He studied it closely. 'I think I'll have it mounted and keep it on my desk in the Kremlin.' He dropped it back in his pocket. 'Has the speech I'm meant to be giving tonight been released to the press?'

'Yes, Mr President,' replied Titov. 'It's full of the usual platitudes. You can be confident that not a word of it will ever be printed.'

'And what about my spontaneous reaction after Fitzgerald has been killed?'

'I have it here, Mr President.'

'Good. Give me a taste of it,' said Zerimski, leaning back in his seat.

Titov removed a file from the case by his side and began reading from a handwritten script: 'On the day of my election, President Lawrence telephoned me at the Kremlin and gave me a personal invitation to visit his country. I accepted that offer in good faith. What happens when I take it up? My outstretched hand is met not with an olive branch, but with a rifle pointing directly at me. And where? In my own Embassy. And who pulled the trigger? An officer of the CIA. Had it not been for my good fortune . . .'

'A *former* officer,' interrupted Zerimski.

'I thought it prudent,' said Titov, looking up from his notes, 'for you to appear to make the occasional error, even to repeat yourself. That way no one will suggest you always knew what was going on. In America, they want to believe that everything is a conspiracy.'

'I shall be only too happy to fuel their paranoia,' said Zerimski. 'Long after Lawrence has been removed, I expect Americans will be writing copious volumes about how I was responsible for the complete breakdown in relations between the two countries. Lawrence's administration will end up as nothing more than a footnote in the history of the resurgence of the Russian empire under my presidency.' He beamed at Titov. 'And after I have achieved that, there will be no more talk of elections. Because I shall remain in power until the day I die.'

—◆—

Connor checked his watch. It was nine fifty-six. He pressed the button beside the service elevator and immediately heard the whirr of an engine as it began its slow journey up to the seventh level.

There were still thirty-four minutes before the stadium would be opened to the public, although Connor knew it would take some time for the crowd to pass through the thirty magnetometers and the personal security checks. But he was keeping to a far stricter timetable than anyone else in the stadium. Forty-seven seconds later he removed the tray and pressed the button to let the staff in the basement know he had received it.

He walked quickly along the seventh-floor concourse, past a concession stand, and up to the door marked 'Private'. He balanced the tray on one hand, turned the key in the lock with the other and slipped inside. Then he switched on the lights and strode down the covered walkway at the back of the JumboTron. He checked his watch again – eighty-three seconds. Too long, but as the final run would be without a tray, it should be possible to complete the whole exercise, from roof to basement, in under two minutes. If it all went to plan, he would be out of the stadium and on his way to the airport before they had time to set up any roadblocks.

Connor balanced the tray in one hand and knocked on the door with the other. A few seconds later it was opened by a tall, heavily-built man who stood silhouetted in an oblong of light.

'I've brought you a snack,' said Connor with a warm smile.

'Great,' said the sharpshooter. 'Why don't you come in and join me?' He removed a pastrami sandwich from the tray, and Connor followed him along a thin, galvanised steel platform behind a vast screen made up of 786 televisions. The Secret Service man sat down and dug his teeth into the sandwich. Connor tried not to let him see how closely he was studying his rifle.

The JumboTron was on three floors, one above the platform and one below. Connor put the tray down beside the officer, who was sitting in the middle of the flight of stairs that led to the lower ramp. He took more interest in his can of Diet Coke than in Connor's roaming eyes.

'By the way,' he said, between swigs, 'I'm Arnie Cooper.'

'Dave Krinkle,' Connor replied.

'So how much did you have to pay for the privilege of spending the afternoon with me?' asked Arnie with a grin.

—◇—

Marine One landed at the heliport to the north-east of the stadium, and a limousine purred up even before the copter's steps had touched the ground. Lawrence and Lloyd emerged a moment later, and the President turned to wave to the large gathering of well-wishers before climbing into the back of the waiting car. They covered the quarter-mile to the stadium in under a minute, passing through every security check without hindrance. John Kent Cooke, the owner of the Redskins, was waiting at the stadium's entrance to greet them.

'This is a great honour, sir,' he said as Lawrence stepped out of the limousine.

'It's good to meet you, John,' replied the President, shaking the slim, grey-haired man by the hand.

Cooke guided his guest towards a private lift.

'Do you really believe the Skins can win, John?' Lawrence asked with a grin.

'Now that's the sort of loaded question I might have expected from a politician, Mr President,' Cooke replied as they stepped into the lift. 'Everyone knows you're the Packers' number one fan. But I'm bound to say the answer to your question is "Yes, sir." Fight for old DC. The Skins will win.'

'The *Washington Post* doesn't agree with you,' said the President as the doors opened at the press level.

'I'm sure you're the last person to believe everything you read in the *Post*, Mr President,' said Cooke. Both men laughed as he led Lawrence into his box, a large, comfortable room positioned above the fifty-yard line, with a perfect view of the whole field. 'Mr President, I'd like to introduce you to one or two of the folks who have made the Redskins the greatest football team in America. Let me start with my wife, Rita.'

'Good to meet you, Rita,' Lawrence said, shaking her by the hand. 'And congratulations on your triumph at the National Symphony Ball. I'm told they raised a record amount under your chairmanship.'

Mrs Cooke beamed with pride.

Lawrence was able to recall an appropriate fact or anecdote about every person he was introduced to, including the little old man wearing a Redskins blazer who couldn't possibly have been a former player.

'This is Pug Washer,' said John Kent Cooke, placing a hand on the old man's shoulder. 'Now, he . . .'

'. . . is the only man in history to make the Redskins Hall of Fame without playing a single game for the team,' said the President.

A huge smile appeared on Pug's face.

'And I'm also told that you know more about the history of the team than any living person.'

Pug promised himself he would never vote Republican again.

'So tell me, Pug, in Packers versus Skins games, what were Vince Lombardi's regular-season points when he was coaching the Packers, compared to his year with the Skins?'

'Packers 459, Skins 435,' said Pug with a rueful smile.

'Just as I thought – he should never have left the Packers in the first place,' said the President, slapping Pug on the back.

'Do you know, Mr President,' said Cooke, 'I've never been able to come up with a question about the Redskins that Pug wasn't able to answer.'

'Has anyone ever stumped you, Pug?' asked the President, turning to the walking encyclopaedia again.

'They try all the time, Mr President,' Pug replied. 'Why, only yesterday a man . . .'

Before Pug could complete his sentence, Andy Lloyd touched Lawrence's elbow. 'I'm sorry to interrupt you, sir, but we've just been informed that President Zerimski is only five minutes away from the stadium. You and Mr Cooke should make your way to the north-east entrance now, so that you'll be in time to welcome him.'

'Yes, of course,' said Lawrence. He turned to Pug and said, 'Let's continue our conversation just as soon as I get back.'

Pug nodded as the President and his entourage left the room to go and greet Zerimski.

◄○►

'It's a bit cramped in here,' Connor shouted above the noise of the large ventilation fan in the ceiling.

'Sure is,' said Arnie, finishing off his Diet Coke. 'But I guess it goes with the job.'

'Are you expecting any trouble today?'

'Nope, not really. Of course, we'll all be on full alert the moment the two Presidents walk out onto the field, but that only lasts for about eight minutes. Although if Special Agent Braithwaite had his way, neither of them would be allowed out of the owner's box until it was time for them to go home.'

Connor nodded and asked several more innocuous questions, listening carefully to Arnie's Brooklyn accent, and concentrating especially on any expressions he used regularly.

As Arnie dug his teeth into a slice of chocolate cake, Connor looked through a gap in the rotating advertising boards. Most of the Secret Service officers in the stadium were also taking a snack break. He focused on the lighting tower behind the western end zone. Brad was up there listening intently to an officer who was pointing towards the owner's box. Just the sort of young man the Service needed to recruit, thought Connor. He turned back to Arnie. 'I'll see you again at the start of the game. A plate of sandwiches, another slice of cake and some more Coke suit you?'

'Yep, sounds great. But go easy on the cake. I don't mind my wife telling me I've put on a few pounds, but lately the SAIC has begun to comment on it.'

A siren sounded to let all the staff in the stadium know it was ten thirty, and the gates were about to be opened. The fans began to flood into the stands, most of them heading straight for their usual seats. Connor gathered up the empty Coke can and the plastic container and placed them on the tray.

'I'll be back with your lunch when the game kicks off,' he said.

'Yep,' replied Arnie, his binoculars now focused on the crowd below. 'But don't come in until after the two Presidents are back in the owner's box. No one else is allowed in the JumboTron while they're out on the field.'

'OK, I understand,' said Connor, taking a last look at Arnie's rifle. As he turned to go, he heard a voice coming over a two-way radio.

'Hercules 3.'

Arnie unclipped the radio from the back of his belt, pressed a button and said, 'Hercules 3, go ahead.'

Connor hesitated by the door.

'Nothing to report, sir. I was just about to run an eye over the west stand.'

'Fine. Report in if you see anything suspicious.'

'Will do,' said Arnie, and clipped the receiver back onto his belt.

Connor quietly stepped out onto the covered walkway, closed the door behind him and placed the empty Coke can on the step.

He checked his watch, then walked quickly down the covered walkway, unlocked the door and turned off the lights. The concourse was swarming with fans heading for their seats. When he reached the lift shaft, he checked his watch again. Fifty-four seconds. On the final run it would have to take less than thirty-five. He pressed the button. Forty-seven seconds later the service elevator reappeared. Obviously no one on the second or fifth levels had been calling for it. He placed the tray inside and pressed the button once again. It immediately began its slow journey down to the basement.

No one gave Connor, dressed in a long white catering coat and a Redskins cap, a second glance as he strolled casually past the concession stand towards the door marked 'Private'. He slipped inside and locked the door behind him. In the darkness he walked noiselessly back along the narrow walkway until he was a few yards from the entrance to the JumboTron. He stood looking down at the vast steel girder that held the massive screen in place.

Connor gripped the handrail for a moment, then fell to his knees. He leaned forward, grabbed the girder with both hands, and eased himself off the walkway. He stared fixedly at the screen which, according to the architects' plans, was forty-two feet in front of him. It looked more like a mile.

He could see a small handle, but he still had no idea if the emergency trapdoor that had been clearly marked on the engineer's plans really existed. He began to crawl slowly along the girder, inch by inch, never once looking down at the 170-foot drop below him. It felt like two miles.

When he finally reached the end of the girder, he dropped his legs over the sides and gripped tightly, as if he was on horseback. The screen switched from a replay of a touchdown in the Skins' previous game to an advertisement for Modell's sporting goods store. Connor took a deep breath, gripped the handle, and pulled. The trapdoor slid back, revealing the promised twenty-two-and-a-half-inch-square hole. Connor slowly hauled himself inside and slid the door back in place.

Pressed in on all sides by steel, he began to wish that he had added a thick pair of gloves to his clothing. It was like being inside a refrigerator. Nevertheless, as each minute passed he became more confident that should it prove necessary to fall back on his contingency plan, no one would ever discover where he was hiding.

He lay suspended inside the hollow steel girder 170 feet above the ground for over an hour and a half, barely able to turn his wrist to check the time. But then, in Vietnam he'd once spent ten days' solitary confinement standing upright in a bamboo cage with water up to his chin.

Something he suspected Arnie had never experienced.

33

ZERIMSKI SHOOK HANDS WARMLY with everyone he was introduced to, and even laughed at John Kent Cooke's jokes. He remembered the names of all the guests, and answered every question that was put to him with a smile. 'What the Americans call a charm offensive,' Titov had told him: it would only add to the horror of what he had planned for them that evening.

He could already hear the guests telling the press, 'He couldn't have been more relaxed and at ease, especially with the President, whom he kept referring to as "my dear and close friend Tom".' Lawrence, the guests would recall, did not show quite the same degree of warmth, and was slightly frosty towards his Russian visitor.

After the introductions had been completed, John Kent Cooke banged on a table with a spoon. 'I'm sorry to interrupt such a pleasant occasion,' he began, 'but time is marching on, and this is probably going to be the only opportunity I have in my life to brief two Presidents at once.' A little laughter broke out. 'So here goes.' He put on a pair of glasses and began reading from a sheet of paper handed to him by his public affairs assistant.

'At eleven twenty I will accompany both Presidents to the south entrance of the stadium, and at eleven thirty-six I will lead them out onto the field.' He looked up. 'I have arranged for the welcome to be deafening,' he said with a smile. Rita laughed just a little too loudly.

'When we reach the centre of the field, I will introduce the

Presidents to the two team captains, and they in turn will introduce them to their co-captains and the coaches. Then the Presidents will be introduced to the match officials.

'At eleven forty, everyone will turn and face the west stand, where the Redskins band will play the Russian national anthem, followed after a short pause by "The Star-Spangled Banner".

'At precisely eleven forty-eight our honoured guest President Zerimski will flip a silver dollar. I shall then accompany both gentlemen off the field and bring them back here, where I hope everyone will enjoy watching the Redskins defeat the Packers.'

Both Presidents laughed.

Cooke looked up at his guests, smiling with relief that the first part of his ordeal was over, and asked, 'Any questions?'

'Yes, John, I have a question,' said Zerimski. 'You didn't explain why I have to flip the coin.'

'So that the captain who correctly guesses whether it's heads or tails can choose which team kicks off.'

'What an amusing idea,' said Zerimski.

◄○►

As the minutes slipped by, Connor checked his watch more and more frequently. He didn't want to be inside the JumboTron for any longer than necessary, but he needed time to familiarise himself with a rifle he hadn't used for some years.

He checked his watch again. *Eleven ten.* He'd wait for another seven minutes. However impatient you become, never go early – it only adds to the risk.

Eleven twelve. He thought about Chris Jackson, and the sacrifice he had made just to give him this one chance.

Eleven fourteen. He thought about Joan, and the cruel and unnecessary death Gutenburg had ordered for no reason other than that she had been his secretary.

Eleven fifteen. He thought about Maggie and Tara. If he managed to pull this off, it might just give them a chance to live in peace. Either way, he doubted if he would ever see them again.

Eleven seventeen. Connor slid open the trapdoor and eased

himself slowly out of the confined space. He gathered his strength for a moment before swinging his legs over the girder and gripping it firmly with his thighs. Again, he didn't look down as he began the slow forty-two-foot crawl back to the walkway.

Once he had reached the safety of the ledge, he pulled himself up onto the walkway. He held onto the rail for a few moments, steadied himself, and began a short series of stretching exercises.

Eleven twenty-seven. He breathed deeply as he went over his plan for the final time, then walked quickly towards the JumboTron, pausing only to pick up the empty Coke can he had left on the step.

He banged loudly on the door. Without waiting for a response, he opened it, marched in and shouted above the noise of the ventilation unit, 'It's only me.'

Arnie peered down from the ledge above, his right hand moving towards the trigger of his Armalite. 'Beat it!' he said. 'I told you not to come back till the Presidents were off the field. You're lucky I didn't put a bullet through you.'

'Sorry,' said Connor. 'It's just that I noticed how hot it gets in here, so I brought you another Coke.'

He passed the empty can up, and Arnie bent down to take it with his free hand. As his fingers touched the rim of the can, Connor let go of it, grabbed him by the wrist and, with all the strength he could muster, pulled him down from the ledge.

Arnie let out a terrible scream as he came crashing over, landing head first on the galvanised walkway, his rifle skidding away across it.

Connor swung round and leapt on his adversary before he had a chance to get up. As Arnie raised his head, Connor landed a straight left to the chin that stunned him for a moment, then grabbed for the pair of handcuffs hanging from his belt. He only just caught sight of the knee flying towards his crotch, but deftly moved to his left and managed to avoid its full impact. As Arnie tried to rise to his feet, Connor landed another punch, this time full on his nose. Connor heard the break, and as blood began to flow down his face, Arnie's legs buckled and he sank to the ground. Connor sprang on him again, and as Arnie tried to get up he delivered a blow to his right shoulder that caused him to go into spasms. This time when he collapsed onto the walkway he finally lay still.

Connor tore off his long white coat, his shirt, tie, trousers, socks and cap. He threw them all in a pile in the corner, then unlocked Arnie's handcuffs and quickly stripped him of his uniform. As he put it on he found that the shoes were at least two sizes too small, and the trousers a couple of inches too short. He had no choice but to pull up his socks and stick with his trainers, which were at least black. He didn't think that in the mayhem he was about to cause anyone would recall that they had seen a Secret Service agent who wasn't wearing regulation shoes.

Connor retrieved his tie from the pile of clothes in the corner and bound Arnie's ankles tightly together. He then lifted up the unconscious man and held him against the wall, placed his arms around a steel beam which ran across the width of the Jumbo-Tron, and clamped the handcuffs on his wrists. Finally he took a handkerchief out of his pocket, rolled it up into a ball and forced it into Arnie's mouth. The poor bastard was going to be sore for several days. It wouldn't be much compensation that he would probably lose those extra pounds the SAIC had berated him about.

'Nothing personal,' said Connor. He placed Arnie's cap and dark glasses by the door, and picked up his rifle: as he'd thought, an M-16. It wouldn't have been his first choice, but it could do the job. He quickly climbed the steps to the second-floor landing where Arnie had been sitting, picked up his binoculars and, through the gap between the ad panel and the video screen, scanned the crowd below.

Eleven thirty-two. It had been three minutes and thirty-eight seconds since Connor had entered the JumboTron. He'd allowed four minutes for the take-over. He started breathing deeply and evenly.

Suddenly he heard a voice behind him.

'Hercules 3.'

At first he couldn't work out where the sound was coming from, but then he remembered the small two-way radio attached to Arnie's belt. He snatched it off. 'Hercules 3, go ahead.'

'Thought we'd lost you there for a moment, Arnie,' said the SAIC. 'Is everything OK?'

'Yep,' said Connor. 'Just needed to take a leak, and thought I'd better not do it over the crowd.'

'Affirmative,' said Braithwaite, breaking into a laugh. 'Keep scanning your section. It won't be long before Red Light and Waterfall come out on the field.'

'Will do,' said Connor, in an accent his mother would have chastised him for. The line went dead.

Eleven thirty-four. He looked around the stadium. Only a few of the red and yellow seats remained unoccupied. He tried not to be distracted by the scantily-clad Redskinettes kicking their legs high in the air directly below him.

A roar went up from the stands as the teams emerged from the tunnels at the south end of the stadium. They jogged slowly towards the centre of the field, as the crowd began to sing 'Hail to the Redskins'.

Connor raised Arnie's binoculars to his eyes and focused on the lighting towers high above the stadium. Almost all the agents were now scanning the crowd below, looking for any suggestion of trouble. None of them was showing any interest in the one location it was actually going to come from. Connor's gaze settled on young Brad, who was peering down into the north stand, checking it row by row. The boy looked as if this was the nearest he'd been to heaven.

Connor swung round and lined the binoculars up on the fifty-yard line. The two captains were now facing each other.

Eleven thirty-six. Another roar went up as John Kent Cooke proudly led the two Presidents out onto the field, accompanied by a dozen agents who were almost as big as the players. One look and Connor could tell that Zerimski and Lawrence were both wearing bulletproof vests.

He would have liked to line up his rifle on Zerimski and focus the mil dots on his head there and then, but he couldn't risk being spotted by one of the sharpshooters on the lighting towers, all of whom held their rifles in the crooks of their arms. He knew that they'd been trained to aim and fire in under three seconds.

As the Presidents were introduced to the players, Connor turned his attention to the Redskins flag which was fluttering in the breeze above the western end of the stadium. He cracked the rifle open to find, as he'd expected, that it was in 'gun-box' condition – fully loaded, off-safe, off-cocked. He chambered the first round and slammed the breech shut. The noise acted on him like the crack of a starting pistol, and he suddenly felt his heart rate almost double.

Eleven forty-one. The two Presidents were now chatting with the match officials. Through the binoculars, Connor could see John Kent Cooke nervously checking his watch. He leaned across and whispered something into Lawrence's ear. The American President nodded, touched Zerimski's elbow and guided him to a space between the two teams. There were two little white circles on the grass, with a bear painted inside one and an eagle inside the other, so the two leaders would know exactly where to stand.

'Ladies and gentlemen,' said a voice over the loudspeaker. 'Will you please stand for the national anthem of the Russian Republic.'

There was a clattering of seats as the crowd rose from their places, many of them removing their Redskins caps as they turned to face the band and choir at the western end of the field. The bandleader raised his baton, paused, then suddenly lowered it with gusto. The crowd listened restlessly to a tune few of them had ever heard before.

Although Connor had stood through the Russian national anthem many times in the past, he had found that few bands outside the country knew either at what tempo it should be played or how many verses ought to be included. So he had decided to wait for 'The Star-Spangled Banner' before he took his one chance.

When the Russian anthem came to an end, the players began

to stretch and jog on the spot in an attempt to calm their nerves. Connor waited for the bandleader to raise his baton once more, which would be his cue to line up Zerimski in his sights. He glanced at the flagpole on the far side of the stadium: the Redskins banner was now hanging limp, indicating that there was virtually no wind.

The bandmaster raised his baton a second time. Connor placed the rifle through the gap between the triangular ad panel and the video screen, using the wooden frame as a rest. He swept the telescopic sight across the field, then focused on the back of Zerimski's head, lining up the mil dots until it completely filled the centre of the rifle's sights.

The opening bars of the American anthem struck up, and both Presidents visibly stiffened. Connor breathed out. Three . . . two . . . one. He gently squeezed the trigger just as Tom Lawrence's right arm swung across his chest, his hand coming to rest over his heart. Distracted by the sudden movement, Zerimski glanced to his left, and the bullet flew harmlessly past his right ear. Seventy-eight thousand out-of-tune voices ensured that no one heard the soft thud as the inch of metal embedded itself in the grass beyond the fifty-yard line.

Brad, lying flat on his stomach on the lighting platform high above the executive suite stared intently down at the crowd through a pair of binoculars. His eyes settled on the JumboTron. The vast screen was dominated by a larger than life President Lawrence, hand on heart, lustily singing the national anthem.

Brad's glasses swept on. Suddenly he jerked them back. He thought he'd seen something in the gap between the triangular ad panel and the screen. He double-checked . . . it was the barrel of a rifle, pointing towards the centre of the field from the gap where he had earlier seen Arnie peering through his binoculars. He touched the fine focus and stared at a face he'd seen earlier that day. He didn't hesitate.

'Cover and evacuate. Gun.'

Brad spoke with such urgency and authority that Braithwaite and two of his counter-snipers instantly swung their binoculars round to the JumboTron. Within moments they had focused on Connor lining up his second shot.

'Relax,' Connor was murmuring to himself. 'Don't rush. You've got plenty of time.' Zerimski's head again filled the scope. Connor lined up the mil dots and breathed out again. Three . . . two . . .

Braithwaite's bullet hammered into his left shoulder, knocking him backwards. A second bullet whistled through the gap where his head had been an instant before.

The national anthem came to an end.

Twenty-eight years of training had prepared Connor for this moment. Everything in his body screamed out to him to make good his escape. He immediately began to carry out plan A, trying to ignore the excruciating pain in his shoulder. He struggled to the door, switched off the light and clambered out onto the walkway. He tried to run to the far door that led out onto the concourse, but found he needed every ounce of energy just to keep moving. Forty seconds later, just as the two Presidents were being escorted from the field, he reached the door. He heard a roar from the crowd as the Redskins prepared to kick off.

Connor unlocked the door, staggered to the service elevator and jabbed the button several times. He could hear the little engine whirr into action as it began its slow progress towards the seventh level. His eyes were darting right and left, searching for the slightest sign of danger. The pain in his shoulder was becoming more and more intense, but he knew there was nothing he could do about it. The first places every law enforcement agency would check were the local hospitals. He stuck his head into the shaft, and watched the top of the elevator heading towards him. It was about fifteen seconds away. But then it came to a sudden halt. Someone must be loading or unloading at the executive level.

Connor's instinctive reaction was to fall back on his contingency plan, something he had never had to do in the past. He knew he couldn't hang around – if he waited for more than a few more seconds, someone would spot him.

He moved as quickly as he could back towards the door that led to the JumboTron. The service elevator resumed its journey. A tray of sandwiches, a slice of Black Forest cake and the Coke that Arnie had been looking forward to appeared a few seconds later.

Connor slipped back through the door marked 'Private', leaving it unlocked. He had to summon up every ounce of willpower in his body to cover the seventy yards along the walkway, but he knew that agents from the Protective Intelligence Division mobile team would be swarming through that door within moments.

Twenty-four seconds later, Connor reached the massive girder that supported the video screen. He gripped the rail with his right hand and eased himself over the edge of the walkway and onto the ledge just as the door to the corridor swung open. He slipped under the walkway and heard two sets of feet run towards him, pass above him and stop outside the door to the JumboTron itself. Through a gap in the walkway he could see an officer clasping a hand gun pushing the door open. Without stepping inside, he fumbled for the light switch.

Connor waited until the lights went on and the two officers had disappeared inside the JumboTron before he began to crawl along the forty-two-foot girder for the third time that day. But now he could only hold on with his right arm, which meant that his progress was even slower. At the same time he had to be sure that the blood dripping from his left shoulder fell the 170 feet to the ground and not onto the girder for all to see.

When the leading Secret Service agent entered the JumboTron, the first thing he saw was Arnie handcuffed to the steel beam. He moved slowly towards him, constantly checking in every direction until he was standing by his side. His partner covered him while he unlocked Arnie's handcuffs and gently lowered him to the ground, then removed the handkerchief from his mouth and checked his pulse. He was alive.

Arnie raised his eyes to the ceiling, but didn't speak. The first Secret Service man immediately began to mount the steps to the second level, while the other officer covered him. The first man edged cautiously along the ledge behind the vast screen. A deafening roar went up around the stadium as the Redskins scored a touchdown, but he ignored it. Once he had reached the far wall, he turned back and nodded. The second officer began to climb to the top level, where he carried out a similar reconnaissance.

Both officers were back on the lower level, double-checking every possible hiding place, when a message came over the first agent's radio.

'Hercules 7.'

'Hercules 7, go ahead.'

'Any sign of him?' asked Braithwaite.

'There's nobody here except Arnie, who was cuffed to a beam in his underwear. Both doors were unlocked, and there's a trickle of blood all the way to the concourse, so you definitely winged him. He has to be out there somewhere. He's wearing Arnie's uniform, so he shouldn't be too hard to spot.'

'Don't count on it,' said Braithwaite. 'If it's who I think it is, he could be right under your nose.'

34

THREE MEN SAT in the Oval Office listening to the tape. Two were in evening dress, the third in uniform.

'How did you find it?' asked Lawrence.

'It was among the pile of clothes Fitzgerald left in the Jumbo-Tron,' said Special Agent in Charge Braithwaite. 'In the back pocket of his jeans.'

'How many people have heard it?' asked Lloyd, trying not to sound anxious.

'Just the three of us in this room, sir,' said Braithwaite. 'As soon as I'd listened to it, I contacted you immediately. I haven't even briefed my boss.'

'I'm grateful for that, Bill,' said the President. 'But what about those who witnessed the incident in the stadium?'

'Apart from myself, only five other people were aware that anything happened, and you can be assured of their discretion,' said Braithwaite. 'Four of them have been on my personal staff for ten years or more, and between them they know enough secrets to sink the last four Presidents, not to mention half of Congress.'

'Did anyone actually see Fitzgerald?' asked Lloyd.

'No, sir. The two agents who searched the JumboTron immediately after the incident found no sign of him except a pile of clothes, a lot of blood and one of my men handcuffed to a beam. After I'd played the tape, I gave an order that there was to be no written or verbal report concerning the incident.'

'What about the man who was hanging from the beam?' asked the President.

'He just lost his footing and slipped off the ledge. I've put him on sick leave for a month.'

'You mentioned a fifth person,' said Lloyd.

'Yes, sir, a young trainee who was up on the lighting tower with us.'

'How can you be sure he won't talk?' asked Lloyd.

'His application to join the Secret Service is on my desk as we speak,' said Braithwaite. 'I think he's hoping to be assigned to my division as soon as he's completed his training.'

The President smiled. 'And the bullet?'

'I made a hell of a mess digging it out of the field after the stadium had been cleared,' said Braithwaite, passing a spent piece of flat metal across to the President.

Lawrence rose from his desk, turned round and stared out of the bay window. Dusk had fallen over the Capitol. He looked across the lawn while he thought about what he was going to say.

'It's important that you realise one thing, Bill,' he said eventually. 'It certainly sounds like my voice on that tape, but I have never suggested to anyone, at any time, that Zerimski or any other person should be the target of an assassin.'

'I accept that without question, Mr President, or I wouldn't be here now. But I must be equally candid with you. If anyone in the Secret Service had realised that it was Fitzgerald in the JumboTron, they would probably have helped him escape.'

'What kind of man can inspire such loyalty?' asked Lawrence.

'In your world, I suspect it's Abraham Lincoln,' said Braithwaite. 'In ours it's Connor Fitzgerald.'

'I would have liked to meet him.'

'That's going to be difficult, sir. Even if he's still alive, he seems to have disappeared off the face of the earth. I wouldn't want my career to depend on finding him.'

'Mr President,' interrupted Lloyd, 'you're already running seven minutes late for the dinner at the Russian Embassy.'

Lawrence smiled and shook hands with Braithwaite. 'Another

good man I can't tell the American people about,' he said with a wry smile. 'I suppose you'll be on duty again tonight.'

'Yes, sir, I've been detailed to cover the whole of President Zerimski's visit.'

'I may see you later then, Bill. If you pick up any new information about Fitzgerald, I want to hear about it immediately.'

'Of course, sir,' said Braithwaite, turning to leave.

A few minutes later, Lawrence and Lloyd walked in silence to the south portico, where nine limousines with their engines running stood in line. As soon as the President was in the back of the sixth car, he turned to his Chief of Staff and asked, 'Where do you think he is, Andy?'

'I have no idea, sir. But if I did, I'd probably sign up with Braithwaite's team and help him escape.'

'Why can't we have someone like that as Director of the CIA?'

'We might have had, if Jackson had lived.'

Lawrence turned to look out of the window. Something had been nagging at him ever since he had left the stadium, but when the motorcycle escort drove through the gates of the Russian Embassy he was still no nearer to dragging it up from the recesses of his mind.

'What's he looking so angry about?' said Lawrence, spotting Zerimski pacing up and down outside the Embassy.

Lloyd glanced at his watch. 'You're seventeen minutes late, sir.'

'That's hardly a big deal, after what we've been through. Frankly, the damn man's lucky to be alive.'

'I don't think that's something you can use as an excuse, sir.'

The motorcade drew up at the feet of the Russian President. Lawrence stepped out of the car and said, 'Hi, Victor. Sorry we're a couple of minutes late.'

Zerimski made no attempt to hide his displeasure. After a cool handshake, he led his guest of honour silently into the Embassy and up the steps to the packed reception in the Green Room without uttering a word. Then he made a perfunctory excuse and dumped the President of the United States on the Egyptian Ambassador.

Lawrence's eyes circled the room as the Ambassador tried to interest him in an exhibition of Egyptian artefacts that had recently opened at the Smithsonian.

'Yes, I've been trying to find a gap in my schedule to see it,' said the President, on autopilot. 'Everybody who's been tells me it's quite magnificent.' The Egyptian Ambassador beamed, as Lawrence spotted the man he was looking for. It took him three Ambassadors, two wives and the political correspondent of *Pravda* before he managed to reach Harry Nourse without causing undue suspicion.

'Good evening, Mr President,' said the Attorney-General. 'You must have been pleased with the result of the game this afternoon.'

'Sure was, Harry,' said Lawrence expansively. 'Always said the Packers could whip the Redskins any time, any place.' He lowered his voice: 'I want to see you in my office at midnight tonight. I need your advice on a legal matter.'

'Of course, sir,' said the Attorney-General quietly.

'Rita,' said the President, turning to his right, 'it was such fun being with you this afternoon.'

Mrs Cooke returned the smile as a gong sounded in the background and a butler announced that dinner was about to be served. The chatter subsided, and the guests made their way into the ballroom.

Lawrence had been placed between Mrs Pietrovski, the Ambassador's wife, and Yuri Olgivic, the newly appointed head of the Russian Trade Delegation. The President soon discovered that Olgivic didn't speak a word of English – another of Zerimski's subtle hints about his attitude to opening up trade between the two nations.

'You must have been pleased with the result of the game this afternoon,' said the Russian Ambassador's wife, as a bowl of borscht was placed in front of the President.

'Sure was,' said Lawrence. 'But I don't think most of the crowd was with me on that one, Olga.'

Mrs Pietrovski laughed.

'Were you able to follow what was going on?' asked Lawrence, picking up his soup spoon.

'Not really,' she replied. 'But I was fortunate enough to be placed next to a Mr Pug Washer, who didn't seem to mind answering the most simple questions I asked him.'

The President dropped his spoon before he'd taken a sip. He looked across the room at Andy Lloyd, and placed a clenched fist under his chin – the sign he always used when he needed to speak to his Chief of Staff urgently.

Lloyd murmured a few words to the woman on his right, then folded his napkin, placed it on the table and walked over to the President's side.

'I need to see Braithwaite immediately,' Lawrence whispered. 'I think I know how to find Fitzgerald.'

Lloyd slipped out of the room without saying a word as the President's soup bowl was whisked away.

Lawrence tried to concentrate on what the Russian Ambassador's wife was saying, but he couldn't get Fitzgerald out of his mind. Something about how much she would miss the States once her husband had retired.

'And when will that be?' asked the President, not at all interested in her reply.

'In about eighteen months,' Mrs Pietrovski replied, as a plate of cold beef was placed in front of the President. He continued the conversation as first one waiter served him some vegetables, and a moment later another brought some potatoes. He picked up his knife and fork just as Lloyd walked back into the room. He was at the President's side a moment later.

'Braithwaite's waiting for you in the back of "Stagecoach".'

'I hope there isn't a problem,' said Mrs Pietrovski as Lawrence began folding his napkin.

'Nothing important, Olga,' Lawrence assured her. 'They just can't find my speech. But don't worry, I know exactly where it is.' He rose from his place, and Zerimski followed his every step as he left the room.

Lawrence walked out of the ballroom, down the wooden

staircase and through the front door of the Embassy before jogging down the steps and climbing into the back of the sixth car.

Lloyd and the driver stood by the limousine as a dozen Secret Service agents surrounded it, scanning in every direction.

'Bill, if Fitzgerald is still in the stadium, there's one man who'll know where he is. Find Pug Washer, and my bet is you'll find Fitzgerald.'

A few moments later the President opened the car door.

'OK, Andy,' he said, 'let's get back before they discover what we're up to.'

'What *are* we up to?' asked Lloyd as he chased the President up the stairs.

'I'll tell you later,' said Lawrence, striding into the ballroom.

'But sir,' said Lloyd, 'you'll still need . . .'

'Not now,' said Lawrence, as he took his seat next to the Ambassador's wife and smiled apologetically.

'Did you manage to find it?' she asked.

'Find what?'

'Your speech,' said Mrs Pietrovski, as Lloyd placed a file on the table between them.

'Of course,' said Lawrence, tapping the file. 'By the way, Olga, how's that daughter of yours? Natasha, isn't it? Is she still studying Fra Angelico in Florence?' He picked up his knife and fork.

The President glanced in Zerimski's direction as the waiters reappeared to remove the plates. He put his knife and fork back down, settling for a stale bread roll with a pat of butter and finding out what Natasha Pietrovski had been up to during her junior year in Florence. He couldn't help noticing that the Russian President appeared nervous, almost on edge, as the time drew nearer for him to make his speech. He immediately assumed that Zerimski was about to deliver another unexpected bombshell. The thought put him off his raspberry soufflé.

When Zerimski eventually rose to address his guests, even his most ardent admirers would have been hard pressed to describe his efforts as anything other than pedestrian. Some of those who watched him particularly closely wondered why he appeared to be directing so many of his remarks to the massive statue of Lenin in the gallery above the ballroom. Lawrence thought it must have been put there recently, as he didn't remember seeing it at Boris's farewell dinner.

He kept waiting for Zerimski to reinforce his message to Congress the previous day, but he said nothing controversial. To Lawrence's relief he stuck to the bland script that had been sent to the White House that afternoon. He glanced down at his own speech, which he should have gone over with Andy in the car. His Chief of Staff had scribbled a few suggestions in the margins, but there wasn't a witty phrase or memorable paragraph from page one to page seven. But then, Andy had also had a busy day.

'Let me end by thanking the American people for the generous hospitality and warm welcome I have experienced everywhere I have been during my visit to your great country, in particular from your President, Tom Lawrence.'

The applause that greeted this statement was so loud and prolonged that Lawrence looked up from his notes. Zerimski was once again standing motionless, staring up at the statue of Lenin. He waited until the applause had ended before he sat down. He didn't look at all pleased, which surprised Lawrence, as in his opinion the speech's reception had been far more generous than it deserved.

Lawrence rose to reply. His speech was received with courteous interest, but hardly with enthusiasm. He concluded with the words, 'Let us hope, Victor, that this will be the first of many visits you make to the United States. On behalf of all your guests, I wish you a safe flight home tomorrow.' Lawrence reflected that two lies in one sentence were a bit much, even for a politician, and wished he had had time to read the line before delivering it. He sat down to respectful applause, but it was nothing compared with the ovation Zerimski had received for an equally banal offering.

Once the coffee had been served, Zerimski rose from his place and walked over to the double doors at the far side of the room. He soon began saying 'Goodnight,' in a voice that carried across the room, making it abundantly clear that he wanted his guests off the premises as quickly as possible.

A few minutes after ten had struck on several clocks around the Embassy, Lawrence rose and began moving slowly in the direction of his host. But, like Caesar in the Capitol, he found he was continually stopped by different citizens wanting to touch the hem of the emperor's clothes. When he eventually reached the door, Zerimski gave him a curt nod before accompanying him down the stairs to the first floor. As Zerimski didn't speak, Lawrence took a long look at the Nzizvestni statue of Christ on the Cross that was still in its place on the first landing. Now that Lenin was back, he was surprised that Jesus had survived. At the foot of the stone steps he turned to wave to his host, but Zerimski had already disappeared back inside the Embassy. If he had taken the trouble to accompany Lawrence beyond the front door, he would have seen the SAIC waiting for him as he climbed into the back of his limousine.

Braithwaite didn't speak until the door had been closed.

'You were right, sir,' he said as they passed through the Embassy gates.

The first person Zerimski saw as he walked back into the Embassy was the Ambassador. His Excellency smiled hopefully.

'Is Romanov still in the building?' Zerimski bellowed, unable to hide his anger for a moment longer.

'Yes, Mr President,' the Ambassador said, chasing after his leader. 'He's been . . .'

'Bring him to me immediately.'

'Where will I find you?'

'In what used to be your study.'

Pietrovski scurried away in the opposite direction.

Zerimski marched down the long marble corridor, hardly breaking his stride as he shoved open the door of the Ambassador's study as if he was thumping a punchbag. The first thing he saw was the rifle, still lying on the desk. He sat down in the large leather chair normally occupied by the Ambassador.

While he waited impatiently for them to join him, he picked up the rifle and began to study it more closely. He looked down the barrel and saw that the single bullet was still in place. As he held it up to his shoulder he could feel its perfect balance, and he understood for the first time why Fitzgerald had been willing to fly halfway across America to find its twin.

It was then that he saw the firing pin had been replaced.

Zerimski could hear the two men hurrying down the marble corridor. Just before they reached the study, he lowered the rifle onto his lap.

They almost ran into the room. Zerimski pointed unceremoniously to the two seats on the other side of the desk.

'Where was Fitzgerald?' he demanded before Romanov had even sat down. 'You assured me in this room that he would be here by four o'clock this afternoon. "Nothing can go wrong," you boasted. "He's agreed to my plan." Your exact words.'

'That was our agreement when I spoke to him just after midnight, Mr President,' said Romanov.

'So what happened between midnight and four o'clock?'

'While my men were escorting him into the city early this morning, the driver was forced to stop at a set of traffic lights. Fitzgerald leaped out of the car, ran to the other side of the road and jumped into a passing taxi. We pursued it all the way to Dulles Airport, only to find when we caught up with it outside the terminal that Fitzgerald wasn't inside.'

'The truth is that you allowed him to escape,' said Zerimski. 'Isn't that what really happened?'

Romanov bowed his head and said nothing.

The President's voice lowered to a whisper. 'I understand you have a code in the Mafya,' he said, clicking the breech of the rifle shut, 'for those who fail to carry out contracts.'

Romanov looked up in horror as Zerimski raised the gun until it was pointing at the centre of his chest.

'Yes or no?' said Zerimski quietly.

Romanov nodded. Zerimski smiled at the man who had accepted the judgement of his own court, and gently squeezed the trigger. The boat-tailed bullet tore into Romanov's chest about an inch below the heart. The power of its impact hurled his lithe body back against the wall, where it remained for a second or two before slithering down onto the carpet. Fragments of muscle and bone were scattered in every direction. The walls, the carpet, the Ambassador's dress suit and white pleated shirt were drenched with blood.

Zerimski swung slowly round until he was facing his former representative in Washington. 'No, no!' cried Pietrovski, falling on his knees. 'I'll resign, I'll resign.'

Zerimski squeezed the trigger a second time. When he heard the click, he remembered that there had been only one bullet in the breech. He rose from his seat, a look of disappointment on his face.

'You'll have to send that suit to the cleaners,' he said, as if the Ambassador had done no more than spill some egg yolk on his sleeve. The President placed the rifle back on the desk. 'I accept your resignation. But before you clear your office, see that what's left of Romanov's body is patched together and sent back to St Petersburg.' He began walking towards the door. 'Make it quick – I'd like to be there when he's buried with his father.'

Pietrovski, still on his knees, didn't reply. He had been sick, and was too frightened to open his mouth.

As Zerimski reached the door, he turned back to face the cowering diplomat. 'In the circumstances, it might be wise to arrange for the body to be sent back in the diplomatic pouch.'

35

THE SNOW WAS FALLING HEAVILY as Zerimski climbed the steps to the waiting Ilyushin 62, creating a thick white carpet around its wheels.

Tom Lawrence was standing on the tarmac, wearing a long black topcoat. An aide held a large umbrella above his head.

Zerimski disappeared through the door without even bothering to turn and give the traditional wave for the cameras. Any suggestion of this being the time of year for good will to all men was obviously lost on him.

The State Department had already issued a press release. It talked in broad terms of the success of the new Russian President's four-day visit, significant steps taken by both countries, and the hope for further cooperation at some time in the future. 'Useful and constructive' were the words Larry Harrington had settled on before the morning press conference, and, as an afterthought, 'a step forward'. The journalists who had just witnessed Zerimski's departure would translate Harrington's sentiments as 'useless and destructive, and without doubt a step backwards'.

Within moments of its grey door slamming shut the Ilyushin lurched forward, almost as if, like its master, it couldn't wait to get away.

Lawrence was the first to turn his back on the departing aircraft as it lumbered towards the runway. He walked quickly over to his waiting helicopter, where he found Andy Lloyd, a phone already pressed against his ear. Once the rotor blades began to turn, Lloyd quickly concluded his call. As Marine One lifted off, he leaned across and briefed the President on the outcome of the emergency operation that had taken place early that morning at the Walter Reed Hospital. Lawrence nodded as his Chief of Staff outlined the course of action Agent Braithwaite was recommending. 'I'll ring Mrs Fitzgerald personally,' he said.

The two men spent the rest of the short journey preparing for the meeting that was about to take place in the Oval Office. The President's helicopter landed on the South Lawn, and neither of them spoke as they made their way towards the White House. Lawrence's secretary was waiting anxiously by the door.

'Good morning, Ruth,' the President said for the third time that day. Both of them had been up for most of the night.

At midnight the Attorney-General had arrived unannounced and told Ruth Preston that he had been summoned to attend a meeting with the President. It wasn't in his diary. At two a.m. the President, Mr Lloyd and the Attorney-General had left for the Walter Reed Hospital – but again, there was no mention of the visit in the diary, or of the name of the patient they would be seeing. They returned an hour later and spent another ninety minutes in the Oval Office, the President having left instructions that they were not to be disturbed. When Ruth arrived back at the White House at ten past eight that morning, the President was already on his way to Andrews air base to say farewell to Zerimski.

Although he was wearing a different suit, shirt and tie from when she had last seen him, Ruth wondered if her boss had gone to bed at all that night.

'What's next, Ruth?' he asked, knowing only too well.

'Your ten o'clock appointment has been waiting in the lobby for the past forty minutes.'

'Have they? Then you'd better send them in.'

The President walked into the Oval Office, opened a drawer in his desk and removed two sheets of paper and a cassette tape. He placed the paper on the blotter in front of him and inserted the cassette in the recorder on his desk. Andy Lloyd came in from his office, carrying two files under his arm. He took his usual seat by the side of the President.

'Have you got the affidavits?' asked Lawrence.

'Yes, sir,' Lloyd replied.

There was a knock on the door. Ruth opened it and announced, 'The Director and Deputy Director of the CIA.'

'Good morning, Mr President,' said Helen Dexter brightly, as she entered the Oval Office with her Deputy a pace behind. She too had a file under her arm.

Lawrence did not return her salutation.

'You'll be relieved to know,' continued Dexter, as she took a seat in one of the two vacant chairs opposite the President, 'that I was able to deal with that problem we feared might arise during the visit of the Russian President. In fact, we have every reason to believe that the person in question no longer represents a threat to this country.'

'Could that possibly be the same person I had a chat with on the phone a few weeks ago?' asked Lawrence, leaning back in his chair.

'I'm not quite sure I understand you, Mr President,' said Dexter.

'Then allow me to enlighten you,' said Lawrence. He leaned forward and pressed the 'Play' button of the tape recorder on his desk.

'I felt I had to call and let you know just how important I consider this assignment to be. Because I have no doubt that you're the right person to carry it out. So I hope you will agree to take on the responsibility.'

'I appreciate your confidence in me, Mr President, and I'm grateful to you for taking the time to phone personally . . .'

Lawrence pressed the 'Stop' button.

'No doubt you have a simple explanation as to how and why this conversation took place,' he said.

'I'm not sure I fully understand you, Mr President. The Agency is not privy to your personal telephone conversations.'

'That may or may not be true,' said the President. 'But that particular conversation, as you well know, did not emanate from this office.'

'Are you accusing the Agency of . . .'

'I'm not accusing the Agency of anything. The accusation is levelled at you personally.'

'Mr President, if this is your idea of a joke . . .'

'Do I look as if I'm laughing?' asked the President, before hitting the 'Play' button again.

I felt it was the least I could do in the circumstances.'

'Thank you, Mr President. Although Mr Gutenburg assured me of your involvement, and the Director herself called later that afternoon to confirm it, as you know, I still felt unable to take on the assignment unless I was certain that the order had come directly from you.'

The President leaned forward and once again pressed the 'Stop' button.

'There's more, if you want to hear it.'

'I can assure you,' said Dexter, 'that the operation the agent in question was referring to was nothing more than a routine exercise.'

'Are you asking me to believe that the assassination of the Russian President is now considered by the CIA to be nothing more than a routine exercise?' said Lawrence in disbelief.

'It was never our intention that Zerimski should be killed,' said Dexter sharply.

'Only that an innocent man would hang for it,' the President retorted. A long silence followed before he added, 'And thus remove any proof that it was also you who ordered the assassination of Ricardo Guzman in Colombia.'

'Mr President, I can assure you that the CIA had nothing to do with . . .'

'That's not what Connor Fitzgerald told us earlier this morning,' said Lawrence.

Dexter was silent.

'Perhaps you'd care to read the affidavit he signed in the presence of the Attorney-General.'

Andy Lloyd opened the first of his two files and passed Dexter and Gutenburg copies of an affidavit signed by Connor Fitzgerald and witnessed by the Attorney-General. As the two of them began reading the statement, the President couldn't help noticing that Gutenburg was sweating slightly.

'Having taken advice from the Attorney-General, I have authorised the SAIC to arrest you both on a charge of treason. If you are found guilty, I am advised that there can only be one sentence.'

Dexter remained tight-lipped. Her Deputy was now visibly shaking. Lawrence turned to him.

'Of course it's possible, Nick, that you were unaware that the Director hadn't been given the necessary executive authority to issue such an order.'

'That is absolutely correct, sir,' Gutenburg blurted out. 'In fact she led me to believe that the instruction to assassinate Guzman had come directly from the White House.'

'I thought you'd say that, Nick,' said the President. 'And if you feel able to sign this document' – he pushed a sheet of paper across the desk – 'the Attorney-General has indicated to me that the death sentence would be commuted to life imprisonment.'

'Whatever it is, don't sign it,' ordered Dexter.

Gutenburg hesitated for a moment, then removed a pen from his pocket and signed his name between the two pencilled crosses below his one-sentence resignation as Deputy Director of the CIA, effective nine a.m. that day.

Dexter glared at him with undisguised contempt. 'If you'd refused to resign, they wouldn't have had the nerve to go through with it. Men are so spineless.' She turned back to face the President, who was pushing a second sheet of paper across the desk, and glanced down to read her own one-sentence resignation as Director of the CIA, also effective nine a.m. that day. She looked up at Lawrence and said defiantly, 'I won't be signing anything, Mr President. You ought to have worked out by now that I don't frighten that easily.'

'Well, Helen, if you feel unable to take the same honourable course of action as Nick,' said Lawrence, 'when you leave this room you'll find two Secret Service agents on the other side of the door, with instructions to arrest you.'

'You can't bluff me, Lawrence,' said Dexter, rising from her chair.

'Mr Gutenburg,' said Lloyd, as she began walking towards the door, leaving the unsigned sheet of paper on the desk, 'I consider life imprisonment, with no hope of parole, too high a price to pay in the circumstances. Especially if you were being set up, and didn't even know what was going on.'

Gutenburg nodded as Dexter reached the door.

'I would have thought a sentence of six, perhaps seven years at the most, would be more appropriate in your case. And with a little assistance from the White House, you need only end up serving three to four.'

Dexter stopped dead in her tracks.

'But that would of course mean your agreeing to . . .'

'I'll agree to anything. Anything,' Gutenburg spluttered.

'. . . to testifying on behalf of the prosecution.'

Gutenburg nodded again, and Lloyd extracted a two-page affidavit from the other file resting on his lap. The former Deputy Director spent only a few moments reading the document before scribbling his signature across the bottom of the second page.

The Director rested a hand on the doorknob, hesitated for some time, then turned and walked slowly back to the desk. She gave her former Deputy one last look of disgust before picking up the pen and scrawling her signature between the pencilled crosses.

'You're a fool, Gutenburg,' she said. 'They would never have risked putting Fitzgerald on the stand. Any half-decent lawyer would have torn him to shreds. And without Fitzgerald, they don't have a case. As I'm sure the Attorney-General has already explained to them.' She turned again to leave the room.

'Helen's quite right,' said Lawrence, retrieving the three

documents and handing them to Lloyd. 'If the case had ever reached the courts, we could never have put Fitzgerald on the stand.'

Dexter stopped in her tracks for a second time, the ink not yet dry on her resignation.

'Sadly,' said the President, 'I have to inform you that Connor Fitzgerald died at seven forty-three this morning.'

BOOK FOUR

THE QUICK AND THE DEAD

36

THE CORTÈGE continued its slow progress over the brow of the hill.

Arlington National Cemetery was packed for a man who had never sought public recognition. The President of the United States stood on one side of the grave, flanked by the White House Chief of Staff and the Attorney-General. Facing them was a woman who hadn't raised her head for the past forty minutes. On her right stood her daughter; on her left her future son-in-law.

The three of them had flown over from Sydney two days after receiving a personal telephone call from the President. The large crowd assembled at the graveside could not have left Maggie Fitzgerald in any doubt how many friends and admirers Connor had left behind.

At a meeting the previous day at the White House, Tom Lawrence had told the widow that Connor's last words had been of his love for her and his daughter. The President went on to say that although he had only met her husband once, he would remember him for the rest of his life. 'This from a man who meets a hundred people a day,' Tara had written in her diary that evening.

A few paces behind the President stood the newly appointed Director of the CIA and a group of men and women who had no intention of reporting to work that day. They had travelled from the four corners of the earth to be there.

A tall, heavily-built man without a hair on his head stood

slightly to one side of the other mourners, weeping uncontrollably. No one present would have believed that the most ruthless gangsters in South Africa would have been delighted to know that Carl Koeter was out of the country, if only for a couple of days.

The FBI and the Secret Service were also present in large numbers. Special Agent William Braithwaite stood at the head of a dozen sharpshooters, any one of whom would have been satisfied to end their careers regarded as the successor to Connor Fitzgerald.

Higher up the slope of the hill, filling the cemetery as far as the eye could see, were relatives from Chicago, academics from Georgetown, bridge players, Irish dancers, poets and people from every walk of life. They stood with their heads bowed in memory of a man they had loved and respected.

The cortège came to a halt on Sheridan Drive, a few yards from the graveside. The eight-man honour guard lifted the coffin from the gun carriage, raised it onto their shoulders and began the slow march towards the grave. The coffin was draped in the American flag, and resting on top were Connor's battle ribbons. The Medal of Honor lay in the centre. When the pallbearers reached the graveside they lowered the coffin gently to the ground, and joined the other mourners.

Father Graham, who had been the Fitzgeralds' family priest for over thirty years, raised his arms in the air.

'My friends,' he began. 'Priests are often called upon to sing the praises of parishioners who have passed away, with whom they were barely acquainted and whose achievements were not always apparent. But this cannot be said of Connor Fitzgerald. As a student, he will be remembered as one of the finest quarterbacks the University of Notre Dame has ever produced. As a soldier, no feeble words of mine could possibly match the citation written by Captain Christopher Jackson, his platoon commander: "A fearless officer in the face of danger, who always placed his men's lives before his own." As a professional he gave almost three decades' service to his country; you only have to look around to see the high regard in which he was held by his peers. But most of all, as a husband to Maggie and a father to Tara, we will remember him. Our hearts go out to both of them.'

Father Graham lowered his voice. 'I was lucky enough to count myself among his friends. I had been looking forward to playing bridge with him again over the Christmas holiday – in fact, I was rather hoping to win back the $10 I lost to him in a rubber just before he went away on his last assignment. Dear God, I would happily give everything I possess just to be able once again to lose a game of bridge to him.

'Sportsman, soldier, professional, lover, father, friend, and for me – although I would never have had the courage to mention it in his presence, simply because he would have laughed at me – hero.

'Buried not far from you, Connor, is another American hero.' The elderly priest raised his head. 'If I were John Fitzgerald Kennedy, I would be proud to be buried in the same cemetery as Connor Fitzgerald.'

The pallbearers stepped forward and lowered the coffin into the grave. Father Graham made the sign of the cross, bent down, picked up a handful of earth and scattered it on the coffin.

'Ashes to ashes, dust to dust,' intoned the priest as a lone Marine bugler played Taps. The honour guard folded the flag from the coffin until it ended as a neat triangle in the hands of the youngest cadet, a boy of eighteen who, like Connor, had been born in Chicago. Normally he would have presented it to the widow with the words, 'Ma'am, on behalf of the President of the United States.' But not today. Today he marched in a different direction. Seven Marines raised their rifles in the air and fired a twenty-one-gun salute as the young cadet stood to attention in front of the President of the United States, and surrendered the flag.

Tom Lawrence received it, walked slowly around to the other side of the grave and stood before the widow. Maggie raised her head and tried to smile as the President presented her with the standard of the nation.

'On behalf of a grateful country, I pass to you the flag of the Republic. You are surrounded by friends who knew your husband well. I only wish I'd had that privilege.' The President bowed his head and returned to the other side of the grave. As the Marine band struck up the national anthem, he placed his right hand over his heart.

No one moved until Maggie had been escorted by Stuart and Tara to the entrance of the cemetery. She stood there for almost an hour, shaking hands with every mourner who had attended the ceremony.

Two men who had remained on the top of the hill throughout the service had flown in from Russia the previous day. They had not come to mourn. They would return to St Petersburg on the evening flight, and report that their services were no longer required.

37

AIR FORCE ONE was surrounded by tanks when the President of the United States landed at Moscow airport.

President Zerimski left us in no doubt that he had little interest in giving Tom Lawrence a photo opportunity for the folks back home. Nor were there the usual 'Welcome to Russia' speeches delivered from a podium on the runway.

As a grim-faced Lawrence descended the aircraft's steps, he was greeted by the sight of Marshal Borodin standing in the turret of a tank.

When the two Presidents eventually met at the Kremlin later this morning, the first item on the agenda was President Zerimski's demand that the NATO forces which patrol Russia's western borders be immediately withdrawn. Following the heavy defeat of his Nuclear, Biological, Chemical and Conventional Arms Reduction Bill in the Senate, and the Ukraine's voluntary return to the Soviet Union, President Lawrence knows that he is not in a position to give an inch on NATO's role in Europe, especially since the newly elected Senator Helen Dexter keeps describing him as 'the red stooge'.

Since Senator Dexter's resignation as Director of the CIA last year, in order to 'more openly oppose the President's misguided foreign policy', there is already talk on the Hill of her becoming the first woman President.

*At this morning's preliminary talks in the Kremlin,
President Zerimski made no pretence of . . .*

Stuart looked up from the front page of the *Sydney Morning
Herald* as Maggie walked into the kitchen, dressed in jeans and
a sweater. They had been living in the same house for over six
months, and he had never seen her with a hair out of place.

'Good morning, Stuart,' she said. 'Anything interesting in the
paper?'

'Zerimski's still flexing his muscles at the slightest opportunity,' Stuart replied. 'And your President is having to put a
brave face on it. At least, that's the view of the Russian correspondent of the *Herald*.'

'Zerimski would drop a nuclear bomb on the White House if
he thought he could get away with it,' said Maggie. 'Isn't there
any brighter news to tell me on a Saturday morning?'

'The Prime Minister has announced the date for the election
of our first President.'

'You're so slow in this country,' said Maggie, filling a bowl
with cornflakes. 'We got rid of the British over two hundred
years ago.'

'It won't take us much longer,' said Stuart with a laugh as his
wife strolled into the room in her dressing gown.

'Good morning,' she said sleepily. Maggie slid off her stool
and gave her a kiss on the cheek.

'You sit there and have these cornflakes while I make you an
omelette. You really mustn't . . .'

'Mother, I'm pregnant, not dying of consumption,' said Tara.
'I'll be just fine with a bowl of cornflakes.'

'I know, it's just that . . .'

'. . . you'll never stop worrying,' said Tara, putting her arms
around her mother's shoulders. 'I'll let you in on a secret. There
is no medical evidence that miscarriages are hereditary; only
fussing mothers. What's the big story this morning?' she asked,
looking across at Stuart.

'My case in the criminal court has made the headlines – on

page sixteen,' he said, pointing to three short paragraphs tucked away in the bottom left-hand corner.

Tara read the report through twice before saying, 'But they don't even mention your name.'

'No. They seem to be more interested in my client at the moment,' admitted Stuart. 'But if I get him off, that could change.'

'I hope you don't get him off,' said Maggie as she broke a second egg. 'I think your client is a little creep, and ought to spend the rest of his life in jail.'

'For stealing $73?' said Stuart in disbelief.

'From a defenceless old woman.'

'But it was the first time.'

'The first time he was caught, I think you mean,' said Maggie.

'You know, Maggie, you would have made a first-class prose-cuting counsel,' said Stuart. 'You should never have agreed to taking a sabbatical this year – you should have enrolled in law school instead. Mind you, I suspect life imprisonment for steal-ing $73 might not go down that big with everyone.'

'You'd be surprised, young man,' retorted Maggie.

There was a thud on the doormat. 'I'll get it,' said Stuart, rising from the table.

'Stuart's right,' said Tara, as her mother placed an omelette in front of her. 'You shouldn't waste your time being an unpaid housekeeper. You're far too good for that.'

'Thank you, my darling,' said Maggie. She returned to the stove and cracked another egg. 'But I enjoy being with you both. I only hope I'm not outstaying my welcome.'

'Of course you're not,' said Tara. 'But it's been over six months since . . .'

'I know, darling, but I still need a little longer before I can face going back to Washington. I'll be fine by the time the fall semester begins.'

'But you don't even accept invitations to things you'd enjoy.'

'Such as?'

'Last week Mr Moore invited you to *Fidelio* at the Opera

House, and you told him you were already going out that evening.'

'To be honest, I can't remember what I was doing,' said Maggie.

'I can. You sat in your room reading *Ulysses*.'

'Tara, Ronnie Moore is a sweet man, and I have no doubt that whatever it is he does at the bank, he does very well. But what he doesn't need is to spend an evening with me being reminded how much I miss your father. And I certainly don't need to spend an evening with him being told how much he adored his late wife, whatever her name was.'

'Elizabeth,' said Stuart, as he returned clutching the morning post. 'Ronnie's rather nice actually.'

'Not you as well,' said Maggie. 'The time has come for you both to stop worrying about my social life.' She placed an even larger omelette in front of Stuart.

'I should have married you, Maggie,' he said with a grin.

'You'd have been far more suitable than most of the men you've been trying to fix me up with,' she said, patting her son-in-law on the head.

Stuart laughed and started sorting out the letters, the bulk of which were for him. He passed a couple over to Tara and three to Maggie, and pushed his own little pile to one side in favour of the sports section of the *Herald*.

Maggie poured herself a second cup of coffee before she turned to her post. As always, she studied the stamps before deciding in which order she would open them. Two of them carried the same portrait of George Washington. The third displayed a colourful picture of a kookaburra. She tore open the Australian letter first. When she had finished reading it, she passed it across the table to Tara, whose smile became broader with each paragraph she read.

'Very flattering,' said Tara, handing the letter to Stuart.

Stuart read it through quickly. 'Yes, very. How will you respond?'

'I'll write back explaining that I'm not in the job market,' said

Maggie. 'But not until I discover which one of you I have to thank for it.' She waved the letter in the air.

'Not guilty,' said Tara.

'*Mea culpa*,' admitted Stuart. He had learned early on that it wasn't worth trying to fool Maggie. She always found you out in the end.

'I saw the job advertised in the *Herald*, and I thought you were ideally qualified for it. Overqualified, if anything.'

'There's a rumour that the Head of Admissions will be retiring at the end of the academic year,' said Tara. 'So they'll be looking for a replacement in the near future. Whoever gets this job . . .'

'Now listen to me, you two,' said Maggie, starting to clear away the plates. 'I'm on a sabbatical, and come August I intend to return to Washington and continue my job as Dean of Admissions at Georgetown. Sydney University will just have to find someone else.' She sat down to open her second letter.

Neither Tara nor Stuart made any further comment as she extracted a cheque for $277,000, signed by the Treasury Secretary. 'Benefit in full', the attached letter explained, for the loss of her husband while serving as an officer with the CIA. How could they begin to understand what the words 'benefit in full' meant?

She quickly opened the third letter. She had saved it till last, recognising the ancient typeface and knowing exactly who had sent it.

Tara nudged Stuart. 'The annual love letter from Dr O'Casey, if I'm not mistaken,' she said in a stage whisper. 'I must admit, I'm impressed that he managed to track you down.'

'So am I,' said Maggie with a smile. 'At least with him I don't have to pretend.' She tore open the envelope.

'See you both outside and ready to leave in one hour,' Stuart said, checking his watch. Maggie glanced over the top of her reading glasses and smiled. 'I've booked a table at the beach café for one o'clock.'

'Oh, you're so masterful,' said Tara with an adoring sigh.

uart was just about to hit her on the head with his newspaper vhen Maggie said, 'Good heavens.' They both looked at her in amazement. It was the nearest they'd ever heard her get to blasphemy.

'What is it, Mother?' asked Tara. 'Is he still proposing, or after all these years has he finally married someone else?'

'Neither. He's been offered a job as head of the Mathematics Department at the University of New South Wales, and he's coming over to meet the Vice-Chancellor before he makes a final decision.'

'Couldn't be better,' said Tara. 'After all, he's Irish, handsome, and has always adored you. And as you regularly remind us, Dad only just managed to beat him off in the first place. What more could you ask for?'

There was a long silence before Maggie said, 'I'm afraid that's not altogether accurate.'

'What do you mean?' said Tara.

'Well, the truth is that although he *was* handsome, and a magnificent dancer, he was also a bit of a bore.'

'But you always told me . . .'

'I know what I told you,' said Maggie. 'And you needn't look at me like that, young lady. I'm sure you occasionally tease Stuart about that young waiter from Dublin who . . .'

'Mother! In any case, he's now a . . .'

'A what?' asked Stuart.

'. . . a lecturer at Trinity College, Dublin,' said Tara. 'And what's more, he's happily married with three children. Which is more than can be said for most of your ex-girlfriends.'

'True,' admitted Stuart. 'So tell me,' he said, turning his attention back to Maggie, 'when does Dr O'Casey arrive in Oz?'

Maggie unfolded the letter again and read out:

I'm flying from Chicago on the fourteenth, arriving on the fifteenth.

'But that's today,' said Stuart.
Maggie nodded before continuing:

*'I'll be staying in Sydney overnight and then meeting
the Vice-Chancellor the following day before returning
to Chicago.'*

She looked up. 'He'll be on his way home before we get back
from the weekend.'

'That's a shame,' said Tara. 'After all these years, I would
have liked to meet the faithful Dr Declan O'Casey.'

'And you still could, just,' said Stuart, glancing at his watch.
'What time does his plane land?'

'Eleven twenty this morning,' said Maggie. 'I'm afraid we're
going to miss him. And he doesn't say where he'll be staying, so
there's no way I can get in touch with him before he flies home.'

'Don't be so feeble,' said Stuart. 'If we leave in ten minutes,
we might still get to the airport in time to meet his plane. You
could invite him to join us for lunch.'

Tara looked across at her mother, who didn't appear at all
enthusiastic about the idea. 'Even if we do make it, he'll probably
say no,' said Maggie. 'He'll be jetlagged, and he'll want to
prepare for his meeting tomorrow.'

'But at least you'll have made the effort,' said Tara.

Maggie folded the letter, took off her apron and said, 'You're
right, Tara. After all these years it's the least I can do.' She
smiled at her daughter, quickly left the kitchen and disappeared
upstairs.

In her room she opened her wardrobe and picked out her
favourite dress. She didn't want Declan to think of her as middle-
aged – though that was rather silly, because she was, and so was
he. She inspected herself in the mirror. Passable, she decided,
for fifty-one. She hadn't put on any weight, but one or two new
lines had appeared on her forehead during the last six months.

Maggie came back downstairs to find Stuart pacing up and
down in the hall. She knew the car would already be loaded,
probably with the engine running.

'Come on, Tara,' he shouted up the stairs for the third time.

Tara appeared a few minutes later, and Stuart's impatience
evaporated the moment she smiled.

As she climbed into the car Tara said, 'I can't wait to meet Declan. Even his name has a romantic ring to it.'

'That's exactly the way I felt at the time,' said Maggie.

'What's in a name?' said Stuart with a grin as he manoeuvred the car down the drive and out onto the road.

'Quite a lot when you're born Margaret Deirdre Burke,' replied Maggie. Stuart burst out laughing. 'When I was at school I once wrote a letter to myself addressed to "Dr and Mrs Declan O'Casey". But it didn't make him any more interesting.' She touched her hair nervously.

'Isn't it just possible,' said Tara, 'that after all these years, Dr O'Casey might turn out to have become amusing, rugged and worldly?'

'I doubt it,' said Maggie. 'I think it's more likely he'll be pompous, wrinkled, and still a virgin.'

'How could you possibly have known that he was a virgin?' asked Stuart.

'Because he never stopped telling everybody,' Maggie replied. 'Declan's idea of a romantic weekend was to deliver a trigonometry paper at a maths conference.'

Tara burst out laughing.

'Though, to be fair, your father wasn't a lot more experienced than he was. We spent our first night together on a park bench, and the only thing I lost was my slippers.'

Stuart was laughing so much he nearly hit the kerb.

'I even found out how Connor lost *his* virginity,' Maggie continued. 'It was to a girl known as "Never Say No Nancy",' she whispered, in mock confidentiality.

'He can't have told you that,' said Stuart in disbelief.

'No, he didn't. I would never have found out if he hadn't been late back from football training one night. I decided to leave a message in his locker, and I found Nancy's name scratched inside the door. But I couldn't really complain. When I checked his team-mates' lockers, Connor had by far the lowest score.'

Tara was now bent double with laughter, and was begging her mother to stop.

'When your father finally . . .'

By the time they reached the airport Maggie had exhausted all her stories of the rivalry between Declan and Connor, and was beginning to feel rather apprehensive about meeting up with her old dancing partner after so many years.

Stuart pulled into the kerb, jumped out of the car and opened the back door for her. 'Better hurry,' he said, checking his watch.

'Do you want me to come with you, Mom?' Tara asked.

'No, thank you,' Maggie replied, and walked quickly towards the automatic doors before she had time to change her mind.

She checked the arrivals board. United's Flight 815 from Chicago had landed on time, at eleven twenty. It was now nearly eleven forty. She had never been so late to meet someone off a plane in her life.

The nearer she got to the arrivals area, the slower she walked, in the hope that Declan would have time to slip away. She decided to hang around dutifully for fifteen minutes, then return to the car. She began studying the arriving passengers as they came through the gate. The young, bright and enthusiastic, carrying surfboards under their arms; the middle-aged, bustling and attentive, clutching their children; the old, slow-moving and thoughtful, bringing up the rear. She began to wonder if she would even recognise Declan. Had he already walked past her? After all, it had been over thirty years since they had last met, and he wasn't expecting anyone to be there to greet him.

She checked her watch again – the fifteen minutes were almost up. She began to think about a plate of gnocchi and a glass of Chardonnay over lunch at Cronulla, and then dozing in the afternoon sun while Stuart and Tara surfed. Then her eyes settled on a one-armed man who was striding through the arrivals gate.

Maggie's legs felt weak. She stared at the man she had never stopped loving, and thought she might collapse. Tears welled up in her eyes. She demanded no explanation. That could come later, much later. She ran towards him, oblivious of anyone around her.

The moment he saw her, he gave that familiar smile which showed he knew he'd been found out.

'Oh my God, Connor,' she said, flinging out her arms. 'Tell me it's true. Dear God, tell me it's true.'

Connor held her tightly with his right arm, his left sleeve dangling by his side. 'It's true enough, my darling Maggie,' he said in a broad Irish accent. 'Unfortunately, although Presidents can fix almost anything, once they've killed you off you have no choice but to disappear for a little while and take on another identity.' He released her and looked down at the woman he had wanted to hold every hour of the past six months. 'I decided on Dr Declan O'Casey, an academic considering taking up a new appointment in Australia, because I remembered your once telling me that you'd wanted nothing more from life than to be Mrs Declan O'Casey. I was also confident that I wouldn't be unduly troubled by too many Australians testing me on my mathematical prowess.'

Maggie looked up at him, the tears streaming down her cheeks, not sure whether to laugh or cry.

'But the letter, my darling,' she said. 'The crooked "e". How did you . . . ?'

'Yes, I thought you'd enjoy that touch,' said Connor. 'It was after I saw the picture of you in the *Washington Post*, standing by the grave opposite the President, and then read the glowing tributes to your late husband that I thought, Declan, my boy, this could be your last chance to marry that young Margaret Burke from the East Side.' He smiled. 'So how about it, Maggie?' he said. 'Will you marry me?'

'Connor Fitzgerald, you've got a lot of explaining to do,' said Maggie.

'I have indeed, Mrs O'Casey. And the rest of our lives to do it.'